OVERTHROWN

The Dream Fades

Enjoy the read

ALAN ROBERT LANCASTER

Alan RL

12/10/14

New Generation **Publishing**

RAVENFEAST

Acknowledgements & Dedications

I have to thank my family, Kath my wife, my daughters Joanne and Suzy, and my son Robert for their patience, forbearance and untold assistance with producing this book. Thanks also go to my son-in-law Ash for 'cleaning up' my laptop. The assistance given by my offspring has been of a technical nature, whilst my wife's has been of a historical nature, furnishing some useful information about the old Roman roads that were still in use at the time of the Conquest, and about London in the years 1066 and after.

Thanks also go to Barrie Nichols, my former Geography and Maths teacher who has encouraged me to proceed with the saga, and shown interest in the project.

To some of my former colleagues at Mount Pleasant Sorting Office for their input and suggestions on the storyline and content whether used or not, thanks again.

Alan R Lancaster, London 2010

KIRKJUVAGR

LJODHUS

SOME OF THE CHIEF SETTLEMENTS IN LATE 11th CENTURY
BRITAIN

DINAS EIDIN/DUNEDIN
BERUWIC
BAEBBANBURH

CARDEOL DUNHOLM

MAN EOFERWIC

DYFLIN CEASTER LINDCYLNE
MENAI SNOTINGAHAM
DEORABY

HLIMREKR NORWIC

VEIGSFJORDR STAEFFORD
SCROBBESBYRIG
CORK VEDRAFJORDR RHOSGOCH LEAGACEASTER
NORTHANHAMTUN
LUNDEN
CANTUAREBURH

WINTUNCEASTER
EXANCEASTER
WIHT

4

RAVENFEAST HISTORICAL BACKGROUND & NOTES

Historical Background

The historical characters of this saga are known from numerous sources, including Snorri Sturlusson's Icelandic Sagas and the Saxon Chronicles.

King Harold is known to have had many Danes and Anglo-Danes amongst his household troops - or huscarls. His mother, Gytha, was aunt through marriage to King Svein and Jarl Osbeorn of Denmark through her brother Ulf. There had been many Danes living in England, some first generation, others whose families had lived in Danelaw Mercia since the 9th Century division by Aelfred. Their ancestry was celebrated in the bringing of the BEOWULF and HROLF KRAKI sagas to England in the ninth century.

After the Conquest many English nobles, churchmen and warriors left for Denmark and Flanders, raiding with the Danes on England's shores. Others roamed further afield, joining the Byzantine emperor Michael's Varangian Guard at Constantinople - known to the Norsemen as Miklagard (the Great Fortress City) = changing the composition of this elite body. Having originally been composed of Swedes (Rus), the make-up of the Varangian Guard changed over the years via West Norse to Anglo-Danish.

Harold Haroldson was born to King Harold's queen, Aeldgytha in early 1067 at Chester. Mother and son were spirited away to Dublin to keep them from possible harm from the Normans.

Nothing is recorded of them beyond that.

Eadgytha 'Svanneshals' (Swan neck) fled from Winchester with her youngest son Ulf and daughters Gunnhild and Gytha to Exeter together with Harold's mother Gytha. They were joined there by Harold's older sons by Eadgytha, Godwin, Eadmund and Magnus. Even as the Normans gained entry to the city the family went their separate ways, the womenfolk and children initially to Steepholm in the Bristol Channel, and then to Flanders once the hue and cry had died down.

Godwin, Eadmund and Magnus left for Dublin, where they were given men and ships by King Diarmuid. They raided in the West Country, on the Bristol Channel coast of Somerset where Godwin's lands were, and were beaten off by the local fyrd and Normans under the Breton Count Brian. Godwin and Eadmund are known to have survived, but Magnus is thought to have died of his wounds. There is also a story that Magnus did not die of his wounds but lived out his days in his native Sussex as a monk. His older brothers are said to have left for Denmark.

Ulf, Harold's youngest son by Eadgytha is thought to have been captured and imprisoned by William, later freed under an amnesty in 1087. He was befriended, along with Eadgar the Aetheling by Robert 'Curthose', William's eldest son, and is thought to have gone with them on Crusade in the early 12th Century. King Eadweard's widow, Eadgytha retired to the nunnery at Wilton Abbey along with Harold's daughter Gunnhild after surrendering Winchester to William. Wulfnoth, Harold's youngest brother, was brought back to England long after the Conquest and taken to Winchester, where he died an old and lonely, broken man.

Harold's elder daughter by Eadgytha, Gunnhild, is believed to have been abducted from the nunnery at Wilton by Alan 'Fergent', Lord of Richmond, who had received lands of her mother's. In fact she fled the nunnery to be with him. She later 'took up' with his kinsman Alan 'the Black', despite Archbishop Anselm's attempts to get her back to Wilton.

Harold's daughter Gytha began a dynasty when she married Prince Vladimir 'Monomakh' of Smolensk and later Kiev. Her eldest, a son called Mstislav – or Mistislav - Harold was born in Novgorod. From him stems King Valdemar of Denmark and later Queen Elizabeth II of England by way of Queen Margrethe of Denmark.

Historical Notes

To familiarise you with Anglo-Saxon terminology and place names used in the saga of Ivar:

Burhbot work on burh (town/city) defences, alternative to *fyrdfaereld* when defensive work needed to be upgraded or replaced under threat of siege/invasion

Brycgegeweorc upkeep of bridges as part of defensive strategy under threat of siege/invasion

Butsecarl seagoing *huscarl*/warrior

Ceorl commoner, free peasant/freed man

Discthegn/Hraegle thegn household steward/general steward

Ealdorman Anglo-Saxon predecessor of Earl

Earl/Eorl Anglo-Saxon equivalent of Norse *Jarl*

Earldoms status given to former kingdoms of England from and including the time of Knut/Canute

Fyrd regional militia or territorial forces were raised by the king to defend the realm for limited periods only, to repel invaders – not for aggressive purposes

Fyrdfaereld territorial military duty, a form of national obligation for limited period from several weeks to a couple of months before being stood down

Hersir West Norse landowners, latterly household warrior retainers, similar to *huscarls*

Hundred a southern or south-western shire district, charged with up-keep of law and local defence (see also *Wapentake*)

Huscarl household warrior, often landed, Danish origin, introduced by Knut into England

King's thegn obligated to answer king's call to duty

Norns three old crones, seers, *Skuld*: Being, *Urd*: Fate/ *Wyrd,* and *Verdandi*: Necessity

Shire reeve later sheriff

Scramaseaxe scramasaxe, the weapon associated with the Saxons, a curved blade on the top side with a concave split-edged blade on the other

Skalds Norse hall poets, retained by kings and/or jarls to recite the heroic deeds of their paymasters

Skjaldborg Norse, shieldwall, literally shield fortress, defensive/offensive formation of overlapping shields, used both in England and Scandinavia

Thegns or thanes, commoners ennobled by the king, usually held '*book land*' from king or ecclesiastical establishment

Thrijungar or 'Thirdings' (Ridings), the divisions of Yorkshire and Lincolnshire, each with its own *thing* or parliament

Wapentake/Vapnatak district within 'Thirding' in regions of northern and eastern (Danelaw) England, similar to Wessex Hundreds, literally *weapon take*, or weapon store

Wyrd fate, woven by *Urd*, one of the three *Norns* who sat at the roots of *Yggdrasil*, the World Ash Tree – decided the personal outlook of everyone born to man in *Midgard*, (Middle Earth)

I have attempted to maintain the early mediaeval geography in the saga with the use of the 11th Century communal and regional references or names. The spellings use modern-day characters, as some of the original ones were never translated into the Gutenberg alphabet when printing was introduced to England in the 15th Century by Caxton. The main place/regional references and names used are:

Aengla, Aengle, Aenglish Anglia, English – people, English language and collective noun for people inhabiting Aengla Land: England

Andredesleag Andreds Weald, the thickly wooded hills across southern Sussex and south western Kent

Beornica Bernicia, northern half of *Northanhymbra* (Northumbria), ruled from *Baebbanburh* (Bamburgh)

Bretland Brittany

Cantuareburh, -byrig Canterbury, capital of Kent

Ceaster Chester, capital of Mercia

Centland, Centish Kent, Kentish

Danelaw formerly Eastern Mercia, the lands east of Watling Street offered by King Aelfred to Guthrum and the other Danish lords as part of the Treaty of Wedmore

Deira the southern half of the kingdom and later earldom of Northumbria, ruled from *Jorvik/Eoferwic* (York), in 10th Century ruled as separate Kingdom of York by Eirik 'Blood-axe'

Deoraby Derby, one of 'Five Boroughs' of Danelaw, with Lincoln, Leicester, Nottingham and Stamford

Dyflin Dublin, southern Ireland

East Seaxan, East Seaxe East Saxon(s), Essex

Eoferwic and *Jorvik* York, the first is the Anglian, and the latter is the Norse name from which the modern York stems

Five Boroughs are the main towns of the *Danelaw,* Derby, Leicester, Lincoln Nottingham and Stamford (Lincs.)

Frankia France

Laegerceaster Leicester

Lindcylne Lincoln

Lunden London, there were other versions in the Saxon Chronicle, this version was used in the pre-Norman era

Lunden Brycg London Bridge

Middil Seaxan, Middil Seaxe Middle Saxon, Middlesex

Mierca Mercia

Miklagard Constantinople, 'great city/fortress'

Norse the West Norse are the modern Norwegians and their colonists in the Atlantic islands, including the British Isles; the East Norse are the Danes, Goths and Swedes, historically also settlers in the *Danelaw* in England and Ireland; also Rus, an ethnic group largely absorbed by their Slavic neighbours, originally in northern and central western Russia/ Ukraine.

Northanhymbra Northumbria, see *Beornica, Deira*

Northfolc North folk/ Norfolk – a sub-group of *East Aengle*/East Angles - see also *Suthfolc*

Northmandige, Northman/Northmen Normandy, Norman(s)

Norwic Norwich

Seaxan, Seaxe Saxon(s)

Snotingaham Nottingham, one of the 'five boroughs

Staenford Stamford, Lincolnshire, another of 'five boroughs of the Danelaw

Staenfordes Brycg Stamford Bridge, East Yorks

Suthfolc South folk/Suffolk, East Angles

Suth Seaxan, Suth Seaxe South Saxon, Sussex

Wealas, Wealsh Wales, Welsh – term was applied by the Saxons, meaning 'foreigner'

West Seaxan, West Seaxe West Saxon, Wessex – abolished by the Normans as retribution for Harold's 'perfidy', he was regarded as a usurper, and traditionally he still held his lands in Wessex until his death

West Wealas name given by the Saxons to Cornwall

Wintunceaster Winchester, capital of Wessex

Alan Lancaster, 2011

'...Then on midwinter's day Archbishop Ealdred hallowed him to king at the West Mynster, and gave him possession with the books of Christ, and also swore him, ere that he would set the crown on his head, that he would so well govern this kingdom as any king before him best did, if they would be faithful to him...'

The Saxon Chronicle, (E) 1066

Hindsight

'My Lord King, I have word from Earl Leofwin. The Northman duke and his host have made landfall on the south coast!' The rider was still short of breath, kneeling cap in hand before the king at the feast to mark the defeat of the Norse king. The young stubble-bearded fellow who brought the unwelcome tidings reeked with sweat, his hair rank, matted. The waist-length black leather jerkin he wore was spattered with dried mud from countless river crossings, the dust from old highways. Yet Harold did not hold back from thanking him warmly. He gripped the fellow's right hand firmly, bade him stand,

'You are my guest, good man. You must have food and drink. Rest overnight before you take the long road back ahead of us. Ride like on ahead and ask my brother Earl Leofwin to meet me at Wealtham. Meanwhile, he should send out riders to all points east, south and west to summon the thegns with their fyrdmen. I shall try to swell the ranks on my way south, to make up for my dead and those too wounded to ride back now. Go, eat, drink, rest and we will see one another soon at Thorney!'

King Harold pressed south from Eoferwic, driving his long-suffering men hard. He spent a week in Lunden settling matters, sent out more riders to the nearer shires in the east summoning thegns and fyrdmen who had not yet answered the call to arms.

With his brothers Gyrth and Leofwin, he rode to deal with Duke Willelm. Men gathered from far afield to meet at the Hoar Apple Tree overlooking Haestingas. His aim was to block the Lunden road and await more men to strengthen his bargaining hand.

However, the duke had already sent out his scouts. Word reached him during the night that Harold was camped nearby with no greater numbers than he had himself. He needed to break Harold's stranglehold on the Lunden road. During the night Harold's men rested, unaware Willelm knew they were there. They were awakened in the early morning by the men on watch to find the hill across the narrow dale filling with the outlanders.

To the left of the duke the Bretlanders waited under Willelm's son-in-law, Alan Fergant. Frankish and Flemish cohorts were posted on the right side of Willelm's Northmen, the horsemen behind men on foot. There were men sent from the south with the Holy Father Alexander's banner. Bowmen were posted on either end of the massed ranks. With them stood men armed with crossbows, weapons unknown to many a thegn or fyrdman. They would inflict heavy losses with bolts to cut through shields, split them as if made from wicker.

Flapping amidst Willelm's men was his raven standard that looked *strongly like the stark black outline of Harald Sigurdsson's fated banner, the Land Oda, or land-waster.*

Close by, barely flapping in the feeble morning breeze was the great many tailed banner of the Holy Father, the cross of Peter marked in gold thread, four smaller crosses filling the corners.

Behind his front ranks Willelm sat proudly astride a fine black Arab stallion, admired by friend and foe alike but fated to a short life. The horse was a good luck gift given to him by the king of Aragon, to carry Willelm against the sinful Aenglish king who dare flout his vows. Noteworthy amongst the ranks of the Northmen were the duke's half-brothers, Odo of Bayeux and Count Rodberht of Mortain. Their staffs of office held stiffly at their sides, these two would hold sway over the middle of their line.

Atop the hill, at his strongpoint, stood King Harold with his huscarls, behind him on one side his own Fighting Man banner, the outline of the Cerne Abbas giant picked out in fine gold thread and encrusted with gemstones. In a breeze that gathered strength from the sea below the red dragon banner of the West Seaxans began to swell. The beast needed more than this breeze, however, to show itself fully in all its glory; he had to fly freely for Harold's foes to stand in awe of his spell!

The eager warriors in the long shieldwall hurled insults at the outlanders, crashed spears, axes and swords against the backs of their new shields, yelling,

'Ut! Ut! Ut!' - Out! Out! Out!

The Northmen yelled their hatred with their own war cries. Men traded insults which neither side could understand, yet knew it was needed to awaken the fighting spirit, to still their fears. Brothers from Wealtham sang praises to the Lord of Hosts, Franks and Northmen sang the song of Rolande, and the rest laughed or yelled until they were hoarse.

From when the bell tolled at a nearby chapel all went well for Harold, until some time before midday when Earl Leofwin fell leading his huscarls in attacks on Willelm's horsemen. During the day-long struggle the duke's black stallion and a further spare horse were killed from under him. The hill ran red with gore, dying, horses and men screaming in fear and pain. Many a man who thought he had the upper hand, set to render his foe lifeless lost his own footing and was brought crashing to the blood-crimson grass. No man could break from his wyrd. It either hung from a man like chains, or he could clasp it close to his bosom like a friend. Luck was no friend to the heedless! After a lull in the fighting Earl Gyrth fell to the outlanders' arrow-hail unleashed by the Flemings and Northmen.

His brothers fallen, Harold stood grim amongst his huscarls. Now he led only with his stallari, Ansgar. Yet soon even Harold was wounded by a Flemish arrow in his right eye. Unbowed, he fought on after Brothers from Wealtham tended to his wound.

When the Northmen gained a foothold on the hill he was cornered, tormented and slain by three of Willelm's nobles. The day was lost to Willelm. One of Harold's tormentors, Walter Giffard had done the unthinkable and hacked off the battered Harold's manhood, for which he was sent home in shame. It is a dark day if a fallen leader can be humbled in this way after death! .

Thegns and their fyrdmen were coming onto the hill through the woodlands even after the king's untimely death, to fight their way back again, withdrawing hastily into the safety of darkness. Word of Harold's grisly end quickly spread through the southern shires. If a Northman could inflict such a foul wound on the body of a dead Christian king, a stand had to be made to hold Duke Willelm back from taking Lunden burh, and thus the kingdom.

Although passed over by the Witan for the stronger and highly skilled Harold, Eadgar 'the aetheling' did not sulk when the Witan offered him the crown. In a manner befitting a true heir of Cerdic, Eadgar readily answered his calling. It was his wyrd after all. For all his youth, the young king showed himself a true leader of men.

A shieldwall was formed at the Suthgeweorce end of Lunden Brycg against five hundred of the duke's picked men on horseback. Having weathered the brunt of the Northman onslaught, those who had outlived their king and friends were brought together with the young king and his earls Eadwin, Morkere and Waltheof.

None shrank from the clash with the Northmen, noble or commoner alike. Duke Willelm's march on Lunden thwarted, his men thrown back with great losses under a withering arrow-hail that had been lacking at Haestingas. The Northmen turned to rendering houses in Suthgeweorce around the bridge by fire in the hope of spreading fear. That did not pay off either, if anything, the will of the defenders was stiffened to fight on and show Willelm he could not enter Lunden burh.

Willelm withdrew into Centland to lick his wounds and think of a new way of taking the crown. He knew now he would not come by it easily, and that his own fate hung upon securing it. Unless he made good his promises to his own men and to his allies he was undone. All he had ever worked toward would unravel before him, his half-brothers Odo and Rodberht stood to reap the rewards he felt were his due.

Eadgar, Ansgar, the earls and the plucky fyrdmen withdrew to the inns and alehouses to drink to the health of their new king...

13

1

As I cross the bridge with my friends, all the while looking to see if I can find Wulfmaer, I see Theodolf with Oslac and Sigegar. They are cheering him on as he recounts bringing down the horseman who threatened Lord Ansgar. From here on, with their help he will broaden his marksmanship skills, not that he is lacking there.

Hrothulf's son makes friends easily, that skill will stand him in good stead in the years to come. I think also Aethel will be out of reach to both of us if Eadgytha takes her into her household, as I think she wishes to.

Eadgytha should be leaving for Wintunceaster shortly, and that is some way off my way north.

Where *is* Wulfmaer? Men and women pass me on their way back over Lunden Brycg laughing, joking, waving their arms about and mimicking the Northmen falling from their horses. Flailing arms and shaking spears make hard work of looking for anyone. We are close to the north bank of the river now and I have still not laid eyes on the East Seaxan miller.

Sigeric is lively, and with his bow annoys someone just behind him. Unaware of hindering those behind him, he laughs at something Theodolf has told him and raises his bow arm again, onto the man's nose.

'*Foolish* young pup!' The big man booms at him. 'Foolish young pup! *I* should give you a lesson in *manners.* Give that bow here so I can thrash you with it! Did your father not tell you about throwing your weight about with folk trying to pass?'

'It seems to me *you* are throwing your weight about *now!*' Oslac puts himself between his friend and the newcomer, who turns to speak to one of his men and sees me.

Wulfmaer sees me ahead of him on the bridge and calls me,

'Ivar, come here, help me teach this young whippersnapper a lesson in manners!'

I thought Wulfmaer was some way *ahead* of me! In striding back toward him to tell him about Aelfwin, I ease my way through the thronging bodies. At least everyone should be in good spirits this evening, after defeating Willelm's men, looking forward to ale and hearty cheer at any alehouse or inn they can press themselves into without starting a riot.

'Do you *know* this dolt?' Oslac asks me, staring hotly at Wulfmaer, balling his fists in readiness for a fight. 'Why did he not give himself more room to pass? He could plainly see Sigeric is enlivened by our win. It is the second time in as many days Sigeric has seen the Northmen suffer from our bowmanship!'

Wulfmaer stares back at Oslac and brings his arm back, as if to strike the smith.

'*Just you try, East Seaxan!*' Oslac snarls at Wulfmaer.

Those behind them glare at Oslac and Wulfmaer. Thwarted in their haste to get to the feasting, they try to jostle my friends out of the way. Unless I bring these two together in friendship or part them before their enmity ruins my evening, I fear some rough and tumble is in the offing.

'*We are all fighting for the same king, are we not?*' I try to humour them both. 'We are all tired and in need of cheer. There will be a time for fighting again!'

'That fighting will come soon enough. Sigegar, Oslac, this is Wulfmaer. Wulfmaer, this is Sigegar, and the handsome one there is his friend Oslac. You will have seen how their handiwork had the Northmen stopped in their tracks in the first attack. They saved *our* lives yesterday when we left Medestan, and Theodolf made light work of the Northmen's leader, *did you not, young man?*'

Theodolf, standing behind the three of them now is bemused by Oslac. This is wholly unlike the calm, peace-loving fellow I thought I knew. He modestly answers me,

'Aye, Ivar, I did. What tidings do you have for Wulfmaer? We will walk on whilst you tell him', Theodolf thoughtfully steers the young bowman out of the way. 'Sigegar tell me the end of that tale about the salmon in the Medwaeg whilst we walk back to the 'Eel Trap''.

I hear nothing more of that. Theodolf and his new-found friends leave us for the darkness beyond the flickering torches on the bridge. I have to square up to Wulfmaer to tell him about Aelfwin's end, saving my life. It is the hardest thing, to tell a man of his brother's untimely end. Wulfmaer stares heavenward. The few left on the bridge are there to guard against any renewed attack They stand looking at the East Seaxan, wondering why he did not join the others in the search for somewhere to quench a raging thirst, and to raise a cup to the new king Eadgar.

'Hail, wassail - there should be *many* more days like this!' The call will echo around the many inns dotted about Lunden burh.

At last Wulfmaer speaks,

'What do I tell *mother?*'

I put my hands on his shoulders. His face is drained of its ruddiness, as if he were suddenly aware of his own mortality. He had been fighting alongside the others in the shieldwall.

He was plainly unaware of his brother's death, otherwise he would most likely have risked his own and his comrades' lives by trying to kill the horseman who speared Aelfwin, or be killed doing so.

He turns quickly, hurries over to the bridge rails and begins to heave. The men on watch turn away and busy themselves, looking over their axes, swords or shields for cuts and cracks. His plight is none of their affair. They may know how it feels to lose a dear one.

Two of a mother's three sons have been lost to the Northmen within the last week. Losses of this kind would be felt today by the kin of many around the south and east of the kingdom, all of whom will feel powerless – even with the best will in the world - to change anything for the bereaved. The able-bodied can only look on, or try to re-kindle cheer.

He sees me standing to one side of him,

'Ivar, do not feel you must wait for me... I will be with you soon. Go to the inn by Billinges Gata, the 'Eel Trap'. Most are going that way. There are others, but I heard that Lord Ansgar is taking the king there because he has his eye on the landlord's widow'.

Many a man has taken a liking to Aelfthryth, I take it. It is understandable enough, as she has drawn my own thoughts from both Braenda *and* Aethel.

Was she merely flirting with me when she told me she hoped to see me again, the way a woman might to bolster a man's spirit in times of war? Can I think of her as a bedfellow?

'We shall see you there, then, Wulfmaer', I take his hand and grip it with both mine. This earns me a crooked grin and he slaps my back with his free hand,

'Go, Ivar. I will see you there', he slaps my back again and we part company for the time bring. I understand his wish to be alone with his grief.

My next thought is whether all my friends have gone on. There is no sign ahead of Theodolf. He has melted into the darkness with Oslac and Sigegar. The shadows have swallowed everyone at this end of the bridge.

Theorvard stands talking to Burhred by the last bridge post, head and shoulders above the mass of men.

'Hey, who have we *here?*' Theorvard calls out to me, glad to see me again. 'Are we going back to the same inn to eat and drink?'

'Aye, but the inn will be *full* by now, surely', Burhred echoes my own thoughts.

'We are going there because we are awaited', I tell them despite my own misgivings. 'I think King Eadgar and Lord Ansgar await us there'.

'The landlord's widow, Aelfthryth might have something to do with your wanting to go back there', Theorvard looks sideways at the grinning Burhred and winks. Their loud laughter draws the eyes of the few still standing around, thinking of which way to take from here.

'Firstly, though, we should wait for Wulfmaer', I tell them.

'Why wait for *him?*' Burhred looks bewildered at me and up at Theorvard, who in turn shrugs and asks me,

'Aye, *why* do we have to wait for Wulfmaer?'

'He is Aelfwin's and Aelfwig's older brother, at a loss as to how he will tell their mother that she has lost two sons'. I turn to Theorvard and ask him,

'Would you leave a man in the wilderness of his tormented soul without words of cheer?'

'*Are you turning poet now?* It depends on whose tormented soul are you thinking of saving, anyway', Wulfmaer has come up behind me and makes me jump. Theorvard and Burhred begin laughing again, Burhred holding onto the rail to keep himself from falling into the river in his mirth.

'I was saying we should await you and keep you company', I tell Wulfmaer once I have regained my wits, 'to give you words of comfort when you tell your mother of her losses'.

He looks from me to Theorvard, then to Burhred and back to me. With a sigh he looks down at the river and answers me,

'All I need right now is enough ale and I will go home strengthened, to do my duty as a son - now the *only* son of the house. I would be glad of company on my way home, though', Wulfmaer tells us.

'Where are your fellow fyrdmen?' Theorvard asks him.

'We will not be taking the same road beyond Cingheford', Wulfmaer looks up at the young giant. 'Does anyone ever tell you they get neck ache talking to you?'

'Often enough for me to no longer take it as an insult', Theorvard grins at Burhred and winks down at Wulfmaer to show he is not offended. 'My friends in Snotingaham all asked me what it was I ate that sent me shooting up like a tree'.

Wulfmaer strides up to me and rubs his nose,

'I shall come with *you,* with the three of you', he looks Theorvard up and down, 'wherever it is you are going. Can I?'

'What about your mother?' I ask and try to let him know he could not cope with the life we lead. 'You know what will happen tomorrow, how, when and what you will do at any given time'.

Theorvard tells him how we spend our time, and what might await us,

'We have days of doing nothing, sharpening our swords, our axes,

17

looking over our shields closely to see whether we need to have new ones made, and then everything happens at once. We are surrounded by our foes, we surround *them*. Hours are spent locking shields and just pushing, trying to push the foes harder than they can us so that we can roll them back, head-over-heels', Theorvard spits onto the bridge planks. His mouth is no doubt dry and he dearly wants to wet the back of his throat with good ale, and to bed a woman – *tonight*, as soon as he can, and this miller is keeping him from both.

'We might we hook our long-handled axes over the foes' shields and pull so that our comrades can shove their spears into the foes' ankles or knees. Furthermore, we do not know when or where our next meal comes from, eh, Burhred?'

'Oh, *never*', Burhred answers absently, looking elsewhere.

'He is eyeing the talent again', Theorvard looks around and sees four young women walking the way we are to take,

'As it happens, I do not', Wulfmaer brings them both back to what they were talking about. 'My work takes me into the small hours and I am usually asleep during the morning when the women are about, buying in food for the thegn's household and his friends'.

He looks down at the ground, and at me, and puts them right about his day,

'It is back-breaking, dusty and thirsty work in the mill. All we can drink is water. Milk would curdle in the heat of the mill and ale would not help, only send us to sleep', Wulfmaer tells us and he too casts a keen eye on the young women as we follow on in their footsteps.

'You are doing the work you are suited for, *are you not?'* Theorvard sees Wulfmaer's thoughts are on other things and does not press for an answer.

'Theorvard, I have just had a thought', I recall Brother Earnald, and that he was taken to the 'Eel Trap' to get drunk. 'Brother Earnald will be at the inn still. He is of no use to us any more, nor is he a threat –'

The young giant chews his tongue briefly and enlightens me about Earnald's fate,

'King Eadgar has told me to send him on his way, but I may not need to do so. He is in a small room at the back of the inn and they may have found him, sent him away with a flea in his ear. Eadgar and the earls will have been guzzling for some time there now'.

'The king will have his eyes on Aelfthryth, anyway', Burhred laughs. 'Would he know what to do with her?'

They both cackle knowingly and Theorvard raises an eyebrow,

'She is almost old enough to be his grandmother, *surely*', Theorvard has trouble stopping himself from grinning at the thought of the callow youth chasing after Aelfthryth.

'I think Ansgar will drink Eadgar under the table, and charm her for himself', my thought brings gales of laughter even from Wulfmaer.

'*You know her?*' Theorvard asks.

'Her husband, Wynstan learned his war-craft with us in the Wealtham Hundred's fyrd. He is an East Seaxan like me, and his son Cyneweard took over the inn when he was away – not that Wynstan trusted him, *but he trusted his wife less*', Wulfmaer tells us offhandedly.

Sigeric says nothing but sniffs and smiles knowingly up at me.

'According to Aelfthryth, Wynstan may have been killed in the slaughter that took King Harold, and their son left before that because his father bullied him', I tell Wulfmaer as we leave the street to enter the yard of the 'Eel Trap'.

'She told you *that*?' Wulfmaer asks, whistling. He throws me a wide-eyed, disbelieving look. A wide grin then follows the look of disbelief, 'You *believed* her?'

'Why should I *not?*' I push open the door to the main room of the inn. Theorvard and Burhred stand beside me looking into the darkened room. There is no-one there.

'A man might well trust in what a woman tells him, as long as he can have her. Then he will be laughing inwardly as he gives her some silver, and leave by the back door as her husband enters by the front', Wulfmaer says, to sage nods from the other two.

A new candle burns where some hours earlier a shorter one had almost gutted when we left.

'Oh, she *is* a good looking woman, and can make herself believed by any man she takes a liking to', Wulfmaer grins gleefully.

'Where *is* everyone?' Theorvard cranes his head around the door, to be greeted by a dour welcome, if it can be called a 'welcome'.

'Where is *who*?' a voice booms out from behind the heavy oak store room door.

'Where are all the guests, the king, Ansgar, Waltheof and the others?' I ask a stout fellow who looms from the darkness, looking half-asleep with boredom after waiting for someone to show. 'They were meant to be here drinking to the king's health and to our win over the Northmen and their bastard duke!'

'*Ho*, Wynstan!' Wulfmaer greets him, 'What he means is he wishes to know where your woman is hiding, *never* mind Lord Ansgar and King Eadgar?'

'Lord Ansgar and who else...? Who are you talking of? Our king was killed by the Northmen', Wynstan growls.

19

'We have a new king', I enlighten him.

'Well, this new king, whatever his name is –', Wynstan begins to answer me.

'King Eadgar', Burhred offers.

'*King* Eadgar is it? Since when did that snotty-nosed little fool earn the kingship?' Wynstan is bemused that the Witan picked Eadgar to be our new king and leader.

'How is it *you* know him?' Theorvard asks.

'He has been in here almost daily since Lord Ansgar first brought him to fill his gills with my ale!' Wynstan answers Wulfmaer sourly. 'He was here the day we set out for Haestingas, trying to sweet-talk my wife into bed. I felt like giving him a good hiding there and then! And then he tries to get that fool son of mine to leave the inn for his house-hold as a *discthegn*. God, of all things he is *not* suited to, being disc-thegn to a king is one of them, so I sent him packing!'

'How long had you been sitting here, Wynstan?' Burhred asks of our host.

'Long enough to think out for myself that my woman is likely to be with her friends, as she calls them at the 'Crooked Billet', down there', he waves eastward with one thumb.

'Why would they be there when you have an inn here, with all this room, and with a nice cosy fire to warm us all up?' Burhred asks, fid-dling with an empty ale cup on the rough wooden table.

'If you are hoping for a drink, young man, there is no ale in my vats!' Wynstan growls sullenly. 'I have already had to turn away trade, so there is no sense in you twiddling with that cup!'

Wynstan spits on the straw-covered floor, shakes his head and adds,

'Her best friend, Gunnhild owns the 'Crooked Billet'.

He glowers into the air before going on, looking up at each of us in turn,

'The woman's husband must have taken the ale there on his wag-gon'.

'*How would they know we would win?*' I ask Theorvard, 'It was not clear until when Willelm's men made their last attack on us. That last arrow-hail finished his hopes of taking Lunden quickly. It would have taken hours to move all that ale from one inn to the other'.

'Aye, we were there for *hours!*' Burhred adds.

'I know. What went on between Earnald and Willelm alone took time', I think back to the young king's dislike of the Brother. 'He dis-trusted Earnald all along. And then there was *Eadred*, mumbling to Willelm'.

'So they *had* time enough. If Willelm had won they would no doubt have drunk to *his* health with his men!' Theorvard snorts at the thought of the two women touting themselves, although none of us knows what Gunnhild looks like

'Where *is* Cyneweard anyway?' Wulfmaer takes our thoughts away from Aelfthryth and Gunnhild making free with the Northmen.

Wynstan prods a shapeless heap on the floor by the next table

'*How should I know?* You may as well ask *him*'.

Theorvard walks over to take a close look at the heap Wynstan showed us and guffaws when he sees what it is,

'*Earnald* - he is still *here!*'

'Who is *he?*' Wynstan asks. 'As I came in through this door here, he was slurping the dregs of the ale in his beaker. God only knows *where* he could have found it – '

Theorvard grabs the empty beaker from Earnald's left hand and holds it upside down over the floor. Only a few droplets splash onto the straw. The young giant laughs,

'He must have been awakened when the women and their helpers took the ale vats. He would have shuffled from the little room I left him in with this beaker, and drained the last of the ale before he fell asleep again!'

Burhred stands over Earnald and shakes his head, laughing,

'That will teach him to enter a drinking bout with *you*, Theorvard. You could stand your ground against your namesake'.

'Drink the *sea* dry, you think?' Theorvard beams back at Burhred. 'No, I only had a cupful. I wish I *had* taken more. My throat now feels as if someone had set fire to it!'

I recall the tale my aged foster father told me many years ago, of Thor being given a drinking horn by Utgard Loki, the sorcerer king of the Frost Giants, and how he drank the sea dry without knowing he was being tricked.

'If *only*', Theorvard sighs ruefully and turns to Wynstan. 'Where is this other inn, did you say?'

Wynstan looks up at my friend and snaps,

'Theirs is an *ale-house*, not an inn. Do you want to go there *now?* By all means', Wynstan does not wait for an answer and heads for the yard through the still open door.

'What about *him*?' Burhred nods toward Earnald.

'What *about* him? Come on, you three', Theorvard beckons to Burhred, Wulfmaer and me, 'or we shall lose him in the darkness'.

A feebly burning rush light nearby guts and Earnald is left sound asleep in the darkness. I follow my friends out onto the street and we chase after a fast- walking Wynstan, past boarded-up shops and narrow

21

alleyways to the 'Crooked Billet'.

A chorus of shouting and laughing echoes down the street. 'The Crooked Billet' stands beside a small timber-framed church. In the darkness, his left shoulder lit from the ale-house I see a beggar sitting by the oaken, iron studded door of the church.

He is fast asleep, an empty cup by his right knee. I try my hand at tossing a silver penny into the cup.

'What in God's name are you doing, Ivar?' Wulfmaer asks and shakes his head when he knows what I have done, 'That is young Cyneweard, not a beggar. Hey, lad, wake up, this is not the time of the year to fall asleep out of doors. Come *on* now, son we are going in to the 'Crooked Billet'. *Is* that you, son?' Wynstan turns on the still dozing fellow and kicks his feet until he is fully awake and groans.

'That is *not* Cyneweard', I tell Wynstan. He does not look like the fellow who told me where to find the 'Eel Trap'. He was shorter and fair-haired.

'You are right, you know', Wynstan stares wide-eyed at the fellow by the church door. 'What are you doing with my son Cyneweard's cloak?'

Wulfmaer has to fend off Wynstan before he tramples on the poor fellow's feet.

'In God's name, can a man not catch up on his sleep? Who is Cyneweard?' the fellow groans, 'Someone threw this thing over me before I went to asleep. He said I would catch my death'.

'Saeward what are you doing here, *in Lunden?* ' I know this heavily built 'beggar' when he gets to his knees and stands shakily, still half asleep.

The cloak falls to the ground and Wynstan bends down to pick it up, nearly bumping the unsteady Saeward off his feet.

'Hey, what are you *doing?!* Have the damned thing if it means so *much* to you!' Saeward half throws the cloak at Wynstan.

'You are that lay Brother from Wealtham', Wulfmaer knows of him, too, 'the one who murdered the Northanhymbran'.

Bad tidings travel faster than good ones. I can see Saeward balling his fists, ready to strike out.

'Not so much murdered a man as avenged his brother's death, on a fool named Garwulf', I put myself in front of Saeward and look back over my shoulder at him. 'Put your hands down, Saeward. Fists will settle nothing here!'

'It *might* save me from being insulted like this again!' Saeward's fists are still balled, ready to strike Wulfmaer.

'Wulfmaer has lost brothers to the Northmen, you lost your brother to a foolish Northanhymbran oaf with a love of ale, so who between you should be afforded greater sympathy?' I ask Saeward, staring into hate-filled eyes, and make him mindful of what we are about,

'I would sooner you took your hatred out on the Northmen. Put up your fists, Saeward. Greet Wulfmaer as a comrade –',

I am not allowed to finish

'When he tells me he is sorry for calling me a *murderer!*' Saeward demands, hatred boiling within him.

'All right, all right, I will ask him. Wulfmaer', I plead with the miller, 'tell Saeward you are sorry for calling him a murderer?'

'To what end? The story of what he did in Northanhymbra was spread by the lay Brothers and working folk of Wealtham. I had nothing to do with it, and to me this fellow', Wulfmaer means Saeward by a nod of his head, 'was due his revenge. I will get my own back on the Northmen for the deaths of Aelfwin and Aelfwig'.

He looks over my shoulders at a still furious Saeward, and asks him,

'Do you have a mother, Saeward? What I feel now is emptiness for her loss. Our mother will sorely feel sorrow when I tell her'.

'I cannot say it is anything to do with you whether I have one or not. As it is, mine died years ago, a short time after my father. From then on I only had my brother', Saeward spits out his answer.

'As far as I can see, no it has *nothing* to do with me, whether or not you have a mother. I am sorry for your loss, but if we are to be companions on the road ahead, it helps if we can talk like friends. Wulfmaer holds out his right hand in friendship.

He stands there, arm outstretched to take Saeward's. The miller is right. There is nothing worse than having men around you who are torn by hatred. I do not know if that was what killed Hrothulf, the sudden emptiness between him and Aethel that pulled them apart on their ride, although she kissed him before they parted.

Somehow, perhaps it is the sight of the forbearing Wulfmaer, his right hand held out – Saeward sees sense and stretches out his hand. Wulfmaer solemnly takes his hand, but cannot stop a broad grin creasing the corners of his mouth upward.

Theorvard and Burhred break out in grins and I cannot hide my own relief at seeing Saeward gain another friend. They have more in common with one another than I with either of them, and I am not merely talking of the loss of brothers.

'My mother took herself to a nunnery when my father died. Beorhtwulf and I swore to take holy orders one day. Beorhtwulf was close to taking his final vows when he was struck down. Dean Wulfwin rightly warned me about my temper', Saeward shamefacedly admits to his new friend.

He has come a long way on the road to finding himself. Perhaps the sooner he settles into a new mould the sooner he will be able to master his moods. He may have a life ahead of him that will fulfil him, a friend to Theorvard, Burhred and me on our long road.

Theodolf might be with us, too, although Oslac may talk him into going back to Centland with him and Sigegar.

We enter the 'Crooked Billet' in pairs. I look around at the happy faces. Men quaffing ale from horn beakers in one corner seem to be vie-ing with one another. Women standing with them are egging on their men. A chant goes up,

'*Inwaer - down that ale!*' one of the women by him crows to the de-light of those around her.

'How much is riding on Inwaer?' someone asks next to me.

'That pile of silver on the table by his right elbow', the answer comes quickly from another bystander, 'is what is at stake'.

Saeward looks at the silver and bridles.

'*What is it, Saeward?*' I ask him, not wanting him to start a fight in here that he cannot win. Inwaer's friends look many and able, little worse off for the ale they may have already downed.

'That silver was mine', he answers grimly.

'Was that the silver you had with you when we came across Hrothulf?'

He answers with a sharp nod.

'*How did you lose it?*' is my next question.

'Like *that*, in here - earlier', he nods at Inwaer, guzzling from a great beaker, slopping ale into a scruffy, un-combed beard.

'Who did you lose the silver *to*?' Theorvard asks Saeward.

His answer rakes me aback,

'*I lost it to Inwaer!*' he answers angrily. I have my work cut out to hold him back.

'Wait', Theorvard tells Saeward, clutching at his elbow to stop him making a fool of himself, 'my name is not Theorvard for *nothing!*'

Saeward looks baffled at me. How do I tell him the story of Thor drinking the sea in a few words? It is a saga in its own right. I put on a grin and tell him for now,

'I will tell you *one day*, when we have time. For now let Theorvard do your bidding when this drinking bout ends.

Inwaer is in the midst of taking another bet, and his woman is busy taking the new challenger's silver. When he has wiped the ale from his scruffy beard and shoved another small pile of silver sideways to the woman, Inwaer looks up at Theorvard. Gunnhild makes her way toward the young giant, her fat hips bouncing like those of a prize cow as she waddles.

Inwaer smirks up at Theorvard, waving to the bench opposite,

'Well now, have we another - a *better* bet?' He casts a loving eye on his gains as if the silver were his love child, and eyes Theorvard's stake.

'Give your silver to Gunnhild here', Inwaer tells Theorvard.

'As far as I can tell, *you* are the one drinking for gain, my friend', Theorvard smiles and hands over his coins to the woman, 'and as I see there *is* only the one of you'.

Gunnhild takes the coins from him and smacks them down onto the board in front of Inwaer with a look of unbridled glee. Around Inwaer are King Eadgar, Ansgar, Waltheof and Morkere. Eadwin goes on talking to Aelfthryth, and pays no heed to us.

'To make this bout fair', Theorvard answers, 'I will drink as much as you have already had'. He hands more silver coins to Gunnhild, who casts a wary eye over him but cannot stifle a snigger.

Inwaer looks at Theorvard, grins and leans over to Gunnhild,

'Get Sigegunde to bring seven full horn beakers of ale', he tells her, looking sideways up at Theorvard and grins again,

'Sit, friend. *What is your name?* Your manner of speech is not of this burh, nor would I say even of East Seaxe'.

'I am Theorvard, from Snotingaham', Theorvard shakes hands with his host and seats himself on the bench by him.

A buxom woman with hair the colour of straw brings a wooden tray on which stand seven horn beakers of ale.

'Set five of them on the table in front of Theorvard, Sigegunde. Theorvard, when you are ready', Inwaer tells my friend with a smirk, 'and the other two will be the ones we drink together. Take your time'.

Theorvard sets to draining his ale, one beaker after another. Inwaer's eyes are wide open by the time Theorvard bangs his last beaker down on the table in the manner of a dare. The hush in the great room could be cut with my axe blade. The king, his *stallari* and the young earls are standing now, gawping open-mouthed. Eadgar trades glances first with me, and then with Ansgar, who seems to be speechless for the first time since I met him. Waltheof eyes Theorvard warily. It looks to me as though the young earl knows him.

'We should drink to the health of our lady hostess, Gunnhild', Theorvard stands and salutes her with his beaker, then sits again and nods at Inwaer. Gunnhild blenches as she watches Theorvard calmly gulp down the ale a little faster than Inwaer, who spills almost as much as he drinks. When Theorvard bangs down this beaker on the board in front of him, Inwaer is still guzzling, slopping ale into his lap.

A second, a third and then a fourth beaker follow.

My young friend puts his last beaker squarely down on the tray, well ahead of Inwaer who seems to be breathing heavily. A loud cheer greets Theorvard's win. Men he may never see again throng the table to shake hands with him.

Inwaer's head rests in his hands in front of him on the rough wooden board, unaware that Theorvard is holding out his hand to him in friendship. The drinking champion has been beaten by a true champion! Gunnhild is too taken aback to give Theorvard his winnings and sits there gaping at her husband, unable to say anything. Aelfthryth asks one of the waiting women to bring a cloth bag for the pile of silver, and then shovels handfuls of silver coins into it, all the while looking meaningfully at me.

With the last coins scooped up into the bag, she walks over to Theorvard and sets it down in front of him.

A smiling Aelfthryth calls out loudly across the hum of the awed onlookers to Theorvard for everyone to hear, and bobs to him,

'My *Lord* – I give you your *winnings!*'

'*Nonsense woman*, much of the silver belongs to Saeward over there', he lifts the bag and beckons Saeward over. Unable to understand why Theorvard has done this for him, he meekly obeys.

'Here, Saeward, I trust these coins to your safekeeping. Do not enter into any more drinking contests'.

Theorvard looks up at him and rebukes him sharply to resounding laughter,

'Next time keep to drinking with your friends. *We* will not rob you'.

By the look Inwaer throws at Theorvard, should we be foolish to stay within striking, I would say trouble may come from that quarter before long. He has already lost the goodwill of his esteemed guests. Eadgar, Ansgar and the young earls take their leave of their host. Before he leaves, the young king pours silver into Gunnhild's hand in thanks for her hospitality,

'Inwaer, we wish you farewell. Take care, and do not enter drinking bouts with those you do not know', Eadgar counsels earnestly without wishing his host ill and turns aside to the earls. 'We must return to Thorney to pay our respects to the Lady Eadgytha before she leaves for Wintunceaster'.

I would guess we shall hear more from Duke Willelm before too long, and we must be ready for him. I will come again one day soon to this inn and you can be our host. Until then I bid you farewell, and you too, Ivar'.

'A thousand thanks, my - *good Lord!*' Gunnhild's eyes glow at the sight of his silver and begins to count even as he leaves, forgetting her manners.

Inwaer stands and bows from the waist, although to look at him no-one would know where his waist started. Years of doing nothing but drinking ale have taken toll of him. By the roughness of his hands and the lines on his forehead, I will allow he might once have looked manly.

Theorvard beckons to me,

'Do you think there is anything to eat here? I could eat a horse - as long as it was *cooked* well!'

'I would have to ask Aelfthryth. It looks as though there *was* food earlier, but these good folk must have had hungers to match their thirsts after the fighting'.

'There *is* no food left!' Gunnhild tells me without taking her eyes from the silver Eadgar gave her.

'There you have it, Theorvard. Does anyone around here have food to sell?' I ask Gunnhild.

'At this time of night, there will be *little,* if anything I should think, anywhere. You should have come *earlier*, everyone was hungry!'

'Aelfthryth has left with Wynstan', Inwaer adds gleefully when he thinks we will have to go hungry until morning, 'nothing will be forth-coming *there* either'.

Theorvard casts Inwaer a withering look, stands, picks up his axe and looks for Burhred.

'Did you see where Burhred went?' Theorvard asks me.

'I think he headed for the kitchen, wherever that might be', I answer, also looking around. Saeward cranes his neck to look over the heads of the merrymakers and pulls my mailcoat sleeve.

'*Over there*', he points to where Burhred has shown from the depths of the inn. 'He has something wrapped in a cloth'.

'So he is, and is heading for the door. Come, Theorvard, it may be our prayers have been answered', I put a hand on his shoulder to steer him toward the door and head that way myself.

Inwaer eyes us mistrustfully as we leave for the door.

Saeward is the first to reach Burhred, followed by Wulfmaer and me. Theorvard takes up the rear as we leave the 'Crooked Billet', casting one last look back at our mistrustful host.

'Not only the alehouse name board needs looking at twice', he notes disgustedly as we walk back along the street to the 'Eel Trap. 'I would not even throw up in there! God knows what the *king* was doing in there!'

27

'I have food for us all', Burhred nods at the bundle he carries with both hands, 'where were *you?*'

'We were watching Theorvard drink Inwaer under the table. Where did you get all that from?' Wulfmaer eyes the bulging cloth bag hungrily.

'The two young women you saw me staring after at this end of the bridge', Burhred laughs, 'were working in there and let me have all this for a little show of friendship'.

'You know them?' I ask. I am looking forward to tasting the spoils of Burhred's and Wulfmaer's foraging.

'*I do now!*' he grins knowingly. We all laugh loudly and turn into the yard of the Eel Trap.

Aelfthryth sits in the corner, a single candle burning on the rough wooden board beside her. She says nothing about whether she has made up to her husband, but tells us,

'Wynstan went up to bed. He has an early start'. She stands to do likewise as we spread bundled food from the bag over a table and giggles at the sight of us falling on Burhred's rifled hoard, 'We have some ale you can have with this. Gunnhild would be furious if she knew you were raiding her kitchen'.

'As was Wynstan furious when he told us all your ale had been shipped along the street whilst the fighting was going on over the bridge', I tell her as she leaves through a door behind us.

When we see her again she has a pitcher. Theorvard takes it from her and sets it down on the long table in front of us. Whilst we set to sharing out the food, Wulfmaer looks around for beakers. Once everything is set for our late feast, Aelfthryth turns to me,

'I will show you where your rooms are, Ivar. You can show your friends to their rooms when you have finished down here'.

'*Keep some for me lads!*' I call out as I rise and stretch, to follow Aelfthryth into the bowels of the dark stairway. A cheer goes up as I try to keep up with her, looking to all and sundry as if I am chasing her.

'Not that *you* will need any feeding before the morning meal. *This lot will be worm-ridden or stale by then!*' Burhred shouts after me, thinking me to bed her there and then.

'Our lady innkeeper is only showing me where the rooms are', I call back through the closed door.

'So *you* say!' Theorvard cackles knowingly.

'*I hope Wynstan can sleep through this infernal noise!*' Aelfthryth hisses at me.

The laughter follows me until I follow Aelfthryth through a last door into a fair-sized room, out of earshot of my friends downstairs.

'This is your room. It used to be Cyneweard's', Aelfthryth tells me in hushed tones.

'Why would he not come in during the night and turf me out of his bed?' I only ask because I still have not had my fill of sleep. I am sure I will not be alone in the bed for long, as long as it is not *Cyneweard* who shares it with me.

She puts a finger to her mouth,

'*Hush*, Wynstan is in the next room, in our bed. He is not a light sleeper, but any sudden noise or loud talking will awaken him. I must go in there and see that he is still asleep'. She throws me a foxy smile as she adds, 'As long as I am in the bed next to him when he wakes in the morning he will know nothing. I will show you your friends' rooms and then I must leave you to your late feast. It will be a long day tomorrow and we have to buy the means to fill our vats again'.

Aelfthryth leads me from my room along a narrow gangway, telling me in a whisper as she leads,

'There are three rooms a side on either side of this gangway. Your friends can choose whether they will share a room, as each has two single width enclosed bed-closets. Our cook will start the morning meals shortly after the sun rises. Good night Ivar'.

As she lights another candle for me I bid her good night.

My friends chide me for not having stayed with our hostess when I rejoin them to eat my fill. We sit talking for a little longer, until the flame on our candle sputters.

'We should take our cue from this candle and give ourselves up to sleep', Theorvard speaks like a hall poet.

'Aye, *before* we drop, *dog tired* on our way to bed!' Burhred whispers hoarsely, 'Hush, think about what Ivar said about Wynstan!'

'Aelfthryth will be dropping off by now, too', Saeward guesses. It is likely, although I hope to see her again before morning.

The others settle between them which rooms to take. Burhred and Theorvard file into one room, the young giant nearly dropping his axe on the way in. Burhred catches it before it clatters to the floor and saves Theorvard a heavy cursing from Wynstan. Saeward and Wulfmaer have come to terms and share another room.

A rush light burns on a small stand by the door, casting a dull glow across the room, but not enough to light the bed. Having closed my door and taken off my sword belt, I begin the struggle to strip off my mailcoat. A creak from the bed warns me there is someone in there and I stride over to take a look.

'You took your time', Aelfthryth chides. This is what I had dreamed of since first setting eyes on her, hoping against all odds for it to come about. I take the light to the bedside bench to see her by.

'You know how us fighting men are, talking of fights fought, reliving days gone by, likening women –'

'Were you likening *me* to anyone?' she asks as I pull off my tunic at last. A knowing smile spreads across her youthful, kissable mouth. Long hair curls over bare shoulders, showing she is ready for me.

'I would have to know you well enough first', I assure her. 'Then I would sing your praises to everyone I know not likely to talk to your man'.

'You need have no worries on that score. He has no time to listen to idle gossip', Aelfthryth sounds sleepy.

'He has ears – 'I begin to answer.

'You have a mouth on you that will not spread such small talk within this burh', she murmurs. 'Now shut up before I fall asleep on you, *and blow that candle out!* They are not cheap to come by these days'.

I climb into bed beside her, feeling her nakedness. She wraps her left leg around me and caresses my neck and back with her long fingers. Warm kisses are planted on my neck and my chest. Aelfthryth takes my hands and presses them to her breasts. Although they feel smaller than Braenda's, they fill my hands. The kneading I give them brings a low, throaty moan that gives me a start.

It sounds as if Braenda is here with me! She rubs herself on me, heedless of my alarm and moans,

'I want you, Ivar. *I want you now!* I *have* wanted you since I first saw you!' Aelfthryth bites into my chest and feeds my swollen manhood greedily into her, her long hair covering my nakedness. She pumps me wildly, thrusting harder. All too soon we are both spent and she slumps on top of me.

Moonlight, having crept from the corner of the shutter, now beams fully through a gap between the boards. The room is lit all too briefly, allowing me to take in her nakedness, the copper hues of her hair...

Have I been making love to Aelfthryth, or to Braenda?

2

The morning dawns brightly, the light streaming brightly through the gaps in the shutter and my stomach rumbles as though the earth is shaking. And I am alone in my bed. Was I dreaming, or is Braenda playing havoc with me again? For all the bright sunlight outside it is bitterly cold, even in my room. There are noises out on the street, of waggons being drawn by heavy animals, of children running and shouting, and of Wynstan bawling at someone.

My stomach rumbles; that much is real to me. I need to eat, and soon! The sound of shuffling feet beyond my door gets me to my feet and I go to see what is happening out there.

'Good morning, Ivar', Saeward greets me, half asleep still. He shuffles back to the room he shares with Wulfmaer, 'I was looking for somewhere to wash. There is no water in our room'.

'You would have to go down into the yard where the horses are. There must be a water butt somewhere to swill our faces', I tell him. 'Come', I steer him to the stairs, 'we can go down together. The worst that can happen is that we get under Wynstan's feet'.

Saeward laughs,

'I heard the way he shouts at his ceorl. If he tried that with me he would find me harder to shove out of the way'.

'We need no more fighting than we have had already', I warn Saeward off from picking a fight with our host. He seems to be spoiling for one on whatever grounds.

'Anyway, he might be helpful to us'. I could think of why Wynstan might not be helpful toward me, but I would also like to think Aelfthryth reached her bed before he awoke and began searching for her.

'I wish you all a good morning, my friends', Wynstan salutes in friendly fashion when we show in the yard, half-clothed and still groggy. When I scratch under my armpits, then at my right ear Wynstan chortles,

'You should have stayed in bed for longer, Ivar. Still, you are awake now and I see you need a wash. The tub there can be used to freshen yourselves up'.

He points to what looks to be a chest-high wooden vat.

'Is there someone to look after our horses?' I ask before swilling my head and chest, allowing Saeward to it first.

'Gudheard comes later in the morning to wash down the animals and feed them', Wynstan answers quickly. 'He will be back soon from buying bran for your horses. My woman let things slip whilst I was away with the fyrd'.

Back in my room I set about pulling on my clothes. When I lift my tunic a brooch falls from the folds, as if someone had left it there for me to find. Made of gold, it has a dark red, polished stone mounted at its heart. Not the one Aethel handed to me, that she said was Braenda's, this is much older craftsmanship. It may belong to Aelfthryth but there are no marks, either on the front or the back that show ownership. If I leave it on the table in front of me when I am eating, she may see and claim it.

She sees it lying near my bowl and asks,

'This is a beautiful piece of jewellery. Is it yours?'

'What is it?' Wynstan thumps heavily past me from behind and picks it up to look at it closely.

Aelfthryth looks longingly at it, not knowing whose it is,

'It is a brooch, husband. It looks old, perhaps Celtic craftsmanship'.

Wynstan holds it up to the light, the plum-coloured stone glowing in a shaft of daylight from the yard that cuts through the smoky murk of the room.

'It might be Wealsh craftsmanship. Where did you get it from, Ivar?'

Aelfthryth looks up at it in Wynstan's grubby hand.

He sets the brooch down on the table and looks at his wife. Her eyes are wide open, like an owl's, taking in the fine work.

'What do you want for it?' he asks me.

'I cannot say whose it is. It might belong to someone who stayed in my room before me', I answer, cursing my foolish honesty. There they are admiring the brooch, neither of them knowing where it came from and he is asking me how much I want for it.

'You *found* it in your room?' Aelfthryth looks from the brooch to me, at Wynstan, and back at the brooch, 'Can I have it?'

'Well, if he found it there, it should belong to him. The last guest who stayed in that room said she was on her way to the Holy Burh, where Christ was put on the cross', Wynstan tells me as he looks searchingly at Theorvard, who has taken to the brooch.

'This guest was a woman, what did she look like?' Theorvard asks Wynstan.

'She was a fiery red-haired woman who came before I was summoned by the fyrd. She left on the same day as I did, saying she had a long way to go, to Dofnan', Wynstan thinks back.

'She had the most wonderful hazel eyes', Aelfthryth recalls, adding,

'I would say this must have been made for her by a Wealshman. It could be she had been to Wealas, or she came from there'.

'Did this woman have a *name?*' it is my turn to search her memory.

'She may have told someone, but it was not *me*', Aelfthryth looks at her husband again. I do not know how far she will take this pretence, but Wynstan does not suspect for one minute that she was in my bed last night.

'She told *me*', an elderly woman has just come into the room, her best days long since slipped by. She has been listening in and suddenly wishes to show knowledge of the matter.

'She *did?*' Wynstan sounds hardened toward the woman. 'What was her *name*, Ymme?'

'She told me her name was Braendeswitha', Ymme tells him flatly, turns back for the kitchen and comes back for another look.

My blood freezes. Braenda left one brooch at Aethel's steading with Theodolf. Now she has left this one here. Is she homing in on me? Was it because of that I saw her when I thought I was making love to Aelfthryth?

'You look worried, Ivar, have you seen a ghost?' Theorvard knows what I am thinking, knowing she also showed when I fought Brand.

'Get back to *work,* woman!' Wynstan scolds Ymme when he sees her standing looking at the brooch on the table. The old woman scurries away scowling, and looks back at me before vanishing into the kitchen.

'Get your porridge eaten before it goes too cold and stop worrying about this woman', Aelfthryth tells me, as if I were a child.

I do as she says, but still cannot help wondering about the brooch, as if it were a sign. She seems to have brought me good luck so far, but if I dally with another woman she may call in the debt! Have I been given another warning? If I stay here too long at this inn, Aelfthryth may think she has a claim on me.

'What are we doing today?' Theorvard brings my friends' thoughts to bear on me now.

'Are you leaving for the Danelaw, Theorvard?' I do not wish to lose his company, but by outstaying my welcome in Lunden I may bring Braenda's wrath upon both me and my friends.

'Do you want to be rid of me?' Theorvard gives me a look of mock hurt.

'The thought would curdle my blood! No, my friend, I am thinking of going north again myself. I do not belong here in the south any more'.

There is nothing for me here now. I need to see if Braenda is in Jorvik. I want to see her again, to ask her whether she bedded Brand at some time. Perhaps if I find Aethel and Theodolf the homesickness might take them. They will be safer for our being with them if they wish to ride on, back to Deira.

'Will Earl Morkere not see me as an unwelcome guest again?' Saeward frets.

'No more than I would be', I tell Saeward with a grin. 'We would not need to go into Eoferwic. There *are* other burhs. Besides, he and Earl Eadwin are here in Lunden with King Eadgar, did you not see them at the 'Crooked Billet'?'

'You recall drinking for silver', Theorvard laughs. 'How much did you bet on beating Inwaer? There must have been enough to fill a belt purse in front of the fat bastard!'

Saeward scratches his growing beard and looks up into the darkness of the eaves. He shakes his head as though chiding himself for his lapse of forethought and opens his eyes wide as though trying to awaken himself,

'You may be right, Theorvard, although I do not recall putting a full belt of silver on the board. He would have won that from the other drinkers'. He turns to look at me and spreads his hands, 'Ivar, I have only ever laid eyes on either of them twice in my days, but you are right, aye, I do know them both by sight now. There is something about them that chills the bones'.

'What about you, Wulfmaer, do you think you are up to a long ride?' I ask the miller. 'You need to tell your mother of your brothers' deaths, and let her grieve for them in her own way'.

'As long as you think I will be of use to you?' Wulfmaer wants to come with us, wherever it is he thinks we are going. But he is unsure of his worth.

'I think Theorvard and Burhred are at one with me. They have grown used to you, and you proved worthy in the fight yesterday. We will ride with you to Saewardstan but you must tell her on your own'.

He nods gravely and we get on with our meal. Theorvard looks at me, unsure of something – or someone. I try to draw him on his doubts,

'When we have finished this meal Theorvard, can you come with me to the stable?' I ask. If he is unhappy about Wulfmaer riding with us we should have it out now, sooner than later. He rises from the bench with a heavy sigh.

'Aye, Ivar - whatever you say'.

The other three are still finishing their cheese, bread and ale, as we go out into the yard.

'Have you had second thoughts about taking Wulfmaer north with us? Shall we sit down on these sacks? Looking up at you gives me a pain in the neck', I laugh and try to make light of his worry, seating myself on a low stack of grain bags.

'Do you think this will be wise, taking *him* with us? We could be days in the saddle, you know that better than I, already having ridden to Jorvik with King Harold and Earl Gyrth. You were halfway back again when Brand caught up with you. I dare say for a seasoned warrior like yourself it begins to tell when you start in the morning. His work is in a mill, a few days every so often with his local fyrd and he thinks he is ready for the warrior's life. Tell him of the days of doing nothing, feeding horses, taking turns to make a meal and so on'.

Theorvard knows he is right. Perhaps I was misleading myself if I thought Wulfmaer could last out. Then there will be the winter. *Where do we stay?*

If I knew where Aethel was, or Theodolf, with her say-so we might overwinter at her steading.

Taking shelter with Morkere and Eadwin would be of no use, either. As the sons of Aelfgar and grandsons of Leofric they are deeply mistrustful of the Godwinsons. As one of Harold's kin, this dislike of all things to do with Godwin passes on to me. Even though their sister Aeldgytha married Harold after being widowed from Gruffyd, with him now being dead the enmity may begin anew.

As for Waltheof and Eadgar, neither of them has a following that Eadwin and Morkere can not deal with. Morkere's holdings were second only to Harold's. Although it would make more sense to swear ourselves to Eadgar, he is still only like a figurehead on the bow of a ship without being as frightening.

As for making ourselves worthy of being called Eadgar's retainers, Theorvard, Burhred and I have our own proven skills, but on our own we cannot hope to make our mark. We must draw more men to our ranks. Wulfmaer might pass as a huscarl if we give him weapons, mailcoat, clothing and a good horse. The same could be said for Saeward, but that does not make either of them a warrior. Their skills, such as they are, must be honed and they must learn to deal with fear, and all that takes time. As things stand, we have neither the time nor the numbers. More seasoned sword-hands are needed.

'You went quiet suddenly', Theorvard looks closely at me. 'Are you thinking up an answer, or have you thought of something that could bring trouble?'

'Could you see yourself as a king's huscarl?' I ask him plainly.

'Can I see myself - a *king's* huscarl?' he echoes. 'You want to pass off Wulfmaer and Saeward as huscarls to King Eadgar too? I can not see it, somehow'.

Can he read my thoughts, or has he a greater insight than his years might lead me to believe?

'We *can* make it work; we *have* to. There will be scant time for Eadgar to test their mettle before Duke Willelm shows again. Saeward kills when he is seized by bloodlust. We must teach him to tame his rage. Wulfmaer was with us when we beat off the Northmen at the bridge, and Eadgar must have seen him fight because he was nearby', I am in the throes of cobbling together the makings of a king's retinue, true to him only. 'Between us we should amount to *something*'.

If I can find Theodolf again, talk him, Oslac and Sigegar into joining us, we may have more men in whose skills Eadgar can put his trust. Theorvard is thinking, his arms crossed, brow furrowed deeply and strokes his soft beard with a forefinger and thumb.

'Since I put my trust in you after you killed Brand, I have found it well founded', he tells me. 'You know these high-born folk, so if you say it will work I will trust you in this, too'. Theorvard rises and makes his way to the yard door, turns, looks back at me and grins,

'With time it can work, *why not?* Come on old man, we have to find them something to fight with'. He helps me to my feet and we stride in step to the door of the inn.

'After you', he stands aside to let me through and is still grinning broadly when we sit down by Burhred, Saeward and Wulfmaer.

'What have *you two* been cooking up together?' Burhred frowns and looks at me as if I had sprouted another head.

'What would you say of becoming king's huscarls?' Theorvard blurts out before I can outline my thoughts to them, 'I *am* sorry, Ivar. *You* tell them'.

The three of them look from Theorvard to me. Burhred folds his arms as though he thinks there is worse to come. Nevertheless, when I finish telling them what has been churning through my head he is as much for it as is Theorvard. Saeward looks bemused, Wulfmaer nonplussed.

Burhred still has his doubts and goes over them aloud,

'*One thing*, Ivar, where do we get the swords, axes, shields and so on to arm these two? As a rule huscarls have their own made, and pay for them from their own purses, with silver gained from their own five hides of land. Only Saeward seems to have silver, but we do not know *whose* it is, do we? Who pays for Wulfmaer's, or do we ransack someone's weapon store?'

'Aye, King Eadgar is unlikely to be happy with us if we go to Thorney and say to him that we want to be his huscarls, but *he* has to pay for them to be given mailcoats and everything else they need, horses as well. He will laugh, and his earls will laugh as loud if not louder', Theorvard groans at the thought of being laughed at by Morkere and his brother.

Then he thumps the table, hard, shaking the dust from them. Wynstan almost jumps out his skin but regains his wits quickly enough to scold Theorvard. He yells from one corner of the room where he has been talking with someone as yet unknown to us,

'Hey you, *stop that!* We have to *buy* these tables!'

'Ivar, *so this is where you have been hiding!*' Theodolf shows from the shadows, where he has been talking with our host.

'Theodolf, I was wondering how I might *find* you! What became of Oslac and Sigegar? I thought you were going to Centland with them', I get to my feet and take my young friend's hand.

'They went back to Medestan. Their wives and families needed to be shielded, they said. So I came back to look for you. 'The innkeeper here', Theodolf nods at Wynstan, 'said he had some fellows staying here, who had been fighting at the bridge. I see your horse in the stable now, Ivar. There is no mistaking *Braenda!*'

'Aye, there is no mistaking her', Theorvard butts in. 'It seems her namesake has been staying here on her way somewhere'.

'Is this true?' Theodolf looks from Theorvard to me, 'I saw a red-haired woman in the 'Crooked Billet' last night. When she turned my way she winked at me as if she knew me. *You could have floored me with a dishcloth!*'

'You sound as if someone *had* floored you with a dishcloth', Wulfmaer laughs. 'How much did you have to drink last night?'

'Most of these women who hang about in alehouses are like *that*, lad. One day you will learn the ways of the world', Burhred grins lopsidedly at me.

'Those young women at the hall in Saewardstanbyrig will be waiting for you still, will they not?' Theorvard teases Burhred.

'Like as not mine will be in someone else's bed by now', Burhred sniffs, as though mourning the passing of a friend. 'She was like that, that is how I came by her. She used to be cosy with a thegn before he was killed by one of Tostig's huscarls'.

'The tears had hardly dried on her cheeks before she hopped into *my* bed', he finishes.

'*Women, eh* - you cannot live with them, and you have a hard time living without them', Saeward notes thoughtfully.

'Saeward, since when were you such an old hand with women?' I chide. Everyone laughs affably when I add, 'Is there something you have not told me?'

Theorvard raises his right eyebrow.

'What do you think of becoming a king's huscarl?' I ask Theodolf when the merriment has died down. 'King Eadgar thinks highly of your skill as a bowman since yesterday, bringing down that horseman the way you did. Everyone in Lunden must be talking about it today'.

'Do you think he will give it a second thought?' Theodolf asks, still unsure.

'Whyever would he *not?* With a young man like yourself at his side do you think he would ever feel unsafe? He would be a fool to let you leave', I assure him.

'You have better things to come with this king', Theorvard adds. 'When we are old men talking of our days in the shieldwall and

'Aye, when we are addled with too much ale and dribbling in our breeks, you will still be at the king's side', Burhred laughs.

'You will be watching Earl Morkere and Earl Eadwin dribbling in their breeks, too', Saeward jokes, 'but Ivar here will be *ahead* of us all into his old age'.

Theorvard gives Saeward a sour look and turns to me,

'We will have to buy a bridle for this one', he taps Saeward on one shoulder, 'to curb his tongue. Otherwise he will land us *all* in hot water!'

Burhred, Wulfmaer and Theodolf nod wisely, like old men at the *Thing*, but Theodolf cannot hide his glee.

'Oh, what is the joke?' Burhred elbows the lad.

'I can see you all dribbling into your *beards*', Theodolf tries but fails to hold in a giggle, like a young maid.

'By our good Father in his Heaven', Burhred casts a weary eye skyward. 'What was that you said about him fighting for the king? He will have his work cut out holding his bow straight for tittering. *Our* seats at Eadgar's table are assured until we fall dead into our graves!'

'*Amen to that!*' I sigh and wink at Theodolf, 'We may never have the time to sit back and dribble into old age after all'.

Theorvard laughs and thumps the table again, drawing more oaths from Wynstan about wrecking his inn.

'Then we are assured a ride with the Valkyries to Valholl!' es.

'*Oh God, you heathen!*' Saeward pouts. 'Why were you sent to try *me?*' He has taken Theorvard's riding lightly. This is a side of him that has grown since his trials in Northanhymbra.

'You will have to get used to it', Theorvard grins. 'There are still many of us about, eh Ivar?'

'*Hah*, leave me out of it!' I answer tersely. 'I need to think of a way of arming the two East Seaxans without losing too much of Saeward's silver!'

'You said something about offering our skills to our new king', Saeward offers. 'Why can King Eadgar not use the silver in *his* treasury to arm them? Come to think of it, you need new mailcoats, even you would agree on that'.

'He cannot draw silver without the say-so of the Witan', I counter.

'We can try him *first*, before giving up the ghost?' Theorvard cuts in.

'Well, all right, let us see what he says-', I begin.

'*Hey*, I have been told the Northmen are burning their way through Suthrige!'

Someone passes through the yard door into the inn and yells the tidings to us. Heads jerk up on hearing him. After their bleak showing yesterday I might have thought Duke Willelm would stoop to that.

'*God's teeth man*, what did you say?' Wynstan bellows.

'I said the Northmen are burning their way through Suthrige. He has reached Acstede, only just west out of Centland. Where can he be *heading* for?'

'Who told you this, *and when?*' I ask the fellow.

'A grain trader was out that way yesterday, buying corn. He saw smoke rising and went to see what was happening', he tells me.

'He said he was lucky to come away unscathed. A score or so of them were slashing at ropes holding down the hay ricks, running off the animals, killing anyone who stood up to them. He told me he was lucky to be on his best horse and was able to outrun his pursuers, three of them with long spears and he only had a sword to fend them off with!'

'Where is this trader now?' I ask again. 'Who is he?'

The poor fellow is out of breath from running and has to gulp for air. He takes a mouthful of the ale that Theorvard offers and answers,

'He is Wigmund of Suthgeweorce. Having come back today to find his house a burnt-out shell, he said he was going to Lord Ansgar to find out who set fire to his house whilst he was gone', the fellow answers.

'He has gone to seek out Lord Ansgar?' Wynstan shouts from the back of the room, '*Where* has he gone to look for him?'

'He must have gone to Aethelmentun, where else?'

'He will be hard-put to find him there. Nor will the ride out do his horse any good, if he has ridden all the way here from Suthrige. Ansgar is likely to be still with the king', Wulfmaer puts in.

'Someone will have told him that already, surely?' I turn away to ask Wynstan about any nearby weaponsmiths. 'Do *you* know any we can trust, to arm these two', I ask and wave at Wulfmaer and Saeward.

'Nowhere near *here*. There *is* one near the River Fleot, on the river bank beyond Lud Gata, his name is Gudbrand. Then again there is Asmund who has a forge by the river, near Dow Gata'.

'What do *you* say, Theorvard, Gudbrand or Asmund? They sound equally good to me', I sigh.

'Which way are we going to Thorney?' he asks me in turn.

'We have to cross the Fleot', I begin, 'before going west'.

'How do we go there from here?' he knows the answer already, I think.

'By way of the church of Saint Paul, atop Lud Gata hill', I must have echoed his thoughts because he nods and grins.

'I thought so. This Dow Gata, is it *far* from here?' Theorvard asks Wynstan over one shoulder.

'It is along the river bank, beyond where a small river called the Weal brook flows into the Temese. Asmund is a tall fellow with grey hair and beard, and runs a small smithy. Gudbrand has a number of men working with him, churning out weapons for the fyrd', our host answers thoughtfully. 'But I would not set store by any of those goods, not like Asmund's. His weapons are well made and last a long time. He is the weaponsmith Ansgar chooses for his own war gear'.

Theorvard is bemused. He looks at me, then at Wulfmaer, at Saeward, lastly at Burhred,

'*Burhred which way would you jump?* I know what Ivar would say, *go for the peerless*'.

'Ask Asmund what kind of deal we can strike with him for swords and axes, perhaps? Gudbrand sounds as though he can put some shields together quickly. We must see how much time we have'.

'Aye, we must find a horse for Saeward, too.

'I walked from Wealtham', he affirms what I already half knew.

'Plainly Wulfmaer gets his brother Aelfwin's horse', Burhred sees the sense in that.

'Do you have a horse for sale, Wynstan?' I think I know the answer to that, too.

'*I* have no horses for sale, *but Inwaer does*'.

Looking at Wynstan, I can see he does not think Inwaer will let it go cheaply if he knows it is for any of us.

'*God*, we might as well give up now!' Wulfmaer's shoulders sag as though already carrying the weight of our failure.

'*Never* give up', Theorvard slaps him on one shoulder.

'*I* can buy him for you', I hear someone say from my right.

'Why would you do that for us, what could you hope to *gain*?' I ask the newcomer.

'I am Wigmund of Suthgeweorce. You have the king's ear and I have tidings that will make him sit up and listen. Duke Willelm is slashing and burning his way around Lunden to cut us off from our food supplies. The good folk of Lunden will fight for their king, but if their bellies tell them his is a lost cause, they will give in', he answers bleakly.

His answer is so straightforward it hits me like the stone on the giant Goliath's forehead. I cannot say I did not think it unlikely, but I have been hoping against hope that I might be wrong. Eadgar would be the best king we could want...For now.

'You think Eadgar should yield the kingdom to Willelm?' Theorvard asks Wigmund angrily.

'*No*, by Christ, *never* give in! I myself was chased out of East Suthrige by his horsemen!' Wigmund turns on Theorvard.

'No, that was not what I was thinking. But the king needs to think about cutting off the Northmen from *their* own food. If he is slashing and burning, who brings him *his* food, and from how far?' Wigmund's answer is straightforward, and carries a ring of truth. It was what Harold should have done had he used his cunning, as he did when we chased Gruffyd back to his hills. If we can make Eadgar, and even only half the Witan listen to Wigmund, *then we might win yet!* Duke Willelm only seeks to wreck our food supplies because his lines must be weak.

Wulfmaer has been ogling Wigmund's sword whilst we were talking and plucks up the nerve to ask the trader about it,

'Wigmund you have a beautifully crafted sword, if the hilt and pommel are anything to go by. Is the blade as good, *show me*?'

'You like it?'

Wigmund draws the sword for Wulfmaer to look up and down at the craftsmanship.

'My weaponsmith is Asmund, who has his workshop is not far from here, along the river. Shall I take you to him? If not in his slumbers, he should be hard at work – his hours are not set in stone'. Wigmund is glad that his gear has drawn acclaim, but treads unwarily with his next question,

'Where are you *from*, my friend? I find your manner of speaking a little odd'.

Wulfmaer growls a warning like an angered bear, to show his feelings about Wigmund's slur on his manner of speech,

'I am an *East* Seaxan, as are both Saeward *and* Burhred here!'

Burhred wheels to look askance at Wulfmaer,

'*Did you say something to me?*' he asks Wulfmaer tersely.

'*He said my manner of speaking is odd!*' Wulfmaer growls again. I was only giving his sword the onceover and he started on me, about the way I speak.

Wigmund is troubled now. He does not know where to put himself and clearly feels awkward with us. I think he might try to wriggle out of coming with us to see Asmund so I make light of Wulfmaer's anger,

'Wulfmaer my friend, it sounds as though Wigmund's Centish speech and your East Seaxan miller's way of talking have bumped into one another in the night and are trying to get to their feet! Wigmund meet Wulfmaer, Burhred and Saeward, my friends from east of the burh of Lunden', I turn the other way and catch Theorvard's elbow, 'and this is Theorvard from the Danelaw. Behind him is Theodolf, a North-anhymbran from near Tadceaster. I am Ivar and I am a Dane'.

It takes Wigmund a few blinks before he takes everything in and asks further,

'Did you *all* come to Lunden to fight the Northmen?'

'Aye we did. We fought alongside King Harold. There were more of us then', Theorvard adds.

'We were told of your tidings for the new king and Lord Ansgar, and thought we might head to Thorney to let them know what was happening around Lunden. The fellow who told us of you thought you might be on your way to Ansgar's hall. Were you told he might not be there?'

'I asked the way from a woman near Wudu Straet. When I told her why I wanted to go there she told me he was at Thorney. It is only a matter of *luck* that I came across you here!' Wigmund happily burbles to me.

'*Luck,* you say?' Wulfmaer snaps huffily.

Wigmund looks nervously aside at Wulfmaer, who turns his back on him. He then asks me,

'What happened yesterday at the bridge?'

'We gave the Northmen a drubbing. That is what happened!' Wulfmaer growls again, still with his back to Wigmund.

'We want Wigmund with us when we go to see the king, Wulfmaer. We do not want him haring off on his own because you put the wind up him', Theorvard snaps at Wulfmaer, '*do* we, Ivar?'

'We want each and every one of you!' I try to assure both Wigmund and Wulfmaer. 'First, if Wigmund would be so good as to buy the horse for Saeward, then we can go and ask Asmund how much his work will cost us'.

'His swords are not to be bought cheaply, I must add. This sword cost me a fair amount of silver. A year's worth of trading paid for this beauty', Wigmund tells me, drawing his sword fully, raising it to the

42

light for all to see the pattern-work.

Theorvard and Burhred let out low whistles in chorus. I have to smile. I *have* seen such fine workmanship, but only in the scabbards of kings or nobles.

'Why does a trader need such a fine piece of weaponry?'

Theodolf has come closer to look over Wigmund's sword. His words echo my own thoughts. 'This is a sword an earl or king would wish to own!'

'I have to fend off outlaws when I ride through the thickly wooded southern uplands. Even though I do not ride alone, I have to show I can look after myself', Wigmund has been taken aback by Theodolf's questioning, almost as if he had been asked why he needs to eat and sleep.

'Let him go and get Saeward's horse', I nod to Wigmund, to send him off on his way. 'We can see Asmund's craftsmanship for ourselves when we come to his workshop'.

He dithers, or he is waiting for someone to escort him to the Crooked Billet,

'Am I going alone?'

'I *would* send one of my men with you, but Inwaer knows us all from last night', I fail to think why I should tell him about Theorvard regaining Saeward's silver in a drinking match. 'If he sees any of *us* he will demand more silver than the beast could ever be worth'.

'You *trust* me with your silver?' Wigmund stares at me openmouthed.

'I am thinking you will use *your* silver, and we will repay you'.

My answer puts him off his stride.

'I take you for an honest man and that you will tell me what you paid. I am no fool, mark my words! Theodolf, Burhred or Theorvard would go with you, but as I said they are known to him'.

'What about a saddle? If Inwaer says he has a saddle - ?'

'*I* have a saddle Saeward can have', Wynstan assures the worried Wigmund and shoos him away.

'Buy only the horse', I know Wigmund will not cheat me. My friends have plainly over-awed him.

He nods quickly again and leaves the yard on foot to see Inwaer at the 'Crooked Billet'. A little later Wigmund shows at the yard gate leading a bay mare. Only a hand taller than Braenda at the shoulders, the mare looks healthy enough for the task we have in hand.

'How much did you say?' Saeward asks. He expects he will have to stump up the silver for his own horse, after all.

'Twenty ounces of silver', Wigmund answers warily, as if he thinks his head might be bitten off by one of us. To go by Saeward's stare, that might not be altogether unthinkable.

Theorvard mouths the answer soundlessly with a pained look on his face, then says it aloud,

'You paid twenty ounces of silver - *for her?*'

'Are you sure Inwaer was unaware the horse was for one of us?' Saeward coughs with laughter.

'What would *you* pay for a horse? This animal is young yet, good for years to come!' Wigmund sees the looks we give him and snaps,

'This is not East Seaxe or the Danelaw, and I do not know what anyone might care to pay for a horse in Northanhymbra. In Lunden twenty ounces in silver is fair for a horse. *I* might keep her for *myself* if you ingrates are not careful!'

'Wigmund, *Wigmund,* do not take on so!' I try to humour him, 'We are all misers, forgive us our niggling. You did well buying her! Saeward, get out your purse, this man needs repaying for his sweat. We want to be at Thorney by this afternoon at the very latest or else someone *else* will give the king Wigmund's tidings - wrongly! Come, Wynstan, can we have this saddle now and how much do you want for it?'

Wynstan vanishes into one of the stalls and proudly shows off a well-crafted piece of leatherwork, but which I would hardly call a man's saddle,

'*Whose* was this?' I knit my brow in a frown that tells Wynstan his wares are ill suited for the trials we think it may have to bear.

'It was Aelfthryth's saddle', Wynstan allows, downcast.

He knows he has fallen short of the mark.

'You thought I would put that on *my* horse?' Saeward snorts scornfully. 'I would never lower myself so far as to do to you what I should!'

'Just as well then', Wynstan sniffs, offended by the threat. It is not so much from fear of Saeward, but that his well meaning was not taken into account.

'*What do we do now?*' Saeward turns to me.

I have let him down once in allowing Morkere's huscarls to take him to Jorvik for trial. This time I can do something for him, I think.

'Let us see if Asmund has one to sell', I offer. He nods readily and Wynstan shrugs glumly, throwing his hands up, and leaves us to ourselves.

'Come, then let us be off to meet Asmund', Theorvard and Burhred lead to the stable stalls to saddle our horses, to ready them for our short way to see this weaponsmith. We lead our mounts out onto the street and ease ourselves into our saddles.

With Saeward holding on to my saddle, between my horse and Theodolf's, we let our mounts walk unhurriedly to Dow Gata by way of a rubble-strewn roadway, and down to the river.

'*Asmund, I have custom for you!*' Wigmund calls out, looking around and not knowing where the man will emerge.

'Who calls for me when I am trying to rest?' an unseen Asmund booms out from the darkness, 'Come back later and I will see what I can do for you!'

'What fool turns away custom when silver beckons?' Theorvard leans into the doorway with his hands resting on the lintel.

'The kind of fool who thinks I turn away custom is the kind of fool who will not come back to see what I can do for him. *Now leave me in peace!*' Asmund answers gruffly, still without showing.

'We do not have the time to wait about', I call out, 'because we have tidings that cannot wait to pass on to King Eadgar!'

'That is your bad luck. It has nothing to do with me', Asmund growls. He sounds as though he cares nothing for custom.

'Then we will take our custom to Gudbrand instead. Thank you, and goodbye', Theorvard makes to walk away, his parting footfalls draw scorn from Asmund.

'When you see that old fool you can ask if his spear points still bend when they hit a man's shield'.

Saeward laughs loudly, the rest of us grin foolishly. We have to wait if we want worthwhile weapons for Saeward and Wulfmaer.

He has us between a rock and a sword blade.

'How long should we leave it *before* coming back?' I shout back into the darkness.

'Take time for a couple of beakers of ale each and a good chinwag!' Asmund yawns. 'Be thinking about what it is you want from me'.

I look at Theorvard and Burhred, and then at Wigmund. They nod and we walk away slowly, Saeward trailing closely behind me like a hearth hound.

'Where is the nearest inn, Wigmund?' I ask the trader.

He thinks about that briefly, looks up and down the street, and jerks his head westward,

'Not far from here, just a short walk further on is an inn'.

'Very well, so much for *our* thirsts – but what about our horses?' Wulfmaer looks closely at our new-found friend and guide Wigmund and scratches his beard.

'Young Hearding, the yard lad will do that for us, I think', Wigmund looks back at Wulfmaer and gives him a winsome smile.

A little later we pull open the side door of the 'Three Cranes' into the stable yard and blink at the bright sunlight. Doubtless Eadgar knows by now what we were going to tell him.

But we need swords and axes for Saeward and Wulfmaer. Burhred needs to have his axe blade re-worked, as it looks as if he had been swinging it onto rocks! Young Hearding smiles up at us as we drop pennies into his open hands for looking after our horses. A short walk, leading our mounts, takes us back to Asmund's workshop.

When we see him again he is hard at work hammering. Sparks fly as his outsized right hand swings a hammer rhythmically, bringing it down onto three white-hot bars of iron twisted around one another. We stand admiring his skill until he becomes aware of us being there.

'*This show of sparks pleases you?*' Asmund growls his acknowledgement of us.

'I think it is more to do with your looking like the god Thor, the way you swing that hammer raising showers of hot, white sparks', Theorvard has the measure of Asmund, I think.

'I look like Thor?' Asmund growls back. Whether he is angry at Theorvard for being likened to a heathen god, or whether he is astounded that anyone thinks back on the old gods, he gives no inkling.

'He is a heathen and a man of the Danelaw', I say of my friend, 'and he knows the value the good workmanship'.

'*You* think I am a good smith?' Asmund asks Theorvard, his hammer still in his right hand, resting it on the flat of the anvil, ready to strike again.

I nod at the sword in Wigmund's scabbard before Theorvard can answer and tell Asmund,

'We have seen your work'.

Asmund's follows my eyes and rests on the hilt of his friend's sword.

'Oh, *that!*' Asmund looks up at me. He clearly likes having his work admired, but he will not allow it to show, 'I put that together in one afternoon, whilst he went into the 'Three Cranes' and frittered away more of his silver!'

'You do not drink?' I ask, but Wigmund takes Asmund's thoughts away from my question with flattery for the workmanship on his own sword.

'He is a fast worker when he puts his back into it', Wigmund laughs.

'That was because Earl Gyrth had asked for another one to be made for his younger brother, Leofwin', Asmund grins at me. 'He wanted a gift that was worthy of a young man being made an earl! Anyway, since when did you know about putting your back into anything? All you ever do is ride about, buying and selling, and that weapon only ever gets an airing when you show off! He brings me trade, so why should it bother me if he only ever draws his sword to let men drool over the pattern welding on the blade?'

So, Wigmund's sword had been made some years ago when Harold was still the Earl of West Seaxe. It still looks as good as new! Hopefully *my* sword still looks as good three years from now. I had never given much thought to Leofwin's sword before we took on Duke Willelm. Doubtless it now fills a corner of some young Northman noble's gear, unless he has chosen to wear it at his side. I hope he knows good workmanship when he sees it!

'You want something like that for yourself?' Asmund asks me, waving his hammer at Wigmund's sword.

'There are two workmanlike swords that we need you to make. One is for Wulfmaer here', I shake my head at his question and rest my right hand on Wulfmaer's shoulder, whilst with my left I playfully pull Saeward's tousled hair. 'The other is for Saeward here. More than the two swords, we need axes for them both. Burhred would you show Asmund your axe, to see what he can do for it'.

Asmund looks at the two Wealtham men as though he thinks his craftsmanship would be wasted on them. He says nothing about that but asks instead,

'How many axes do you want?'

'Two, one each for Saeward and Wulfmaer', I tell him again, 'and one more for Burhred if you think his is beyond working over'.

On seeing Burhred's chipped axe blade, Asmund winces,

'You were waging war on rocks?' At seeing Burhred's vexed look Asmund adds with a wink, 'I thought you only went to fight the Northmen. Do you have to be taught how to use an axe as well?'

This raises a laugh from us all and Burhred shakes his head in disbelief.

'My axe was already old when I fought the Northmen. It was given to me by my thegn, Thorfinn, from the pile of weapons the Wealtham Hundred had left him. You just make the weapons, re-work my axe blade if you can, and I will *split* the Northmen's skulls with it!' Burhred grins and leans on the head of his axe.

'Not if you treat your axe blade like that! Mark my words young fellow, when you learn the craft of caring for and making weapons, you learn to fight the right way', Asmund warns Burhred, '*I* was a huscarl with Earl Harold years before I came here to make their swords and axes, *ask him*'.

Asmund points his hammer at me now, but I do not recall him being in Harold's household. He makes me mindful of what he thought about me then,

'I know you, 'the know-it-all', you with your white blond hair. Are you sure you do not recall me? Try seeing me with dark russet hair', Asmund ruffles his shock of iron grey hair, 'This grey is a fairly new thing. Having customers like *you* does not help a lot!'

Asmund throws a dark look at Wigmund and grins as the trader mockingly whines,

'What have *I* done?!' Wigmund's voice grates, 'I bring you trade and you grumble!'

'You do not recall me, *do you?*' Asmund is at pains to remind me, pumping the bellows at the side of the forge to heat up the burning coals piled up ready for new work.

'I have had a few knocks on the head since then', I have to allow. 'I am sorry but you will have to tell me something else about yourself'.

I look hard at him, trying my best, but no good comes of it.

'Who rounded up the horses in Wealas with you before we showed them to Earl Harold? You pulled out your silver to buy this red-maned one for yourself', he nods toward Braenda, 'and your kinsman told you to wait until when we had brought them to Thorney. He wanted to offer your horse to King Eadweard'.

Asmund takes a few bars of iron from behind his forge and sets them, side by side on the edge of the by now red hot coals. It is true what he says. It is also true no-one knew Harold wished to bring me to Lunden as one of his own household. Tostig had argued light-heartedly whether Harold was worthy of taking the best huscarl in the kingdom.

They were Tostig's words, not mine. Harold had agreed that I would only be here in the south until I *wanted* to go back to Jorvik. None of my friends knew about that, so could not have told him before we came here. We had not given him any thought until Wigmund showed us his sword and offered to bring us.

'...And who was it who mended your sword pommel in the smithy at Menai, before we came back with Gruffyd's head bundled in the blood-soaked cloth bag his followers gave Harold?'

'It *is* all coming back to me', I answer, the mist clearing in my head, 'although I had to ride back to Eoferwic to gather my things before coming on south'.

'Well, take your time. *Anyway,* when do you want these weapons ready for? I cannot finish them today. By the time I shut up shop tomorrow afternoon, at this time, they should be fettled and ready for use. They will not *look* like the work of a master craftsman, *but they* will *be usable for a long time to come!'*

Saeward and Wulfmaer nod eagerly. Burhred shrugs.

Wigmund stares down into a dark corner of the workshop and Theorvard is unaware of me looking his way, too.

'We will come by for them tomorrow', I agree, looking at Saeward who gives a start, thinking I was talking to him. 'You will want a down payment?'

'The goodwill, aye, it will cost you ten silver pounds. There is something I should ask, too', Asmund looks at Saeward too.

'What is that?' I ask, perhaps knowing what he wants.

'What is your friend going to sit on when he rides away? The road there is stony, and by the time you all climb down from your horses, he will be numb down there', Asmund looks across to Saeward and points at his manhood.

'A saddle, aye - *have you one?*' I have been thinking about when I saw him last. His dry wit, which harks back to Thorfinn, comes back to me now. Theorvard shares the dry wit more than anyone else I know.

'You want a lot for your coins, Ivar Ulfsson', Asmund notes drily with those same words that he used when I talked the Wealshman into parting with bridles to put on the horses as well as the animals themselves. He adds with a wink, 'It *will* cost you a little more silver'.

I grin broadly at him. He has *not* changed, only greyed.

'I see you recall me now', Asmund grins back and gives me a friendly thump on one shoulder with the dish-sized palm of his hand.

Theorvard grins in sympathy and grimaces with shared pain. The smack of Asmund's heavy palm feels as if it had bruised me,

'I felt that as well, *oh God!*'

'*Wha-at*, grow up man, I only *tapped* his shoulder!' Asmund laughs and walks over to one wall of his workshop and comes back with a sol-id-looking piece of leatherwear I would be hard put to call a saddle for *any* horse, let alone Saeward's bay mare.

'I think he would be just as well off without a saddle as with that', I stare at it in disbelief at it.

'As I said, you expect a lot for your silver. Try it, my friend', he heaves the thing onto the back of Saeward's horse. The animal nearly keels over with the sudden heavy weight and snorts its unwillingness to bear the load.

'What kind of animal did you put that thing on before?' Theorvard asks as Asmund lifts the saddle from Saeward's grunting mount.

'You think it too great a burden for your friend's mount?' Asmund answers in mock disbelief. He laughs as he lets it drop onto the dusty flagged floor of his yard. 'It was worn by an *ox* before. A fellow tried to sell it to me. His ox had died and he was unable to use it, but I told him if anyone wanted to buy the thing, I would give him the payment. He was killed fighting with King Harold, poor man!'

49

'*I can well believe that!* An ox saddle, eh?' Burhred raises his eyebrows, stands his axe against the anvil and steps back.

Asmund trudges to the back of his workshop and comes back with something that looks more like a saddle for a horse. He tosses it to Saeward, saying,

'You had best try *this* one, then'. With a smirk he tosses it to Saeward, who catches the saddle on his chest and almost falls backward onto his horse.

'*You* have not changed, Asmund', I chide. He most surely has not. I recall well now the jester that he was.

Asmund nods, winks, and with that we part company. Saeward has strapped the saddle onto his mare and climbs gingerly into it. The rest of us mount and turn toward the setting sun beyond Lud Gata.

I turn to give a salute, but Asmund is out of sight, back at his work. Sparks fly, lighting the little workshop as our horses walk away along the street, drawing admiring looks from shopkeepers and passers-by alike.

3

Our ride west to Thorney leads past the tiny church of Saint Bridget on our left. All around is the noise of bustling and shouting as the few shopkeepers here ready themselves for the night. Once beyond the old Seaxan settlement outside the walls of the older burh, all is quieter. A look across the falling meadows to my left in the failing light shows the Temese flowing like molten gold in the evening light, a sight I should look back on in my thoughts in the days ahead..

There are few on the road, aside from a small company of huscarls riding our way. Lit from behind by the sun settling on eastward bearing cloud, they are almost level with us when one of them calls out,

'Ivar Ulfsson, why are you out on this road at this time of the day?' one of them hails me and wheels his horse around. 'I would have thought you to be drinking with a good looking woman on either arm'.

'Osgod, *what gives?* Has Morkere sent you out to look for me?'

Saeward, behind me, is resentful at my friendship toward Osgod but that cannot be helped. That Osgod is now a thegn could prove useful one day.

'He and Earl Eadwin were talking with King Eadgar about what to do in the light of the lack of news from Duke Willelm. Earl Morkere thought you might know–'

Osgod does not say very much before I stop him,

'How would *I* know? For that you need a spay wife or a seer. If you need counsel about what Duke Willelm is doing, I know someone who could throw some light on that. It is a good thing we were on our way to see King Eadgar right now. This man here can tell you what you need to know. Osgod meet Wigmund the grain trader', I wave for Wigmund to come forward.

'Wigmund here has seen something that should give the king and the young earls something to think of'.

'I saw Duke Willelm's men burning–'Wigmund begins to tell Osgod.

'Leofstan ride back to Earl Morkere. *Tell him we are coming*'.

The fellow has already wheeled his horse and spurs the animal so sharply it rears before hurtling off towards Thorney.

'*Leofstan is eager*', I note drily to Osgod.

'He is new to Earl Morkere's household and still trying hard to earn his spurs', Osgod allows himself a wry smile. 'Nor does he know much about horses'.

'That much I can see', I turn to Theorvard who has just come up alongside me and point at Leofstan kicking his spurs into the animal's flanks.

'He *is* hard on his mount', Theorvard winces at the reckless way the man rides for Thorney.

'We all learn', Osgod smiles thinly and watches after Leofstan until the young fellow vanishes into the fading sunset. The sun has set behind the clouds and the cold begins to nag. 'With some the learning takes longer. Come, let us ride', he turns back to me and we urge our horses into a fast canter to keep up with Osgod's huscarls.

Torches splutter on the walls of the king's burh at Thorney, their flames dancing wildly in the strengthening westerly breeze. The West Mynster church with its younger abbey stands eerily silent across the way from King Eadweard's lodge.

Long ago, in the days before Aelfred an East Seaxan king Saeberht built the first church on this site, which was soon razed by my fellow countrymen before Guthrum took the Christian faith, baptised with the name Aethelstan.

The late King Eadweard had the church rebuilt, added an abbey and is now buried there. Eadgar uses the hunting lodge to rule his kingdom from, instead of Wintunceaster, as did Harold and Eadweard at times before him.

As we enter the hall, Eadgar is laughing at something Ansgar has been telling him. He turns to watch me near him and bow my head.

'What is it that you have to tell me, Ivar?' Eadgar rises from his high seat and strides forward to greet me. Eadwin and Morkere look at one another askance. They share a sharp intake of breath.

Hakon grins at the pair and berates them good-humouredly,

'Would you have a stuffy king, who sits like a wooden box, or would you sooner have a more welcoming king?'

'My King, it is Wigmund who has the tidings for you', I beckon the trader forward and he almost falls over his own feet in kneeling.

'Up, Wigmund - stand up and tell me', Eadgar laughs. 'This is almost like in the east!'

Eadwin and Morkere come up behind their young king and watch as Wigmund straightens himself and gathers his wits to tell Eadgar what he saw,

'My Lord King, I was chased from Acstede, a few miles within Suthrige from Centland, where I saw Duke Willelm's men on horseback burning steadings, chasing off sheep and cattle. Folk were begging on their knees tor pity, struck down where they knelt, killed by the horsemen for trying to save their livelihoods'.

Wigmund is clearly shaken by the suffering he witnessed, but staunchly finishes telling Eadgar was he saw,

'Having been seen, I was chased off by three of the horsemen. I think they wanted to take me back to be questioned by their duke but my horse was too fast for them', he pants. 'They were well armed, wore heavy mailcoats and their saddles were plainly heavier than mine, that is how I was able to outstrip them!'

'You did well, Wigmund', Eadgar puts a hand on the fellow's shoulder. 'How can I reward you for such worthy tidings?'

'By allowing me to tell you my tidings, your lordship has rewarded me richly already', Wigmund gushes. Eadgar cannot hide that he finds him bothersome, but his upbringing demands that he must offer some sort of reward for the man's efforts,

'Eat with us this evening, Wigmund', Eadgar smiles as he asks. 'I have to thank you somehow for your tidings. Taste my fare whilst I talk with Ansgar about our next step. You too shall sit with us, Ivar. as you have had dealings with this Northman duke'.

He has had little to do in the past with leadership matters and has only the Witan, his *stallari* Ansgar, his churchmen and his own eagerness to guide him during these bleak days. Beating Willelm at Lunden Brycg is only the beginning of what may be a long struggle. Willelm has already shown that he will not let his claim to Eadweard's crown falter on the outcome of one lost fight.

'My Lord King', I draw breath before I launch into what Harold should have listened to. 'We can only guess at what Willelm will do now. The next rider will make clearer what he is aiming for. Meanwhile, shall I take some riders to the south coast to see what is happening there? Their other leaders, Alan of Bretland, Odo of Bayeux and Count Rodberht of Mortain will be with Willelm. A few men could sneak in at night and see what is coming, ask questions of the local men'.

'Are you offering to do this for me?' Eadgar asks, looks me in the eyes and turns to Ansgar, 'Do we have anyone who speaks the Northmen's tongue?'

'I do not, my Lord King, I am sorry. None of my friends speaks their tongue, either. Thorfinn did, but he was killed with Harold'.

'I know a man, but could not swear to his loyalty', Theorvard has overheard and nears me, 'Earnald may still be in the burh'.

'Do you think you could *trust* him not to betray you as soon as he is able?' Eadgar squints at Theorvard in disbelief. 'I know I could never, and I would throw up at the smell that follows him. You are welcome to try'.

'As long as he knows there is a knife in his ribs if he says anything that warns the Northmen', Theorvard answers, 'we will be safe'.

'*Should* be safe, you mean. Is he still in Lunden burh? He may have sneaked away by now with whatever news Willelm could glean from him'. I do not recall seeing Earnald since the last evening.

'Since I showed him the delights of a good drink of Lunden ale, he will not be too far from an inn or an alehouse', Theorvard grins broadly at the king.

He shows gaps in his teeth that I know must be the outcome of his own liking for a good brew.

'He may fall *asleep* when he is needed, perhaps?' Eadgar asks, unsure about the wisdom of our errand.

Eadwin and Morkere look on, bored but the king has shown a thirst for knowledge about what I have in mind, so they have to make a show of wanting to know, too.

'He had best *not* fall asleep, my Lord King', I answer for Theorvard, 'for his own safety. If we are harmed, *he* dies first'.

'What is it you are looking for on the coast?' Eadwin asks. He may really want to know, or he is hoping for my errand to fail, so that he can ride north with his brother in the hope that Willelm lets them rule the north between them.

I stand with my feet firmly planted on the floor, my arms folded and answer Eadwin levelly,

'The hope is, armed with the knowledge we bring back from Pefense and Haestingas, that you the king might order the sending of ships around the east coast of Centland to Haestingas. If we break their supply chain we starve Duke Willelm of men and food'.

'You are sure this is the way to go about it?' Morkere asks now, thinking very likely that he could hide beyond the Hymbra.

His brother Eadwin would be the first to be given a rude awakening. The Northmen would be fools to let them sit fast, their wildwoods used as safe havens for rebels from the south.

'You are taking *these* fellows with you?' Eadgar asks, nodding toward my friends behind me and wondering perhaps if my thinking is wrong.

'I am, my Lord King. They are well proven'

'These two cannot surely be proven', Morkere sneers, trying to belittle Wulfmaer and Saeward in front of the king and his nobles.

'I saw that one bring down several riders before my very eyes', Ansgar lauds Wulfmaer loudly. 'He did as well as that young fellow with his bow, bringing down the knight who rode full tilt at me with his lance, ready to send me to my maker. Everyone there saw that, even *you,* Morkere!'

'I did not bring the *bowman's* skills into question. Anyway, where did you learn to use a bow so *well?'* Morkere tries to swing Ansgar's anger from himself to fend off well-earned mockery.

'My Lord Morkere, I learned from my father Hrothulf'. Theodolf saves the best part of his answer for last, 'My father was one of Earl Tostig's huscarls'.

Everyone in the room falls silent. Morkere's downward-twisted mouth betrays a sudden hatred for the young warrior.

'King Harold told you and your father to stay close to his banners', Ansgar thinks back, 'as we had few enough good bowmen and Harold wanted to be able to guide their aim himself to best effect. You gave a good showing with your father. What is your name?'

'My name is Theodolf, my Lord Ansgar', Theodolf stands straight, chest out, his bow grasped tightly in his left hand, unused to being held in awe by men of such high standing.

'Is your father still with us, Theodolf?' Eadgar asks, wanting to show that as king he wishes to learn about his underlings.

'No, my Lord King, my father was killed before King Harold was wounded'. Theodolf is holding up well. He has a pride in his bearing that was not there when Saeward and I first met him. He has become a man.

'Shame - from what I have heard, your father was a master bowman if he could teach you your craft so well, Theodolf'. Eadgar seems moved by Theodolf's bravery. Being of an age, they have much in common and could learn from one another.

His father, Eadweard 'the Exile', spent much of his life in the east, married Agatha, a kinswoman of the High king Heanric. He brought her together with his young son Eadgar and daughters Margaret and Christina. Agatha is still a good-looking woman and draws the eye of many a hopeful noble, but hers is the blood of kings and no matter how hopeful the retainer, she spends much of the time with her ladies-in-waiting. The old king treated Agatha as a queen in her own right, to make amends for the loss of her husband.

Theodolf only nods. Although the pain of losing his father is going, nevertheless he still feels it.

'What is *your* name? I recall seeing you, I think, at Wealtham when Earl Harold took me to see the building of the abbey. Dean Wulfwin asked for some horses to be shown in the yard', Eadgar looks closely at Saeward, thinking back.

'Now I know, you were one of the handlers. You had not handled horses before, had you?'

'I was not used to horses, my Lord King, and still am not - having spent my early days in the fields before Beorhtwulf and I entered into the laity. Beorhtwulf was to have made his final vows...'

Saeward stands crestfallen, unable to say more.

'Beorhtwulf was killed by a drunken oaf in the yard of the Earlsburh in Eoferwic', I tell Eadgar for him.

'Was the killer brought to book, Earl Morkere?' Eadgar turns to the young earl and, on hearing nothing from the earl snaps, '*Was* he brought to book?'

'Garwulf, the killer was in turn heinously killed by *him*'. Morkere points at Saeward. As he could not pay *wergild* to the man's kindred, he was stripped to the waist on Stan Gata and whipped for his crime-'

'Morkere, what *sort* of law do you keep in Northanhymbra? This man's brother was killed by one of the revellers in your burh and you have him *whipped?*' Eadgar has missed Morkere's saying Saeward took the law into his own hands.

I step in again to tell Eadgar,

'He threw an axe into the man's back from two-score paces'.

'He... *did what?!*' Eadgar stares at Saeward, thumps his beaker down onto the table behind him, knocking over one of the pitchers of Frankish red wine. Everyone looks worriedly at the king. Not having foreseen his outburst, they are unsure whether there might be another in the offing.

'Have you tried him out *again*, to see if that was not a fluke?' Eadgar asks once he has calmed himself.

'We have only just met again, my Lord King. Last night was the first time I had seen him since he was taken to Eoferwic by Osgod', I answer, looking at Morkere's thegn, who acknowledges me with a nod.

'Set out a target for him in the morning, Ansgar', Eadgar asks his *stallari*. 'I want to see if he can do it again. *If he can*, I want him as a huscarl along with these other four, and Ivar. You have a good eye for a warrior, Ivar. It may be something to do with your Danish forebears'.

He turns to me and laughs, perhaps unaware that it was Knut, my uncle, who brought about the downfall of Aethelred, his grandfather. Morkere and Eadwin breathe out, thankful that Eadgar's drinking leads to his thinking being so easily befuddled.

'Ivar, you and your friends should eat and drink your fill. I do not envy the task you have set yourself', Eadgar regales us.

'Sleep well, all of you. Good night one and all. We will meet in the morning to see if Saeward has lost his touch – or not, as the case may be', our new king takes his leave of us to go to his rooms. We all echo his farewell and find room either side of Ansgar after others also take their leave for the night.

'You have made your mark with the king, Saeward', Ansgar tells my friend but his words fall on deaf ears.

Saeward eats, and sips his ale half-heartedly. Having been reminded of his brother, he may now be at one with Beorhtwulf, buried far away in Jorvik.

My thoughts wander too and I wonder if who I saw in my bed last night was really Aelfthryth. Or did I bed Braenda again? Whoever I bed now, whatever the shape of her body, she will look like Braenda.

Even when I only looked longingly at Aethel on the way to Lunden I saw Braenda smiling back at me. Are my thoughts playing tricks on me, or is she using others to see me, to use me as a plaything?

Theorvard looks at me and away again. He says something to Burhred, who turns, looks my way and shakes his head.

'I should sleep', I say to Ansgar, who looks at me and nods.

'We should *all* put ourselves in the care of our dreams', Ansgar smiles, 'but unluckily we have no young serving women here to sleep with you'.

'I would be of no use to any woman. When I put my head onto the bolster I shall be away, *far* away from here', I draw my hands down over my brow and shake my head in a bid to rouse myself enough to find my bed before I fall asleep.

I look across at Theorvard and Burhred, raise both hands in salute and wonder aloud to Ansgar,

'Where is Aethel?'

'The Lady Eadgytha took her to Wintunceaster today as a companion. Widows together! I think she has taken to your friend's woman. She may have taken Eadgar's younger sister Christina with her, too. Perhaps she took Aethel to be fit company for a young lady of high birth', Ansgar rises and rests against the table, knuckles down on the rough cloth stained by the wine beaker Eadgar knocked over.

I do not know why I feel downhearted at the thought of Aethel being taken along with Christina to Wintunceaster. It may mean she will be safe from Willelm's men if they should take Lunden. I should be happy for her, but I am not. As long as we did not upset Theodolf I wanted to get to know her better.

'Let me show you where you are resting', Ansgar tells me.

'Saeward, Burhred and Theorvard will be shown when they tire of Morkere's company. Waltheof plainly knows him better. He and Eadwin will let him know when they have had enough of his prattle'.

Ansgar finally makes to leave the table.

'Ansgar, are you leaving us so soon?' Morkere's speech is slurred.

He stands, sways, and sits again when he sees Eadwin scowl at him and finishes telling Ansgar, 'The night is young yet and our host Eadgar's *hraegle thegn* has offered to send us some young women to play with'.

'I am a married man, Earl Morkere. My nights of carousing are long past. Enjoy yours, by all means', Ansgar answers him cheerfully, knowing the young earl will be unable to pleasure any woman now, let alone a young one. Eadwin gives Ansgar a little wave, as if to send him away like one of the household retainers.

Oddly, Waltheof sees himself away too now, and earns Morkere's scorn when he too turns down the offer of womanly company. I think he has his sights on Eadgar's sister Margaret, but he would be wise to steer clear of her. The Scots' king Maelcolm has set his sights on her, a man of proven skill with the sword.

The morning dawns grey, though dry like any afteryear day in this part of the kingdom. Saeward has been warming up with a war-axe since I came out into the yard of Thorney's small burh.

He has two more propped up against a drinking trough behind him and straw has been strewn thickly on the ground close to a thick wooden target. This way the axe blades will not be too chipped if they drop onto the flagstone-laid yard.

Morkere, Waltheof and Eadgar have not shown yet. Ansgar watches, lost in thought as Saeward limbers up with the axe, swinging it, mill-like around his right shoulder. He takes aim and sends the axe hurtling at the target, over two-score paces away - too far, I would say. The axe thumps loudly onto the outer rim, and drops with a dull clatter onto the stone-set yard. None of us says anything. When Garwulf was killed only Hrothulf, Theodolf and I were there. We saw nothing other than the fool drunkard fall backward with my axe firmly planted in his chest. When we looked up, Saeward was at least as far away as he is from the target now.

He might have taken a short run-up to hurl the axe, but I took it that he had thrown it that far and he had followed it a few paces further. It chills me to think it could as easily have hit me!

He is getting a feel of the axes now, and weighs them before throwing.

Eadgar shows, with Morkere trailing. He looks at Ansgar, who merely shrugs and looks sideways at Saeward. My friend knows he is being watched closely, and might be unsure of himself.

'Bring the other axe back, someone', Eadwin calls out to one of the stable hands here given the task of stewarding. The burly fellow strides across to the target, bends and picks up the axe, hands it back to Saeward, and walks slowly back to where he was standing.

The next axe sticks in the inner ring of the target briefly before dropping again.

'Better luck – ', Theorvard begins to cheer Saeward.

'*Hush there,* that man!' Morkere scolds.

Saeward looks around for me, sees me and walks back a few steps. He quickens his stride for another throw and hurls the axe.

With a loud thud the axe buries itself in the outer ring. Those of us who think ourselves his friends cheer loudly. Eadgar claps wildly, as does Waltheof. Eadwin and Morkere stand behind Eadgar, arms folded, saying nothing.

Ansgar grins reassuringly at Saeward and calls loudly,

'You should hit the inner ring with your next axe, Saeward!'

Saeward says nothing but takes the next axe from the stable hand.

Quickening his stride as he nears the scraped throwing line, Saeward lets fly... and hits the inner, just below the first axe. We all hold our breath as he is handed one more and strides up to throw it... The third axe not only hits the inner ring, but splits the shaft of the second axe, raising a whoop from Theodolf.

Theorvard stands dumbstruck, mouth agape. Eadgar cannot believe what he has just seen either and stands, hands over his mouth, eyes popping.

Waltheof and I are the first to come back down to earth and stride up to Saeward. I am first to open my mouth but cannot say anything for short gasps of laughter and can only give him a bear hug to show him how taken I am at his sheer skill.

'You have earned your right to be a king's huscarl', Waltheof is first to hail him and gladly takes Saeward's right hand and pumps it with both his.

'You need to rest now, my friend', I pat his left shoulder as Eadgar strides up to add his own acclaim for such a feat.

'I am glad you are one,of *mine,* not Duke Willelm's!' Eadgar clasps Saeward's shoulders tightly, 'Tell me again you want to my huscarl! For that matter, all *five* of you! Go, see what it is you have to, come back safe and sound to stand with me in the shieldwall against Duke Willelm in the *next* fight!'

Saeward throws his head back and gives a throaty laugh, something I have rarely seen since the day I first set eyes on him at Wealtham. It is a welcome sight, I have to say. Morkere still baulks at his king's kindness,

'That he is a killer does not go against the grain with you my Lord King?' Morkere puts his head on one side, testing Eadgar's goodwill. Is he trying to wrongfoot his new king?

Whatever his thoughts, Morkere is not allowed the slur on Saeward. Eadgar rounds on him, ring finger aimed at the young earl's now open mouth,

'*He avenged his brother's death, Morkere!* It is something that my kinsman King Eadweard should have done when he came to the throne. His brother Aelfred the *Aetheling* was slain, coming to further his claim to the crown as was his right. Eadweard was sent away back to North-mandige by their mother Ymme to cower whilst Knut lorded over the kingdom - *his kingdom!* It was widely held that Ivar's kinsman Godwin had him blinded. Aelfred later died from his wounds in a cell at the monastery of Elige, dumped like a sack of carrots without a Christian burial!' Eadgar looks sorrowfully at me, as if ashamed at his outburst, 'Ivar you had to be told one day. I do not hold your kinsman's deeds against *you.* I still wish you to be a huscarl. You should be made thegn one day, if not an earl'.

He holds out a hand, which I take in the spirit of friendship it was offered, and finishes,

'Perhaps also, like your half-brother Beorn before you, you will be the one of *your* kin to truly be of use to one of Cerdic's line without furthering your own aims or killing another of *my* kin!'

Morkere looks happy that Eadgar has made me mindful of Godwin's misdeeds. His father Aelfgar lost out to my kinsman, Harold after his first clash with Eadweard, marked for answering back when charged with faithlessness. There was a claim he had been aiding the Wealsh in the west, raiding in Svein Godwinson's earldom.

I am no threat to Eadgar. He knows I rely upon his open-handedness, and that he must in turn to me for my help in banishing the Northmen from his kingdom.

'It is time we left to see how Willelm's men are fed and armed', I offer. 'We must gather Saeward's and Wulfmaer's weapons from Asmund the smith on the way to the bridge'.

'*Are they paid for?*' Eadgar suddenly asks, following us back to the stables, 'What have you asked him to make?'

'Saeward paid silver on a pair of swords and axes', I tell him.

'You must show me them when I see again after your exploits, Saeward', our young king stops and turns to speak to Ansgar.

He catches up with us as we set off to the stables,

'I have asked Ansgar to speak to my *hraegle thegn* to bring silver for the weapons, Ivar. Having seen *your* saddle I must press you to buy good ones for Saeward and Wulfmaer'.

Some of the stable lads bring our saddles and help to strap them on-to our mounts. For all his youth has already earned the loyalty of Harold's household. He had time to watch, and learn the way my kinsman spoke to his servants and has learned well. They will stand him in good stead for as long as he is king.

Agatha and Margaret, having stayed in the background during Saeward's show of axe-throwing, have left for the ease and warmth of the hall, leaving Eadgar to wave us off from the burh gates. Ansgar and Waltheof stand behind the king, on either side of him, and raise their arms in salute as we ride out through the gates. I have still be unable to speak to the young earl about leaving Caldbec Beorg before the fighting began. Eadwin and Morkere walk back into the hall without acknowledging our leaving.

I have a feeling Leofric's grandsons will have to look to their own before too long. They will find themselves at odds with their king if we are to stand against Willelm again one day soon.

Asmund must have been working through the night.

He has not only had time to make the heads and shafts for two Dane axes, even pattern-welding the blades, but has made two swords and put them into a pair of handsome sword scabbards.

Asmund sees my look of awe and laughs deeply,

'You did not know I could work magic? Thor is a mighty friend for a smith!'

My broad grin of disbelief brings enlightenment,

'No, *honestly*, Ivar if you do not believe me, ask him yourself. Thor, my friend, come here. I have a man who does not believe in you'.

A giant of a man, taller than Theorvard and near twice his age comes from the back of the workshop and stretches out a hand to greet me.

'Ivar, I give you Thor', Asmund nods sideways at him.

'Who *gave* you that name?' Theorvard cheekily asks the giant.

'Who would you *suppose* gave me such a name?' Thor beams warmly, shaking with laughter.

'*Well*, my friend I for one am glad to meet you!' Theorvard booms.

'I am Theorvard, this is Burhred and behind him is Theodolf, our bowman', Theorvard holds his left hand to his mouth and speaks behind it to the smith,

'The other two are committed Christians and would question the wisdom of speaking to a man their faith would not let them see'.

'I can see him, as plain as that bulb-like nose of *yours!*' Wulfmaer comes over to admire the handiwork of these gifted craftsmen and shakes Thor by the hand. 'What fool would think of *me* as a staunch Christian? The last time I went to church the priest did not know me from *Adam!*'

Saeward only looks at his sword, and at me.

'*Why so sad?*' Asmund asks before I can. 'You have a new sword and axe. It is a proud day for most young men. Your king has seen fit to show you his open-handedness with silver to pay for your weaponry'.

Saeward cannot bring himself to answer, staring at the sword in his hand.

'What is the *matter*, Saeward?' I ask him.

'I am saddened that I have come so far through life without knowing the true worth of my fellow man', Saeward answers finally.

We look at one another, trying to fathom what it is he means.

After what seems like an age, Thor himself asks Saeward what is meant by that. His face twisted in self-loathing, Saeward almost spits out an answer he thinks will tell us everything,

'I am being geared up to fight and kill my fellow man. Where has *my* faith gone that I should be ready to take *another* man's life?'

'Saeward', Thor grips my friend by the shoulders, 'I too am an un-swerving follower of the same god you claim to have faith in. I make these weapons with Asmund here for men to kill others. When your sword bites, when your axe sings in the wind and cuts into the North-man who would otherwise kick you onto your back for him to skewer you with his pig-sticker, I shall feel that man's pain'. Thor stops to let Saeward take in his words before going on, 'If I did not feel his pain I could no longer make these weapons, because I would then have be-come a thrall to the anvil that I work on! I praise the Lord that I am a brother!'

'*What* - you are a man of *God* with that heathen name?' Saeward almost coughs in disbelief.

'Aye, friend, I am a brother', Thor reaches behind me and pulls down a brown habit from a shelf. 'With a name such as mine, what else could I be now that none trusts in the old gods?'

The laughter that follows echoes around the small workshop, Saeward's being the loudest.

'What will you do with the silver *you* have been paid?' I ask Thor. As I am the first to speak after all the laughing and more hoarse cough-ing, I think we should know what he has aforethought for his pay.

'The silver would go far to renew some of the stonework on the nearby church of Saint Clement. The door needs caulking against the damp from the river mists that eats away at the timbering. Come, fol-low me and I will show you my church. The late king came by often, and gave me silver to pay for new timbers in memory of his namesake who was buried here. The worshippers do not care for silverware on the altar, being honest hard working fisherfolk. They ask only for plain

things, such as a cloth for the altar table to put their wooden cross on...
and for a prayer to be said for the Harold who was buried here before
Eadweard was crowned in his own right'.

He pauses because he knows there will be at least one of us who
does not know which Harold he means.

'But King Harold was killed by the Northmen only weeks ago',
Theodolf is the one who does not know, being young. The lad stares
hotly at the smith, awaiting his answer. Thor smiles at Theodolf, at
Saeward and then around at the rest of us except me, thinking I know
the answer anyway,

'I am talking of Harold, the one nicknamed '*Harefoot*'.

'He was the son of Knut by his handfast wife, Aelfgifu of Northanhamtun. He held the kingdom for his half-brother and was briefly our
king before Harthaknut came to claim his right. Harold was torn from
his slumbers in God's hands and cast into the Temese by his foes', Thor
recounts. 'A fisherman found him spread-eagled, filthy – weeds
brought in by the tide strewn across him where he lay on the strand -
and brought him here to be buried in the care of Clement. He has rested
here since', Thor shows us to a corner of the churchyard, where a hog-
backed tombstone marks the last resting place of another Harold who
reigned only months for all he was well-liked. Harthaknut's only saving
grace was that he offered to share the throne with Aethelred's son by
Emma, his half-brother.

We are steered around the church yard, Thor pointing to graves he
thinks we should know about. When he comes to an overgrown one by
the wall of the church itself he tells us gravely,

'Here lies Marthe, a woman who came to Lunden from Flanders.
Her ship was beset by Frieslander freebooters in the mouth of this river.
Her crew of four were all killed, but she lived long enough to tell the
tale. Marthe had steered her boat alone on the east wind with a deep
spear wound in her chest. King Aethelred sent ships downriver but to
no avail. The Frieslanders had left by then, knowing what would pass
should they be caught', Thor makes the sign of the cross with his hand
and passes on.

'We had best be leaving, my friend', I tell our kind guide. 'There is
a long ride ahead of us and we must skirt the Centish burhs lest we are
seen on our errand by Duke Willelm's men. I thank you for showing us
your kingdom, Thor. Hopefully soon we shall meet again'.

'I too look forward to seeing *you* again, friend Ivar. May your gods
go with you and one day you will tell your grandchildren that you knew
a man of God who went by the name of Thor', he grins broadly down at
me. 'They will laugh because they will not believe you, *thinking you to*

be simple!'

'Nevertheless I *will* tell them', I grip his arm and turn to my friends.

'We need to find Earnald', Theorvard reminds me as we leave the church.

'Are looking for the fat Frankish priest?' Thor calls after us. 'He left Lunden this noon, by way of Suthgeweorce. I saw him heading east on a small horse, poor creature. He will not have gone very far, a man of his size!'

'I thank you again, Thor. *I owe you!'*

We make our way back to our horses, tethered near the river bank, mount and turn them onto the road east to Lud Gata over the Fleot. We have to press them into a gallop to make up for lost time.

Theodolf's horse reaches the bar at Lud Gata first and he calls out for the watchman on duty to open up.

'Open up, by *whose* order?' someone calls out from within.

'Open up on the orders of *both* King Eadgar *and* Lord Ansgar!' I shout back, having arrived with Theorvard and Burhred.

Braenda snorts and whinnies. She, too, would sooner be on her way than have to wait for some old watchman to lumber up behind the creaking doors. We hear him curse as he fumbles with the chains and after a long wait the doors creak back. A half-bent old man peers through the gap and blinks at the sight of the six of us in the half-dark in our mailcoats.

'*Come on old man,* we need to reach the bridge *before the* Angel Gabriel blows his trumpet for the second *coming!'* Theorvard pushes his side of the great oak door wider with little effort.

'Do *you* want this work?' the gatekeeper croaks up at Theorvard as we file through behind Theorvard and press our horses into a gallop again, up the hill past the great church of Saint Paul. We are soon on our way through the streets, down to the river past Dow Gata again. Soon the bridge stretches out ahead of us. The long planks are covered with the sheen left by a mist from downriver on its ghostly way up to Thorney. Ansgar's huscarls stand aside at the Suthgeweorce end of the bridge to let us through.

I rein in Braenda and ask of Earnald,

'Did you see the Frankish priest pass earlier, a stout fellow on a small horse?'

'He *did* pass, before the sun passed over Thorney. I think it must have been some time after we let the others off duty in the early afternoon. I said something about him wearing out the poor animal and asked why he had not bought a bigger one. He snorted and cursed me, told me to watch my lip or answer to Saint Peter. Then he said something about churchmen riding stallions being out of keeping with church teachings. I asked if it also meant priests should drink heavily. He smelled *rank!* Well, *whatever* - it takes all kinds – '

Before he finishes telling me I am halfway to the first of the ruined houses on this side of the river, trying to catch up with the others. Someone has made a start on pulling down a few of them, ready to start building anew, but that is as much as I can make out before I pass between them. Braenda strikes sparks off the dry stones half-buried in the muddied road as we hurtle past the last buildings along Watling Straet toward the darkening shadows around the hamlet of Grenewic.

My friends have slowed their horses to a canter. I can barely see them in the murk ahead, their talking becoming louder as I close on them.

'*Ah*, Ivar, have you news of Earnald?' Theorvard breaks off and Saeward turns in his saddle without reining in to watch me ride up to them. Saeward and Wulfmaer are further along down the road, and Theodolf has taken the lead.

'I think *I* can see something on the road ahead!' Theodolf reins in his horse for us to catch up and I strain my eyes to look eastward.

'I think I can see something, too', Saeward agrees. 'But whatever it is I cannot say'.

'Do you think the Northmen will be waiting for someone to come along this way?' Burhred asks.

None of us wishes to be taken captive. Theorvard must be well-known to them by now, the easiest to recall after the skirmish on the bridge. When Theodolf slows his horse to an easy trot, we all follow suit. Theodolf puts a finger to his mouth.

'*That* is no warhorse!' Wulfmaer laughs, 'We have caught up with Earnald. He is by the roadside, sleeping off another few beakers of ale'.

True enough, as our horses slow to a walk I see the shapeless heap by the roadside, which must be Earnald.

'Thor said he saw Earnald leave at around noon. Where he saw him must have been near the bridge, but there are no inns there'.

I dismount to pick up a bundle, knowing it to be Earnald's by the smell. As he has pulled his dirtied habit over himself there is nothing I would know to be a man in the darkness. Nevertheless when I lean over him, the rank smell of soured wine and piss rises to my nostrils.

'He has found some *wine* somewhere. Take a sniff – no, *perhaps not.* The smell is enough to make even a seasoned warrior gag!'

'Who *is* this fellow?' Saeward demands, disgusted a man of the cloth should have sunk so low.

'He is Earnald, a Frankish priest. He was our go-between with Duke

Willelm before the fight at Lunden Brycg. King Eadgar asked someone to get him drunk so he would not run off to Willelm and tell him about our true strength. Theorvard took him to the 'Eel Trap' and plied him with ale', I stand well back, away from the smell.

'Aye, he is harmless enough, though. He must have already had a great liking for strong drink before I showed him to Aenglish ale', Theorvard comes up between Saeward and me and bends down.

He straightens again, lips curled,

'*Ugh!* You are right, Ivar. He smells *rank!*' Theorvard looks set to heave, for all his size.

Burhred is happy there is no need for him to come any closer,

'Well, we are agreed it *is* him'.

'Is there running water nearby?' I ask, should any of my friends know our whereabouts.

We all fall silent, listening. There is no sound of a beck, so Wulfmaer clambers up onto a high stone wall, holds onto a low tree branch and looks out over the moonlit landscape.

'To the north of us is a mere. Have we anything to carry water in?'

'Why do we need to *carry* water?' Burhred asks in a way that makes me think he is asleep on his feet.

'We need to awaken Earnald because we have to take him along to the south coast', I tell him.

'He can speak the Northmen's tongue as they do'. Theorvard cuts in, trying to make it clear to a half-asleep, nodding Burhred.

'Why do we not rest and keep a watch on our friend until morning?' Burhred answers slowly. He may think we are slow on the uptake. It may be we are the ones who are half asleep. Theodolf is the first to see sense.

'The Northmen may keep an eye on this road, although no-one would use this road in the dark. We are safe for now, but in the morning things might not be so easy for us', the lad points out.

'I for one do not wish to be prodded with a pig sticker between my shoulder blades when we try to cross this open land!'

'Point taken, Theodolf', I acknowledge his fear about the Northmen being this close to Lunden.

'We *still* need someone to get water', Theorvard grumbles, eyeing Wulfmaer. The miller folds his arms and sets his teeth, feeling he is about to be called on to search for this water.

'Why do we need to go over *there* for water', Saeward asks, 'when we each have drinking water?'

'The water is not for *drinking*. It is for throwing over Earnald, to awaken him and take him somewhere safer whilst it is still dark', Theorvard enlightens him as if he were talking to a child.

'Why do we not just *piss* on him? That would wake him up enough for us to prod him toward the mere and push him in. At least he might smell *fresher* then', Wulfmaer does not seem to be full of the milk of human kindness toward Earnald.

Theorvard calls heavenward, as if asking his maker for the words to set Wulfmaer right,

'He would catch his death of cold. I am no priest killer, but we might as well shove a sword into his belly now as throw him in the mere! Good God man, have you no *kindness* in you?'

'He is a Northman spy, is he not?' Wulfmaer laughs humourlessly. 'We would be doing well by King Eadgar'.

'Aye, and if he is alive he will be a spy for *us* when we get to Haestingas and Pefense', I look Wulfmaer in the eye as I tell him *why* I wish to take Earnald with us. 'He is to be our tool until we have done with him, to ask the Northmen what we can not. Do you know their tongue? When he has done our bidding, *then* you can do what you like with him as long as you leave me out of it', Theorvard is beginning to lose his temper. This long-suffering son of the Danelaw finds the East Seaxan testing. I can hear it from the way he speaks slowly, measured-ly.

'Mealy-mouthed *fool* –'Wulfmaer begins to jeer at Theorvard.

'The only fool I can see is *you!* Wulfmaer, listen. I will tell you once, I will not abide bickering. If you are going to carry on like this you can go back to your mill, *now*', I grab his right arm as I stare into his eyes, to stop him drawing his dagger on me, '*whatever* King Eadgar might have said about your weapon skills'.

Wulfmaer falls silent and I step back whilst Saeward rasps something into his ears I am unable to hear. He seems to have Wulfmaer's ear. If what Saeward tells him keeps him quiet until we reach safety again, so much for the better.

'What do we use for bringing water?' I ask everyone.

'Has *he* anything?' Theodolf asks looking down, bored at the sleeping Earnald.

'He might have a wine skin with him, either on his saddle or hidden somewhere in his habit', Theorvard's thinking sounds useful.

'There is nothing on the saddle, but he may have a skin cradled within his habit', Burhred turns his nose up at the thought of having to rummage through Earnald's stinking habit.

'Turn him over', Theorvard counsels without making a move to do it himself, 'with your foot'.

I stride across the grass, wringing wet with dew in the cold night air, grip one corner of Earnald's habit with both hands and pull sharply. The brother rolls over, still asleep. His hands now cover his head, his eyes closed.

'*There*', I tell Theodolf, and point my boot at a skin, half covered by the greasy, dirty habit.

Theodolf bends forward, snatches the skin and undoes the stopper cap. He pours out the sour wine onto the road and then pushes the stopper back into the spout.

'*Where* did you say the mere was?' Theodolf asks Wulfmaer.

'*Give it here*, I will take it', Wulfmaer offers.

Swallowing his pride he takes the skin from Theodolf's hands, scales the wall at the roadside and vanishes into the darkness. Whilst Wulfmaer is gone we stand and wait. Earnald rolls back and pulls his habit back over him, still fast asleep.

'I wish I could sleep as soundly as that, like a baby', Theorvard shakes his head at the brown, shapeless heap.

'He will be wide awake soon enough', Saeward laughs and nods at a gleeful Wulfmaer, who clambers back over the wall with a bulging skin full of water.

'That mere smells about as rank as Earnald himself', Wulfmaer says when he reaches us, 'Still the water in this skin is not as dirty as his habit, and it is *cold!* He looks as though he had been rolling in the horse muck back in Wynstan's stable, so he will gain by a dousing!'

'Well *un*-stopper it, man! Get this over with. All this standing around in the dark bores me, and I am getting damned well cold!' Burhred snaps at Wulfmaer and darts a look at me. He will not be the only one before long.

'All right, *all right* - I am *doing it!'* Wulfmaer is in no mood to be nagged.

'God in heaven - is it *raining?*' Earnald sits, awake as Wulfmaer shakes the last of the brackish water onto him. He looks up at Theorvard, coughs and rolls over onto his knees.

Pressing awkwardly down on the grass he tries to rise to his feet, stands, falls back onto his knees and is dragged to his feet by Saeward.

'I thank you, my son', Earnald seems to bless Saeward and sags to his knees again.

Theorvard lifts Earnald by his right elbow so hard the priest whitens.

'*Hey,* not so hard, good fellow, I am not a sack of turnips. *See,* I am standing!' Earnald yells out. '*I am standing!'*

He almost whimpers when he sees who it is he shouted at. Theorvard scowls darkly at the priest and turns away from him.

'What am I *doing* here?' Earnald squeaks, looking up at each of us in turn.

'We would all like to know that one, Frankish priest! Were you scampering off to your master to tell him something?' Wulfmaer spits, 'This is *our* land, should you have forgotten!'

'It is *God's* land', Earnald tries to put him right, 'and your king was an oath breaker...' Seeing us all scowl down at him he tries to lead us on a new line of thought, 'What did you do with my *wine?* That was good wine that Count Rodberht gave me a few days ago, when he sent me to Lunden'.

'It was sour, rank – like you. Who sent you to spy on us?' I demand, but think I know what he is going to tell me anyway, that he was sent to speak to King Eadgar. Willelm *himself* could not have known Eadgar had been made king in Lunden. No plea will help the priest.

'I am a *monk*, not a warrior. I was sent to speak to your king, Eadgar', Earnald swears foolishly, as I thought he would.

'You only need a good pair of ears to be a spy! Did you *know* what Eadgar looked like?' I stare at him and step back, gagging at the stale smell of sour wine on his breath, 'He stood as close to you near the bridge before the fight as *I am* now to you, and you did not know him until Lord Ansgar told you who he was. That was when he asked you to speak for him to your duke in his own tongue'.

'I merely *spoke* for him with Duke Willelm!' Earnald whines pitifully, chins jiggling as he jerks his head, looking from me to Theorvard and back to me. On peering up at the others he only sees blank stares.

'You spoke long together about *something* that can have had little to do with what King Eadgar asked you to say', I snarl at the cowering Earnald, reminded of being told by my father about the unwillingness of some of these clerics to stand on their own feet when faced by fighting men.

There are a *few* men of the church bold enough to stare back, like Thor, but broadly speaking they are craven.

'Fear not, priest. We will not kill you', Theorvard takes in the sorry looking fellow, 'at least not yet'.

'No, Earnald, we will not kill you because you will be of use to us in the days ahead. You will do the same for us as you did for Duke Willelm', I tell him, watching his eyes widen in fear. 'You will do our bidding and ask for what we want to know of your fellows'.

Trembling, wide awake, wet and fully sobered, Earnald asks me,

'Where are we *going?*'

I let him sweat before answering. Unsure of what we want from him, he may do my bidding better than if I tell him what he wants to know,

'We are to ride first to Pefense - and from there to Haestingas. From there we will ride back through the Andredesleag to Lunden, but I will free you well before we reach Grenewic again'.

Theorvard coughs to catch my ear, but I will let my friends know my aims when Earnald is too far off to hear me. With a wink at Theorvard I try to show him that I am not giving anything away.

Earnald is still unaware of what is going on even after I have told him, still much the worse for wear since downing at least half the wine. The shock from the skinful of water Wulfmaer poured over him has worn off. He looks dazed again and flops onto his backside on the dew-laden grass.

'Oh no, you are not due for a rest yet!' Theorvard hoists him to his feet. 'Mount your horse'.

'Why do we have to leave now? I need to sleep if you are taking me to the coast', Earnald wheedles. 'Can I rest first and then we will be able to ride in the morning?'

'We are riding on to the marshes to find shelter for the night', I look sideways at the overweight cleric, feeling sorry for the poor creature that has to bear him, 'Until then, doze while you are riding. Fear not, we will not let you fall off your horse'.

As Earnald gives me a baleful look and climbs with effort into the saddle of his overworked horse, Theorvard asks,

'Ivar, what would you say to stealing a bigger horse for him to ride? He is going to find it hard keeping up with us on that nag. *He will hold us back!*' he protests loudly to me. 'Without him holding us back we could be near Haestingas by morning. With him we will still be on the way when evening comes again'.

I try to reassure him that we will be faster than that,

'If we see a suitable beast that looks as if it belongs to no-one, Theorvard, by all means take it for him'. The likelihood of that happening is slight. As anyone, Centishfolk take care of their horses. He gives me an odd look and mounts. When we are all mounted, I wave to move off.

There may be at least an hour's ride ahead of us before we find shelter, and then we will have to ride from dusk to dawn, skirting Hrofesceaster and Medestan. When we reach the Andredesleag we can ride most of the time if we need to, no-one will see us on the wooded upland tracks.

It is fairly easy riding, even with the moon dipping into the clouds now and then. The land here is mostly even, and the men who built this road knew how to lay stones and dig ditches. It has lasted long and well, although at times I think the Centish folk might have taken stones to build their homes with where we ride through drying mud. I can let

Braenda find her own way, surefooted animal that she is.

My friends' horses slip from time to time, raising loud curses. Theorvard and I take turns quietening them, so that the cursing does not get too loud. On a quiet night such as this, sounds carry and jar on the ear if there are Northmen scouting the land. After all, we are not meant to be here.

The miles do not fly by, with Earnald on his little horse between Burhred and Wulfmaer. I know Theorvard has misgivings about the priest riding with us. Finding a bigger mount for him would be welcome, but unlikely.

To the north and east the land looks flatter in the moonlight. Having come off the road, the track we are on now is deeply rutted by heavily-laden waggons. There are huge stones and rubble inset in the track and these make the going awkward for some of the horses where they are half buried.

The six of us dismount and walk our horses. Earnald rides, his short-legged long-suffering horse suddenly stands stock still and pulls back when Theorvard catches the reins to pull it along.

'Earnald, you will have to dismount and walk your horse a little way', I tell him.

Seeming not to have heard me, he stays in his saddle. I tell him again,

'Dismount, Earnald. Your horse cannot carry you. We are all walking our horses, as you can see'.

There is a low building along this track that I know of, where we can all rest out of sight through the daylight hours.

'*Get off the damned nag!*' Theorvard tells him this time.

He still turns a deaf ear.

'*Earnald, get down off that horse!*' Saeward snaps. I hope Earnald has the sense to know he has sorely tried us.

Theorvard stands, feet spread wide, his right hand resting on the pommel of his sword, threatening. Earnald seems not to understand how close he is to losing his hold on this world, whether he is useful to us or not.

'*Dismount* priest, before I drag you down off that damned creature!' Theorvard warns him again and grabs his left elbow.

Earnald falls dead onto me from the saddle.

'What do we do *now?*' Burhred asks. From the looks I am getting, I am the one who has to supply the answer.

'We will not be able to learn anything useful now, that much is understood. We will only be able to watch and learn from what we can see, rather than finding out through Earnald', I tell them what they already believe.

'We will have to sneak about at night time when we are nearer the coast, or try to find some useful clothing to make ourselves look as though we are merchants'

'I should have guessed as much', Theorvard for one has read my thoughts, 'with our swords ready under our cloaks'.

'What do we *do* with Earnald?' Theodolf asks. 'Do we bury him, *or leave him for the wolves?*'

'Do we have any digging tools?' Saeward wants to do right by the priest.

Theodolf casts a baleful look at Saeward. He would sooner be rid of the old sot.

'Put him over his horse, like a bag of corn', Wulfmaer offers with a snarl. 'It has to be used to the smell of him by now. I would not want him on *mine*'.

Theorvard and Burhred bend to lift Earnald's lifeless, muddied corpse. Burhred, being shorter than Theorvard by a head and shoulders finds it hard going to help the young giant.

'Steady, man, just hold his shoulders and lift, like a sack of grain', Wulfmaer laughs.

'You would know more about that sort of thing, miller! This damned priest is a dead weight, my friend. I am *already* out of breath, having manhandled him only this far!' Burhred puffs under Earnald's bulky shoulders, made worse by the loose habit.

'Then let *me* take his shoulders. I cannot think for the life of me why *you* took them', Wulfmaer mocks, shaking his head, and bends down to be ready when Theorvard lifts the feet.

Wulfmaer drops Earnald quickly, holding his nose, and yells out,

'Oh my God in Heaven, *what a shit smell!*'

'What is it *now?!*' Theorvard groans and stands straight. 'Wulfmaer pick up his shoulders and help fling him over his horse!'

Burhred laughs hysterically at the now heaving Wulfmaer, earning himself dark looks from Theorvard.

'I thought perhaps you would be better doing this than Burhred, being used to the smell of cow shit and lifting heavy meal sacks', Theorvard growls at Wulfmaer.

Wulfmaer looks around at the rest of us and, finding no sympathy, lifts Earnald with Theorvard onto his saddle,

'Ready? - *heave!*'

Wulfmaer snorts like a bull and, with Theorvard at the dead man's feet, between them they hoist him onto his stump-legged mare. '*Hey there*, what is it that has fallen from his habit?'

A small, tightly tied packet has fallen from the folds of Earnald's habit, into one of the muddy ruts. Saeward goes down on one knee and fishes for it with his long fingers. He scoops the thing up, stands and gleefully whoops like a child,

'*Found it!*'

'Unwrap it then, whatever it is', I let him fumble with the string, as he was willing enough to get his hands and knee dirty.

The last knot undone, he turns the loose bundle over in his hands and unfolds it. When he sees I want him to show what is in it, he holds up a heavy key.

'Why does a priest carry a carefully wrapped key in the folds of his habit when he could so easily have lost it?' Saeward wonders aloud.

'He was a sot. My guess is the fool had forgotten he was carrying it. As I see it, that is all there is to know', Theorvard looks at the dead priest slung over the horse's back and shrugs off any doubt about the key.

'What shall I do with it?' Saeward asks of me.

'Keep it. You never know we might find a use for it', I tell him. I do not believe we *will* find a use for it, but weeks of being with seafaring men, sailing between the Danish isles and the eastern sea teaches you not to throw anything away. Seamen can be hoarders, and I find it hard to throw things away myself.

'Maybe *you* should keep it safe, Ivar', Saeward holds out the key to me.

I look the key over as we trudge on beneath a now overcast sky. When we rode for Lunden after losing to Willelm, I saw a low building out here that looked as though it could be useful as shelter were we to come this way again one day. That day has come.

For its size the key is heavy. It may be cast bronze but over years grime has masked the metal. In turning it over and over in my hand, digging my thumb nail into the dirt, I see there are letters scratched into it. Even with my lowly reading skills I can see the letters are nothing to do with Earnald.

'What would you say 'W.DUX' stands for, Saeward?'

Saeward mulls over what I have asked him all the way to our shelter for the night.

The long, low building I remember looks as though no-one has been here for a long time. If the Northmen *had* been here, they did not think it worth razing. Have they earmarked it for their own use?

We are in the midst of relieving the misery of Earnald's horse by removing the weight of his corpse from its back when Saeward calls loudly,

'The key must have something to do with Duke Willelm, Ivar. I think the letters mean, 'Willelmus Dux''.

4

'All we have to do now is find a lock that the key fits', Burhred yawns.

Theorvard laughs, although my mood is grim. I do not know how we *can* find out. I dreamed up this whole errand to find my mark, and to show Eadgar I wish him no ill in his bid to take the throne. I need to do some earnest thinking, to make up for the loss of Earnald. The finding of a key to any of Willelm's property is only of any use if we can find a casket or trunk to open with it.

'What *kind* of lock would this key fit?' Saeward asks.

'Forget about it for now. Get some sleep', I yawn.

Burhred has fallen asleep. Saeward rubs his eyes and the other three are seated on the rubble-strewn floor, leaning back against the wall, dozing after the strain of lifting Earnald from his horse.

Although I cannot stop myself yawning, having drawn lots I am to take the first watch. Only by an underhand stroke of bad luck would anyone trouble us in this god-forsaken corner of Centland. Nevertheless somehow I have to stay awake for my few hours until Theorvard takes over.

A rush light set in a sheltered corner to show the passing of time flickers with gusts that find cracks in the rough wattle and daub wall behind it. From its smell, the daub is made from cow dung mixed with lime. The owner did not have to go very far for his building means, at least.

My watch passes slowly, giving me time to check my sword and axe for chipping, and give them a rub with grease from a spare flame. My weapons have worn well in these last few weeks since leaving Jorvik. A good rinse in Wynstan's stable yard took the encrusted blood from the blades, and the wide groove in my sword blade had let most of the blood to drain away.

With my thoughts wandering, to stop myself being overtaken by drowsiness I feel I have to stand and move about. I take in some fresh air whilst looking up at the heavens and see the wind is picking up from the west. We may see rain during the day, meaning Saeward and Wulfmaer will have to be told to find cloth binding to keep their swords dry. They will need to grease their swords and axe heads, or see their weapons suffer in the damp.

Stirring in the bushes across the way breaks my thoughts. Given the way the wind has picked up, I would not normally see anything wrong in the bushes shaking. But there has to be someone, or something amongst them, as they are shaking too much for the wind to have brought it about.

'I heard it as well', Theodolf stands behind me, his father's knife to hand. However, his worried frown tells me he is unlikely to use the knife in anger.

With a nod from me he slowly follows me the few strides it takes to clear the track, stopping and waiting for the rustling to start again. When it does it is to our left. Theodolf freezes. He must think we will be attacked by a bear again. He stays put when I go on ahead to look closer. Earnald's corpse is no longer where we left it. Drag marks and flattened grass lead to undergrowth yet further away, where the bushes are still shaking.

'You go on by yourself', Theodolf tells me. Night creatures still dwell in his world after the setting of the sun, in the way the Celts believe, and he fears the darkness, however brave he might be in the daylight hours. Or he is wiser than I am, and wishes to hold on to this life a little longer.

'What is happening?' Theorvard whispers hoarsely from behind, where he stayed by the trackside.

The bushes are still, but for when gusts of wind pull at the outer branches.

'Earnald's body has been moved', I whisper, and show him the drag marks in the mud and grass that lead to where the undergrowth and bushes were shaking.

'It *has* to be the work of some damned fox or brock!' Theorvard stands beside me now. He grunts in disbelief at my thinking there is a bear about.

'What kind of foxes or brocks do you *have* in your part of the world? *Neither* could have moved him. It *has* to be a *bear!*' I try not to sound mocking, but he will have none of it.

'*We shall see!*' With that Theorvard strides quickly into the thick of the bushes. I look back at the still frozen Theodolf and follow Theorvard into the blackness. Once again the bushes shake. The sharp, high-pitched bark of a fox tears into the still night air and Theorvard shows again, his sword brandished in one hand. A dead dog fox dangles by its brush in the other.

'Caught the damned creature red-handed', Theorvard grins and waves the animal around his head, shouting 'I *told* you it was a fox!'

'You will catch something *else* if you hold onto that fox for long. Think of all the mites and other crawling things that share their holes with them!' I warn him.

Theodolf shivers all the same and tells Theorvard he thought some-

76

thing bigger still lurked in there.

'*You* thought there was a bear here too, Theodolf? There is not the sort of woodland for bears for miles around. This creature', Theorvard gives the fox another shake and dumps it onto the muddied grass, 'lives over there in the bit of woodland that would not shelter *any* bear with a shred of pride!'

'What did the fox do to Earnald?' I ask Theorvard.

'Nothing much that I could see in this light, at least nothing I could think of that would spoil his good looks', Theorvard answers breezily, and makes for the door where Saeward and Burhred stand scratching their heads, wondering what the noise is about.

'A fox dragged Earnald's corpse into the bushes', Theorvard tells them as he passes through the doorway. Their askance looks tell me they do not wish to argue at this hour, and turn to take their rest again. Knowing he is not usually as foolish as this they follow him meekly back in again, Wulfmaer yawning aloud and stretching on his way back to sleep behind them. Theodolf, deeply shamed by his show of fear enters the shed, leaving me out in the open on my own.

Before I sit again I turn to look at the melting candle. Theorvard stands looking at Theodolf and shakes his head in dismay as I pass him to where my saddle-blanket stretches across the floor.

As he passes me to go outside again he whispers,

'Why did I bother coming back in?' He says nothing of the child-like way Theodolf bore himself.

Burhred shakes me awake, grinning,

'We have to bury Earnald, or what little there is left of him. There *was* something bigger than a fox outside after all. Theorvard went to look at the body just now when I woke him and he told me there were bigger paw marks on the priest than a fox could have left - so much for *his* knowledge of bears!' He laughs and walks away again, then comes back and asks, still grinning, 'Why bother even burying him? These woods must be teeming with beasts that could tear him to shreds. They would even dig him up again unless we dropped him into a bear pit'.

Theorvard stands to one side of the doorway, brow knitted, deep in thought.

'Things could have turned out very differently for me last night when I went into the bushes over there', he admits sheepishly when I stop and look around for somewhere the owner might have left a shovel.

'*Oh*, why would that be?' I turn to look up at him, stifling laughter.

Wulfmaer and Theodolf stand in the doorway looking at him, too, their faces wreathed in smiles. Theodolf now knows he *was* right not to go ahead into the darkness when Theorvard was armed only with a knife.

'I *may* have made a mistake about the fox', Theorvard allows, laughing.

'You made no mistake about a fox, Theorvard. *It was the bear you erred on*', I try to stop myself from doubling up, which is more than the others are able to.

Burhred thumps on the wall of the shelter, knocking pieces of daub from the wattle, trying to fight the pain of laughter that threatens to double him up with pain. Wulfmaer and Theodolf are only just able to hold themselves. I have not laughed so much in weeks.

'Anyone can make a mistake', Saeward tries to champion the big man, himself now aching with silent laughter.

'Only if you know nothing about foxes and bears', I cannot hold in the laughter any longer. Gales of laughter start afresh, Burhred turns red in the face and almost chokes. As quick as it started the laughter stops. The bushes shake again and a bear's growls are heard.

'Get the horses before they bolt!' I shout. 'Grab the reins and hold them back from bolting!'

Braenda does not care to be so close to bears either, since the close shave we had with the one on our way to Newerce.

'*Hold the horses*!' I snap at Wulfmaer and Burhred whilst Saeward, Theodolf and I snatch up our weapons.

Theorvard struggles with Braenda and his own horse. The growling goes on. There has to be more than one bear here but I would not want to take a head count, rushing around instead, gathering as much as I can carry, Theodolf and Saeward do likewise.

'Is that everything?' I turn to ask Theodolf, who looks frozen to the earth floor.

Beyond him is Saeward, still gathering our gear in the other corner, unaware of Theodolf's gaping mouth. It is only when Theodolf drops everything that Saeward looks up and sees a bear rearing on its hind legs outside.

With horses whinnying and screaming in fear, men shouting and the bear's roaring, a fearful din is being raised. I drop the war gear and reach down for Theodolf's bow. His arrow bag is half full, but I would only need one if I do the same as Hrothulf meant to bring down his bear when he tried the first time, before I stumbled across his aim.

The beast is still on his hind legs, as tall as me, his paws flailing. I aim the arrow for his jaw, draw the bow – and he keels over toward me before I can let the arrow fly. I can only think of taking a few steps back as he crashes onto his jaw, less than a foot away from me. Not an arrow flight can be seen, no spear point in its back.

We are all still looking down at the dead beast, wondering what killed it when three fellows step out from the bushes and stand looking at us. One of them, balding, thickset, strides toward us and looks down at the bear. He points to the back of the animal's skull and asks,

'See how deep the stone went in?'

I look, as do Saeward and Theodolf. Through the thick, matted fur at the back of its skull I see a bloodied wound where something bigger than an arrow head has passed through.

'That was a *stone*?' Theodolf stares in disbelief that a bear this size could have been brought down by a stone from a sling.

'*Of course* it was a stone! It is still in there as there is no way it could come out through the nose!'

'Well, whatever felled him we owe you', I tell the newcomer. 'Whom do I thank for coming to our help?'

The tallest of the three stares levelly at us before answering,

'We did not come to help *you*. This bear is a sheep killer'.

He looks down again at the dead creature and back at me before giving his name,

'I am Oswold. My friends', to his left he puts a hand on the shoulder of a gaunt, dark haired fellow with a lantern jaw. The other is a short, fair-haired youth, 'are Brihtwulf and Theodred. Brihtwulf cast the stone. May I ask who are you, what are you doing in *my* bar*n*, and what is that half-eaten corpse of a man doing back there in the *under-growth?*' Oswold is rightly annoyed at finding us on his land if he is indeed the owner.

'I am Ivar, these are my friends. The tall one holding the two horses is Theorvard. On your right is Burhred, to your left Wulfmaer', I tell him.

Oswold follows my hand with his eyes and looks each of my friends up and down without showing fear at our number.

'Beside me is Theodolf, with Saeward', I finish.

'You have still not told me what you are doing here, nor about the corpse', Oswold presses. 'For all I know you are robbers and ambushed the priest'.

'He was no common priest. Duke Willelm was his paymaster', Saeward tells him.

Oswold stares bleakly at him and then asks me,

'This Duke Willelm, is he the one they say was King Eadweard's kinsman?'

'It is true, through Eadweard's mother, Ymme', I agree, although I fail to see what it has to do with anything,

'He believes Eadweard made him his heir, but the Witan made Eadgar the young aetheling king in Lunden and we beat Willelm's men at Lunden Brycg the day before yesterday. Without telling you what we are about, we have been sent by King Eadgar – '

He stops me there,

'*King* Eadgar is it? Last I heard he was passed over for Harold. Who made *him* king?'

'Duke Willelm brought a host to help him take the crown from King Harold, who together with his brothers was killed near Haestingas. Our king was beset by three of Duke Willelm's men after being struck by an arrow in his right eye. They cruelly cut him down in the manner of hounds tearing down a stag. You do not know of this?'

Oswold looks at me, and back at his friends, to see what they think of my tale. Looking at each of us he must see that I am not joking.

'How do you know of King Harold's death?' asks Oswold. 'Were *you* there?'

He seems still unable to take in the news.

'Burhred, Theorvard and Theodolf were there with me. As were a number of our friends who were killed. Another was killed in the fight with the Northmen at Suthgeweorce', I give him the latest news.

'There was a fight at *Suthgeweorce?*' Theodred breaks in, staring disbelievingly at me.

'The first of my two brothers, Aelfwig was killed fighting near Haestingas. The *other*, Aelfwin was killed at Suthgeweorce!' Wulfmaer growls at Theodred. 'What *is* it with you Centishmen? Do you know *nothing* of what happens on your doorstep?'

Theodred points his spear at Wulfmaer and snaps,

'We know as much as we need to know, whatever that has to do with *you!'*

'Theodred, lower that spear and *hold your tongue!'* Oswold barks, warning Wulfmaer in the same breath, 'And *you* had better keep a civil tongue in your head, my friend. Theodred would think nothing of ripping it out'.

'*He can try!'* Wulfmaer spits back and bends to pick up the still unused sword that he dropped trying to stop his horse from bolting. When I put my foot on the sword and push him he falls back, knocking chunks of daub from the wall.

Oswold scowls darkly,

'Keep the fool away from Theodred and I will hold my friend from tearing *him* apart. I will forget this meeting ever happened if you make good the mess you have left. I do not want to see you again, *right?'*

'You will one day be fighting the Northmen *alongside* us!' Saeward foretells, only to be scowled darkly at by the heavy-jawed Brihtwulf.

Oswold leads his friends to a corner of the building where they talk earnestly amongst themselves and I turn to Saeward, agreeing with him that we could well find ourselves in the same ranks fighting Duke Willelm before long,

'You may well be right about that, Saeward. At this time, however, I do not think they are altogether worried about the Northmen. They are thinking of their own small world here, watching for outsiders, although I doubt Willelm's men would bother arguing if they were to come here'.

Oswold comes back to talk to me, his friends skulking at the corner of the barn, Theodred stares sullenly at Saeward.

'We are at one about the ways things may go for us all. We may well face a foe better skilled than we are in the craft of warmaking', Oswold allows.

'Nonetheless we marsh folk feel a threat from such as they pose is less likely than it is for you. We know these lands as well as we do the palms of our hands. We will know when to fade into the shadows if they come in overwhelming numbers. Our womenfolk and children are in hamlets hidden by reed beds. If we have to defend ourselves we *will* hit hard, make no mistake about that. When the *thegns* came to call us for the fyrd we were out cutting reeds. They did not come back this way'.

'Many of the Centish *fyrdmen* we met were unable to stem the Northmen when they came. The king was already dead and we had to cut our losses'. I point to Burhred, Theodolf and Theorvard, 'My friend Theodolf there, held some of our Northman pursuers back in the gulley by the side of Caldbec Beorg, along with some of the Suth Seaxans who escaped with us'.

Oswold looks from my giant friend to the others, shakes his head but says nothing.

'We do not know what became of King Harold's body. We may learn of his fate from the good folk on the coast', I add, hoping Oswold will think that is what we were sent here for. If he and his friends were caught by Willelm's men, he would not be able to tell them a lot.

Shaking his head Oswold goes back to his friends and talks with them for some time. Meanwhile, we ready ourselves for the ride on. Oswold calls across to me, asking,

'This Frankish priest, what was his name?'

'His name was Earnald', I answer and look away, making sure that my axe is well down into its strapping on my saddle, fastened well.

'*Right*... Earnald it is then. We will give you time to bury what there is left of him'. Oswold tells me, 'There are two shovels in the barn - near the far end, covered by sacking. You may use them'.

'I thank you, Oswold. Where shall we bury him?' I tie my bed roll behind Braenda's saddle and turn back to him to hear his answer.

'*Bury him where he is!* The woodland creatures are not likely to be able to get at him if they are tucked in between the roots of the bushes, are they? That is how we bury *our* dead', Oswold grins thinly and waves his friends away. They leave through the bushes vanishing into the reed-beds as quickly as they first showed.

'It is time to get digging', I tell Theodolf as I enter the barn once more. 'He said there are two shovels in there'.

An hour later we have hidden Earnald's corpse, secured safely amongst the tree roots, the shovels back where we found them. We are ready to leave at long last.

'*I see horsemen!*' Wulfmaer follows them with a finger.

There are perhaps a score or more of them, riding along the track we followed from the west. A quick look eastward reminds me of the woodland Theorvard said no self-respecting bear would live in, so I turn Braenda that way,

'Mount quickly, we ride for the woodland!' I swing myself into the saddle and turn for the woods.

We leave along the track that passes the barn, on from the way we came, bending low in our saddles as our horses pick their way between low trees and bushes, pressing them into a canter where we can on the other side, out of sight of the Northmen. As we reach the woodland Theodolf looks back over one shoulder and laughs,

'What does this remind you of, Ivar?'

I look at Theodolf, thinking of our flight from Brand after leaving Thegn Eadmund's hall, and smile at Theorvard. He gives me a bemused look in return and looks away behind us.

'What is it about these Northmen?' Theorvard asks.

'Do they *never* give up?'

'Just as Brand kept on after us', I tell a grinning Theodolf.

Our pursuers are still following, at a canter, leading me to believe we have not been seen, or they may think we are friendly.

We let Earnald's little horse find its own way back to wherever it came from. As we ride on it runs after us for a time. When the gap widens it slows and stops to crop the lush greenery at the side of the field. Let the Northmen have it, by all means. Let it slow *them* down.

We can ride faster now without Earnald's horse. Fairly soon we are out of sight of them at the south-western corner of the woodland, with more trees behind us. Another track leads southward. With the trees behind us, and the sun on the other side of the trees, we will hardly be seen. I have a feeling this new track may be the same one we followed behind Leofwin only days ago.

'How far do we ride to reach Pefense? Surely the Northmen will have mounted lookouts along the way. It may be that is what *they* are?' Burhred points back over his shoulder.

I look back. We still have our shadows, and as far behind as they were the last time I looked.

'If we had some of their gear would we not be taken for Northmen?' Saeward calls out over the drumming of our horses' hooves as they trot along on the near-dry earth of the track.

'He might be right about that', Theorvard calls out from behind us. 'Have you thought about that, Ivar?'

The horsemen behind vanish behind a thick copse some way behind and I turn to answer Theorvard,

'I had thought of that, but they are too many for us to tackle'.

They are soon in sight again. Had we been Northmen, might we not have waited for them to catch up with us, to ride into their camp together? Their leader must be wondering who we are, taking this track, at this time of the day. Have they taken us for Bretlanders, as we carry no lances?

Before long we enter thicker, broader woodland. I begin to look for a way off the track and call ahead to Wulfmaer as we ride on between the trees,

'Give a shout if you see a break in the trees on either side, and we will follow you. I am thinking of going round to get behind, to see if there are any stragglers'.

Wulfmaer jerks his head down in a nod. He has heard and understood my thinking.

'Good thinking, Ivar', Theorvard agrees.

The drumming of the hooves lessens as we ride over a thickly grassed and overgrown stretch of track where the sun catches us at a shallow angle through the trees. Wulfmaer takes a woodsman's trail to the right and we leave the broad track, up through tightly bunched trees behind him. The going is steep, rocky in places, but this trail can be followed with little hardship for our mounts.

It bends to the right again and I wonder if we are doing the right thing following it. However, we soon find a turn that leads back to where we should see them ahead of us.

'Wait', Wulfmaer mouths when we come to where the main track bends, and waves us down.

Below us the Northmen' horses canter along the main track, around a bend and out of sight. This is better than I thought it could be. By the time we reach it our pursuers have passed. We halt where the two tracks meet again and I dismount.

'I am going to walk down there, perhaps hear the last of the Northmen ahead of us. We follow on until they either stop at their camp or ride out of sight', I tell a nodding Theorvard, who seems to know what I am about before I have told him.

My boots slip on the grassy slope as I fight to keep my footing. Before I set foot on level ground I hear hoofbeats to my left and scramble to hide behind a clump of bushes. Two riders abreast press their horses into a fast canter to catch up with their comrades, horses snorting with the effort of carrying riders in full mail, weapons and shields. They carry yellow and red pennons on the ends of their lances, below the spear points. Their long shields are yellow, with well-painted outlines of red prancing horses on them. What this means is beyond me. It is a shame Thorfinn is no longer with us.

Having sailed often to Northmandige, he might have known. This much is clear to me, that there will be others with the same outlines on their shields. Likewise the pennons will be the same. If we could somehow catch these two, we would have some of our number looking right. Who knows, we may all get ourselves kitted out in this fashion?

I wave my arms for the others to join me. Lagging behind them, Saeward on his horse makes the track look heavy going, holding Braenda's reins, slithering.

'You want the last two taken for their gear?' Theorvard is the first to answer once they understand the need to catch up with them.

'I should think so', I acknowledge with a cheery grin. Turning to Saeward and Theodolf I beckon them closer. When they draw close I let them know what I want from them,

'Can you ride on, catch their eye so they ride back after you?'

'What about their *boar stickers*, Ivar?' Theodolf makes me mindful of the lances, as if I need it.

'If you leave enough time to turn about, and you are sure they have seen you, then you should be safe enough. *Off,* away you go', I wave him away. Of Theorvard I ask, 'You kept the rope after freeing Brand and his friends?'

'You knew I kept it?' Theorvard stares open-mouthed at me. Fumbling behind his saddle he pulls out a length of rope from within his bed roll, 'Here, I was keeping it for you anyway. You saw the rope *end?*'

'*Quick,* we have too little time to waste', I tell him, nodding. 'Ride to the bend and tie the rope tightly to one of the trees on the left. Draw the rope loosely with a hitch around a tree across the way, but not above a horse's knee height. Then wait'.

'Thy will be done!' Theorvard salutes and sets about the task I have given him.

'Wulfmaer', I ask the miller next, 'can you dismount and walk around the bend? Wait in the bushes for Saeward and Theodolf to pass back, then wave and duck out of sight when you hear the Northmen's horses'.

I grin at the miller, who sets off and waits in the trees.

'Burhred, can you wait here with me? When the Northmen have been unhorsed by the rope stretched across the track, take the nearest one and kill him', I draw my dagger and he does likewise. 'A good, clean cut around the side of the throat should be enough, and will not shed too much blood on the collars of their mailcoats. Wait here by this tree. I will be over by Theorvard'.

Burhred dismounts, tying his horse by its reins to a tree nearby.

I meanwhile cross the track to Theorvard and we settle for a wait. Across the way Burhred whittles away at a stick with his dagger to while away the time. Even if the wound itself does not kill the Northman, his blood will be poisoned by the bark scrapings on the blade. While Theorvard waits for Wulfmaer's shout, I stroke his horse's muzzle. All is quiet again. The birds begin singing again. Rustling in the undergrowth behind me tells me a squirrel is foraging for nuts. The high-pitched bark of a fox can be heard some way away behind us.

The birds go quiet again and start for shelter. The rustling stops and hoofbeats echo between closely-grown trees south of us.

'Ready?' I call to Burhred, who nods once. I look to Theorvard, standing behind the tree, his hands on the rope. 'Let Theodolf and Saeward through and take tight hold of the rope – all set?'

I fidget with my dagger and draw blood from my thumb. Theorvard knows what this waiting can do to a man and does not answer. However often you have fought, or taken part in an ambush, you still become edgy.

The muffled thunder of hooves on the overgrown track grows louder.

'Our men are coming - *now!*' Wulfmaer yells. Saeward comes first, followed closely by Theodolf.

Theorvard watches the track, waiting. Then we feel the trackside quake with the galloping of heavy mounts as they near us. Wulfmaer waves, drops back into the bushes and the rope rises! Both riders are pulled back over their horses as they turn the bend. Burhred falls on the one on the far side. His dagger finds the man's throat and quickly draws the blade back. The Northman's struggles die as quickly as he does.

The one on my side has been winded by his fall and puts up no fight. Theorvard smiles thinly as I draw my blade deftly around the man's windpipe.

'*Quick,* pull them into the trees and strip them of their padded coats and mail!' I tell my friends. Theodolf and Saeward have caught their horses and lead them back. I call out to them, beckoning, '*Come on,* the pair of you. Help strip these two and load their gear onto the saddles?'

As he sets off I listen for other horses, but no-one else seems to be coming from that way.

'We need to have them soon, before any more come from either way. If they find us here like this, they will not take kindly to our killing their comrades'.

'Is that *more* of them coming this way?' Saeward cocks an ear to the east. 'I would say we have little time before they show'.

'Hide the corpses', I tell my friends. 'Theorvard, can you take down the rope? We want to be able to use this ruse again'.

Theorvard reels in the rope and stows it back behind his saddle. The others busy themselves with the Northmen's gear and over-clothing, load it onto their horses and take the reins. Wulfmaer and Saeward grab the lances that fell to the trackside, and Burhred helps me drag the corpses into the bushes.

Before we melt back into the woods Theorvard looks around to see if we have forgotten anything in our haste and, with Theodolf follows with our horses. We are well back into the trees as the next *conroi* passes behind a young noble. As they pass I catch sight of three riders between them who do not seem to belong. It looks as though Oswold, Brihtwulf and Theodred have been *caught!*

Saeward's horse shakes her head, snorting. Theodolf takes the horse by her bridle, blows into her nostrils and strokes her forehead slowly. It seems to work, because she stops the snorting and quietens. Meanwhile the Northmen ride on westward around the bend with their captives, unaware of us. Soon they are out of hearing down the track. The birds catch up on finding food and guarding their homes again.

'Was there food in their saddle packs?' Wulfmaer asks when the Northmen have gone.

'*Trust you to think of food at a time like this!*' Burhred looks in their saddlebags anyway, but finds nothing, 'There must be somewhere close by where food to be had. What do you say about finding something to eat, Ivar? My stomach has begun to rumble now with this talk of food'.

I nod to show I have heard him, but there is something I need to know first,

'First let us see what we have that will let us near them'. I think

Saeward and Burhred would be best suited as lures. 'These two are good matches for you Burhred, you and Saeward. Why not try their clothing and mail coats for size? They should fit, and perhaps you can find us all something to eat when we come to a camp. There has to be one somewhere near here, where they are tented'.

Saeward and Burhred try out the apparel. The hauberks are not unlike our *huscarls'* mail coats, but it is as well to have the real thing to look believable.

'Leave the throat flap down', Theorvard counsels, grinning. It is odd to see a one-time lay brother don Northman war gear.

'You look every inch the warrior', I tell him.

Saeward frowns at first. He then lightens, taking me at my word. Burhred beams happily,

'Just look at this, Ivar! Do you think maybe I should change sides?'

'Do that, friend, and you will see how friendly I am toward *you!*' Theorvard growls at Wulfmaer's foolish cackling, scowls and looks to me.

'Ride', I tell everyone. We mount, Theodolf leads the two spare horses behind him and we set off at a steady canter along the track through thickly wooded hills for Pefense. None of us says a word until when we round another bend some miles further. Burhred warns,

'There are horses behind us'.

I turn in my saddle. Thankfully they are far enough away, too far yet to know we are not friends,

'Leave the road everyone, except Burhred and Saeward! We will see how well they fit in with these new riders. The rest of us take this trail and keep out of sight. We do not know yet how many they are', I point to another, lesser trail that takes us uphill, around the back of the main one. Out of sight, we can see who passes below us. And what is more, they will be within hearing. Should they be fewer than us in number we can take them on, but we will have to cut them all down if we do not want anyone raising the hue and cry. We would then be chased back empty-handed with our tails between our legs.

I think the riders are Bretlanders, who yell cheerfully at Burhred and Saeward in their own tongue. My friends wave stiffly at the Celts as they pass noisily.

Was that a blessing! At least our friends are taken to be haughty Northmen. We may not be able to count on our luck again. Wulfmaer waves them back again to join us and we ride on. Feeling saddle sore, I am heartened at the sight of a woodman's hut.

'Hopefully there will be only the woodsman, his wife and any young ones', Burhred echoes my thoughts.

'Theodolf, can you look around the back? The last thing I want is a fight with Willelm's men here *if* it is a trap. It could turn ugly if they hold his wife or any of their children, making us drop our weapons and give up without a fight', I ask the lad. 'Watch out for any lookouts amongst the trees. They could be dozing if they have waited long'.

Theodolf nods, dismounts and stalks around the modest shelter. Whilst he is away the horses crop the moist grass.

'There *is* no-one - no owner, no wife or young ones, *no-one!*' he tells us on his return.

Theorvard touches two fingers to his lips, takes the reins of his horse and walks her to the front of the dwelling.

'I will take a look inside', I whisper, dismounting, and hand Braenda's reins to Burhred. Theorvard and Wulfmaer are further away from the dwelling than the rest of us, talking. Wulfmaer looks up and notes drily,

'They keep their home warm, whoever or wherever they are', he points at wispy smoke rising through a hole in the roof.

It may have been for my sake he said it, because I slow down as I near the door. *How did everyone else miss the smoke?* The door creaks on worn leather hinges. I push it back, holding it, and look around it into a dark, smoke-filled room. My eyes take time to get used to the darkness. There is a small pen in one corner, but no household animals in it. The woodsman might very well be out, herding his livestock right now to drive them back here to a warm hearth.

Pots and beakers stand on a rough wooden table near the hearth. Benches are covered with pelts, drying out. A bed closet abuts the far wall, clothes scattered about on the straw-strewn earth floor as if some-one left in haste. A door leads out from one end of the dwelling. I leave through here, stride warily around to the front and wave the others to enter,

'There must be food somewhere in here, although what livestock they might have owned is away', I tell Theorvard. He ducks under the lintel and stares until his eyes become used to the gloom.

'See if there is anything hanging on the other end wall outside?' I ask. 'There could be wildfowl or chickens to be plucked'.

Wulfmaer, the next in, looks around and sighs. This must look like home to him.

Peering into all the nooks and crannies he finds some oatmeal cakes, still warm as if freshly drawn from the mud oven by the hearth.

'It is a start, *however lowly*', he shows his find proudly.

Saeward finds strips of meat in a pot by the fire,

'They must have been getting ready to cook this when they were shepherded out of here'.

'*What did you say, Saeward?*' I ask him.

'They must have been moved out by someone, *whoever,* who was hoping to take over this dwelling, although I cannot think why. If they only wanted to drive them out everything would have been kicked over. We could be in trouble if we stay here'.

Is it instinct that tells me we may be in a trap after all?

'Who is outside with the horses?' I ask Theorvard.

'Theodolf - *why?*' he answers, unaware of what Saeward has said just now.

'Saeward, Theorvard, outside, *hurry!* Wulfmaer, *get out - now!*'

Outside, Burhred is talking to Theodolf and looks up startled when we show suddenly again in the doorway,

'*What is it?*' he asks, taken aback that we are out again so soon.

'*Nothing yet*, but if we do not leave soon there might be!'

I look around as I tell him, worried lest the Northmen are waiting for us to settle in before swooping. This is a trap too well set not to be sprung quickly.

'*Come*, we have to get away', I almost take flight up onto Braenda's saddle from the ground. The others follow suit and we turn our horses away from the dwelling. I do not know why it took me so long to see the signs.

Arrows hiss past our ears as we press our heads close to our horses' necks to make ourselves smaller. Several bowmen run across from behind the bushes and aim at us, but we are too fast for them. They waited too long to spring the trap and their bowstrings are not strong enough to take us from our saddles.

Two men stand in our way at the western end of the thwait. One holds a crossbow, the bolt levelled at my chest ready to be loosed off. The other brandishes a spear, a stabbing spear, too short and too well made for throwing. As I draw closer to them the one with the crossbow takes aim, his comrade grips his spear with both hands, ready for me.

Out of the corner of my eye the shadow of one of my friends hurtles at the spear bearer. Feinting, he brings his sword down on the bowman's helm. I bring my sword down on the right shoulder of the spearman.

His scream rents the air as I bring Braenda round to see Saeward reining in his horse. He draws up to me, shouting,

'*This is just like when we crossed the Hvarfe!*'

I can only laugh. He still has the knack of catching out even me never mind the foe. He is as taken aback as Hrothulf and his men were. When I get my breath back I tell Saeward to make his way to catch up with the others, who have gone the other way,

'We have to find them, but to do that we have to leave here and give this steading a wide berth! *Here - with me!*'

As I look back Northmen are running out from the undergrowth past the dwelling. Shouting, unable to catch us, they must be a foot troop, left here to spring their trap on any unsuspecting Aenglishmen who might have thought of waiting for the homeowners to show up. We must find another track to meet up with the others.

'Have they gone back by way of the track we were following?' Saeward asks me as we look for the nearest turn.

I answer, looking ahead for another way around,

'They must have - look for a trail that brings us back the other way. Hopefully they know we left from this side'.

As our horses trot side-by-side he nods, then looking to his right points,

'What about that one?' A track climbs steeply away from the one we are following now, a few score yards further on. Without a word we press on ahead at a trot. On reaching the start of this new track we stop and look uphill. It looks so quiet up ahead, *too* quiet.

'What do you think, Ivar, will it do for us?' Saeward looks over his shoulder at me.

I weigh our choices, screw up my eyes against the light and shake my head slowly,

'I would say it looks as though it would be hard work for our horses', I have a change of heart almost as I shake my head, 'but not so much that I would say 'no' outright. I have to be honest, I like it now'.

There are no undue hazards that I can see, but there are mud patches across the trail that might make climbing hazardous. If the worst comes to the worst, we can always dismount and lead our horses for part of the way.

'No risk, no gain', I nudge Braenda with my knees and she walks on. There is spiny gorse on either side where we leave the shelter of the trees. The way ahead looks to be more of a bridle path as we climb, turning back around and above the steading. Smoke still drifts in the gentle breeze from the dwelling below us, out of sight through the trees.

We make a halt whilst I look out for tell-tale signs of someone waiting amongst the bushes, not wanting to ride straight into another ambush. If the men we escaped from had fanned out on either side of the thwait to cut us off, they would not make the same mistake again.

It is hard to say whether the bushes are moving in the breeze, or are being moved by men lurking amongst them. After some hard thinking I tell Saeward to ride on, adding,

'Should there be anyone there, we might catch them unawares', I scratch my beard and nudge Braenda on. 'We should be able to hit hard and get past them quickly'.

We pass quietly through between the trees and gorse. Saeward steers his mount wide of mine so that there is room between us to draw our weapons should we be attacked. If anyone were to leap out from the undergrowth, then either one of us could help the other without coming to any harm. Before we reach the bushes the path splits, allowing us to pick our own way, skirting the bushes on either side. On the right hand side the path drops a little. I signal to Saeward that I will take that side. Before we have gone very far Saeward turns onto the path I have picked for myself. We take the lower path together, still wide apart, he a little way behind me to my right. I look back at him over my shoulder, wondering why he chose to follow on the lower path.

He shrugs and we ride on. The bushes shake madly to my left and one of the Northmen lumbers out at me with a spear aimed at my thigh. I draw my sword and slash down at him with it. Saeward behind me is beset by two of my attacker's comrades, so I round on the second man, taking his shoulder with one swipe of my sword. He drops to his knees in agony, but his mouth does not open for him to scream. Saeward has rammed his sword through the fellow's ribs from behind and the point shows, bloodied, through his chest.

'Behind you Saeward - *look behind you!*' I shout.

He wheels around in his saddle and rams the boss of his shield into the jaws of another attacker, a stout fellow who collapses back onto others of his troop, flooring them with his sheer size. The rest fall back to safety, allowing us past on our way to find our friends.

Saeward gives out a high-pitched laugh. It is the laugh of a man who feels he has dealt well with a meddlesome foe. I join in the laughter, glad that we are still free, alive and on our way again. My laughter is short-lived. Ahead of us are two of Willelm's men on horseback, lances levelled. They set their mounts at a steady canter to take us on in an uneven fight. There is no way we can face these two with their 'boar-stickers', as Theodolf likes to call them.

I look sideways at Saeward, who has reined in his horse alongside mine,

'Turn, we have to find *another* way around!' I tell him.

'What, you mean we have ride *back* into the midst of *them* back there?' He looks worried now. Nevertheless he does as I tell him, and turns his horse to run the gauntlet of the heartened Northmen that we have just fought our way through.

One of the mounted Northmen raises his lance. He grins invitingly.

The second does likewise, and raises the nosepiece of his helm to show we are looking at Burhred. He and Theodolf have come to look for us! Seeing *them* here cheers me. On looking back I see the Northmen have melted back into the woodland. They must have seen that these two were not going to hand us to them and have taken the hint, to withdraw without further loss.

Theodolf is the first to reach us and gleefully shouts,

'Theorvard and Wulfmaer await us a little way back!'

'Where in God's name did you *go?'* Saeward demands. *'We were beside ourselves with worry that you might have been taken!'*

'We found a track that led the same way. Following it we came across another dwelling. This one looked just like the last, with food on the table even, but no fire was lit, and no-one was there to eat the food that lay scattered about on the board. There was bread and fruit lying around on the floor and we thought more Northmen would fall on us, but instead a wizened old man and his wife came'.

Burhred reaches into his saddle pack, draws out a small apple and sets to munching it. Saeward begins to drool watching him.

Theodolf pulls out an apple from his saddlebag and bites great chunks from it. Not being one to keep things to himself, he draws two more and tosses them, one each to Saeward and me.

'At least there is *some* cheer in this world of ours', I tell Saeward between mouthfuls of sweet, juicy apple flesh. My friend only nods, finishes the fruit hastily, belches and tosses the core into the bushes behind him.

'Follow us', Burhred tells me, and having finished his apple also tosses his core into the bushes and turns his horse.

'Do you think there are any more Northmen around?' Saeward asks me.

I swallow the last mouthful, look back to where I last saw them and answer,

'I just hope they have black eyes from us throwing our apple cores away', I laugh and throw mine ahead of me into a gorse bush.

If any of them were still around, they were not keen to lock horns with us and have left to us ride free. They would have to admit to their lord that we had slipped their clutches, and he would not be at all happy with them.

He would be even less happy if he knew they had let me off the hook. Of all the prizes for him to gain here, my neck in his noose would be a feather in his cap. If by sleight of hand he *were* to lay his hands on me, I have no doubts about the rough handling that would be meted out to me. I shall do my level best to stay clear of his grasp.

The ride to where Theorvard and Wulfmaer await us is quiet enough. In passing through dense woodland and skirting fields, I wonder how or why the Northmen missed this break to rid themselves of another thorn in their sides. We come upon an even smaller thwait than the last one. There is no steading here, just a ceorl's dwelling, crudely crafted with wattle and daub, roof pitched steeply and covered with long-stemmed reeds and mosses.

Within this humble dwelling, blue woodsmoke drifts upward to a hole in the thatch. The tempting smell of cooking river fish tells me not to fret too much about the smoke.

'So you are the Ivar these fellows talk of', an old man speaks to me. Bent with age, parchment-pale skin drawn taut over his face and bony hands, he sits hunched on a short bench in the middle of the smoky room. In front of him on a wide-planked board stands a beaker, half full of ale. Seated on either side of him on tree stumps are Theorvard and Wulfmaer. Burhred seats himself next to the old man. Theodolf makes himself at home, resting on a log by the blazing fire.

The old man feels Saeward's unease and, without looking at him, tells him to take a seat,

'Young man, please feel at home here. We will soon be eating. Ale is there for the asking. My woman will see to your needs if you speak loud enough to make her hear'.

Saeward still holds back, so the old man calls over to a crone bent over a pot by the fire,

'*Woman, give this young fellow a beaker of our finest ale!*'

Not without grumbling, and wincing with the smoke driving into her dry old eyes, she hobbles to a far corner in the room and lifts what looks like a heavy pitcher to a horn beaker. Some of it spills on the rushes and Saeward strides across the room to help her.

'Allow me', he offers, but she flaps her hand angrily for him to go away.

'Braendeswitha, let the young man help you!' the old man commands.

I stare at her. She grumbles but allows Saeward to lift the pitcher.

'Does anyone else wish more ale?' the old man offers. 'Oh, I am sorry Ivar, *you have had none yet*'. He laughs at his own forgetfulness and chides the old woman,

'Get Ivar a beaker, Braendeswitha. Are you thirsty, Ivar? I would say you must be. How *foolish* of me for asking. Sit yourself down, young man, and look forward to some good food!'

I am still staring at the old woman, but neither of them seems to be aware of my bad manners. Theorvard sees me watching the old crone and tries to take everyone's thoughts away from her,

'Tell me your name, my friend', he asks the old man. 'You may have told me already, my friend, but I forget – you know'.

'I am Sigurd, Theorvard. I came here many years ago with my woman and son Oslac from the Danelaw', the old man begins to tell us all of his days as a huscarl in the household of Godwin.

When I ask him to tell me what this Oslac looks like, he draws a picture, in words, of a barrel-chested fellow with strong bowman's arms and a keen eye for game. A smith and talented bowman, this Oslac, he has won prizes and wide renown in Centland.

'And he has the eye of King Eadgar on him', I tell Sigurd, 'I think we know your son. He saved us from the Northmen when we were fleeing from Haestingas to Lunden. He fought, together with his young friend Sigegar, his Centish friend, and Theodolf here at Lunden Brycg'.

'*Theodolf has fought at my son's side?*' Sigurd's eyes light up, hearing me speak well of his son. Yet something is amiss here.

'Theodolf is a good Danelaw name, is he from there?'

'He is from near the old Celtic kingdom of Elmete, within Deira', I tell Sigurd.

'Well now, *you are all welcome to my supper!* I shall rest happy tonight in my bed, knowing the king thinks well of my son for his bowmanship', the old man thumps the table hard enough to upset the beakers. Ale spills from Theorvard's and Wulfmaer's freshly re-filled beakers. 'No matter, Theorvard, have more'.

We feast on Sigurd's freshly caught river trout and sup his foaming ale, but not once does his woman look my way. It is almost as if she is hiding from me. Finally we bring in our bedrolls from our saddles and settle down to sleep on the warm, rush-strewn earthen floor. Sigurd limps to his cot-bed and is covered with a great bear skin by his woman and Burhred takes the first watch.

We awake cold and hungry. Mist gathers in the trees and rolls eerily across the small thwait. There is something wrong here. Where is the dwelling? Where is the old man, Sigurd and Braendeswitha – or *Braenda?* What did they put in the food, wild mushrooms?

My friends are curled up in their bedrolls and awaken one by one. Burhred sits, still dozing, leaning against a tree stump. A wisp of smoke rises lazily in the thin morning air. The embers in a makeshift hearth still glow faintly amid our circle of bedrolls.

'Saeward had misgivings about this dwelling last night', I tell a yawning Theorvard.

'Right or not, my stomach was filled last night, but now house and host have gone. I would say my dreams had the better of me, but who could explain the food in my belly and the good-looking red-headed woman who regaled me when you had gone to sleep?' Theorvard is of a sudden more awake at the memory of the old woman, whatever she did for him.

I can only stare disbelievingly at him. He winks and looks at Burhred as he tells me,

'Believe me, Ivar, *as sure as you are standing there!* When you had gone to sleep Sigurd's daughter came to see them. What happened to the old crone is anyone's guess, but I did not miss her'.

Theorvard laughs hollowly, telling me,

'The tales the daughter told me were just beyond this world. I, too, fell asleep in the early hours, long after the rest of you had dropped off. I would dearly love to see *her* again!'

'Did she tell you her name?' I ask Theorvard, hoping she had left him in the dark there.

'Would you believe it? She was named for her mother. Her name was Braendeswitha too. She had these wonderfully soft hazel eyes. You might say she was bewitching!' Theorvard laughs, 'Come to think of it, that is what she was, was she not? The three of them must be hwicce'.

Has he been making all this up, to taunt me? Am I still within reach of Braenda? I am so tired still that I cannot think straight, unsure whether this is good or bad. She seems to have kept us all out of harm's way for a night. The Northmen may have been hunting high and low for us.

On the other hand Theorvard had been listening to talk of her from Theodolf, Aethel or Hrothulf, or even from me. Is he playing on my darkest thoughts, having fun at my cost, or are Braenda's spells as strong as ever? But why did she not show herself to me when I had need of her?

'You are suddenly very quiet, Ivar. What are you thinking about?' Burhred comes over to my side, his thoughts resting on his stomach, as ever. 'More to the point, what are we going to do for a morning meal?'

Wulfmaer seems to agree with Burhred. The pair of them cast odd looks at me, and at one another.

'I *am* thinking about food – about our next meal', I tell Burhred. 'Perhaps you can tell me *your* thoughts. What would you offer by way of counsel?'

If he could weave our wyrds and bring us to food I would be grateful. I put the same question to Wulfmaer, Theorvard and Saeward. Burhred shakes his head and looks at his feet, as though the answer might be down there on the ground. Theodolf tries to catch my eye, as though he has an answer - something we have not thought of.

'Has anyone thought of riding into one of their camps and *taking* food?'

'That is all very well, but have you thought what would happen if we were stopped? You wear Northman war gear, but you do not speak their tongue', I reason with him. 'They would flay you alive for having a hand in killing one of theirs to get that gear. Even if I were to don one of their mail coats and helm, where would that leave *me?* My own tongue is Danish, not Frankish'.

Standing, arms folded, I add,

'Thorfinn spoke their tongue, but we cannot raise him from the dead. At least, none of *us* can'.

'We have to hope to find a camp where no-one will challenge us', Theorvard offers bleakly.

'At this time of the day, how will *that* happen?' Saeward chimes in.

Theodolf turns to me suddenly, almost knocking me off my feet,

'How about luring them to another part of their camp? That would take eyes away from whoever goes to their food store'.

'*Could we do that?*' Burhred is not sure.

'*If we are hungry enough, we can make it work!*' I am for such a raid. We have to set out our thoughts.

'We could have our own Lammas Supper, stolen from the North-men, *who have in turn stolen the food from the folk of Suth Seaxe!*' Saeward claps his hands gleefully. The thought of living off the North-men's stores makes me feel better, even though they *have* most likely been taken from these poor folk around here.

The sound of his clapping echoes around the thwait.

'Be quiet!' I put my hands over his to stop him clapping, at worst alerting our 'hosts' to our being here.

If luck has it, there will be no-one else about. If there were any Northmen in the neighbourhood we would be ringed already.

I would not put it past Odo to have scouts in these parts looking for us, with orders to bring us in. Once he is done with us he can send us to our maker with the blessing of his half-brother. There would be less meddlers for Willelm to deal with.

'Let us be away from here. I have a bad feeling about this thwait!' I have to hurry them, to be back on the road before we come to any harm.

'We have been kept from *harm* sleeping here', Theodolf puts in as we mount. Whether or not the others agree with him, they say nothing and we head our horses from our overnight encampment, such as it was, although I would say it felt as if a spell had been cast by *someone*.

The woodland opens out on either side of the main track. There are signs of tree felling, where Odo's men have been clearing the trees

96

from the trackside to make it harder for his men to be ambushed. A wide swathe has been cut here, so the Northmen cannot be far off.

I can hear everyone's stomachs rumbling and only hope our plans for our first meal of the day come to something.

'Saeward, take to the right with Theorvard and hide between the trees if you can when we see any Northmen. Likewise, Wulfmaer come with me on the left. Theodolf stay with Burhred on this track. If you see Northmen and they speak to you, just nod and keep riding'.

'Should they challenge you or stop you, we will close on them', I go on. Everyone nods their agreement and we part company with Burhred leading Theodolf along the track. Because the Northmen have cut down many trees, I am not sure of our whereabouts.

Nothing happens for a while and our horses trot on steadily, albeit watching the skyline. The shadows have shortened before we see any-one who might threaten us. Saeward looks back at me when he sees our foe before anyone else,

'Back there, *look*', he calls across to me and prods a thumb in the air over his right shoulder.

My eyes light on the half dozen mounted Northmen behind us, rid-ing our way. I nod to him. He and Theorvard melt into the trees. Wul-fmaer jerks his head around, and sees my hand wave him to the left, into the closely-grown trees.

5

I hope they have missed us and see only our friends on the track ahead. They take little time to draw level with Burhred and Theodolf and merely glance sideways at them as they ride on. They have rounded the last bend before Burhred dares to look round, over his shoulder. Even I can see him breathe out. He slaps Theodolf on his back and laughs,

'*Well done my lad*. This time we passed for Northmen', Burhred tells him. He turns in his saddle to see where I am. Before he can say anything else there are four more on the way. Against the light it is hard to see what colours the pennons are on their lances, but I have an ill feeling this time. We could have a fight on our hands.

'*Get back into the trees!*' Hissing at Wulfmaer, who has inched his horse forward, I wave Theorvard and Saeward on. We need to keep up with Burhred and Theodolf below.

'Wulfmaer, keep up', I turn back to Wulfmaer to make sure he knows what I want him to do. If anything was to go wrong now, and we unwittingly gave the edge to these Northmen, they would make a meal of us. It would be our last mistake.

The first rider draws closer to Burhred and calls out something that sounds like a greeting - or it might be a shout in anger. By the way the other three spur their mounts, it has to be the latter. They close on our friends. Just as the first rider thrusts his longsword at Burhred he raises his shield and yells at Theodolf to do likewise. The lance-wielding riders are making for Theodolf when I wave to the others to break cover. They fall on the unwary Northmen like wolves, Saeward with his axe held forward ready to pull the nearest foe's shield down. Theorvard gives an ear-splitting war cry as he drives his axe down on a young rider who has not seen the giant behind him.

A scream rents the air with the pain of Theorvard's axe crashing through his collar bone. His nearest comrade, seeing the blade rent the mailcoat tries to get away and backs into Saeward's axe-blade.

'*Tur aie!*' the leader yells in defiance and turns on Theorvard. His last underling parries Burhred's lance but is knocked from his horse from behind by the young giant's shield.

The leader makes to turn his horse but when his shield is caught by Theodolf's axe he is toppled from his saddle. Unhorsed he howls with anguish, yet scrambles to his feet and throws himself bodily at me on Braenda as I draw near.

She shies away from him and he stumbles on a tree root as he tries

to throw me from my saddle. I kick him back he and falls onto Theorvard's axe blade, the blood surging from his mouth as he stands held
fast by the sharp blade.

Theorvard grimaces and scowls as he shoves the Northman to the
ground with his boot, straight away checking the blade of his axe for
chipping.

'Damned Northman, *he must have a hauberk with strengthened iron
links!* There is a small dent, look', Theorvard holds his axe under my
nose to show me and nearly shaves off my beard doing so.

'These things happen', I look down at the crumpled fellow. His mail
coat has been shredded where Theorvard's axe bit into his back and had
to be robustly pulled back. A pool of blood grows around him. If I had
not become used to the sight of killing over the years I too would be
retching the way Saeward is now.

'Never mind, this killing will be part of your everyday life. Before
you know it, you will not turn a hair at the sight of men dealt their death
blows', Burhred assures him.

'You should have been with us fighting them on Caldbec Beorg
with King Harold - *the hill was awash with blood!*'

'Be glad you can be sick', I tell my friend, 'if nothing else, it shows
you are still *alive!*'

Burhred laughs. He is not unfeeling, but he has become used to the
pain and death of others, as Saeward will be one day. That is, unless he
takes to the cloth. Dean Wulfwin would gladly take him in now he has
seen our world for what it is.

For now we have the task of hiding the corpses after first stripping
them of their war gear. It will be useful to us to help us escape when we
have fulfilled our errand. But we have to take care not to let their horses
loose. Stray mounts will warn the Northmen that there is something
amiss here. We must also keep our own horses in hiding, and we have
to stay out of the clutches of Odo or any of his henchmen. First and
foremost, however, we really *have* to find food.

As with the other two we waylaid yesterday, these Northmen carried
no food in their saddle packs. This means that their camp cannot be far.

'Perhaps they came from just over the rise, up there', Burhred offers
by way of answer to my unasked question, 'I see a banner above the
trees, atop the hill'.

Theorvard looks up, one hand shielding his eyes,

'Aye, Ivar, look up there'.

I shield my eyes and stare up at a colourful banner flapping idly on a
gilt-tipped post.

'Well seen Burhred. Instead of just two of you riding into their

99

camp, I think we could send three or four. Two can just as surely send them the wrong way, and four can carry more food than two', I tell him, beckoning the others closer. I outline my thoughts and ask for theirs. Saeward has a better plan, he says,

'What if the four ride in from the other side of the woods', Saeward waves his hand eastward, 'then whichever two carry out the ruse hide over to the west. That would take the Northmen away from where we *want* to go, to the south?'

I look at Theorvard and Burhred. Both nod agreement, but Theorvard raises a finger,

'You say 'hide', as in the two taking the Northmen out of our way hide to the west, thus drawing off your pursuers. Here is another '*what if*'. What if they catch the two, whatever the said ruse?'

Would three not fare better than two?

We look back to Saeward, to find out whether he knows what might draw the Northmen away from the camp, but I have something else I wish to do before working out our ruse,

'Shall we take a look at this camp first?' I ask. Then we can see how to take their eyes from the food stores?'

We now have six spare horses, two each for Theodolf, Wulfmaer and Saeward to lead. With their high fronted saddles, these war horses are handsome beasts and for now seem happy enough carrying their riders' gear. Our way to the camp skirts the woods to the east, as the hill there is higher, to overlook them without being seen.

There is a God in his heaven, after all.

We find somewhere south by east of their camp, which affords a good outlook. Burhred points to where he thinks is the food store,

'Would it not be better for just two of us to go down there and take enough to keep us going for a day?'

'They are going to stand there and let you walk in, steal their food', Theorvard scoffs,

'No my friend, we have to look the part and, as Saeward said, two can take their thoughts from our mischief. What kind of ruse was it you were thinking of?' he asks Saeward.

'As there are few of them, we could take their eyes away from their camp by us banging our shields and shouting in the woods nearby', Saeward answers.

'You think that would be enough?' Wulfmaer scoffs.

'Would they not send a few to see who was making the noise and keep the rest in camp? We may not see many, but that does not mean there is not a whole host of men around in the camp or the woods around'.

'Have you thoughts of anything better?' Theorvard folds his arms and fixes Wulfmaer with a steady gaze.

Saeward looks hurt at Wulfmaer's attack on his long-thought-out offering.

'Well, why not send *three* of us in for the food, *and three can draw the Northmen away?*' Wulfmaer stares back smugly at the young giant. He smacks his lips and waits for us to mull over *his* offering.

'Three could make more noise than two, I will give you that', I agree.

'Three could take enough food to last until late tomorrow, by which time we should be well away from here', Burhred warms to Wulfmaer's insight.

'Has anyone *else* anything to say about this before we agree on the matter?' I glance sideways at Theodolf, who looks as though he has second thoughts about stealing from Willelm's men.

'Should we not look around, to find the safest hiding places?'

'That is the first useful thing anyone has said thus far!' Wulfmaer snorts and earns himself an icy glare from Theorvard. His sheer size sways even the doughtiest of men.

'It would be worthwhile looking. We cannot leave this too much to fate', I agree with Theodolf. The others nod sagely.

'Who rides with Theodolf and me?' Burhred asks.

'Have we any takers – Saeward, do you want to ride in with these two?' I ask, showing him the mailcoat from one of the dead men. 'There would be no need to speak. You would just ride into the camp when we begin crashing our shields with our axes, and you look as though this would fit you'.

Saeward nods as if fated. All is set for this side. Burhred and Theodolf help Saeward struggle into the Northman's mailcoat. As Wulfmaer, Theorvard and I make ready to set off for the far side of the camp I turn and wish them luck, adding,

'When you hear the din, wait and see what happens first', I grin at Burhred, who finishes helping Saeward.

'When their eyes are on us, and they look as if they are heading our way, ride in and help yourselves to their stores. Look as if you should be there'.

'But we *should* be there - *the thieving bastards have taken the food from some poor ceorls!*' Theodolf blusters with youthful zeal, to Theorvard's and Wulfmaer's raucous laughter.

'What in hell's name are you laughing at? *It is true, they have!*' Theodolf insists.

'You want to think about what you have just said', Saeward tells

Theodolf. 'You recall taking off into the woods with our silver after we had crossed the River Hvarfe?'

'He did *what?!*' Wulfmaer shakes with laughter as Theodolf reddens, bursting with self-righteous anger,

'At least I did not take the food from anyone's table!'

'Meaning *what?* What are you getting at?' Wulfmaer threatens. He stands, fists clenched as if ready for a brawl.

'I think he means them, not *you*, but he did not put it well', I have to say on Theodolf's behalf. I tell the lad, 'You really ought to learn how to speak to your elders, Theodolf'.

Wulfmaer squints warily at Theodolf. Theorvard frowns as we mount. Saeward pulls down the helm over his short, curly locks.

'You should shed some weight', Burhred grins at Saeward.

'Wearing this heavy thing I will sweat off the fat in no time', Saeward cheerily answers. I think he knows he has been living a fairly easy life at Wealtham and has gained in girth even with all the heavy lifting work around the school.

'But will you be able to *fight* it off?' Theorvard teases, harking back to Saeward's pangs of self-doubt after each bout of killing.

'I shall have to *live* with my demons', Saeward answers dourly, then brightens 'If I tell myself they are sent by Satan, I will be able to bear the sin of killing more easily'.

'Bishop Odo must tell himself that daily', I laugh, to Saeward's rasp of disgust at my talk of Duke Willelm's ilk. Braenda trots off when I press my knees into her withers, followed by Theorvard leading his spare horse, and Wulfmaer with his. We leave the other two spares with Theodolf and Saeward to carry the bags of food we think he and the other two will *'free'* from the camp store.

It might look more usual if the three of them reach the store tent with spare mounts, as though they were to load them to take supplies for men camped elsewhere. When we begin to hammer our shields with our axes or swords, they will ride downhill to their allotted task. Scant enough heed will be paid to them if the Northmen think an attack is about to be launched on them.

After the scare we gave them in Suthgeweorce they would no longer be as cocksure of themselves.

We give the outermost tents a wide berth on our way around, with the camp above us amid the woods. On coming back to the track some way back along our way here, before we cross it, we stop under the trees. I nudge Braenda forward, take a look either way and wave the others on.

'I hear hoofbeats from the north', Wulfmaer pulls sharply on his spare horse as he passes on this news to me.

Theorvard hisses back at him,

'Then, for God's sake, *keep up with us!*' He has a strong liking for the lad and did not take kindly to Wulfmaer's threatening him.

My stepping between them kept him from wrecking our errand, and our search for food, by giving Wulfmaer a drubbing he would no doubt have earned. Nevertheless Wulfmaer makes up our number, and as such is needed.

I am sure the miller would not have spited us by giving away our whereabouts to the Northmen. Whether Willelm's men would have let him leave for Wealtham after betraying us is a moot point. But even supposing he *were* able to ride away north, give the bad news of his brothers' deaths to their grieving mother and gone back to working for his master, no-one there would be any the wiser.

We are unknown to them, save for stopping briefly, and leaving with Thorfinn and his friends.

The spare horses stumble around behind us over the twisted tree roots in the half-darkness of the woods. We finally reach a hollow, ringed by thick bushes. This is useful for our needs and should leave us unseen from above. There is a dip in the rocky ground for us to get away by, should the need arise.

The sun is still low in the sky, and the shafts of sunlight streaming through the trees from the south-east will hopefully blind them to us. Before we begin banging our shields we have to hobble the horses. The Northmen's horses shied when we hammered our shields before their onslaught both at Caldbeck Beorg and Suthgeweorce. The last thing I want is for our whereabouts to be given away by the horses panicking. For safety we bind the horses' mouths to stop them whinnying with fright when the echoes come back louder at us in the hollow.

Our shields finally held ready, Theorvard and Wulfmaer await my nod to start our hammering.

I nod, and begin shouting loudly, bashing with my sword on the shield. Theorvard and Wulfmaer yell, using the butts of their axes. The horses draw together in fright and even I feel awe-stricken, aside from the jarring in my wrists.

There is something to be said for the way this plays havoc on a foe. In frightening them it gives us an edge.

No man could withstand the clamour of shouting, together with the hammering of iron on dry wood for long. Shouting comes from close by and we keep up the din just long enough to hold them here.

As suddenly as I started I stop the hammering. Theorvard stops with me, but Wulfmaer goes on... Long enough for one sharp-eared Northman to know where the noise was coming from. He points our way and the others make for us. They must number a score at least - not easy odds when you are fighting a skilled foe, more so when one of your own barely has the fighting skills needed for a shieldwall.

'You know they are coming straight for us', Theorvard notes drily, and looks across me at Wulfmaer. His doubts on our making a stand here against a score of the Northmen mirror my own.

'Quick, get mounted. *At least they are all on foot!*' I yell at the other two. 'Cut the bindings on their horses and drive them away. *The horses should get between us and hamper them in their chase* '.

The shouting comes nearer as we hasten to free the horses, keeping hold of our own mounts' reins. We smack the hindquarters of the spare horses, setting them loose at our attackers, making it hard for their bowmen to aim their arrows at us.

Wulfmaer is last away again, only just tearing himself free of the first Northman to reach us. Some of them rush down to the dip in the rocks where we are heading. It is the only way out of here without a stiff climb that would unduly tire the horses. They must have known which way we had to ride to be free of them.

Four of them scurry to a low cliff that overhangs the track by which we need to withdraw. One of them unhurriedly takes aim with his bow, looses off his first arrow and narrowly misses Theorvard. His next may strike true.

I drive Braenda through the narrowing gap and bump two of the Northmen off their feet. The bowman takes aim again, following us as we ride toward him.

Theorvard, unaware of the bowman keeps on riding, heading for a gap in the trees. His shield is on the wrong side of him to stop an arrow. I close on him to cover him with my shield, but the arrow lodges in Theorvard's right shoulder and he grits his teeth with the pain. Another tries to head me off, but before he can loose off an arrow I am on him. He turns to run but Braenda is sure-footed, and fast.

The blade of my sword shears through the man's left shoulder and he screams shrilly like a wild sow in its death throes. Another tries to send an arrow at me, to be cut down by Wulfmaer scything through his waist with a low strike, baptising his sword.

He yelps with glee at having killed a Northman and ducks beneath the flight of another's arrow. More bowmen must have been called out to cut us off from our flight! We leave our pursuers behind, but Theorvard is bleeding badly from his wound.

I tell them both to slow their horses when I feel we have outrun the reach of their arrows. A look at Theorvard tells me he will not live until nightfall unless we find Saeward soon. He will surely have a remedy to treat Theorvard's wound.

Thinking of Saeward starts me wondering how the other three fared, whether they pulled off their part of the raid or were almost taken, as we were.

Theorvard crouches over his saddle with the arrow still lodged in his shoulder, but stays mounted nonetheless. His blood may be poisoned by the arrow tip if it had been thrust into the earth before being loosed off at him. Wulfmaer rides closer to Theorvard, should he fall from his horse with the unevenness of the ground. I bring Braenda around to the other side of him, should we have to prop him up between us.

When I look up ahead there are three riders in Northman war gear up ahead of us, but with only one spare horse.

'Are they *ours?*' Wulfmaer asks me. He has his right hand on Theorvard's left shoulder.

'We will soon find out'. I try to see across the still low sun, holding my right hand over my brow to shield my eyes against the sun through the trees.

The three riders stop dead in their tracks up ahead of us. One of them raises something in the air above his head. They spur their horses and close on us quickly.

'*What is the matter with Theorvard?*' Burhred's voice booms in the cold air before he sees the arrow shaft and flights bobbing with the horse's gait. 'My friend, *you are wounded!*' Burhred leans over and looks up into Theorvard's eyes. He is taken aback that we have not tried to pull it from the wound, 'Why has no-one taken this arrow from his shoulder?!'

'It is as well you left the arrow embedded. I shall be able to free it, but I shall need some help. The ruse *worked!*' Saeward holds up a full bag, and there are more on the spare horse. But why is there only *one* spare?

'Where is the other horse?' I ask.

'Where are *your* four? Have you lost our own horses?' Burhred thumps himself on the forehead, 'I cannot believe this is happening. One of them was my *own* horse you lost! This is one of *theirs* I am riding!'

It suddenly hits me that in our haste I did not think of it.

I cannot tell him how sorry I am for my mistake.

'We let them go because the Northmen were closing on us. They had bowmen all around us and Theorvard was wounded!'

I am hurt that Burhred's thinks I wilfully lost his horse, but he will not let go now he sees I am at a loss.

'Were they on horseback? No, you let them get too close, and *were overcome with fear for your own life!* I cannot believe you led us here, with no food supplies, with a stupid priest who died on us, and a this ceorl Wulfmaer', he cuffs the miller over one ear, 'who behaves like a child!'

'We *agreed* to come with him!' Theorvard rasps and coughs with the strain.

Saeward rounds on Burhred now,

'*For another thing, Wulfmaer is no fool!* You should beg his forgiveness for calling him names. We will find somewhere to shelter and rest for the night, whilst I tend to Theorvard's wound. Or would you sooner we rode back to find your horse?' Saeward turns to Theorvard and reaches for his saddle pack, 'I will take the arrow from you now'.

'It can wait', Theorvard waves him away.

'At least let the shaft be broken off', I nod to Saeward to do it.

'I will do it when we call a halt', Saeward tells me, 'as I said'.

'We do not know how far we will need to ride before we find somewhere to rest', I warn him.

'The poison may begin to work on him before long. Snap off the shaft, draw the head and dress the wound. We will stop for the rest of the day somewhere – hopefully soon, Theorvard – and you can work your wonders, Saeward'.

Saeward gives in and snaps the shaft. The young giant winces and bites on his dagger hilt. Saeward edges his horse closer and tries to lever the head from the wound with his small knife. Theorvard's mouth opens wide, letting the dagger fall and he almost bites his tongue out when Saeward draws the tip and throws it to the ground.

'Almighty God - *that hurt!'* The pain of Saeward prising out the head of the arrow from his shoulder clearly racks Theorvard, but he sets his teeth again and tries to smile. 'At least the damned thing is not waggling around in the corner of my eye. Watch out, *I might fall asleep on you now!'*

'We will keep our eyes open for you', I grin at him, '*it would not be the first time you fell asleep off your horse!'*

'At least it is *his* horse!' Burhred snarls.

I have to snap at Burhred,

'*Burhred, be quiet!* It is not as if you treated that horse of yours with any kind of love!' The worry of losing a good friend plays on my thoughts. I would sooner he forgot about his horse.

Theorvard coughs again, and falls silent.

'*Theorvard, wake up!'* Saeward shouts, 'Try not to fall asleep. If we keep talking to you and you answer then I can tend to your wound when we find shelter!'

'Saeward you are worth your weight in silver, *I swear!*' Theorvard is racked with coughing but waves him away, 'I will live'.

'Why not gold?' I ask with a laugh, *'Saeward is surely worthy enough* of *gold!'*

'When did you last see gold?' Theorvard laughs, 'Oh God, this laughing is painful. *Tell me something boring!'*

Wulfmaer takes Theorvard at his word and looks up at the sky,

'Well at least the rain has stayed away'.

'Not *that* boring!'

Theorvard begins to make a snoring noise and we all start laughing, even Burhred.

'Maybe we should not talk so much', he coughs again. 'Just now and then ask me something to make sure I am still awake'.

He says to me by way of mild rebuff,

'There *must* be shelter somewhere near here!'

'Never fear, we will have you fed and that arrow wound dressed before long', I tell him, my fingers crossed at my side.

The afternoon has worn on before we come upon a clutch of dwellings in the half light. No-one shows when I shake open the first willow-woven door. The folk here would have fled when they knew the Northmen were near. If *they* had come across this hamlet, they would have burnt it down.

'Come... In here, there is not a soul to be seen'. I stand back to allow in Saeward and Wulfmaer, who guide Theorvard between them, 'At least there are none that *I* can see'.

Burhred and Theodolf hobble the horses and come in after us.

'We need something for Saeward to see by', Wulfmaer offers to find something for Saeward to work by.

I nod and see Saeward draw a bundle from his saddle pack.

He carefully opens up the bundle. By slight of hand he holds up a candle and asks Wulfmaer to light it for him with a piece of flint. Whilst the miller sets to with this task, Saeward asks me to help him pull off Theorvard's byrnie.

The sleevelet of Theorvard's jerkin is drawn back to show the ugly wound and Saeward peers closely at the pus that seeps from it. The sight of it earns a look of disgust from Theodolf.

'There are some herbs and salves to put on it, and there may be maggots about somewhere to help clean the wound', Saeward tells me. 'He will need a bit to chew on when I clean the wound and rub something into it. Hold him down between you. He is a big man, so the four of you should just about cope'.

Saeward looks up at me and asks me to pass a small, dark blue flask.

'This task is not hard', I tell myself.

'*Are you blind, Ivar?* That one is green, the blue one is *there*', he points to another one. I hold it up to see by the candle light before handing it to him, making sure it is the right one.

'The light by that candle is not enough to see by very well', I tell him, 'dark bottles are best seen by daylight, I think'.

He lets pass my plea and turns to Wulfmaer again,

'Can you make a fire in this hearth, Wulfmaer, and put this knife on the stone with the blade into the fire?' Saeward seems to rely on the miller more now than on anyone else. Perhaps he knows Wulfmaer has helped with this kind of healing craft before.

'Face it, Ivar, *you are getting old!*' Theorvard brings on another coughing fit with his laughter.

'It is not the be all and end all. *Be quiet, Danelaw man!*'

Saeward hisses and dabs the wound with something that makes Theorvard try to pull away.

'Do you want to see yourself in the next world so soon?!'

Theorvard scowls, but does as he is told and says no more. For all he towers head and shoulders above Saeward – who is himself not short on leg length – he lets the East Seaxan order him about.

'Get me some rags - anyone', Saeward demands. 'Any cloth or some such thing will do, as long as it is clean'.

Theodolf strides out into the darkening late afternoon. I find it hard to see the furthest dwelling at the eastern end of this thwait. Hopefully we will not have ridden too far east. The ride on south will be hazardous now.

Theodolf comes back into sight with something that looks like a woman's underskirt.

'How did you come to have *that* on you?' Burhred grins and peers at it as the lad hands it to a grateful Saeward.

'I found it in the inn. I thought it was left for us to dry our hands on, but none of us used it'.

'It is just as well none of us *did* use it', Saeward observes drily, without taking his eyes off Theorvard's wound.

Burhred helps himself to some bread from the bags of food, earning himself a scowl from Saeward and Wulfmaer.

'We will need your help before long, Burhred', Saeward warns. 'Can I have the flask now, Ivar?'

He tears off a strip of the cloth and folds it a few times. Taking the little flask from me, he un-stoppers it and drips some of the blueish spirit onto the cloth. He takes the knife from the fire, ready to press it onto the wound

'This will *hurt* him. Take hold of him - *now!*' Saeward tells us. Theorvard clamps his teeth onto the small piece of wood he was given and we grip him tightly, holding him down on the straw bedding that some ceorl had thoughtfully left for us.

When the cloth is pressed onto the flesh around the wound, Theorvard bucks. Wulfmaer is thrown off where he was holding his left shoulder, but takes his corner again.

Saeward does not chide, but ties the cloth tightly around the wound. Theorvard's snorts with the pain sound like those of a wild hog. His teeth chew through the stick in his mouth and he spits out the chewed wood before he chokes on it. Wulfmaer is still pressing down when Theodolf, Burhred and I have let go.

Saeward grunts at Wulfmaer, still holding Theorvard's elbow,

'You can let go of him now'.

The young giant sits up, squeezes his eyes shut, and when he opens them again shakes like a hound and gives Wulfmaer an odd look.

'Sorry, I must have been thinking of something', Wulfmaer presses his lips together to show he is sorry.

'Well if no-one else is going to eat, you will forgive me for starting', Burhred has gone out of the dwelling and returns laden with bags.

'They look like the flour bags we use at Saewardstan', Wulfmaer offers without being asked.

'I suppose *you* would know', Burhred wearily drops the bags onto the straw and goes out for the other two. He is not interested in what the bags look like as much as what he, Theodolf and Saeward put in them.

With a few knives and the help of a few lengths of willow we set up a rough spit to turn the meat from one of the bags. Later, when the meat has been browned and we are seated on the earthen floor of the dwelling, feasting on our gains, Wulfmaer begins to hum between mouthfuls. Theodolf stares into the darkness, chewing slowly, thoughtfully. He dearly wants to say something, but plainly cannot find the words to put his thoughts to us. Theorvard gnaws happily on the bones after chewing at the meat and suddenly asks,

'What meat is this?'

'Who knows, *or cares.* I am just glad of the food', Burhred has brought skins of drink and opens one of them.

'The meat makes me think oddly of chicken, or piglet', Saeward hazards a guess.

'This is *not* chicken', I mull over the taste between mouthfuls, take a sniff at the meat and chew some more, 'although the bones are small enough. Nor is it from a piglet. I would say from the carcass the animal looks like a short-legged hare. They must have small hares in North-mandige, what do you think, Theodolf?' I ask. The lad has spent his life in the woodlands near Tadceaster, and may know this odd creature.

'As you say, Ivar, it looks like a small hare with short hind legs. Other than that I cannot say', he chews on, still thinking.

Still thinking of what he wanted to say, what it is he is eating does not weigh unduly with him. He wants to fill his stomach, and wants to say what is playing on his thoughts. We all fall silent. Theorvard takes a drink of what Burhred has been guzzling from the skin.

'God, what sort of mead is it these Northmen drink?!' Theorvard holds up the skin to look at it. When I reach out for it he pulls it back and takes another draught. Burhred lifts another skin to his mouth and agrees with Theorvard,

'It *has* an odd taste; sweet but not like mead. This stuff tastes like fermented apple, but it is great!'

'How many skins of it did you bring?' Wulfmaer asks, looking around on the floor.

I count the skins. Eight, they brought away with them... *eight!*

'*This* one tastes more like ale', Theodolf is delighted, and lifts it to his mouth again, drizzling some around his cheeks as he lies back on one elbow.

'You had best hold it with both hands', I tell him, 'or else you will pour most of it across your face like that. Sit up, it would be a shame to waste it, whatever it is'.

Burhred is happy... for now, at least.

He will not have forgotten about the loss of his horse, but does not show it. Everyone is happier with a full belly and good drink. We have eaten our fill and we are sated.

'Before we lose ourselves in this drink, though, had we not best set watches so that we are not taken off our guard? I would swear the old man and the girl were hwicce', I do not want to, but I have to bring my friends back down to earth. 'Besides, the Northmen could well turn up here. They might have overlooked this hamlet before, but that is not to say they will not come this way again'.

We agree watches, Theodolf and I share the first one, Burhred and Wulfmaer will take over during the night. Saeward will keep watch on Theorvard's wellbeing. It is pitch black outside, our horses slowly crop the grass between the dwellings as Theodolf and I look up into the inki-ness of the sky at the pinpricks of light far away.

'Aethel used to tell me that the stars were the souls of the dead who died peacefully in their beds', Theodolf sniffs.

'*Quiet* out there!'

In this still night his voice still carries, despite our being some way away from the dwelling. Burhred has no thoughts about the souls of the dead; he only wishes to make up for lost sleep. His watch is next.

'We will have to speak in whispers', I tell him with a wink.

A look over my shoulder tells me nothing, but Burhred groans, still unable to sleep, despite having emptied the skin.

'Maybe that drink of his gave him wind', Theodolf laughs, earning himself another bout of cursing from the sleepless Burhred.

'We can move a little further away', I pull his sleeve and point to the next dwelling. It is as we move across the heavily dew-laden grass that I sense stirring in the trees behind the lowly dwelling that our friends have taken for the night.

'You heard that twig crack too, Ivar?' Theodolf murmurs.

'Aye, Theodolf, I did. Go, raise our friends. I feel their sleep will be broken very soon anyway. Tell them just to be ready, not to rush out fully armed or whatever'.

He nods and backs away and quietly vanishes into the darkness of our sleeping quarters. Whilst he is rousing them I pick up a piece of wood and begin to whittle it to shape with my dagger. There will not be enough time for me to finish the task. Whatever shape it takes is meaningless. I am doing something merely to look busy. Nothing stirs anywhere now, but I feel I am being watched. The silence is eerie, our horses become skittish and I make a show of turning to see what has upset them.

An arrow thuds into the lintel of the dwelling that I have put myself in front of, so that no-one can get behind me.

Some way ahead of me a tall, rangy fellow shows from behind one of the dwellings with a spear and runs at me with the point levelled at my chest. Theodolf has his knife drawn, ready to take on our attacker but I pull him back, wrench at his right shoulder and bawl loudly at my attacker,

'*We are not Northmen!*'

He falters and stops in his tracks, the spear still held at shoulder height, ready to jab at me. He peers through the darkness at me, unsure whether to follow through the attack. I could be a Northman, trying to stall him.

'I said we are *not Northmen!*' I tell him again, holding my axe by my side to show him we are no threat. 'This is a Dane-axe, my friend. Have you seen a Northman with an axe like this?'

By now another half-dozen poor bedraggled souls have gathered around him, all bearing makeshift weapons of some sort or another, scythes, shovels. One man carries a war bow.

'Who are you?' I ask the fellow with the spear, 'Are these your homes? If we had been Northmen these dwellings would have been ashes by now. We sought only shelter when we came here after fighting the invaders, and I will pay you in silver for what we have taken if you wish'.

The older man lowers his spear and walks warily toward me,

'If you are not Northmen, then who are you? There *are* no Aenglish fighting men in these parts, surely? I thought the outlanders saw to that. I have lost count of the men herded past us in chains'.

'I am a Dane, Ivar Ulfsson, and these men with me are Aenglish. You say men were herded past you, in chains?' I repeat his last words.

'Aye, mostly men called to the fyrd, not huscarls. *They* are all dead', the tall fellow tells me. He does not look like a ceorl, or a freed man. He does not have the gnarled, callused hands you see on land workers, whose lives are filled with hard, back-breaking day-to-day toil.

'You said you saw them herded past you... where were you?' I wonder what he means.

'We were in the woods, *hiding*', he recounts for me as if talking to a fool. 'Their horses passed at a slow trot, their captives chained like thralls, having to keep up with them. They were being led toward Hrofesceaster, but we have no way of knowing why. They may have been led there to work for the Northmen, some of whom came here for us. We were warned of their coming early enough to take our few cows, pigs and chickens further into the Andredes Leag, beyond the main paths, even. We saw the smoke from your fire and came down to take a closer look'.

'If you had been Northmen perhaps you would have fired this hamlet as you say, but you might have used these dwellings to rest in through the night first', the tall fellow tells me. He is not from around here, I can tell by the way he talks.

'I am, Aelfwold, their thegn', he nods backward at the men behind him as if in answer to my unasked question. 'If the Northmen were to find out who I am, I would be amongst the men led away in chains – or worse, because I fought against them with my men beside Earl Gyrth's huscarls. We were making our way past the Hoar Apple Tree when I saw you and your men with Lord Ansgar and his friends. I recall you well, Dane. You were talking with Earl Gyrth as though you knew him', Aelfwold is fishing for knowledge. What good would it do him, knowing my kinship to Gyrth? I let him wait for his answer until I am sure he means no harm. If he is only asking for his own sake this will show itself soon enough.

'I know Ansgar from being one of Earl Harold's huscarls'. I hold back from telling him about being one of Tostig's men before that how would he take it? He may have been called out by Harold to fight off Tostig when he came across with his ships from Flanders.

'You *know* Ansgar? Do you not mean to say you *knew* him?

'He is not dead, Aelfwold. He is now King Eadgar's *stallari*'.

'*King* Eadgar? What of the Northman duke?'

'He may *want* the throne, but he will not find it easy to take now. We have already beaten him once, at Lunden Brycg', I tell the thegn. 'We *do* have able men to lead us against the outlanders, *believe me*'.

Aelfwold nods thoughtfully, searching my eyes to make sure he can believe me, and goes on to speak about how he has spent time with these folk who have so far stayed free,

'The church men here are in league with the Northmen. I believe – no, I *know* they were spying out the land before Duke Willelm launched his fleet, and they secured supplies for the Duke, so that when he landed they could have at least some food ready for his men and horses. War horses need a lot of hay!'

He spits on the dry earth, as though he blames the Northman-born abbots of the Centish hundreds for their loyalty toward Willelm, although they could not behave otherwise, could they?

'*Of course* they do, and Duke Willelm was not going to tire them out by letting his men ride far and wide in search of fodder. The fields around Pefense would have been stripped clean within days', I can only agree with what Aelfwold I already know. Is he going to give himself away by telling me something that is not common knowledge? My ears pricked up when he told me he saw me with Gyrth.

Could he have been turned, if since the slaughter he had been held by Willelm's men?

'Are the Northmen on every road to Pefense?' I ask, hoping to hear something that might be of use.

'You want to go *there* – but *why*?' Aelfwold looks sharply at me.

Does he think *I* would want to offer my sword-hand to the Northmen? I may be wrong to doubt *his* loyalty, or again it could be too early for me to trust in him. If we were ever to cross swords with the foe side-by-side with his men I would soon know, but I have no wish to test him or his men. Yet I may have need of him one day. If I can test him out without risk I shall. To sound him out I give him the bare bones of our errand,

'King Eadgar has entrusted me to find which way the duke's stores reach these shores. He wishes to send ships around eastern Centland to cut their seaward lines. We have yet to see how they are reaching him through Suthrige'.

'Is that how far he has reached now?' Aelfwold stares at me, and turns to speak to one of his men before asking me again, 'How did *you* know this?'

He shakes his head in disbelief, as does the fellow who stands closest to him.

It could be they really do not know – or understand. I turn to speak to the fellow myself but Aelfwold sees me and stops me from doing so.

Aelfwold speaks for his follower.

'Brihtwig understands you. He cannot answer. His tongue was torn from his mouth for answering back when Lord Odo shouted orders at him'. Aelfwold fights back a torrent of grief. 'Show him, Brihtwig. He does not believe what I tell him'.

Brihtwig gapes for his thegn. Besides showing a set of blackened teeth, some good ones, he wags a stump of a tongue. Aelfwold sees me turn my eyes from the sight and grimaces.

'*This man is a great warrior in these parts!*' Aelfwold slaps the grinning ceorl hard on his back and looks around him, at his men and at my friends. His eyes light up at the sight of our horses cropping the grass past Brihtwig's fellows.

'You have spare horses', Aelfwold notes.

'We have *one* spare horse. One of my friends is in there. He was hit by one of the Northmen's arrows when we raided their camp in the woods back along that way', I point back through the woods, roughly to the north-west of here.

'*You* raided at Benenden? *That is Odo's main camp! God, it* is little wonder, then, that they are everywhere like wasps on a rotten apple! You know of Odo?' Aelfwold stands there with his mouth agape. There is a hint of great warrior worship until he asks, 'Were there many in the camp, or did you wait until most of them had gone out to scour the land?'

'In answer to what you asked first, I do know of Odo. I know him in the flesh. He nearly had me hanged, along with a friend of mine who was killed fighting the Northmen. When we were with Earl Harold in Northmandige on the old king's behalf Odo accused us of trying to free Harold's youngest brother, Wulfnoth. As to what you asked next, you are right. We made sure there were few left in the camp before we raided. We are not fools! All the same we nearly lost Theorvard to their arrows. We were lucky to find these dwellings so soon'. Aelfwold is worthy of my telling him that much. I am sure he is no lickspittle for Odo, not after seeing his friend tortured.

'We need to be clear of here by morning if the Northmen know we are in this hundred', Burhred warns. He shows distrust in these folk by casting a wary eye on Aelfwold.

'Your friend thinks I will betray him, perhaps?' Aelfwold has not misread Burhred.

I laugh, trying to set aside Aelfwold's misgivings,

'He distrusts *all* those he does not know'.

Aelfwold roars with laughter when I add,

'He was no different toward us'.

I sense someone else coming from behind and turn to see Theorvard nearing in the half-dark.

Brihtwig draws back at the size of my friend, unsure of what to do until I tell his thegn Theorvard is a friend. Aelfwold also looks over-whelmed,

'This is Theorvard, Aelfwold. He took an arrow in his shoulder yesterday morning. Once he laid into the Northmen's fare that we freed from their camp kitchen, the pain of having the arrow pulled left him. Their apple ale helped send him to sleep – until now', I present the young giant to the Suth Seaxan thegn.

'You are a lucky fellow, Theorvard. That bowman must have pulled his arrow straight from the bag. If he had pulled it from the earth, you would not be here to tell the tale!' Aelfwold warms to my friend, despite being dwarfed by him.

'Luck seems to walk hand-in-hand with him, aye', I look the bemused Theorvard up and down.

Theorvard warns, lest I forgot,

'We must move on, Ivar. The dawn is coming, and I dare say Odo's men will not be far behind' He nods sideways at Aelfwold,

'Who is he, and who are his friends?'

'These folk live here, this is their hamlet and I have thanked Thegn Aelfwold that these homes were here when we needed to rest', I tell him thoughtfully, bearing in mind we are outnumbered should they suddenly show themselves to be unfriendly.

'*The huts smell, though!*' Theorvard puts a finger under his nose.

'If you shared your home with your pigs, I would say that about *your* home', Aelfwold growls.

Theorvard only grins and waves his hand as if to wish Aelfwold away.

'He does not suffer from manners, does he?' Aelfwold turns to me.

'He is right, though', I have to laugh.

'Oh, *is he* indeed, how so?' Aelfwold sniffs. Perhaps he thinks we say he smells too.

'He is right in that we need to leave these quarters, and very soon', I smile at Aelfwold.

My smile is met by an icy stare. Where Theorvard may not suffer fools, to be even-handed I have to suppose Aelfwold is no different.

I would say we are of an age, rough living has aged us both in much the same way. He would have had little enough to tax him before the Northmen came, but for being called out to fight off Tostig in the summer.

These last two weeks will have seen him called from the comfort of his hall to fight Willelm's men, and then having to take to the woods to hide from them after fleeing clutches. Now he has to live like this. Do his men look up to him, or do they think of him as being one of them?

'Brihtwig saved my life when he took Odo's fury upon himself. It was otherwise very likely that the Northman bishop would have found out who I was. Life would then not have been worth living. As it happens, I do not know where my wife or kindred are, now that our home has been razed. When I last saw my home, there were only the charred stumps of my hall pillars. My grandfather built that hall when Aethelred made him thegn in thanks for raising a ship levy to fight the Danes - your kindred, I think?' Aelfwold looks up at the greying sky, and back at me. The eyes that hold me in a long gaze are now a deep cornflower blue. He looks down at his boots and frets about the dirt on them, 'I stood in some sheep shit during the night when we were creeping up on you!'

As he laughs at his bad luck and gives orders to his men someone calls out,

'There are riders along the path, coming from the south west!'

'Theorvard, can you ride?' I ask my friend.

He stands there, stripped to his waist, his wound dressing bulging across his shoulder. He begins to shiver.

'It seems I will have to!' Theorvard shrugs and walks back to the dwelling that he had been sleeping in.

'Theodolf, can you help Theorvard with his clothes and byrnie?' I ask, unaware Saeward was coming out with Theorvard's torn jerkin and chain mail until he brushes past me, 'Oh, Saeward, *you* are helping him. It just goes to show a man can never have too much help these days, can he? Theodolf, you had best un-hobble the horses, then. Aelfwold, if you need a horse, I have one spare mount. Thank the Northmen for her, not me'.

'You are sure you do not need her? One thing is sure, she is a handsome beast. Still, I have been walking with my men for days, and I do not see why I should not go on doing so for a little longer. Ride, Ivar. You have some way to go, do not let us keep you. We will keep the newcomers busy until you are safely away from here', Aelfwold pats the rough-coated mare on the neck. She gives a snort, shakes her head and goes back to cropping the grass.

6

When we are mounted I take my farewell from him and nudge Braenda into a brisk trot. When we have only just left the thwait I look over my shoulder and see a small number of Northmen break cover from the other side of the hamlet. There is yelling and shouting as the Centish-men vent their fury on their tormentors.

Only a half dozen riders have shown, their leader thrashing about him before Brihtwig gets under his shield and heaves him from his stir-rups. One Northman looks as though he might escape. Panic-stricken he spurs his horse for the woodland that only moments ago he showed from with his comrades.

Saeward has turned his horse and spurred her into a gallop, hurtling over the open ground before I can shout for him to wait. I turn Braenda quickly toward Theorvard's horse.

'Wait here', I tell Theorvard and the others. Burhred shakes his head and raises his eyes heavenward, dumbfounded at Saeward's wilfulness. I press Braenda into a gallop after him.

It is not long before I see Saeward, his warhorse keeping pace with the rider ahead. Freshly rested, his horse should be faster but takes what seems an age before he catches up with his quarry. The man turns in his saddle and, seeing what he takes to be a comrade slows. He turns his mount sideways on to Saeward. It takes little time for the Northman to know he is fated when Saeward draws his axe from its sheath at the front of his saddle and sends it spinning. The axe buries itself in the gaping man's chest, sending him toppling to the leaf-strewn woodland floor. He is still twitching, his lungs filling with blood when I catch up with Saeward.

'Just suppose there were others behind them, waiting for these to call them on, what would you have done then?' I growl at Saeward and grab at his mailed shoulder.

He shrugs off my hand and dismounts, goes over to the dead Northman and calmly puts his left boot on one shoulder. Sneering, he tells me as he wrenches the blade free,

'They are so sure we are beaten that they only come out in small numbers. Their leader was easily pulled from his mount because he failed to understand that we are as yet unbeaten. This callow youth was doomed from the outset'. The axe has sheered through the fellow's ribs. Saeward wipes the blade on the now dead youth's helmless scalp. The helm lies on its crown close by the corpse.

'He is only a lad, like Theodolf', I tell Saeward.

'Are you going *soft?* This *lad*, as you call him, would have meted out as bad or worse to any one of us!' Saeward snarls. I have never seen such a change in a man. Odo himself would be glad to have him for one of his own, as blood-thirsty as he has become. 'If you feel sorry for him, it may be you are getting too old to fight. Give over the leadership of our little band to Theorvard or Burhred and use your axe to cut wood for the fire'.

'Maybe I should use it to cut *you* to size! You have turned into an avenging angel. Until now Aelfwold's men could have vanished into the woodland from whence they came, and we would have been well away from here. Anyway, why would I hand over to Burhred? Merely because the Northmen were quick off the mark and we lost some of our spare mounts, or were you so fond of your horse? You have only had her for a couple of days, and this one is a much better runner'.

'Would you really kill me?' Saeward asks, unblinking. He does not believe that I would do such a thing, and I do not think I *could*.

'Try me hard like that again and I might show you', I threaten through clenched teeth. 'Now come away and leave him. Kick some more leaves over him, poor lad. Some mother will grieve for him. Do you think on what Thor said to you when you were suffering your pangs of self-doubt? Do not take our fight too much to heart. Kill a man if you have to do it before he kills you, but do not turn killer. One day you may become so racked with guilt only a priest would be of use to you'.

Saeward looks down at the dead man, and at me. Shamefacedly he asks for forgiveness,

'I am sorry I threatened you'.

Saeward looks cheerlessly at me, outwardly pleading for under-standing. I suspect he is playing with me and I am beginning to wonder if he means *any* of it. 'I know I must have turned into what you Danes would call a Troll, like Grendel. Burhred might be a leader of sorts, but not as good as Theorvard and *he* looks to you'.

'That much is true, aye. Grendel *was* a Troll'. I am taken aback that Saeward has read these things, 'But he killed men to eat them because he was cursed by the gods'.

'You, Saeward, are a man of learning and thought, or have been. I fear one day you will bury that side of yourself forever, as easily as you sent that lad to his maker. But your deeds will come back to haunt you, that is what I am trying to warn you against. Theorvard is a good warri-or, does not kill without there being reason to do so, and he follows me because I defeated his leader in a fair fight. His loyalty is assured for now, but I do not take it for granted'.

We ride back through the woods to the hamlet where Aelfwold and his men busy themselves hiding the corpses of the other Northmen.

'Did you catch him, Ivar?' Aelfwold asks as we pass.

'He did', I point to Saeward and pull on Braenda's reins to halt her. 'He threw his axe overhand at the Northman when he turned. He must have thought Saeward was one of his comrades'.

'You say he *threw* an axe, *overhand,* from the saddle?' Aelfwold stands there, arms held out wide in wonder. '*God,* if only we had more like him, we would be a match for them. Think what we could do to turn these Northman bastards back and throw them into the sea whence they came?'

'We need the men with such fighting skills, I know. But we should not look on this as a holy war, as their duke does', I nudge Braenda to a walk and wave farewell to these brave men.

No harm should come to them if they leave soon. Before we leave I warn,

'Take care, Aelfwold. I would not want to be here when they come back. These men will be missed. Odo has already lost a number of men to us these last couple of days, and he will not be happy to learn of more losses. *He will be like a mountain on fire!'*

A salute to the brave Brihtwig earns me a grin. He winks and turns away when someone calls him away.

Following Aelfwold's bearings, we have put many miles behind us. I can see the wide bay from between the trees to the west above Pefense. There is no-one about when we come upon what must have been a steading. From the edge of a broad thwait I see ample grazing and growing land. Until only a few short weeks ago cattle were likely to have been seen cropping the grass here, and someone would have tilled the earth with an ox-drawn plough.

'It looks so still here', Saeward is the first to speak, breaking a long silence between us, 'like home'.

Burhred and Wulfmaer nod slowly. Theorvard grunts. Theodolf offers a few words to add to Saeward's,

'Shame the Northmen came here before us, eh?'

'A man could be happy here, content, *even* now', Saeward answers wistfully. 'Yet there would always be the threat of unwelcome guests. Aye, it *is* a shame we cannot see this land as it was. Willelm will one day pay for his short-sightedness'.

'You think he will be here that long?' Theodolf turns in his saddle to look at Saeward.

'We hope he is thrown back before he can do worse, but *he* will

have no second thoughts about what he has done in this land so far!'
Wulfmaer growls and spits on the grass,

'It would be as well for us to achieve that end, before he has time
even to take a breath!' Burhred speaks at last. I thought he was brooding.

'I say '*amen*' to that!' Saeward sets the seal on our hopes.

'Before we can hope to oust Duke Willelm and cut short his dream
of becoming 'King', we must comb the land for the duke's highways', I
join in, hopefully cutting the talk and getting our horses moving again.

'Did Aelfwold say anything about where we could put in for the
night?' Theorvard asks me.

We have been riding all day, skirting what few hamlets we came
across, adding miles to our way. Few, if any Northmen have been seen.
They may have been searching for 'ghosts' where we were last night,
hopefully missing Aelfwold's men. With luck they will not yet have
found their dead. In cutting down that young fellow, Saeward may have
done us a good turn. There has been no hue and cry to the best of my
knowledge.

Saeward looks around, and up into the heavens, seeing only crows
wheeling overhead,

'Since this morning's fighting I have seen no-one. Have you seen
anyone, Ivar, *even from far off?*

He shakes his head wearily and waves a hand in the air,

'These woods should be alive with the sound of wood being
chopped and cut for winter fires, the fields humming with folk sowing
seeds for the early crops'.

I have been watching the crows, and point across the open land, asking,

'Wulfmaer, or Saeward, when you see crows wheeling, would it be
they are awaiting the death of someone or something?'

'They are too big to be crows... more likely ravens'. Wulfmaer
snaps back. 'Someone *must* be over there, standing by dead comrades
or friends, afraid to come out into the open'.

'God, Ivar, they *are* too big to be crows, and we are near the sea.
They *are* ravens, and someone – or something - must be dying down
there', Saeward chides me for my lack of knowledge about our winged
friends and clicks his tongue for his horse to walk on.

'Not so fast, Saeward, someone could be *waiting* for us down there',
Theodolf seizes him by one elbow before he can leave. 'They may take
us for fools, but there is no need to prove them right!'

'No-one knows we are here, surely?' Saeward's protests go unheed-
ed.

Wulfmaer offers another way out,

'We could see what it is the ravens are waiting for, but not straight across there', he waves his hand across the grazing land. 'We should make our way around by the beck there'.

Theorvard cranes his neck to look for water.

'Believe me, there is one down there', Wulfmaer smiles benignly, as though speaking to a child.

'There has to be a burn or a beck, I suppose, by the way the trees line up along the lower edge of this piece of land', I agree.

'Cattle or horses would need to go down for water. What you say makes sense. If the Northmen had seen us, they would want us to be somewhere they could lay their hands on us easily. Up here or along this wooded ridge we can still get away. Anyone might be watching for us crossing that open land'.

Being nearest the trees, Burhred leads. I beckon Saeward to ride close by me, as he is wont to gallop away without telling anyone. Theorvard brings up the rear, with the spare mount trotting along behind him. We are taking turns leading her; in the morning it will be my turn. The other Northmen's mounts were not needed, and might have marked us out if we had been seen by Odo's men.

Skirting the trees, we cross the beck at the head of the rise where the land is firm, but the lower reaches are boggy from where kine have churned up the earth to get to the cool water. Lower yet, there is a cluster of trees around a mere where the beck widens. Where the ravens are overhead we have to be on our guard.

Something stirs in the undergrowth. Nettles and dock leaves shake. Something darts out at us from cover.

'On your side, Burhred, *look out!*' Theodolf calls out as a wiry lad launches himself at Burhred's horse, giving the animal a start. Trying to hold his mount with one hand, Burhred brings down a mailed fist onto the lad's head, laying him out.

'*What in Jesu's name was that?!*' Saeward curses, shaking like a leaf with shock.

'Sweet-tongued fellow that you are, someone has just tried to un-horse Burhred', Theorvard laughs at the wild eyed Saeward.

'It is as well the lad did not jump at *you*. He would have been off with your horse and I would have had to give you this one!'

'He knows his ravens from his crows, but he is not as sure on his toes!' Wulfmaer has a belly laugh at Saeward, who reddens.

'Pay no heed to *him*. The fool would have been off *his* horse even without the lad coming anywhere near him!' Burhred smirks. 'Anyway, whilst he is laid out there we can see for whom or what the ravens were waiting to die'.

Burhred dismounts and leads his horse into the trees as Wulfmaer rides around the edge of the meadow, trying to see through the dense undergrowth. I ride alongside Wulfmaer and the others come single file behind me. With so many pairs of eyes on the ground, looking for God knows what, we do not see Burhred's attacker walking between us until he asks me what we are looking for,

'You are not Northmen?' he asks. Not seeing Theorvard shake his head he asks again in case no-one heard him, 'What is it you are all looking for?'

'We wondered why those ravens are hovering', I answer, pointing in the air.

'I was wondering about the smell. On thinking about it, there must be something dead around here. When I saw you coming down behind the trees on this side of the beck, I waited here to see if I could get *his* horse', the lad points at Burhred.

'Foolhardy lad, what made you think you could get away with it? Here, Saeward, you have a soul-mate', Wulfmaer cackles,

'This lad thinks he could get a horse by attacking a Northman! That is just like you, riding off after that Northman this morning without knowing if he had friends waiting in the woods'.

'Saeward is a brave fellow!' Theodolf defends his friend.

'He might be a dead fellow before we can get back to Lunden!' Wulfmaer cackles again.

'Perhaps he knows he cannot live forever', Burhred jeers at Wulfmaer, '*as you think you can!*'

'Will you shut up, the three of you?!' I yell above the bickering, 'I want to know something from this brave fellow here'.

'What is your name?' Theorvard asks before I can.

'I am named for the blessed Saint Dunstan', the lad answers.

'Oh, bless you!' Saeward cries out, and falls silent when Theorvard glares at him.

'Well, Dunstan, have you *seen* any Northmen here lately, in this neighbourhood?' I ask him.

He shakes his head and then points eastward,

'They are too busy unloading ships down in the bay. When they leave there they seem to head northward from Pefense'.

'Now', I go on, to more useful matters, 'where can we find food and shelter for six hungry fighting men? We have not eaten all day'.

'I have not eaten since *yesterday*', Dunstan calmly tells me. 'I awoke to find myself ringed by Northmen. They were too close to think they just happened upon me. I think they knew I was there, but not resting in the hayloft'.

He laughs, thinking back,

'While they were rummaging around in my home I slipped out through a hayloft door. I have been on the road since then'.

'There always has to be someone less lucky than yourself', Theorvard sighs.

'Well, lad, it is one thing being on the run and another having to fight to get away', Burhred offers an insight.

'When you are fighting, you are using all your muscles and all the fat in your body drains away with the rush of fighting. You should try it some time'.

Wulfmaer takes Dunstan to one side, lays a heavy miller's arm on the lad's shoulder and lets him know why we are here,

'We are here for King Eadgar to spy out the land, Dunstan. Our task is to let the king know where to send his ships, and how many. We have already sent a dozen of Odo's men to their maker. These three are dressed like Northmen to fool them into thinking we are their friends. By the time they know we are not it is too late for them'.

'Do you have kin here?' I ask Dunstan. He is no threat to us, an underdog in his own land. We should take him with us, but I must know if he will be missed.

'My wife and son are with my mother in Medestan since I was called by the fyrd to fight under King Harold. Who is this King Eadgar, and who is Odo?'

'King Eadgar is kin to King Eadweard. He is of the West Seaxan Cerdic's blood line', I tell Dunstan, dismounting and stretching for the first time since climbing into my saddle this morning.

'Odo is Duke Willelm's kin, a bishop in Northmandige. Odo has a ruthless streak and does his duty with a vengeance'.

'Is he a stocky, well-rounded fellow with short russet hair?' Dunstan asks.

'He has the simple understanding of a man of the land, *does he not?*' Theorvard grins at Theodolf, speaking of Dunstan as if he were elsewhere.

'That is one way of drawing him, aye', I nod at Dunstan. 'Duke Willelm is a little taller but looks much like him. They have the same mother'.

Wulfmaer takes his arm from Dunstan's shoulder and turns to me, eyebrows raised in wonder,

'You know, Ivar that is something I did not know. Was that Duke Willelm or Odo who came to fight us at Suthgeweorce?'

'That was the Duke. Odo has others to do his killing. He will not lift

124

a sword to kill, although he is not against using his staff to club men unlucky enough to stray into his path when he is on horseback', I smile at Wulfmaer as I tell him about my old foe.

In my mind's eye I see Odo as he was at Falaise, half-naked, stout, and bellicose. On Caldbec Beorg he was no different in manner. I doubt he has mellowed with all this warring over the past weeks.

'He must be the swine who cudgelled Thegn Aelfwold. I do not know what happened to him after that'. Dunstan's lips curl.

'How many Thegn Aelfwold's can there be in these parts?' Saeward asks, peers around me at Dunstan before asking again, 'Was your Thegn Aelfwold tall and greying?'

Dunstan brightens,

'He was, aye'.

'And did he have a friend called Brihtwig, whose tongue was ripped out at the orders of Bishop Odo?' Wulfmaer asks.

'He was not all that friendly with Brihtwig. Do you say Brihtwig's tongue was torn out because of that Northman turd? *I should kill him if I came near him!*' Dunstan darkens at the thought of one of his friends being hurt on the whims of Odo.

I cannot help but laugh. This lad has spirit! Hopefully he will see the wrongs righted that he and his friends have suffered,

'I cannot say for sure you would ever come near enough to do anything to Odo, but if you ride with us you could see his underlings brought to book', I offer, adding for good measure,

'You never know, we might come across Aelfwold on our way back. You can stay with him, if you want. Or you can come on with us toward Lunden and join your wife in Medestan'.

Dunstan beams. I think I have brightened his day for him. Then he loses his wide smile again,

'Why frown?' Theorvard asks.

'I have no horse, so how can I ride with you?' Dunstan makes a face that goes beyond tragic.

'You jumped at the wrong man', Theorvard laughs and points at the quietly brooding Burhred. 'Instead of leaping out at Burhred there, you should have tried me. I am the one leading our spare horse. You think you can ride this tall mount?'

Burhred grunts,

'I was expecting to find a corpse, or at least an injured man. Then I get you, very much alive, leaping at me through the weeds. You scared me half to death, *you did!*'

'A *likely story* - you look as though you could handle yourself!' Dunstan looks happier now, perhaps for the second time today since learning of our meeting with Thegn Aelfwold. He joins in the banter as Theorvard draws forward the spare mount, 'Just think, I may be riding in the saddle of the bastard who razed my home!'

'*God*, he hardly knows me and already he talks to me as if I were an old friend! Can we find some *food* now?' Burhred grumbles. He has a belly to fill, not unlike the rest of us, although none of us raises that with him.

'We can find something to eat nearby', Dunstan offers.

'Good, but let us hope it is not another Northman supply camp'. Burhred has had his share of thrills for today and wants to find his meal the easy way.

'No, but it came from one when they were not watching the road. They think we are beaten, but we squirrel away their supplies bit by bit, bag by bag. They do not miss what they have not seen, because they get drunk on their fermented apple ale each night and we go in and free more of the meat and root crops from their clutches', Dunstan laughs at the thought of winning back some of the food taken by the Northmen. 'I think they looted the root crops from near here, one of our tithe barns if you ask me'. Dunstan launches into a final rant, 'Having robbed so much, the greedy bastards do not know what goes missing!'

'Who is 'we', my young friend Dunstan? Do you have friends somewhere near that you have not told us of?' I do not want to come across anyone who could cause us trouble. Nor do we want too many riding with us, to needlessly draw the eyes of the Northmen.

'I have a friend called Odd, who lived in the monastery that our Northman abbot allowed his cronies to use for their quarters', Dunstan answers quickly. He will be afraid in the dark, on his own'.

'Will he mind being on his own if you ride with us?' I ask again.

'He has a pony', the lad tells me.

'How come you were not riding it?' Wulfmaer asks, 'Would it not have made sense, if you were going for miles around?'

'He might have been seen', Saeward puts in.

'So why jump at Burhred for *his* horse?' Theodolf cannot see the reasoning behind what Saeward thought made sense.

'Very soon, on his way home in the half dark, he would not be seen as easily', Theorvard says and looks up into the heavens, as if to hope for clouds to douse the light of the moon before we happen on any unwelcome company... or before they happen on us.

On his looking up I do the same and feel droplets on my brow. We need to ride for Dunstan's new home for the night, out of the wet. We also need to see what food stocks he has, and to see who this fellow Odd might be. He might be a layman, as Saeward was, or a brother. If he was a brother, and his abbot is Northman, does he know their tongue? We need luck on our side.

As we turn northward again, I turn to Dunstan and ask him why.

'This is the way to where I live now', is all Dunstan will tell me. As he can help us with our errand, I keep my thoughts to myself for the rest of the ride.

Our way now takes us down into a dale and up another rise before we stop at a small thwait. We must be north of Pefense here. There are two buildings, one of which looks like a dwelling. The other must be a barn, but on looking through the trees neither looks welcoming.

Braenda snorts heavily when I dismount. I have over-taxed her again and more than once in the darkness she has stumbled, tired.

'Are you in there, Odd?' Dunstan shouts out to his friend and slides down from the horse. On hearing no answer he shouts, 'Odd, where are you? I have friends with me who can help us!'

Still there is no answer. I sense a trap and am ready to head off back into the woods again, with or without Dunstan or his friend.

Theodolf pats his horse's neck. She is turning skittish and the eerie silence makes me more wary than I already am. Theorvard stands in his stirrups and looks around. I can see little in the dark but that the thwait slopes to the back where the trees seem to reach heavenward against the darkened eastern sky, creaking in the gathering easterly wind. It feels colder now and I would like to be indoors after all this riding.

'Odd, where –', Dunstan is stopped by Burhred from calling out again and my friend turns to me.

'He may have been taken, or is in the woods, hiding'.

'Dunstan is there a burh, or perhaps a hamlet nearby?' I ask. 'He could have gone there for something'.

'He would not have gone to Weartlinga this late in the day', Dunstan dismisses my thought out of hand.

'Then where could he be, unless the Northmen have him. You say he ran away from the abbey, was he a brother or a layman?'

Theorvard is irked by Dunstan's answer. He wants to rest and eat, as do we all.

'I will look in the outhouse, at the back', Dunstan dismounts and strides up over the steeply sloping green to what I thought was a barn and vanishes into the darkness within, to emerge by another door at the end of this building. 'But first I will see if he is hiding in the barn'.

'Is he in there?' I ask.

The rain has started again. It is colder and we are all tired.

'No he is not in here. He could be in the dwelling house. I will look there', Dunstan answers. He seems on edge, and this does not make me feel any better.

'Has anyone anything against us just dismounting, hobbling our horses and leaving them to graze whilst we rest our weary bones in there?' Burhred is annoyed with Dunstan and his absent friend.

'We could get a fire going in the hearth. By the time your friend comes back the dwelling will be warm and welcoming'.

'You must agree, that would be much better than waiting here for him to show', Theodolf says to me.

I look at Dunstan, who purses his lips. When a branch creaks above us, Saeward and I look up at the same time. Saeward takes a sharp breath and points upward.

'The Northmen *must* have been here, or else there are other raiders about. Look up there'.

Seven pairs of eyes take in the grisly sight above us. Dunstan gives a yelp, like a small dog. He panics and pleads,

'For God's sake, get him down! *Get him down!*' he nearly knocks Wulfmaer over in his haste to get to the tree where some poor wretch swings with the wind.

Theorvard strides across the green with his axe and takes a swipe with it at the securing rope.

'We could have *used* that rope!' Wulfmaer groans. He would have kept it. He must have had a use for it in mind, or he was like that, like a seaman keeping things like rope for further use.

'You do not keep the rope that was used for a hanging, Wulfmaer. It brings bad luck!' Theorvard growls at him.

He throws his axe to the ground, picks up the body and looks down at the shivering Dunstan, wailing, his head buried in his hands.

'Where do you want him?' Theorvard asks.

'Do we stay here for the night, or do we try to find somewhere else? We do not know how much further our mounts will take us before they give up the ghost', Burhred asks me, and looks at Dunstan, shaking in his grief.

'Leave Odd here, in the barn. We can shelter in the dwelling for one night. Dunstan, come inside with us and eat something. What have you got?' I steer him back to the dwelling house and the others follow. Theorvard is last, having laid the still limp Odd onto straw in the barn.

Dunstan is still unable to give us an answer, so we take to foraging in the darkness until Wulfmaer finds rushes and something to light them with. Theodolf takes one lighted rush and wanders aimlessly. With a nose for finding food, Burhred looks elsewhere and calls out soon after starting his search,

'*Hah,* I knew I was looking on the right shelf! Hey, Saeward, give me a hand with this box onto that table!'

Saeward helps and between them they lift a sizeable box onto the four-plank table top. Burhred lifts out bags of roots and fruit.

There are apples and pears in plenty, salted meats and a stone bowl of cooking fat.

'There is more meat in a bag, hanging out at the end of the dwelling', Dunstan swallows his sorrow and points northward.

That would be the coldest side. I wonder what kind of meat he has hanging outside and beckon to Theodolf to come with me, to see what delights await us there.

As we rummage around outside, looking at the hanging game and other rich-smelling meats, Theodolf glances downward and yells fitfully before fleeing for the door. I turn and watch after him as he vanishes around the corner, and then look down myself.

I feel gripped by terror. The corpse has come to life! Somehow Odd has crawled back across the green to the dwelling and looks up at me in a weird sort of way, his neck twisted. He drags himself across the ground toward me just as Saeward and Burhred show. Theorvard, striding up behind them calls out to Theodolf as though he had seen many such pitiful sights as this,

'It is all right, Theodolf, he will not harm you – he has no strength in him beyond crawling!'

Dunstan comes running and goes sobbing down onto his knees, hugging his friend, the rain running down their faces.

Theodolf returns, grinning sheepishly at me. I cannot blame him. The sight of Odd on the ground gave me a turn too. Saeward bends down and unclasps Dunstan's hands from around Odd's waist.

'Let me look at him, Dunstan', Saeward asks. 'I know about these things. I can help him'.

Dunstan stares angrily up at Saeward, but then meekly shuffles to one side on his knees, still pathetically holding on to Odd's right hand.

'Let go of him, Dunstan', Wulfmaer tries to calm the fretful lad. 'Saeward needs to look at your friend, to see what he can do for him. He *does* know about these things, *believe me*'.

Dunstan looks pleadingly at me. I nod, once. He unwillingly lets go of his friend's hand, and, still watching worriedly over Odd stands to let Saeward see his friend.

'Trust me', is all Saeward tells him before looking at Odd's neck and hands. 'Can you hear me, Odd? Open your mouth wide for me?'

We all stand around, as if riveted to the spot as Saeward holds Odd's wrist, puts the arm gently down, holds his hair away from his right ear and presses his head to the lad's chest.

Theorvard stares at Saeward, baffled, unable to understand.

'What *is* all this? We have seen this young fellow is alive, even if not kicking, and Saeward fusses about him as if he were nobility. What is it all in aid of, for God's sake, can *anyone* tell me?'

I put my finger to my lips and stand watching, spellbound. Saeward finally asks Odd to try to speak, if only to say his name. Odd can merely croak, spit and try again, but can still only croak. Tears well in the corners of his eyes and Dunstan rushes to hug him before us all. Burhred shifts his feet and curses, annoyed at this womanly show of feelings by Dunstan. Theorvard stands quietly, arms crossed, taking everything in as do Wulfmaer and Theodolf.

I feel sorry for both Dunstan and Odd, but my belly tells me it is time to fill it before it forgets what food is. When I head for the door, Burhred follows gladly, with Wulfmaer and Theorvard close behind him. Saeward leads the tottering Odd a little later, helped by a much happier Dunstan.

'What gives, life-giver?' Burhred asks. A lump meat in his right hand, he holds a knife in his left, ready to sever the sinews on the leg of this creature that we first came across yesterday.

'*Show some respect!*' Theorvard growls at Burhred, sickened at Burhred's show of blinkered foolishness.

Burhred slams his knife down into the table top and snaps back at Theorvard,

'Why in Christ's name do we have to stand for this?'

'Why indeed, *you tell me!*' Theorvard counters. Turning on his stool, he pulls Burhred's knife from the splintered wood and tells him again, 'Show some manners! *You* should tell him, Ivar'.

With one hand Theorvard grabs Burhred by the throat flap on the Northman's mailcoat and holds the knife under his chin. With his other hand he pulls on Burhred's right ear. Burhred wrenches himself away from the young giant's grip, stands on unsteady legs and holds a hand over his ear.

He smarts with the pain and shame of being spoken to like a child in this way, in front of us all. Theorvard slams down Burhred's knife on the table, close to the beaker that Burhred had been drinking from.

'What Theorvard means, Burhred, is that these two fellows', I point at Dunstan and Odd, 'are our hosts and we have *their* food on *their table* for us to eat. We need only wonder that they have not told you to go and find your own food! I am close to telling you to do that, but if *they* choose not to ask you to leave, who am I to tell them?'

'You could say you are sorry for your outburst and I am sure either one or both of them would find it in themselves to forgive you',

Saeward adds, beetling his bushy eyebrows, 'the sooner, the better'.

We all watch Burhred, waiting to see what he will do next.

We have all been riding, foraging and fighting these last few days. Some inner turmoil was bound to show itself, but Burhred has shown himself to be an ingrate, a guest who abuses his hosts. The feelings behind that abuse cannot be shown by the rest of us to be shared.

Sensing our anger at him, seeing there is nowhere for him to go, he casts his eyes to the floor. I have to press for an answer,

'Well, what is it to be? Do you feel sorry for insulting Dunstan and his friend, or are we to cast you out to fend for yourself?'

I would not wish to make a foe of a man felt to be a friend until he challenged my leadership yesterday, but on the other hand Burhred must learn to bow to reason.

'I am sorry... *No* I am a fool, why *should* I be sorry!' Burhred leans over the table and snatches his knife from the table, upsetting his ale over Theorvard's torn byrnie.

Theorvard grabs again at for the throat flap on Burhred's mailcoat but misses, falling from his stool onto the earth floor with the effort. Burhred makes for the door but is stopped when Saeward leaps to his feet in front of the door.

'Get out of my way, Saeward! I do not wish to harm you, *but I will if I must!*' Burhred brandishes his knife under Saeward's nose.

'Where will you go, you fool?' Saeward pleads. 'There are Northmen everywhere'.

'Should they see you in that war-gear, do not think they will show mercy!' Theorvard adds, 'Think about that. *Think very carefully!*'

'In hell's name, why would *you* care about where I am going?' Burhred snaps at Saeward, 'Odd sort of killer that you are, you nurse feeble fools like him as if he were a child. Tomorrow you will be out again, chopping down the Northmen and then you will find another poor soul to tend to. What am I doing, riding with that fool Dane?!' Burhred points a finger over his knife handle at me.

'Let him be', I tell Saeward. He wants to be the master of his own fate, so why should we stand in his way? 'Go, Burhred, *if you must*'.

'You heard him, *stand aside!*' Burhred pushes Saeward out of the way and pushes the wicker door aside, vanishing into the night. His horse snorts wildly and the thud of hooves on the grass outside tells us he has left. Everything goes quiet again.

'Now what do we do?' Wulfmaer sounds worried.

'We finish our meal, sleep, take turns on watch, and then leave at first light', I tell him calmly.

Theorvard breathes out and nods, pulls apart a short leg that Burhred left on the table and stuffs it into his gaping mouth. Theodolf carries on eating as if nothing had happened. Odd gives me a frightened look and Dunstan fidgets with the food in front of him, unable to eat.

Saeward shakes his head angrily and warns,

'You should *not* have let him go - *this will lead to no good!*'

'Fear not, he will be back with us before long', I feel it in my bones. I am sure of it. But even if not, he will be careful to steer clear of the Northmen, what with riding one of their horses and a wearing a dead man's war gear. They will know soon enough who he killed for them.

'If he is stopped he *may* give us away', Theodolf warns, and takes a mouthful of bread, 'even without wanting to. They would torture him until he gave us away'.

'Do you think he would?' I ask, sure he will not betray us.

'If he were put to torment, he might give us away', Saeward tries to argue with me. I think he is only telling me the same as Theodolf has, but finding me unmoving he gives in and throws his hands up in the air.

I have to try to win my friends over to the way I see it,

'He will keep to the woodland tracks, ride by night and hide in the daytime. We did that when we fled Caldbec Beorg. Burhred has fought alongside us against the Northmen, he is no fool. He has lost his thegn and his two friends, the brothers Aelfwin and Aelfwig and he is still around to tell the tale'.

Theorvard and Wulfmaer nod, chewing still. Saeward will be harder to win over, but Theodolf seems not to be unduly bothered. To him Burhred is someone we met along the way, who fought by our side when Harold was killed. He was another who helped bar Willelm's entry into Lunden, no more.

To all and sundry I am sure of my words. Within, I feel for Burhred. I wish him no ill, but he was testing me hard and I could not be seen to weaken. Where would that have led otherwise? He would have been right in saying I am no fit leader for them.

'Aye, he is right', Theorvard agrees with me, wiping his hands on his tunic sleeve. 'Burhred will come to no harm, nor would he tell them where we are'.

'If you say so', Theodolf has finished his bread and reaches for an apple. He has known Burhred for weeks now, fought alongside him, slept near him and shared foolery with him. He takes the world in his stride. That is his youth. There are many things beside his fears that Theodolf has mastered these last weeks, such as his fears.

Only earlier he was frightened out of his wits by the sight of Odd crawling from the barn. Yet here he is now, eating and drinking as if nothing had happened. Theodolf is a child lurking within a man's body.

Saeward, on the other hand, goes from strength to strength. His beliefs still holds him captive, but his fighting skills have grown. He has made his mark with the young king as an able warrior, but is still seen by Morkere as a killer. He keeps his own counsel, as I do, yet he is an open-handed, caring fellow.

Theorvard is a warrior first and foremost, but thoughtful about the feelings of others. He is young yet, about Leofwin's age, twenty years younger than I. He willingly gives his fighting skills to me, a man he sees as a leader, and will stay true until I am proved unworthy. He did not lightly switch his loyalty from Brand. I feel I have sorely tested his loyalty of late, and that I owe him something to keep his trust. I hope my luck holds out.

'We need to sleep', I remind everyone.

'Who keeps the first watch?' Wulfmaer asks me.

'Do you want to take it with Theodolf, or Dunstan?' I sit, looking at my beaker, then look up at Theodolf, who stands leaning on the table close by me. He nods at sharing a watch with Wulfmaer. 'You will watch for the time this candle burns to the halfway mark'.

'Do we need to be outside?' Wulfmaer asks again.

'If it is still raining, stay within the partly open door', I look from Wulfmaer to Dunstan, who has entered the dwelling from the yard.

'It is no longer raining', Dunstan tells me, 'but it is damp'.

Before they pass through the door, Dunstan adds,

'There is a short bench under the roof overhang that you can sit on. It will be dry enough to sit on, but if you want I have pelts to cover it'.

'I think it best if you stood or moved about so that you do not become too sleepy. If any of Odo's men come and you are asleep when they come, you will be dealt with swiftly', I point at the mailcoat that Theodolf still wears, 'by them'.

'Shall we take off this gear?' Saeward asks. Is he afraid of being captured before we reach Lunden again?

'No, leave it on, Saeward. If I thought we were under any threat I would tell you to take it off, but for now it is not worth doffing your gear. When you get used to its weight, it will seem like a second skin'.

I turn back to staring at my beaker until Theorvard breaks into my half-dream,

'Who shares *my* watch?'

I look up at Dunstan and ask him,

'Have you made your mind up about sharing your watch?'

'Aye, I will take Theorvard', Dunstan answers quickly, as though he were gifting the young giant with his being there.

Theorvard looks askance at him, as if saying to himself, 'Who does this young upstart think he is?' Theorvard will do what is asked of him. He seats himself by me and holds his head in his hands.

'I will take the last watch with Saeward, when the second candle has half-burned out', I tell Theorvard.

'That sounds fair enough to me', he dozes off and is fast asleep almost as soon as he lays his head on the table.

I wonder he can fall asleep like that. It will take me some time, thinking about Burhred out there, wandering aimlessly. Is he likely to head north back to Lunden?

7

Sleep soon overtakes me however, and I wake again shortly as Theorvard and Dunstan go out on watch. The candle is half-burnt through when I am awakened by Theorvard, tapping my boot with his knife handle to rouse me. With some effort I straighten myself up and lift myself from the bench, stand, stretch and yawn.

'Saeward', I shake my friend awake as quietly as I can.

Failing to rouse him I have to shake him again, 'Saeward!'

He raises his head from the table, his eyes still half-closed,

'Oh, I had a *wonderful* dream!' Saeward shakes his head, rubs his eyes, opens them wide and stares around the room as if he does not know where he is.

'I am glad you slept well, but now we should be out there. All manner of things could happen out there whilst no-one is on watch! Come, strap on your sword belt on your way out', I say as I stride out through the doorway into the arms of a smiling Northman noble. Two of his friends stand behind him, beaming at the thought of taking us without a fight.

Before I can draw my sword I am made aware of the tip of a sword blade on my stomach. No words are spoken, the meaning is clear. The owner of the blade jerks his head to the right, and I understand I am to go that way. Saeward, close behind me does not know what is happening before a spear is brandished under his chin by a third.

Saeward and I are kept in check whilst their leader strides through the door to see who else is within. Two more sit astride their horses with their comrades' and our horses roped together.

Theorvard shouts to the other three to get to their weapons. The noble who strode in does not make it back out again through the door. An ear-piercing scream rents the air from within and the point of the sword is pressed harder into my stomach.

The sword bearer stares grimly at me. He would like to rid me of my innards. He grins briefly and draws back his sword hand to strike. Then the grin turns into a look of horror.

'*Aidez* -' His eyes open wide. A spear-point shows through his ribs, twists, and is pulled back sharply.

Wulfmaer turns to deal with one of the other two, still mounted. How did he get behind the rider without his comrades seeing him? An arrow buries itself in one man's chest, the other turns his mount and tries to ride away. Another arrow flies, misses him and is followed closely by a third. This last makes its mark, skewering the hapless rider in the small of his back. Where did the arrows come from? I look around and see Dunstan with a bow. *He* could not have loosed off all three arrows so quickly, could he?

Behind him stands Theodolf with his bow. Only one of our attackers still lives. He does not flinch, but raises his spear in a token challenge and sinks to his knees under a swift, merciful blow from Saeward's sword. The stricken man's body sways and is kicked backward by Saeward. The head, almost cut from the neck, lies oddly angled to the shoulders.

'He was a brave fellow', Theorvard looks down at him, wiping the blade of his axe on the man's tunic sleeve.

'Who - *him?*' I ask, pointing at the one Saeward killed.

'Aye, I mean him. He knew we had to kill him but he did not flinch or plead with us for his life. The one who went inside was foolish'. Theorvard looks around in the half-light, as if there is something – or some*one* - missing. He fingers his beard, looking down at the dead man and tells me, 'Only one thing bothers me now'.

'There should have been six of them', I nod, reading his thoughts and look for another rider. 'Do you think there was another?'

'There had to be. They ride in sixes. Where is the *sixth?*' Theorvard gives a shrug and goes back inside to make up for lost sleep. Theodolf follows him, closely followed by Wulfmaer and Dunstan. Saeward stays where he is, looking down at the dead man, almost as if admiring his own work.

'There is one we still have not dealt with, having only killed five. We need to keep our eyes peeled for more if he got away', I tell him, scouring the nearby trees and bushes in the greying dawn for tell-tale signs of more of Odo's men.

'Do you think it could have been Burhred who led them here?' Saeward wonders aloud.

'I really do not know. But how would he speak to them? He does not know their tongue'.

If he was about, I think he may have done away with one of them and rode behind the rest to make them think they were a full *conroi*, or troop.

'He may have followed the others back here in the dark, letting them think he was one of theirs', I hazard a guess. 'He could have left them before they reached us, unaware one was missing. After all, if the Northmen were likely to kill him when they found him, then *we* were just as likely to kill him thinking he had led them here. No, they were scouting and happened on us, I am sure of it'.

136

'Happened upon us... *at this early hour?* Is *that* what you think?' Saeward sounds as though he is laughing at me. Is he too beginning to question me now?

By the time we have all eaten our first meal of the day the rain has set in again from the east. I look out from the doorway across the green, swallow the mouthful of bread that I just bitten off and down the last of the stale apple ale that Dunstan has poured into my beaker.

'It is no wonder this land is so green, what with all the rain that falls', Wulfmaer drones to anyone who can be bothered to listen.

I have more pressing thoughts, one being the likelihood of more of Odo's men prowling the area.

'*Which way are we headed?*' Theorvard asks, paying no heed to Wulfmaer whining about the rain.

'Dunstan knows the lie of the land, and he knows where Odo's men are likely to be', I answer and put my beaker back on the table for Dunstan to tidy away before we leave. I look to the lad for an answer to Theorvard's question.

Perhaps because he does not know I am looking at him he goes about the business of tidying things away so that the dwelling looks as if it has been abandoned, unlived in. He knows where things go, and Odd mutely helps him with this task. When he has finished he looks at me. I take this as my cue to put roughly what Theorvard asked,

'Which would be the best way to go from here to Pefense?' I ask.

'What is it you need to do in Pefense?' Dunstan asks in turn, having forgotten what I told him last evening. It may be just as well.

'I need to know where the Northmen are bringing their supplies and fresh men in to', I outline the reason for us being here.

Dunstan goes down onto his haunches and draws with a finger on the earth floor near the doorway. He points to the top corner of the outline,

'They are bringing most of their supplies through the bay at Pefense, although some comes by way of the haven at Haestingas. Their leader has had the old burh of Anderida strengthened and put up a wooden tower and wall in its middle', Dunstan tells me everything I need to know and more. 'Another wooden stronghold stands above Haestingas. A further one was begun since ten days or so ago at Dofnan to keep the Centishmen away from the river haven'.

'You say *Dofnan* had a wooden stronghold built ten days since?' Theorvard asks, raising his eyebrows. He is taken aback by the haste with which Willelm's men have strengthened their hold on the coast. 'They must have used the men of Centland and Suth Seaxe to put *them* up. That may have been why men were herded eastward'.

'It has been three weeks now since King Harold was killed', Theorvard puts my own thoughts into words. 'My grandfather told me the burhs of Snotingaham and Deoraby were each fortified in three weeks by the Danes! It is no time at all until you recall so many men have passed this way'.

It seems only days have passed since my kinsmen were killed, when in fact it has been weeks!

I feel my brow knitting suddenly. A sharp pain burns through my head and I feel my scalp before donning my helm.

'Ivar, you should ask Saeward if there is something he can do to help you. You have a nasty bump on your head, with blood caked in your hair', Theorvard points to the back of my head and puts his fingers there,

'Does that hurt? I saw it when we were on our way to Lunden from Medestan, but in the chase forgot about it'.

'You are right. I feel it throbbing now and then, although I have worn a helm and that should have hurt. Luckily I have had no more harm done to my head', I rub the wound now and feel a dull pain, although there is a sizeable bump. What with riding and fighting for most of these weeks, my wound was the least of my worries Now he has spoken of it, if there is anything to be done I should have Saeward treat it.

When I look at Odd Dunstan sees, and tells me,

'He will be able to talk soon, Saeward tells me. He has given him honey beads to suck'.

I nod and point back at his drawing, asking,

'Is there anywhere I can see them without being seen?'

He closes his eyes to think, and scratches the hairs on his chin.

'It can just be overlooked from a hill to the south of here. I will take you', Dunstan offers, staring up at me over one shoulder. 'There are trees in the way and the view is broken by buildings on the landward side. You would see better from the east'.

'How far do we have to ride away from Pefense to see that?' Theorvard asks now.

'It is not far, only a couple of miles that way', Dunstan points over Theorvard's head, 'only be as long as it took to beat the Northmen this morning'.

Theorvard smiles broadly and thanks Dunstan for his part in the skirmish,

'Thanks to your part in that we have more horses. We should be able to get back to Lunden quicker than we came here'.

He looks sharply at me and we both laugh at my foolish sense of passing time. Dunstan understands little about our merriment and stares blankly at Theorvard, he then turns away to finish tidying around the dwelling with Odd.

'When he has finished we can mount', I tell Theorvard. 'Can you tell everyone whilst I ask Dunstan something else? There are a few things I need to clear up with him about our way there, and how we can get closer to Anderida'.

'Why do we need to go to Anderida?' Theorvard wants to know.

'The Northmen are building their wooden strongholds as quickly as they move inland. There must be something we can learn from them. When we were in Northmandige with Earl Harold they had stone strongholds everywhere. They are bringing with them a way of building we have not seen in this land before. We need to see how well they could stand up to our attacks if it comes to that', I hope my answer is enough for him.

King Eadgar may be thankful enough for this knowledge to keep us as his huscarls long after we have sent Willelm back from these shores. Perhaps also he will award me with the deeds and lands of a thegn for my loyalty to him, as Harold had meant to before he was killed.

Theorvard seems happy with my answer. After all it is not every day he can show his skills. A man who lives by the sword will choose the right to die by it. Do my other friends trust me with their lives? Burhred no longer did, which is why he left after first trying to shake everyone else's faith in my leadership.

When they did not take to his show of fickleness he knew he was on his own. That, in his own eyes, set him free from his ties to us. I am not worried at his leaving, as long as he does not lead Odo to us.

We are ready to leave, to see this new wooden stronghold. Odd, still unable to talk has shown Dunstan by signs that he is willing to come with us. He may have become lonely, disheartened and afraid on his own. Being so close to our grasping foe, he tried to take his own life. We may not have reached their dwelling long after his bid to die when we cut him down. But how would he have gone about it on his own? Did he sit on his own horse, if so where is it now? His hands were not tied, so he must have rigged the rope. He only needed to make a slip knot, which would not have broken his neck and cut his windpipe, as a good hangman's noose *would* have done. Looped as it was over the lowest branch of a horse chestnut tree and secured to the trunk, he could have climbed onto the animal and slapped its flank to set it off at a trot. The animal may have gone back to where he took it from. If it belonged to the abbey, the abbot must have let his landsmen know. That might have led to the Northmen coming this morning. He will be stirred to sending more when he finds out his first party have not shown yet.

'Are we set?' I ask Theorvard, who nods and I wave my friends on. We can ride at a steady canter and not tire our mounts before reaching Dunstan's lookout point. From there, it is only a short ride to get closer to Anderida. Depending on how many scouts the Odo has had posted in this hundred, we can be sure of getting close enough for me to see well enough how busy the haven is.

When we are close to the first lookout point, Dunstan sees riders ahead. Theodolf sees them too from our left flank. He waves us down and reins in. Saeward is on the right and does not see that we have stopped short. He only guesses that we have stopped when he has ridden on a short way further and looks for us.

It is too late to avoid being seen now. With Saeward and Theodolf kitted out in Northman war gear, and the rest of us looking very Aenglish, we must be an odd looking band of men. A *serjeant* on the right flank of this small company of a dozen men says something to Saeward, who looks back at him, leans forward in his saddle and spits on the track. It is perhaps because the Northman assumes Saeward is going to say something that we have gained the upper hand again.

Before they draw level with us Saeward draws his axe and throws it at the first rider's chest. He makes his mark, as surprised as the Northman is at the sudden blur of the axe, spinning like a wheel at him. He cannot even draw breath to scream as it digs deep into his upper chest. The other five fan out and level their lances, ready to attack. The five of us form a wedge, with Dunstan and Odd behind us, our shields held forward, ready for the onslaught.

Dunstan has a hunting bow ready, aimed over our heads. Its range will not be as great as a war bow, but its striking power will be enough to unhorse a man. Odd only sits still on his horse, praying.

I glance behind Theorvard's back at Theodolf. He has his bow ready, an arrow hidden from their sight behind his shield. Between them, Theodolf and Dunstan could deal another two their death blows with a second arrow each before the Northmen know what is happening. That will leave eight for us to deal with, because they will not wait for us to finish them off.

'How is your shoulder, Theorvard?' I ask. His is the horse next to mine in the wedge. He says nothing, but nods that he has heard me. His eyes are fixed on the horsemen ahead.

Suddenly, without a sound, the Northmen press on toward us. Not wishing to let us think they are afraid, they set their mounts into a quick trot. Gathering speed, they close the gap at a near-gallop. Theodolf and

Dunstan take aim, loose off an arrow each and find their mark. Two riders drop their lances, one to try to tear the arrows from his throat, the other falls back across his saddle. Another two arrows fly; Theodolf and Dunstan are at one with their choice of target. The others waver. They rein in their mounts and turn to flee.

Theodolf lets loose another arrow, which drills into another's neck. He is left struggling to breathe when the others make for the trees. Wulfmaer looses off an arrow which merely lodges in one man's shield and Saeward catches up with one of the riders, punching his shield at him, almost knocking him from his saddle.

The man's lance is on the wrong side and he is badly hampered by his own shield in trying to bring the weapon round at Saeward. A change of grip does him no good, as it only serves to make Saeward's task easier. The axe scythes through the air as if he was back at Wealtham, cutting hay, and catches the foe at the waist.

Wulfmaer's horse is neither big, nor fast enough to catch the last rider and is overtaken by Theodolf, who launches a lance taken from one of the dead men at the fleeing horseman. The lance overflies the Northman, who turns his horse quicker than Theodolf can stop his.

With his life at stake the Northman urges his horse at Theodolf's and yells loudly,

'*Tur-aie -*'

Theodolf ducks quickly but is nevertheless caught by the lance point on his right shoulder. As he passes Theodolf his midriff is raked by the sword Hrothulf had made in Jorvik when he was still one of Tostig's huscarls.

Theodolf's left shoulder is bleeding badly when he turns to us. He winces with the pain of holding the great kite-shaped shield and throws it down onto the grass. Saeward kicks his horse's flanks and she canters up to join Theodolf's mare.

Wulfmaer, Theorvard and I closely follow after Saeward. Dunstan and Odd trail behind. I want to know how badly wounded Theodolf is. If we now have two men below fighting fitness, we could be hampered if it came to another skirmish.

Saeward has seen the shoulder wound that the Northman has inflicted on Theodolf. He shakes his head, although not with worry,

'He is not badly hurt. It is a flesh wound, and luckily not soiled as with a lance stood by the point in the earth. He will not be able to wield a bow for some time with as much strength as may be needed to kill a Northman through his hauberk. We will have to stay low, what with Theorvard's shoulder also in need of another dressing. You can see the blood seeping through his byrnie. With good wound dressings I can have both of them fighting fit by the time we reach Thorney again. Wulfmaer will have to do the work of two bowmen'.

My hopes of taking a closer look at Anderida will need to undergo some fresh thinking now. Saeward is right. We must keep to the woodland tracks until safely within reach of Suthgeweorce.

Dunstan knows the lie of the land. He will guide me to where I can watch the comings and goings. First I must see the others to safety. Whilst Saeward sees to Theodolf I tell my friends,

'Wulfmaer and Saeward, ride back to Dunstan's dwelling with Odd, Theodolf and Theorvard'.

They nod, relieved that they will be out of harm's way whilst I risk my own hide. Already riding away when I call after them, Theorvard and Wulfmaer turn in their saddles and wave to let me know they have heard,

'Await us there, if you will. Dunstan and I must watch what is happening at Pefense whilst the light is still good. Rain clouds are gathering in the east, and we will be unable to see much when they reach us'.

The Northmen will not be too eager to be out scouting when the weather turns. When the rain begins to sheet in these parts in the after year, no-one wants to be out in it.

'Dunstan we need to make haste for Anderida', I tell him as I press my knees into Braenda's flanks to take me on. He leads to the right and we leave the main track for a low ridge behind Pefense's haven.

'I need to stop to pay my respects to mother earth', Dunstan tells me a short time later, when we are coming up behind the ridge crest.

'Take your time', I answer, looking around. 'I shall ride to the ridge and await you there'.

He says nothing, but dismounts and makes his way to a clump of bushes.

Why he needs to be coy about relieving himself in these woods is beyond me. Anyone else would have just got on with it, first making sure which way the wind blew. I put his show of shyness to the back of my thoughts and ride on.

On reaching the low hill that overlooks Anderida the first thing I see is that the lie of the land is broken by older buildings and trees.

'As I said -', Dunstan has come up behind me and almost catches the blade of my sword in his midriff.

'*Never* creep up behind me like that again, Dunstan. I nearly ran this sword through your belly! You were right about the buildings, though. Is there anywhere I can see better from?'

He finishes what he was going to say with a wide-eyed look of fear on his face,

'*S-sorry, Ivar*, I was only going to tell you that we will need to ride down to a spur off this hill, that looks over the back of the old burh'

'Nevertheless you were right', I try to humour him after threatening his life. There *is* a lot in the way. How much further on can we go before we lose too much height to see what is happening in the burh down there?

Dunstan gathers his wits and takes time to think.

'There is a track that is mostly hidden from that side, out of sight of their new stronghold. When we get there, we will need to be very much on our toes. The walls of Anderida bristle with lookouts. We hardly need to show ourselves and we will have them all down on us. Your friends will not know what has happened to us and get themselves caught looking for us'.

I know Dunstan wants to stay free for as long as he can. He knows what can happen to a any man they take. He would not last if put to work on building for them. It is best for him I am not too bold in my search for knowledge. We cross an open piece of land and enter another copse on our way to the southern reaches of this high ground.

'Stay here', Dunstan dismounts and walks forward, parting the undergrowth carefully as he creeps forward. When he is sure he cannot be seen he waves me on.

I drop down from my saddle, stretch and warily wade through the thicket to where he awaits me. Thorns tug at me as I push through, taking care not to let branches snap back. The view is not a lot better than before but I am closer to Anderida, which is what I asked of him.

'Is this what you wanted?' Dunstan cranes his neck to look at me, hoping I want to go no closer.

'With someone who spoke their tongue I should like to go down and look around', I tell him.

His jaw drops and he almost squeaks his answer,

'I did say I would ask Odd, but that was before we found him hanging. Are you still thinking to go down there?' Dunstan asks in a way that tells me he is apt to flee if I say I do.

'If only he found his voice', I groan through gritted teeth. 'But we do not know whether he *can* speak their Frankish tongue, do we?'

He looks beseechingly at me, hoping I will tell him we are going back soon.

I ask without looking at him,

'Is there anywhere closer, where I can see what is going on?'

Dunstan looks crestfallen at me when I do turn to look his way. He knows his safety is at risk in being with me, but he cannot bring himself to leave. He thinks before answering - truthfully, I hope,

143

'There is *no* way we can go any closer without giving ourselves away, Ivar. If we go any further we might as well tell them we are here', he shifts awkwardly on his feet before adding, 'I do not want to seem overly fearful to you, but I have my wife and son to think of, and Odd. You saw Odd is not above trying to do away with himself, so afraid that he is of being caught and taken back to his abbey. That abbot of his scared him somehow'.

At least Dunstan is open about his fears. But then again, I would be lying if I did not allow for feeling as if something was chewing at my innards as I watch my foe striding up and down behind the wooden palisade. In walking back to Braenda I nod gravely to show Dunstan I value him as a guide. He almost skips back to his mount in his relief at my having seen enough.

Our ride back through the cold, slanting winter rain passes drearily. As I thought, none of their scouts is about. The more the clouds thicken, and the rain falls heavier, the happier Dunstan seems to be. He knows that the Northmen have no taste for our dismal weather. Our afteryear weather is not for the faint-hearted.

'You are in time for some cooked food', Theodolf tells me as Dunstan and I step back into the dwelling through a door frame that looks to be in need of straightening, 'Odd has been showing us his skills that he learned from the abbey kitchen'.

'His skills learned in the abbey *kitchen?*' I repeat Theodolf's last words, almost spitting out the last.

'Aye, Ivar, he was a layman - he worked in the bakery. Nor does he know any words of the Northmen's tongue', Saeward tells me, reading my thoughts.

'How do you know this?' I ask, looking at Odd from the corner of my eye as he puts out freshly-baked bread to eat with a broth made from turnip stock. However good it smells, I would have liked him to be a monk with knowledge of my foe's tongue.

'He seems to be able to say a little', Theorvard tells me now.

'But as he still feels sore', Wulfmaer adds, 'we did not ask him a lot, only what you wanted to ask'.

'And now I know', I sink onto a stool, my elbows on the table and my head in my hands. All that goes through my head is 'what do I do now?' What I wanted was to be able to hear at first hand what these Northman seamen were bringing, and to where it was being taken. Now we have to go back to Eadgar and give him only half the news. At least I know where to send our ship levy to cut the flow of Willelm's supplies and men.

'We go on to Haestingas', I tell everyone to a sucking-in of air through Theorvard's cheeks. When I turn to look at him he shrugs and smiles. I finish, 'But we keep out of harm's way'.

They breathe out to a man. Going back by way of Haestingas is a step along the way to going back to Lunden, nights in a bed, and - most likely - a woman.

'...And from there to Medestan to see my wife and son', Dunstan welcomes what he takes as my good news with a bright smile.

His eagerness rubs off on Wulfmaer and Saeward. Saeward, who tells us that he does not relish killing, even Northmen, rubs his hands gleefully to show his joy at our leaving this woefully beleaguered shore,

'Good, I am sick of running into these invaders'.

'I hope you know we have to pick our way again through Centland, because that is where Odo seems to be making himself at home. We will ride toward Medestan, however, to safeguard Dunstan's return to his kindred. 'When we have left Dunstan to find his way to his kindred, we strike for Lunden by the straightest roads, nevertheless giving Hrofesceaster a wide berth'.

Saeward's smile freezes, but does not fade altogether. If Dunstan thought we were going out of our way he would try to talk us into taking the straightest way back to Lunden from Haestingas. Theodolf nods sagely, and Theorvard yawns. Wulfmaer shakes his head and fidgets with a small knife and a sliver of wood.

'What are you doing there?' Saeward sees Wulfmaer whittling away at the wood.

'I have a piece of meat stuck in my teeth and I can feel it there each time I run my tongue over it to speak', Wulfmaer wails.

'That would suit me. Talk less', Theorvard grins at Theodolf and looks up at me. 'Ivar, what would you say?'

Not wanting to be drawn into the banter I ask instead,

'What is on offer, aside from the stew - or is it soup?'

'Soup - same as yesterday', Wulfmaer answers flatly, 'what else?'

'I would not say no to anything that is dished up right now', Theorvard leans over the table to pick up a piece of dry bread.

'There is little to offer anyway, until we raid their stores again, whenever that may be', Wulfmaer says dully. He looks across the room at Odd, who fusses over the fire like an old maid.

Dunstan takes off his wet cloak and drapes it over the end of the table where no-one is sitting. He skirts around everyone and goes to help Odd. Odd croaks something and Dunstan comes back to the table,

'He wants to do it unaided', Dunstan tells us and Theorvard makes

145

out he is going to sleep, laying his head on the table.

'You had best argue that one out with Odd', I tell Dunstan, 'or we will all be going to sleep cold and annoyed with him about his mulish streak!'

'I will see what I can do', Dunstan agrees and goes back to help Odd.

Odd croaks like an old crow fighting for a mouthful, and waves his friend away. Dunstan finds some wooden bowls and spoons and goes about setting them out for us. When Odd comes to the table with the food we all cheer, however mean it looks.

Wulfmaer, Theorvard and Theodolf shout and drum the table as one, much like the same way as we in the shieldwall drummed our shields on Caldbec Beorg before the slaughter. All I can do is hold my belly to ease the pain of laughing.

It takes little time for us all to finish it off. There is little enough of it to go around, but with the few turnips that softened in the pot with the meagre meat, and some stale bread, the gnawing in our stomachs has been stilled. Hopefully soon we can free more supplies from the Northmen.

In a greying dawn we leave the dwelling, huddled in our woollen cloaks that we have pulled on over our mailcoats and byrnies. Wulfmaer is the only one of us who has neither. All he has to shield himself from sharp weapons is a leather jerkin over a woollen tunic. The cloak Dunstan gives him from his store of 'freed' supplies gives him the look of a bigger man.

However, none of us measures up to Theorvard's towering height. For all his byrnie is losing links to rust, he is too big for any of the war gear that we pulled off some of the riders of the last patrol we skirmished with. Having the arrow pulled from his shoulder did not help things much, either. The links of his byrnie around the arrow-head had to be prised apart to help Saeward remove it. The byrnie given to him by Thegn Eadmund now looks the worse for wear.

We saddle our mounts quietly, keeping our thoughts to ourselves. I am hoping for better weather, but the heavy mist and drizzle will make it harder for the Northmen to follow us if we are seen on our way to Haestingas. Dunstan tells me the ride will only take a few hours by way of Weartlinga and the south-western reaches of the Andredes Leag.

On hearing this I think back on our ride from Lunden, when we picked our way in the darkness over tracks well known by Harold and his forefathers, criss-crossed by tree roots. Many a horse stumbled that night! I am only glad we are taking these tracks during daylight hours. I wonder whether we will pass the meeting place we all gathered at, where Harold awaited us,

'Is the Hoar Apple Tree on our way there?'

'Northmen are posted everywhere around it', he tells me glumly. 'No Seaxans can go near it because of what it stands for'.

When I set my jaw Dunstan asks,

'We have to by-pass it. I am sorry, Ivar. Does it mean anything to you?' He even *sounds* sorry. Even after this time, despite that the almost withered tree is a mere landmark, the Northmen are wary of a rebellion in these parts.

'Why are they afraid, these Northmen? Whoever heard of keeping folk from a *tree?*' Theorvard laughs as we urge our mounts across a low ridge between a long, ragged screen of hawthorn bushes.

'The Hoar Apple Tree is not just some tree, Theorvard. These folk see it as a sort of holy way-marker', I have to tell my friend from the Danelaw, 'It has the standing of an ash tree in the eyes of our forefathers, although it is hardly alive except for the few new shoots that spring from its branches each spring'.

'Well, I would not go as far as to call it *holy*', Dunstan fights shy of allowing it that much of a share in local lore, 'but it *is* known far and wide throughout the earldom, even to the eastern hundreds of Hamtun shire'.

'That is why he chose it for gathering before going on to Caldbec Beorg', I finish for Dunstan.

Theorvard and Theodolf look suitably gripped by all this ado about an old tree. They must have had an inkling of it when we came the first time.

We drop down into a wide, shallow dale that reminds me of Sjaelland with its low rises in the land. As we ride further to the north-east the track climbs steeper. This is prime growing land, and at least the harvest has been gathered in, but I fear there will be no harvesting done for some time after this one. Saeward reads my thoughts,

'There will be no more Lammas feasts until the Northmen allow these folk back onto their land soon', he looks morosely around us as we let our horses find their own rhythm.

'Ahead is Weartlinga', Dunstan tells me, his smaller horse keeping up with Braenda's stride as we follow the steepening road. We come upon a settlement that looks bereft of its inhabitants. 'The few folk here were chased away by the Northmen who came out from Haestingas and Pefense to steal their hay. Their hay and fodder stocks ran low, I think. This was before we fought them on Caldbec Beorg', he recalls. 'I sent my wife Gerda and our son Brihtwin off to her mother's kindred in East Centland before the Northmen came knocking down my door, such as it was'.

'This was where *you* lived?' I ask, more to while away the time than from a wish to know.

'My father's steading was over towards Hamelesham. He was struck by a long spear when he and his friends ran downhill after the Northmen. None came back', Dunstan tells me, his eyes welling.

'The worst thing was, we could see what was happening from where we were', he recalls with deep sadness, having witnessed his own father's death at the hands of Willelm's horsemen.

'*You* held back from chasing after the fleeing Bretlanders?' I wonder at his will, not bowing to his fellows' foolishness.

'We would have gone, too, but Earl Leofwin, or one of his huscarls shouted at us to stay put', Dunstan admits.

'Who is Gerda? For that matter, who is Brihtwin?' Wulfmaer asks, not having heard Dunstan speak of his wife.

'They are my wife and son', Dunstan lets Wulfmaer know and looks askance at me.

'Wulfmaer is a man of the land, as you are, Dunstan. I thought all folk on the land knew about one another's lives', I try to reason for Wulfmaer's rough ways, but Dunstan plainly thinks matters of his kindred are for the ears of those he knows and says no more on the matter. Wulfmaer rides on ahead, in a huff, Dunstan watching him until he thinks the East Seaxan is out of earshot.

'He is some sort of Ceorl, is he not?' Dunstan asks.

'I am a *craftsman*, Dunstan, *not a ceorl*', Wulfmaer eyes the South Seaxan over his shoulder with a cold stare and turns to look ahead again at what there is of Weartlinga.

'Wulfmaer is a miller', Saeward tells Dunstan, 'near where I lived at Wealtham'.

'You were a brother of the cloth?' Dunstan looks taken aback at Saeward.

'I too was a layman, but I *was* thinking of taking holy orders until my brother was killed by some drunken fool in Eoferwic. I killed the man when I saw him near Theodolf's steading', Saeward's own sad story is told to Dunstan and Odd, of how he was flogged in Jorvik on the orders of Earl Morkere, and of how he bethought himself to come with us. He even tells of his misgivings on killing, having taken Thor's counsel on dealing with his fear of crossing his God's commandments.

Odd stares in open wonder on hearing of how Saeward's tale of woe led to his forsaking the plough for the sword. Dunstan nods from time to time, rapt in hearing about the East Seaxan's path to becoming a warrior.

This is something new to both Wulfmaer and Theorvard, who also listen in silence to the tale. Theodolf knows about the killing of Garwulf in the woods, but not of the flogging and winces at the thought of feeling the birch on his back. I have to admit that I would not easily bear that form of punishment being meted out to me. Saeward has reached the lofty heights of heroism n their eyes.

'Yours has to be a tale of warning, if ever there was one, Saeward. I am in wonder of you', Theorvard pats Saeward on the shoulder, being unaware that the weals may not have properly healed on his back.

Saeward nods slowly, bearing his pain. He leans forward in his saddle and pats the horse's neck,

'It matters little to me whose war gear I wear. Whether it is that of an Aenglish huscarl or of a Northman, it is the war gear of a killer. Thor was right when he told me that I should have the best sword or axe that my silver can buy. With the best the pain of dying is foreshortened, and I come closer to God for the suffering I bear'.

If that is how he wishes to see his killing of the outlanders, then so be it. For myself – and I suspect Theorvard and the others feel the same way about our craft – I cannot feel shame at ridding the kingdom of foes. Brand set himself at odds with my king and kinsman, and so he had gone from being an Aenglishman to being a foe, too. I had to kill him. If I came across any other Aenglishmen who felt the need to throw in their lot with Willelm, I shall feel it my sworn duty to kill them too.

We ride uphill between empty dwellings and sheds. Birdsong echoes from the trees on either side of us. What we should hear is the shrieks of children, the calls of men and women to one another.

There is no lowing of cattle or bleating of sheep and goats. Only birdsong fills the air as we pass along the main street of Weartlinga on this quiet Sunday morning. A hound howls pitiably from one of the buildings to our right, drawing Odd to that side of the road.

He jerks his head to where he thinks the howling comes from, dismounts hurriedly and almost trips in running to a great barn.

'*What are you doing, Odd?*' Dunstan yells after him and looks to me for counsel. I shrug and rein Braenda in.

Odd rushes about between buildings, calling out hoarsely and listening for where the howling comes from. When he enters one of the barns, the howling becomes frenzied barking. I would say between the lad's crazed croaking and the hound's baying, we were set to bring down the wrath of the Northmen on us. Odd shows proudly again with a tall grey hound, almost the height of a pony.

'She must have been left here when the Northmen emptied Weartlinga', Odd croaks.

'What do we do with *him?*' Wulfmaer points at the hound, and earns a scowl from Odd and a growl from the animal.

'Silverhair is not *him*, but her', Dunstan tells Wulfmaer. 'Being a good hunting hound, I daresay she could bring down a horseman or two. She belonged to Odd's father. His mother and two younger brothers must have left her here, chained for days'.

'Silverhair would have been getting hungrier and thirstier with each passing day. They would have left her a bowl of water, hoping to come back for her, but when it was they fled I could not begin to guess', Odd tells me hoarsely.

The hound laps water eagerly from a water butt and returns to Odd's side, wagging her long tail.

'How do we feed her, when we have scarcely enough food for ourselves?' Saeward regards the hound grudgingly.

'She will feed herself *and* us if we are good to her', Dunstan turns in his saddle and stares at Saeward. 'If you are good to her she will get to like you, and very likely bring you a good-sized hare for your supper. We are short on meat, and a fighting man needs meat, does he *not?*'

'Aye, Dunstan, we are sold. Bring Silverhair with you if you wish. If, however, the time comes and we are close to the Northmen and she gives us away, I shall slit her throat myself', I warn them both.

'You shall not have to. She is a hunting hound. When she chases her prey she does so in silence. She will keep still when told', Dunstan assures me, eyeing me warily. 'You have hounds where you come from, I would say?'

'I had two hounds for elk hunting', I tell Dunstan.

'What were their names?' Odd croaks and climbs back into his saddle. He still has the hound's chain in his hand.

'You could take the chain off her', I offer, 'unless she is given to running off on her own'.

Odd glances at me, his head held to one side. He nods and dismounts, takes the chain from the hound's collar and hoists himself back into his saddle.

150

8

Silverhair sits, waiting for us to leave Weartlinga.

'We must be away', I tell Theorvard, who leads up through the top end of the hamlet, along the road to the woodland beyond.

'What were the *names* of your hounds, Ivar?' Dunstan asks on behalf of Odd, unable to shout above the clopping of our horses' hooves as we draw away through Weartlinga.

'Their names were Garm and Aern', I tell him as we climb slowly up the bank.

'What sort of names are *they* for hounds?!' Dunstan peers at me, not understanding my hounds' names. Odd rides happily with Silverhair loping alongside, casting loving looks at his father's hound every now and then.

'Garm is the hound that guards the underworld, as tall at the shoulder as Silverhair, darker, with white flashes on his muzzle and chest. Aern had the colouring of an eagle, was smaller than Garm, but fast!'

'Are you a *Christian*, Ivar? Where are you *from?*'

Dunstan does not make me ill-at-ease with his questioning, but I think I have made him ill-at-ease with my hounds' names.

'I am a Dane, kindred to King Harold through his mother, Gytha, and I *am* a Christian - in a way. We still use the names our forefathers had, not being ashamed of our heathen past. Many of your Seaxan fellows still use the names your heathen forefathers bore. Even your namesake, the saint had a heathen name. Our *deeds* mark us out from others, not our names. One day men might call their sons Dunstan, for what you may yet do in these darkest of days. Who knows, you might even name your next son Ivar without thinking too long over what you should call him'.

'I have a few names to pick from', Dunstan grins. 'Winter's nights will be spent telling my children of days fighting Northmen!'

'You plainly hope to have more children than Brihtwin', I smile at Dunstan.

Odd leans back in his saddle to look at his friend, unaware of what has been said whilst he was lost in the worship of the hound. Dunstan grins back at him and turns back to speak to me,

'What made you come to these shores, Ivar?'

'I have no land on Sjaelland, the Danish isle of my childhood. My father was made an outcast by Knut and was sent away from us before coming back and being slain in his own church',

I tell Dunstan the bare bones of my story, careful to leave out my days with Tostig,

'As I was kin to Earl Harold and his brothers through their mother, Gytha, I thought I would come here, as many other Danes have done in the past, to try to make my mark. I was a huscarl in the household of our late King Harold, who was going to make me a thegn. Now I have to begin again with King Eadgar, which is why I am here, with my friends'.

'Was Burhred a friend?' Dunstan helps to pass the time with his childlike questioning.

'He was – would still be a friend if we met again. His friend and leader was a friend of mine, Thorfinn', I tell him, smiling.

'Who was Thorfinn? He sounds as if he was another of your fellow Danes', Dunstan guesses well, nearly rightly.

'Thorfinn was a thegn from Saewardstanbyrig, in East Seaxe. There were three of them with Burhred, who came with us to fight Duke Wil-lelm. Only Burhred lived through. The last to be killed was Aelfwin who died in my stead in a great skirmish by Lunden Brycg'.

My mood turns black thinking of Aelfwin's death. Wulfmaer turns to look at me, hearing his brother being spoken of. He soon gathers why Aelfwin's name arose when he listens to us talking. However, it is not long before he lets his thoughts wander.

Dunstan's questions peter out soon and I too am left to my thoughts, of my fallen friends and those who still choose to ride with me and share my wyrd. Only the chatter of the birds follows us on our ride through the woodland around Haestingas.

We are passing through a thwait on our way around to Haestingas, careful to skirt the Hoar Apple Tree. Dunstan says that this part of the Andredes Leag is patrolled by the Northmen. The way the sun strikes the trees from the west makes it hard to see properly what is behind the tree trunks ahead, so we are taken unawares when a dozen riders lead their mounts from the trees. We are too close to that side of the thwait to take flight, so we have to make a fight of it.

One of the Northmen calls out, not challenging.

I turn to Theodolf and Saeward and nod for them to go forward. It will look as though they are escorting us.

'I think they see us as friendly, because your friends look as though they are taking us somewhere for talks', Odd croaks for the first time since we left Weartlinga.

Silverhair stands guard by Odd's mount.

'I thought you said you did not speak their tongue', I challenge him.

'I am guessing mostly, by the way he spoke. But I know *some* of the words', Odd says defensively.

The Northman speaks to Theodolf, as he is the closest to him of our little column.

'I think he wants to know from your friend where we are being taken', Odd's voice is giving way again and the croak comes back.

He coughs and Saeward tells him to rest his voice for a while,

'...Or else you will start coughing up blood', Saeward finishes.

'How else will Ivar know what to do?' Odd protests and gives another cough.

'It will be you we bury', Saeward makes a show of not caring.

As it is, Theodolf merely points toward Haestingas with the lance and salutes smartly. Saeward also salutes and the pair of them pass the first two of the Northmen before the one who spoke to Theodolf turns in his saddle and calls out again, this time his voice rasps harshly in the cold morning air. He knows there is something wrong about us.

'I hardly think we can duck out of this one', Theorvard groans loudly and leans forward to tell Wulfmaer to ready himself again. *'It is time to teach these Northmen how to fight again!'*

'Odd, get yourself *close* behind us!' I shout out, and urge Braenda at the nearest two Northmen before they can level their lances at me. I yell, 'Dunstan get out your bow, *now!'*

Theodolf brings his lance around and spears the nearest rider in the waist, who yelps like a pup and falls to be trampled by the next horse. Saeward throws his lance at the one who called after them, catching him fully in the chest with such force the lance point pokes from the Northman's back. He topples backward over his saddle, snapping his backbone as the small of his back hits the high saddle back.

One of Dunstan's arrows finds its mark in the gut of a less sprightly member of the troop. His neighbour stops another with his shield and brings down his lance to Dunstan's waist height.

He catches the young fellow off guard as he hastily lays another arrow across his bow, and Odd screams out shrilly. He sends Silverhair at the rider who brought down his friend. The hound clamps her great jaws around the Northman's leg and pulls before the fellow knows what is happening.

His mount rears, panic-stricken by the great hound. Horse and rider part are brought down. I have no time to see what else happens to him because one of his comrades sets his lance to take me on. I raise my shield and hold my sword steady, hoping to parry the lance or push the shaft away from me. He cannot get the speed from his horse that he would need to unhorse or kill me and I easily bypass his feeble effort, jarring his shield with mine so hard he cries out with the shock. Instead of cutting upward with my sword I change my hold on the hilt and strike downward onto his knee. His limb torn around the kneecap, he lets go of his shield and I thrust my sword into his stomach before he can bring his lance across to parry my sword. He slumps over the front of his saddle and flops like a child's rag doll against his mount's neck.

The others of his troop awaken to their plight. Seeing their leader and half the troop dead, they turn and flee. Theorvard is now plainly racked with pain in his shoulder from swinging his axe at two of the horsemen, one either side of him. One trails from his horse, nose down in the dead leaves and nettles, his right foot in the stirrup.

The other has righted himself and seeks to flee after his comrades. Saeward brings his axe around to chop at him, catching him and gashing his left upper arm. Nevertheless, bleeding badly he still ducks Saeward's back- swing and urges his mount away.

Wyrd has not destined him for long life, however.

An arrow from Theodolf's bow hits home between his shoulder blades and he falls forward from his horse.

'*Dunstan is dead!*' Odd is on the ground, cradling his ashen-faced friend, howling with grief. Silverhair, having been guarding the Northman he brought down, leaves him and trots back to Odd to lie meekly beside his master.

Wulfmaer, seeing the Northman is still alive brings down his sword and inflicts a long gash downward on the man's chest.

'Now he can meet his maker', he sighs contentedly like a master craftsman who has followed a task through to its end. He wipes the blade on the Northman's sleeve-end and slides his sword back into its sheath.

'Miller, are you finding your true self in this killing spree?' Saeward grins, showing bloodied lips. A lot of strength is needed to wield an axe hard enough to bite through chain mail, and he has bit his lips with the effort.

'I *know* you have been covering yourself in glory, Saeward. You cannot deny that!' Wulfmaer points at the gore on Saeward's hauberk and laughs insanely, praying aloud, 'When will this killing ever end?'

'We have our work cut out for us'.

Theorvard screws up his mouth and gives his right shoulder a hard rub in the forlorn hope of finding some ease from his pain.

'I have *my* work cut out inflicting wounds on our foes and trying to heal yours when I am done!' Saeward laughs hollowly, dismounts and deftly wipes his bloodied axe blade on a tuft of coarse grass.

'The way we are killing them, they should run out of men around here', I feel I should join in the mirth.

154

'A man can only hope', Theodolf looks around at the dead and sees Dunstan being cradled by Odd with Silverhair now lying nearby on the bloodied grass. 'How long before they come back with *more?* Is there time to give Dunstan the burial he has earned himself?'

'He *has* earned that much', I agree with Theodolf that Dunstan should have a Christian burial, as befits a selfless warrior, 'he died in the saddle, bow at the ready'.

'We should have kept the shovels when we buried Earnald'.

Theorvard screws up his eyes with the pain from his shoulder and affirms my worst fears,

'We will have to scratch a hole in the earth with our bare hands to put him in'.

'Oh God, if only we had *kept* them!' I think back on seeing the three Centishmen riding between their Northman captors. They would not have missed the shovels.

Still, a man cannot foresee his own wyrd, let alone another's.

'We had best put him over his horse', I offer, 'and hope to find somewhere where we can raise a cairn with stones'.

Odd bows his head and helps Wulfmaer heave Dunstan over his saddle. He picks up Dunstan's bow sadly, and pushes it between the saddle and the horse blanket of his own mount.

'Will you bury his bow with him, Odd?' I ask.

'*I will learn to use it!*' he croaks, and coughs fit to drop there and then. 'It is time for me to earn my keep'.

'Try not to speak!' Saeward scolds and jabs a finger over his shoulder at Theorvard and Theodolf, 'I have enough on my plate looking after *them!*'

'You sound like a woman!' Wulfmaer berates his fellow East Seaxan and laughs hoarsely at his own wit.

'If I had been your mother I would have boxed you around the ears more often than she seems to have done', Saeward laughs back at Wulfmaer.

'You two sound like bickering women!' Theorvard cackles like an old spay-wife, raising a laugh from us all except Odd. Young Odd is in deep mourning for his friend and our wit misses him altogether.

He will be over his loss soon enough if he wants to learn how to use that bow. In sapping his strength each day, pulling back the cord, the memory of Dunstan's untimely death will be pushed to the back of his thoughts, I will warrant.

'Come on, you two, we need to find somewhere to bury Dunstan before the smell of his corpse brings the crows down on us!' I shout, 'The Northmen will be back before long, too. If we cannot put enough miles between us and their dead comrades, we will be joining them amongst the leaves!'

'You are ever right, friend. No, we do *not* want to be here when they come back. Like as not, the bastards will turn up - *fourfold!*' Theorvard agrees.

The going is good, even allowing for leading a skittish horse with Dunstan's corpse bundled over the saddle. The horse can smell death. All grazing creatures fear the smell of death. We need to find somewhere where there are broken-up rocks because we have no tools to dig and, as Theorvard said, we cannot claw the cold earth with our bare hands. I cannot help thinking Oswold would not have missed his shovels where he went, but thoughts like that do no good.

'I know where there is a rock-fall', Odd croaks when he thinks we will hear him above our horses' footfalls on soft grass.

'Can you lead us there?' I rein in and look around. 'Is it nearby?'

I do not wish any slur on Dunstan, but from time to time my friends have been casting sidelong glances at his bobbing corpse and I think Odd has taken heed of their growing worries. We are being followed along an open ridge by hungry crows.

'We have to go north, away from Haestingas', Odd clears his throat and points northward.

'Is that not going to be like riding into a storm?' Saeward knows, as I do, that the foe will be there in number. Our way must take us somewhere near to where Odo's men are keeping folk from the Hoar Apple Tree.

'We are going to cut into their patrol lines!' Theorvard also fears heading for another fight, enfeebled as he is.

I turn and look at Odd, who looks downward to duck my gaze. We are being pin-pointed by wheeling crows, and if we do not find somewhere for Dunstan to rest with his maker we may yet join him. I nod to Theorvard to ride ahead. If there are any Northmen about, he will see them and we can hopefully skirt them.

'Theodolf, can you watch out for any signals from Theorvard. You look out to the east, Saeward, because they can just as easily show from that way', I grab at the reins of Dunstan's horse as Theodolf urges his horse ahead of us to watch out for Theorvard. 'You will not need to lead her. Odd and I can ride with Dunstan'.

'What do you want *me* to do?' Wulfmaer sounds as though he thinks I have forgotten about him.

'Keep an ear open for anyone following. They may happen upon us from behind, but it is less likely. All the same, we should keep clear of unwanted company', I tell Wulfmaer.

'Lead the way', I ask Odd and hold out my hand as if he were going through a door ahead of me. He nods gravely and I follow him, leading Dunstan's mount. We understand one another, but I hope he does not mean to dish us up to Odo for a reward. With his friend Dunstan dead, we have to rely on his goodwill.

We are outsiders to this malleable young fellow, who could yet give in to his fears and make a gift of us to another outsider, Odo. The rest of our ride is uneventful and we soon come to where we can build a cairn.

During the summer a bolt of lightning would have felled the tree that now lies dead across the track, loosening the earth around its roots. Earth-covered rocks lie strewn like a child's playthings, doubtlessly from around the roots it was embedded in on this rocky outcrop. They suit our needs well.

'Wulfmaer help me with Dunstan's body', Theorvard asks.

The two of them heave him from his saddle and carry him over to the rocks. Theodolf, Saeward and I dismount to help cover Dunstan with the dry, brownish rocks.

'Would you like us to help cover Dunstan?' I turn and see that Odd is still mounted and wave him over.

He sits staring at the ground where his friend is being covered, and I turn back to help pile the rocks on Dunstan. When I next look Odd is on his hands and knees, scrabbling amongst the rocks.

'What are you hoping to *find*, Odd?' Saeward asks him and stays the lad with his right arm. Odd wrenches his arm away. Saying nothing he takes rocks from our cairn and sets bigger ones where he deems fit.

Theorvard, Wulfmaer and Theodolf stand watching Odd's antics, and Saeward finds himself wiping away a tear.

'*Why so sad?* I ask Saeward.

'I did not oversee the burial of my brother in Eoferwic, and here is this young fellow fussing over the body of a fellow he has only known for weeks', Saeward puts his hands together over his face as if in prayer, the rims of his eyes reddening.

'We can stop off at Beorhtwulf's grave when we go that way', I try to comfort him with my arm over his shoulder. We had so little time to think when we left Jorvik after Beorhtwulf was killed. Then when Saeward was taken back by Osgod and the others of Morkere's huscarls who had come with him, they had not given him time to himself. It is perhaps only now, watching young Odd choose the rocks to bury Dunstan that Saeward sees he does not know what became of Beorhtwulf. Saeward nods and turns away. Again I ask Odd if he needs help and am rebuffed,

'I can do this better by myself, thank you all the same', Odd answers evenly and builds his friend's cairn carefully. 'I will not be long, and then perhaps we can stand in silent prayer before we leave for Haestingas'.

'By all means', I let him finish and we stand there, the five of us, watching as he picks the rocks, and hefts them back to the cairn.

Finally Odd finishes his task and turns to me,

'Do you know a prayer for a warrior?' he asks, showing his grief openly and easily, wet tracks on his dirtied cheeks.

'I know what I *would* say, but I do not know whether you would deem the words fitting', I answer.

'Say what you think', Odd croaks. He has aged in his grief and sounds as if he was used to losing friends. He nods for me to begin and cups his hands in the Frankish manner, copying the way his Northman abbot would have led prayer.

Saeward and Wulfmaer hold their hands at waist level, fingers stretched. Theorvard folds his hands across his chest, the left loosely cupped inside the right. Theodolf and I brace our arms tightly as is the custom amongst the Northanhymbrans. I begin what I understand to be a prayer,

'Lord of the slain, take this man –', I am not allowed to finish.

'What kind of prayer is *that?!*' Odd scolds, 'It sounds *heathen* and *barbaric!*'

'It is a prayer that King Harold would have seen as befitting on the field of slaughter', I try to humour Odd, 'and as we all know, King Harold was as pious a Christian as any'.

Saeward agrees with me,

'Ivar is right, Odd. Let him finish and you will hear how men of the sword honour the dead after a fight'.

Odd's eyes seem to burn like coals in the white heat of a forge.

'Very well then, *finish!*' he tells me, unsure Saeward knows what he is talking about. Arguing would delay us.

'Lord of the slain', I begin again, 'take this man to your bosom. Let him stand amongst the great warriors by your side and shield his kindred from evil. Bless us, his comrades and guide our rightful king, Eadgar. Lord, long may he reign by your grace. Amen'

'That was a good prayer was it not, Odd?' Saeward unclasps his hands, 'I think Dean Wulfwin would have seen that as fitting for a brave, selfless fellow such as your friend'.

'Who is Dean Wulfwin?' Odd asks testily but fails to upset Saeward, who merely tells the young Seaxan,

'Dean Wulfwin is the man King Harold saw fit to lead the canons at

Wealtham's seat of learning'.

'It is time we found something to eat', Wulfmaer is beginning to sound like Burhred.

'I heartily second that', Theorvard claps slowly and heads for his horse. 'I sometimes think you forget you have a belly to fill Ivar. Am I right or am I right?' He laughs, cheered by Theodolf.

Saeward seems to have forgotten his grief with talk of food. Odd is still sullen. He trudges, heavy-footed back to his horse, mounts and takes the reins of Dunstan's horse in his right hand.

'I will still show you the way to Haestingas. From there I will seek out his woman and son in Medestan. You can go straight back to the king', Odd tells me quietly.

I am not altogether sure he will be safe on his own, but if he wants to seek out Dunstan's wife on his own then so be it. He should be safe if he keeps to the lesser tracks and I am sure he will put us on the right road for home when our task is done.

We have met with no more patrols by the time we clear the trees above Haestingas, through another settlement cleared of everyone. A lone cow feeds by the grassy edge of the track, chewing slowly as she stares at us, her jaws working the cud. She may have been driven off by her owners before Odo's men rounded up the good folk who lived here. Whether they will ever see their homes again will be up to Willelm's greedy half-brother. I have a sinking feeling for them that they will be kept where they were driven until they have either outlived their use-fulness or outstayed their welcome.

'Did you know anyone from here?' I ask Odd, pointing back at the charred shells of dwellings and barns. He shakes his head, saying nothing. Nor can he answer what I ask next,

'Do you know the name of this hamlet?'

'Folk on the land do not know much outside their own back yards', Theorvard quips drily to Theodolf.

'Folk from the burhs do not know their way rightly on the land, either', Theodolf answers with a cheeky grin. Theorvard looks heavenward and laughs,

'I thought you were from Jorvik'.

'That is Eoferwic!' Saeward cuts in.

It is my turn to laugh and Theorvard looks askance at me,

'What are you laughing about?' Have I said something funny?'

'Saeward and I had a clash on the very same matter before the slaughter at Stamford Bridge. I said Jorvik and he stubbornly held with Eoferwic', I answer, laughing still, 'now he is turning on you'.

'Oh, I shall pay no mind to him. Jorvik is Jorvik, and there is no argument to it. Jorvik's folk are Norse, more than anywhere else in this kingdom. And you can stop growling like a bear, East Seaxan, because your lords the Godwinsons were half Danish through their mother, Gytha. The sooner you acknowledge that the better', Theorvard grins gleefully.

'Aye but our king, Eadgar is now of the line of the Cerdicingas! A Seaxan rules again!' Saeward is triumphant, but not for long.

'His grandfather Eadmund, known as 'Ironside', married a woman, Ealdgyth who was of the Svear line', I let him know, adding, 'Eadgar's own mother is a kinswoman of Heanric the German. Men of this king-dom have come across the sea from many lands, but their mothers stem from many more. Theorvard, you too must bear in mind that we are all Aenglishmen'.

'Even you?' Theorvard laughs, 'Are you a Dane, or not?'

'I have lived long in this land, and think of myself as Aenglish. One day perhaps, Eadgar will see fit to furnish me with the rank of thegn. With a thegndom comes land, and the need will arise for me to take men of my own into my household. How do you see yourself in, say, five years' time? Do you see yourself roaming the land, looking for a lord, as you were with Eadmund, or settling on your own land as a thegn?'

'I had never thought of that', Theorvard admits, 'I did not think be-yond being a king's huscarl – I mean as you were to King Harold'.

'You have proved yourself, time and again, and you have not been found wanting', I stare at him, wondering how he thinks a man should be judged if not by his deeds. He has been found at the forefront in our struggles against the outlanders, what else does he think he should have to do?

'Would King Eadgar see me as a thegn?'

'I would say so, aye. I would wish you to be a man of means, hold land of your own, be your own master and keep the king's laws', I tell him.

I think at his age he should aim for the highest rewards. He should not allow himself to settle for second-best.

'You still have no land?' Saeward, wide-eyed, asks me this question now after all this time he has known me.

'I have my dreams', I answer.

'Nor have you a woman of your own', Theodolf puts in. 'I wonder that you have not made your mark amongst the Danes. What sort of life did you have here, fighting for your kinsman and reaping no lasting reward? You are kin to kings in your own land –'

I cut into Theodolf's argument,

'I have told you already that my father Ulf was banished by Knut, and I stayed loyal to my father. My half-brothers by my mother's sister Astrid, Svein and Osbeorn were too young to know otherwise. Beorn was given an earldom here by King Eadweard, but was wrested from life by Earl Godwin's eldest. I left on a trading ship long ago, coming here before Earl Godwin's last illness to join his household. Harold's mother, Gytha is my father's sister'.

Odd gapes open-mouthed at me. But for Theodolf he would still think of me as a commoner, an outsider who speaks the tongue differently to himself. He says nothing, but keeps company with Saeward and Wulfmaer, whom he knows to be Seaxans.

Nothing further is said about my being a Dane, kinsman to kings. I would sooner Theodolf and Theorvard think of themselves as being at one with our Seaxan friends. A breach of trust between us now, because of where each of us comes from, is something I will not begin to think of. Our common goal is our errand for a king who is also struggling to win over the witan and set down his Aenglish roots.

'We must make camp soon – or is there perhaps a dwelling we can use nearby for the coming night?' I am thinking out aloud, half hoping that Odd might know of somewhere.

'What was that, you are looking for a roof over our heads?' Theorvard has overheard me, 'I dare say there must be somewhere closer to Haestingas, how about over there?'

He points north-eastward to where a clutch of buildings stands amid the trees. There seems to be no-one about. Either Odo has rounded up everyone for his building gangs, or whoever's home it is has gone hunting. What looks to be the dwelling stands apart from two other buildings, none of which is very big – I would say meant only for a man, his wife and small child.

'We can but see if anyone lives there', I think I have been sitting here on my horse for an age because Wulfmaer and Odd are looking vexed at me. Odd openly sighs when I give the signal to ride on.

Even were there anyone around, the footfalls of our mounts are muffled by the thick, dew-laden grass in the thwait. At the edge of the trees we dismount and walk to the buildings. Theodolf and Saeward stride to the outbuildings. One may be a stable, with tackle hanging on the doors. Theodolf walks back to us, happy that there is nothing there that takes his eye, whilst Saeward takes longer looking in and around over the second building.

Theorvard, Wulfmaer and I walk up to the dwelling house. There is no answer to my banging on the door. As I thought, neither the owner nor his kin are about. I lift the latch and open the door to the creak of un-greased iron hinges. Whoever he is, the owner knows how to build a home, but he knows little of keeping it in good order. Nevertheless, anyone who tried to steal in would not get far when the owner was about.

Odd winces at the sound of the creaking door hinges. I push the door further and look in. All is dark within, nothing to show anyone is here. The hearth is charred black, cold to the touch. The owner and his close kin are long gone.

'Leave the door open', I turn to tell Theorvard, but the door creaks shut again.

I feel a sharp blade held by a strong hand against my neck.

'Do not turn around! You would not see me in this darkness anyway, Northman swine!'

'*I am not Northman!*' I struggle to free myself from the iron grip of my unseen attacker and the blade is pressed harder against my throat. I feel it scraping on the shorter hairs of my beard.

'You and your friends, *you are Northmen!*' the fellow hisses into my right ear and I feel a tickling on the hairs at the back of my neck. 'True, your hair is long for a Northman. You may be one of the Bretlanders. Why should I *care* where you are from?'

'If we were Northmen, or Bretlanders or whatever, how far do you think you could get before either of my bowmen cut you down in your flight?' I ask in a forced whisper.

'What are you doing in that black hole?!' Theorvard yells outside, beyond the closed door.

'*Tell him you are my hostage!*' my attacker hisses into my right ear and rubs his knife blade over my Adam's apple. I find it hard enough talking with his knife at my throat. Calling out to Theorvard will be painful, to say the least.

'Only if you slacken your hold on that knife', I can still only whisper hoarsely, his dagger blade still pressed against my throat.

'Is this any better?' he asks and slackens his hold.

'That is much better, *thank you!*' I ram my left elbow into his chest and pull his knife arm down past my right knee. Holding onto his arm, I pull it against my boot top. His shout is pained and he drops the knife. His left knee punches the small of my back and we fall onto the earth floor, punching and kicking one another in a bid to gain the upper hand.

We scuffle in the darkness until Theorvard kicks open the door to allow Theodolf to dart in under his outstretched arm. Theodolf turns toward me, sees me writhing on the floor and shouts loudly at me,

'Why are you rolling about on the floor, Ivar?'

'What do you mean, *rolling about on the floor?* Can you not see this fellow - *where has he gone?'* I know now I am on my own on the floor, and there is no sign of anyone else. 'There, you see, his knife is down there by the table'.

I point at the knife lying beside a table leg.

'It is yours, Ivar. Look, your sheath is empty', Theorvard has been groping in the dark and found a rush light.

With the lit rush in one hand, he points down at my hunting knife and at the empty sheath. at my waist. I had not thought about the sheath since pulling on the belt this morning and forgotten it was there.

'Why would my knife be on the floor if I was in here on my own? I demand he tells me how else anyone but a fool would see things as they are.

'How should *I* know?' Theorvard grins in a way that makes me think he is talking to a madman. He only sees what his eyes show him, 'If there *was* anyone else in here, where is he *now?*'

Where *is* he? Theodolf looks askance at me. Saeward has come in behind Wulfmaer and looks about the room as if he means to move in for a long stay. Wulfmaer and Theorvard poke about in the half-dark, not knowing what it is they are meant to be looking for.

'There is a cloak here in the corner. It looks like one of the North-man cloaks we took, like that worn by Burhred', Saeward bends down to pick up the cloak, to take a closer look at it and straightens quickly again,

'What was *that?*'

'What was *what?'* Wulfmaer asks, prodding a pile of clothing in a dark corner of the room that he had begun to look closely into before Saeward entered.

'I felt something drip onto my ear', Saeward looks around the room.

'Has it begun to rain again?' Theodolf asks Saeward.

He pulls open the door, looks out and up at the treetops,

'There is *no* rain'.

'Theorvard, hold up the flame', I ask and look upward at the roof beams and the underside of the thatch.

'Well, well – look at *this* will you!' Theorvard cackles, pointing up at the rafters. We already are looking - up at Burhred, who has a cut on his cheek from when I was fighting with him, trying to push my knife from his hand.

Odd does not know who he is looking at, never having laid eyes on Burhred, who had already stormed out of the home he shared with Dun-stan, before he had awakened after his ordeal.

'Odd, this is Burhred. We thought Burhred had left for Lunden', I tell the Seaxan.

Burhred drops down from the beam that he was hunched on when Saeward felt blood dripping onto his ear.

'Were you going to stay there all night whilst we rested on the floor?' Saeward asks Burhred.

'What is more, why did you carry out that stupid attack on me?' I find my anger has begun to boil, 'Oh, and what was this stupid thing about me being your hostage, Burhred? Tell me! Tell us *all!* At least *one* of us may make sense of it!' I grab the neckguard of the hauberk Burhred is still wearing, and hold my balled fist ready to strike him unless he gives me a good answer.

Theodolf stands with arms folded, brow furrowing. He looked at me before as though I was going mad. Saeward has proved me otherwise, and Theodolf most likely thinks I will deal with him in the same manner. But my anger is with a man I thought of as a friend.

'It was foolishness, Ivar', Theorvard tries to humour me and tries to ease my hand away from Burhred's neck.

I push him away with my other hand and grip Burhred tighter,

'*Hold a knife to my neck*, will you?!' I rage at him.

'He did *what?*' Theorvard looks from me to Burhred, astounded at this turn.

'He held a knife to my throat - my *own* knife, *the one you found on the floor by the table!*' I almost spit these last words at a terrified Burhred. 'I should beat you black and blue and leave you here for the Northmen to find!'

I think back to when I saw him at Dunstan's safe haven,

'It was you I saw under the trees when that patrol came in the early morning after you left us! Tell me why I should not fillet you and leave you here for Odo's men'.

'Leave go of him, Ivar', Theodolf pleads with me. 'Where is your horse, Burhred? Ride away and never let us see you again. We will say you were killed by the Northmen and no-one will know any better. You shall have died a great warrior. Go, *now*'.

Theodolf looks at me and puts his hand on my shoulder to try to ease me away from Burhred. I look at Theorvard and he nods his agreement. One by one they nod.

'My horse ran off in the woods near here', Burhred complains.

'Then take our spare mount, Dunstan's. We have enough for our needs', Theorvard waves him away to the door. 'I am sorry it had to end this way, but you have been more than just foolish. *Farewell,* Burhred!'

I say nothing more and turn away from him before I do something idiotic. The door closes behind Burhred.

'Make sure he only takes the one horse', I tell Saeward.

After only a short time outside Saeward returns. I turn to look at him.

'Saeward nods, which tells me Burhred took one horse.

'I do not know about anyone else, but I feel a gnawing in my belly', Wulfmaer announces. No-one says anything more about Burhred.

'What do we have -' Theorvard asks, and seeing our blank looks he adds, '*to eat*, I mean?'

'He has forgotten that we ate everything we had this morning. There is nothing in the bags', Saeward sighs. 'There is nothing here for us to eat'.

'Therefore something must be killed before we go under with hunger', Theorvard acknowledges that our evening meal is in the hands of our only remaining bowman.

'Surely the light is too poor for anyone to go out hunting', Saeward pokes his nose out of the door. In his eyes it is too dark to go out with a bow and arrows.

'Nonsense, *Theodolf can see like a lynx!*' Theorvard will brook no argument.

'There is still light to see, and as long as none of you is out in the woods with me, there should be no mishap. The deer only go by smell, so if I stay down-wind of them we should eat soon', Theodolf agrees and goes out to his horse to gather his bow and arrow bag,

'Get us a good hart, or at least a hind, Theodolf', Theorvard shouts after him.

Saeward looks at our friend from the Danelaw and shakes his head, laughing,

'Give him a list, like at the market. Perhaps he can kill to order?'

He walks slowly back to the table and sits on it, making it creak with the weight of him and the hauberk. He looks somehow right in the Northman's war gear, almost as if it had been made for him. With the weapons made for him by Asmund and Thor, he looks as much like a huscarl as Theodolf, Saeward or I. Only Wulfmaer is still without any chain mail, not even a byrnie keeps him from being struck.

Many of the Northmen that I have seen are shorter on the whole than we are. Saeward, as was his brother Beorhtwulf, is well built but stocky. He looks every inch the Northman, apart from his collar-length light brown hair.

'If I were you I would get off that table, *before we have to eat off the floor!*' Wulfmaer snaps at Saeward with his usual lack of tact, yet with all our welfare at heart.

The table groans again as Saeward takes his weight off it. Theorvard groans too,

'Oh God, what would I not do with a leg from a hart!'

'Would the hind leg of a brock do?' I laugh, and duck as he throws something over my head, 'What was *that?* I hope you do not seek to wreck our happy home!'

'It was only a *wooden* platter', Wulfmaer jerks his head to the bottom of the wall where it has fallen.

I look round to see Saeward peering through the open door into the dark. Is he looking to see whether Theodolf is on his way back? I hardly think he would have found a buck so soon! My belly rumbles again, brought on by the sight of the grease stained wooden platter. Odd shuffles across the room to it, picks it up and walks to the table to set it down in the middle. He looks over Saeward's shoulder, out into the evening gloom and rubs his hands,

'I had best go out and look for some kindling', he tells us, hinting heavily that he wants help from one of us.

'I had *forgotten* about making a fire!' Saeward seems to come out of a waking dream and walks out into the night close behind Odd. Wulfmaer looks up from the empty hearth and grunts.

'It might be as well I go with them, *save me listening to your rumbling stomach, Ivar!*' He follows Saeward through the still open door.

Theorvard pushes the door to after Wulfmaer and grins hugely,

'If they come back with an armful of twigs each, then we should have a fire big enough to burn down the dwelling, us with it! 'Do they have no doors where they come from? If only Burhred had not taken on so!'

'Somehow I am sorry I could not see a funny side to his prank', I admit to Theorvard. 'I honestly think now that I should not have taken his jape as a slight in the way I did'.

He chews on his lower lip, thinking about what I have just told him. Just as I believe he is about to dismiss my words he answers,

'It was not *you*, Ivar, it was *him. I* would have wrung his neck and none of *you* could have stopped me, even with my shoulder wound! No I think things turned out the way they were going to. It was his wyrd to be cast out of our company, whether he was a good fighter or not. Neither Aelfwin nor Aelfwig would have acted in that way, I am sure. Wulfmaer would bear me out on that', he argues for me. 'No, Ivar it was *not* your fault. He is a troublemaker. You are a fair man and could only do what you were apt to. We should forget about Burhred now, there are weightier matters to think about', Theorvard has not spoken to me in this way before, as an equal. I feel rewarded by his opening up to me, and that he thinks me fair. I have often wondered how the others see me. I now know *his* outlook.

On hearing a thump on the door, Theorvard leaps to open it,

'It took them little time to gather that kindling', he looks taken aback, but still has not opened the door.

'I wonder how Theodolf has fared in the gloom out there', I half ask Theorvard. 'Do you think he has got something yet?'

Sitting down on the long bench that runs along the wall beside the door, I fold my arms and stretch my legs.

'Hopefully, right now he is dragging a nice big buck or hind', Theorvard licks his lips at the thought of a meat supper, 'is there any ale here?'

9

He looks over his shoulder at me as he opens the door and is pressed back at the point of a short spear! Two burly Northmen push us back into the dimly-lit room and look about to see if there is anyone else in here. Another follows them and puts himself between Theorvard and me.

'Who are you, *what are you doing here?*' the Northman demands gutturally from me.

'I am Ivar Ulfsson', I answer, and ask of him in turn, 'what are *you* doing here?'

He looks scornfully back at me and turns to Theorvard,

'What is *your* name?'

'I am Theorvard', he looks down at the now uneasy Northman. 'My kinsmen call me 'shortie' where I come from'.

One of the Northman's underlings pushes Theorvard back with his spear. He too is wary of the young giant looming over him. Usually these fellows ride in sixes. I wonder where the other three are, or what they are doing.

The Aenglish-speaking one turns to me now, his hand on his sword pommel. Clearly he thinks that there should be more of us,

'Where are the others?' he demands to know.

'*What* others do you mean?' I throw his question back at him.

'*Do not be foolish*, Aenglishman. There are six horses out there, more than half of which I would say are ours. I shall ask again, *where are the others?*' He says the words slowly, as if talking to a fool, or child.

'I cannot say where they are, not being able to see through walls. One went out to hunt for our supper, the others are looking for kindling, for a fire', I answer, allowing that there *are* more than just the two of us.

'The others are looking for – *what is kindling?*' the Northman squints at me in the poor light.

It is my turn to look at him as if I were talking to a child,

'Kindling is what you light a fire with, twigs, branches, that sort of thing. In this damp weather they will need more than just twigs to start a fire that does not smoke us out of here'.

He stares at me, unable to fathom what it is I have told him. His knowledge of the tongue still has some way to go before he can think of himself as an Aenglish speaker. I peer back at him,

'Usually there would be a stack of logs outside, but your country-men seem to have driven off the folk who lived here before they were able to chop wood for their winter fires'.

'You admit you do not belong here', the Northman notes drily.

'Nor do *you*, even less so than I', I look across from where I am seated on the bench. He crosses the floor quickly and slaps my face hard with the back of his mailed glove.

Theorvard makes a start for him, but is stopped by two spear points. The Northman stands back, shaking with anger, plainly thinking me foolish enough to risk being speared by his underlings, and snarls at me,

'I can have you killed, *if that is what you really want'*.

One of his men leans toward him and says something to him in his ear. When the fellow has finished telling him whatever it is he needed to say, he stands still, listening for something outside.

There may be more of his comrades on their way here, or he may be listening for my friends coming back from the woods. He goes over to the door, flings it wide open and shouts something in his own tongue.

Outside there is a ruck. Whatever is happening calls for the two spearmen to stand guard over us with their points aimed at our throats.

Whatever is happening outside seems to keep their leader unduly and they become edgy, frightened. The one with his spear point at my throat looks at his comrade and back at me, and waves the weapon to-ward the door. I understand he wants me to go to the door, and out into the open. Theorvard and I are prodded through the door.

Outside their leader is nowhere to be seen. I sense something stirring behind me, to my right, and something drops onto my guard. Theorvard is on my left. His guard, now jittery, prods him again. Theorvard turns like a bear, grabs the spear with both hands and wrestles it from the Northman's hands. My guard is beset by someone who has leapt onto him from the roof and is losing his struggle.

'*Mon dieu!*' he screams as a knife is thrust into his stomach by The-odolf with the knife I recall Hrothulf used for gutting game.

Both our guards have been subdued and killed. One by Theodolf, the other by - Burhred!

Why and when did he return, and why do I feel I owe him thanks when he has evened with me?

'Where is the other one?' I ask Theodolf.

'He is resting', he grins lopsidedly at me, drawing a finger around his throat, showing that the man has been dealt with.

'I thought they rode in sixes', Theorvard echoes my thoughts and stares into the darkness. It is not so dark that we are altogether unable to make out shapes, 'Where *is* the sixth?

A look around at the mounts the other five came on tells me we have amassed more horses than we can handle. Wulfmaer shows from behind the second outbuilding, trying to stuff his woollen shirt into his breeks. He grins cheekily when he knows I have seen him.

'I had to hose down the back wall once we had sent them to their maker. We saw the six of them riding up, and when these three went inside, we gave the others the shock of their lives – ahmm, their deaths. The leader is with his other three men over against the wall of that building', Wulfmaer waves one hand toward the stable, and with the other tucks away the rest of the shirt.

'When did Theodolf come back? I ask him.

'Well before us', he nods at Saeward and Odd. 'I was here when the Northmen came, and hid. Then we saw them off'.

'Odd kept our horses quiet whilst the three of us put them out of their misery'.

'You put them out of their misery, *how?*' I ask, grinning.

'They must have been ailing, to come out here in the twilight. I mean, anyone who is right in his head would count his blessings, stay put and down a few cups of ale with his comrades!' Theorvard looks pained, rubbing *his* wounded right shoulder.

'They were as likely to have been on their way back from Pefense to a camp near Haestingas', I offer, 'and they thought they were lucky to find shelter. Then they happened on us. Imagine finding us up here, one wearing stolen war gear!'

'I suppose there is that to it. Think of the rewards Odo would have showered upon them when they told him that they had caught *us* with our Northman hauberks', Theodolf grins again. 'Anyway, *look what I found!*'

He leads us to the back of the stable and proudly shows us a deer carcase, still with an arrow embedded in its neck.

'I see you left your arrow in there, to show who it was killed this creature', Theorvard chuckles, pointing at the flight feathers.

'Ah, *but that is just it'*, Theodolf straightens and points at Burhred. He finishes,

'That is not one of *my* arrows. I did not have to dig into my arrow bag to bring him down. This buck was on a bed of dry leaves when I saw him, panting his last. I had not long been there when Burhred came out from the bushes. He did not have to plead with me to help him bring the carcase back here'.

Theodolf points behind me and I turn and stare at Burhred, who looks down at the carcase at our feet. He then looks up at me and holds my stare. What do I do now?!

'Let him stay', Theodolf pleads. 'He helped me bring the carcase back, and then helped finish off the Northmen, taking the one who stood guard outside. He has earned a seat on the bench with us'.

'I think he may have brought them *upon* us, to make himself look good', I am still staring fixedly at Burhred, who looks down at the buck, and then at Theodolf. 'He has been given more leeway than I might have been given by the four of you, had I done what he did. Theorvard said he would have wrung his neck after the last time'.

Burhred turns to look up at Theorvard, who avoids his gaze, and then walks to the stable,

'Can I at least have a keepsake?' he asks, looking at me over his shoulder.

I have to think before I answer, and give a short nod,

'Aye, if you mean, "can you take something from one of the corpses?", the answer has to be aye', I call after him as he walks toward the dead leader. 'But I would also have to say that you may as well stay and eat your fill. We will think over what to do with you in the morning, when we have rested'.

Burhred carries on walking, stoops to pick something up from one of the Northmen, and picks his way back between the corpses to the door of the dwelling where I await his answer. He stands stock still, looking levelly at me. Then, after taking in all of us one by one he shrugs and walks away again, slowly.

Before he reaches the stable he turns again,

'Ivar your numbers are right, you do not need me riding along with you. I will find something else to kill tonight and eat my fill, keeping company with the other night creatures. Although my thoughts will be with you, I think the brocks and foxes will prove better company. Have a good ride back to Lunden', he waves quickly and vanishes behind the stable, into the darkness.

'*He did not feel welcome*. If you had said something about him having been forgiven he might have stayed', Saeward upbraids me.

'Burhred was in the wrong, he knew that', Theorvard says on my behalf, 'Ivar told him what I would have done in his stead, and I stand by that. There is no telling what he would have stooped to -'

'*He helped kill these Northmen!*' Wulfmaer snaps, not letting Theorvard finish, 'Without him Ivar and you might have been taken by now! Not only that but Theodolf might still have been out hunting now, and the rest of us could have been taken to Hrofesceaster along with Ivar without him knowing where we were!'

Theorvard looks up into the sky and closes his eyes tightly before opening them widely and staring angrily at Wulfmaer, he rages,

'*All right, fine!* If you feel you can trust him, *run after him,* and call out for him to come back! But first ask Ivar what he thinks about having him back. If *he* takes Burhred back, perhaps it is *I* who should leave!'

'*No-one leaves!* Trust me, Theorvard. Go, call Burhred back. If he so wishes, he can keep company with us for the night. In the morning we will talk over whether he rides with us. If you think we should forgive him, let it be thus'.

He struggles as fast as he can to the stable, but Burhred is already headed for the woods. Wulfmaer calls out after him,

'*Burhred, come back!*'

Burhred rides on into the night and Wulfmaer throws his hands up with a sigh and drops them to his sides in a show of despair. The sound of hoofbeats dies and we are left standing in the open. His wyrd now is of his own making.

I can still taste the meat when I rise from a drugged sleep in the morning. Saeward tells me game should be hung out for some three or four days before it is cooked. We do not have that kind of time to waste, as I hope to be safe in Lunden again within the next three days - unless Odo sends men after us. If he does, our road back will be long and hard.

'That meat was *rich!* I do not know how these nobles can eat so much of it', Wulfmaer sounds as if he is griping.

'If the choice is between getting something into your belly and starving, which do you take?' Theorvard growls at Wulfmaer. 'You might like the taste of fox better?'

'We should have had bread to go with it', Wulfmaer whines.

'We *had* no bread, only ale that was well past its best. I do not know why you are moaning, Wulfmaer', Theorvard looks down at the miller from his saddle.

'*Was* I moaning?' Wulfmaer grins shamefacedly.

'It sounded that way', Saeward chides. 'What do *you* think, Theodolf?'

'Leave me out of this', Theodolf answers, trying to keep the look of anger for as long as none of us does not bring him to laughter against his will. He knows it will only lead to a ribbing.

'Do you always bicker like this?' Odd asks, looking from me to Theorvard, and then to Saeward, 'I *liked* that meat, even if though it *was* rich. You should have seen what *we* had to eat at the abbey, when that fat Northman was guzzling his Frankish wines and stuffing his belly with the best cuts of meat!'

'I would sooner not; a good guess tells me the abbot was given the cream of the crop, and that the pigs got better than you ate, *am I right?*' Saeward laughs and swings himself up into his saddle.

'*Something* like that', Odd sucks in his mouth and mounts.

Only Wulfmaer and I are still not mounted. We are hobbling the Northmen's horses so that they do not show up at the nearest camp and alert the foe. We need a head start, to take a look at Haestingas, what is in the haven and guess at which way their waggons take across the land to Willelm.

When the task is done and the Northmen's horses contentedly crop the rich, dew-laden grass in the shade of the woods, we mount and make our way southward. Theodolf has hold of Braenda's reins, and I nod my thanks to him as I take them from him and climb into the saddle.

Wulfmaer makes heavy weather of mounting and earns a groan from Theorvard.

'Wait until you are *my* age', Wulfmaer moans to a chorus of deep groans from everyone.

'It is not so much your age as your appetite. Anyway, how do you rate the likelihood of my living to a ripe old age like you?' Theorvard asks.

I recall watching Saeward mounting in the days before he grew used to handling horses.

'Wulfmaer is not that old. You yourself will die in your bed with your boots off', Saeward laughs.

'I can only hope *not!*' Theorvard's answer comes swiftly enough to make me believe he wishes to be killed before he reaches Wulfmaer's age.

'We need to be quiet from now until we are well away from here', I warn them all, and look from one to the next until my gaze settles on Odd.

He swallows hard, as if I had meant the warning for him alone. I make myself smile to put him at his ease, but he presses his knees into his mount's flanks and ducks my gaze. I give no more warnings until we come to a rise where I raise my hand, palm forward, to stop.

The haven is busy, even at this early hour. Before the sun has cast its shadows behind the ships' masts the vessels are being rowed into the eastern part of the bay to await their turn to unload. We are safe from being seen as long as we watch from the cover of the wood. To the south the bay is shaped something like a woman's thighs, with the burh on her right knee. Unluckily for us Odd does not know these parts, so he cannot point out what we need to know.

'The outlook is good, but there is still a lot that cannot be seen from here', I see a need to get closer, to see Haestingas' haven from another angle.

'What if we go over there to the west and enter behind the burh on that high ground?' Theodolf asks, 'It looks to me as though there are trees and bushes that afford enough cover'.

Theorvard and I look to where Theodolf points out a low ridge, buildings scattered haphazardly around its lower reaches,

'If the buildings here are too close to where you were thinking we should stand, then we may see better from there', Theorvard sounds a little too caring about his safety for a man seeking glory.

'I think I know what he means. The houses are lower than the top of the ridge and we should see down into the haven there', I tell him, waving the others to follow us across the head of the dale. 'You may yet die in your bed, Theorvard'.

The others laugh, even the straight-laced Odd. It takes some time to reach Theodolf's outlook point, and when we do get there, Theorvard is unmoved,

'I thought we would see *more*'.

My own doubts about coming here are borne out by the lack of a wider outlook. Also the rooves below us are closer than I thought they would be and block out what is resting closer in the haven, only a few mast tops can be seen bobbing up and down.

'What do we do?' I am for going down later, when the light has gone and few will challenge us with our Northman hauberks.

Odd, Wulfmaer and certainly Theorvard would be best counselled to stay here, but somehow Theorvard has had his appetite for adventure whetted. My telling him about dying in bed has perhaps stung him. He may have a thinner skin than he would admit to .

'If you say we need to be closer to see better what is going on, then we shall get closer', Theorvard is set on finding something worth our efforts now. 'Wulfmaer and Odd can look after the horses here, and we four walk down between the houses in the dark. What can be simpler than that?' Theorvard sounds confident, even though he would stand out in his Acnglish byrnie with the rip in the shoulder. Theodolf and Saeward nod, although Saeward bites his lower lip and looks less sure of the plan than Theodolf does.

'Then we wait for darkness'. I have another thought, about food, 'Meanwhile, what do we do about eating? Is there a camp about here, where we can find something worth taking?'

'There may be one to the west, over the ridge', Saeward is watching something now. Perhaps he thinks he has learned something worthwhile.

'Why do you say that?' I ask, looking westward past him to see if I can spot anything.

'Mounted men have been coming and going that way', he points westward toward the headland.

We all follow his finger, and what we see are the pennons and the lance points of horsemen crossing, some to the north, others southward and westward. The houses to the north from here hide the rest, but in our thoughts we see what is missing - and what is missing is a troop of Northmen on their way north. They must have begun their ride from nearby, to the west of us, which is where their camp has to be.

'Well seen, Saeward. Theorvard you had best stay with Wulfmaer and Odd when we ride to their camp. You would stand out too much, I think. We would be more likely to find something without you', I tell a vexed-looking Theorvard.

'Are you *sure?* What if you run into trouble? Four are better than three, I think', Theorvard will have nothing of my thought.

'There is a sea mist coming in!' Wulfmaer points to the east. 'It will hide us and we can be away before anyone is any wiser'.

I like what is happening.

'Theorvard, you *can* come with us'.

Surely the mighty Aegir has come from his watery fastness to see what is happening on this shore? Aegir was one of the old gods forsaken for Christianity; the lord of the sea has not been good to the Aeng-lish, favouring the Norse - and now the Northmen.

Aegir's blanket of mist kept him from being seen, when he went to look over Odin's realm. If he thought old 'One-eye' was not looking out seaward from the walls of Asgard, so much the better. As a cloak he would use a thick sea mist, a 'roak', as it is called in the coastlands of Deira. Blessing or not, the mist will be our weapon in relieving the Northmen of some of their stores. They will miss them less than they will miss the men we have killed so far!

Again we have to skirt the burh, which wraps itself around the lower slopes of the pointed ness, to the right of the 'thigh'. When we have passed the last of the dwellings where a shallow river dale crosses, we skirt a loose ribbon of smallholdings.

Their campfires dance between great tents lined east to west, north to south across a long plain. Away to our right a wide, forked inlet shelters ships of all sizes that bob on small waves made by an easterly wind. At the mouth of the inlet empty supply ships await a north-easterly wind to take them back to Northmandige.

A copse to our left looks useful for us to stop and wait until the incoming mist catches us up.

'We can wait here until Aegir's cloak of mist reaches us', I tell them. Odd and Saeward look sharply at me, but the others understand my meaning.

The wind having dropped means there will be longer to wait. Soon, however, the plain is cloaked by the drifting mist. I look to Theorvard and he nods back to show he is ready. Having marked the site of the camp in my thoughts I nudge Braenda into a walk again. Theorvard follows, the others following on with Wulfmaer taking up the rear and only just in sight.

None of us says anything as we pick our way between clumps of trees that rim deserted smallholdings. The folk who lived here would have been the first to suffer Willelm's men in their haste to hunt down fodder for their horses.

Grain for bread, or better still ready-made loaves would have had to be found, too.

The rest of their livelihoods would have gone with the Northmen's need for meat to go with any roots for their meals before the havens had been made safe for the ships. It is time we dipped into *their* stocks of food again, to live off *them* for the next few days. The trick will be to find tents that hold the food and drink. It might have been better had we had the time to watch the camp before the mist set in. Still, I must thank Aegir for his blessing.

'Can you see aught yet?' Theodolf asks.

'No, but I think you and Saeward should ride a little way ahead of us before we reach the camp', I answer. If the Northmen see them first they will not bother us.

Saeward and Theodolf come through between Theorvard and Odd to take up the lead. I call back to Wulfmaer to close the gap behind us and everyone pulls their cloaks around them against the clinging wetness,

'Put your helms on, too', I tell them before we near the first line of tents. 'They will look like theirs in this mist, so they will not think anything is amiss when we ride along the line of tents. Say nothing, either to me or to one another, and follow Saeward's lead'.

A bored sentry waves us past, half asleep I would guess, and goes back to his day-dreaming. After passing something like a score of their tents I catch sight of a higher, longer one.

After looking carefully around for prying eyes, a closer look shows it is open at one end where two men stand talking idly. The back of the tent is closed off. This has to be where the food is kept. Saeward stretches his right arm out for us to halt. Theodolf reins in, looks back over one shoulder at me and waves us on. I press my knees in on

Braenda's flanks and ride up to them.

Saeward takes Braenda's reins when I dismount, Theodolf does likewise and I wave on Theorvard. When he, Odd and Wulfmaer stop behind Theodolf I wave them down, to wait,

'I will signal, like this', I whisper, raising my right arm to show how I will let them know, 'Theorvard will dismount and walk forward to me'.

Theorvard, Wulfmaer and Odd nod and I stride to walk at Theodolf's side. As we make our way to the stores tent someone calls out to the two Northmen talking by the open flap. We slow down, hoping not to be seen, but they walk away briskly leaving us to do what we want without hindrance. This is too easy! I check myself to slow my heartbeat, and look ahead and behind for signs of a trap.

Once inside the tent we pick our way around the stacks of barrels. At the back is a holding area, a smaller store that must be where dry foodstuffs are kept. Although unlit, this part of the tent is not dark enough to hide a fat old fellow resting with his back on grain sacks.

His feet rest on a tun and he has his back to me, but from the jerking of his head, I can see he has fallen sound asleep. I signal to Saeward with a finger on my lips, and point out the sleeping storekeeper.

Quietly poking our noses into bags, sniffing at kegs and looking into barrels that might hold cured fish or meat, we seek out food stocks for the coming days, taking care to take empty bags for carrying them. When we have looked, sniffed and prodded enough, and filled several bags, I raise my eyebrows at Theodolf to signal that we should leave. On my way out I take two large spare bags. He too takes spare bags, as well as a bag of what must be root stocks and a small keg under his arms. I pick up a bag of bread loaves and hoist another keg of whatever drink they have, tucking it under my arm before picking up the bags again. We leave quickly and quietly by the flap through which we entered.

Out in the open again, I make my signal for Theorvard, and wave to Odd to come with him. As Theodolf and I hand over our booty they go back to the horses. We head back to the tent.

The sleeping storekeeper has moved a little but begins to snore, head back and mouth wide open. We help ourselves to salted meat, bagging it carefully so as not to awaken him. He is harmless enough, and I would hate to have to kill him needlessly, thus also forfeit our other supplies when the alarm is raised.

There are more of the skinned small animals that came from the camp in the woods, and as Theorvard liked his share so much we bring as many as Burhred and Theodolf took last time.

177

When we think we have enough, we steal away again. Theodolf apes the now loudly snoring storekeeper on his way past and I am hard put to fight my laughter.

Saeward still has hold of our horses' reins, and as we stride past him he follows us, with our horses in tow. Theorvard and Odd have already stowed away what we left with them, bags tied together and slung in front of their saddles. Now that we have enough for a couple of days, and with the threat of the mist thinning, I wave everyone away. I still think this was too easy and cannot help wondering if a trap was set for us. I look once more over one shoulder. There is a half mile between us and the great camp now and there is *still* no-one coming after us.

The mist has now rolled away to the west and we are on open ground. Heading north again, we pass the landward reaches of Haestingas and climb, turning inland with Pefense to our left..

'Were we not going to see what was in the haven?' Theorvard calls to me as we near the thickening woodland of the Weald.

'By how much we took, I would say they are stocking up daily', I tell him.

He is happy with my answer and we press our mounts to a steady trot. Our ride will take us some way into the Haestingas Hundred, where fields and barns have been stripped, the corn stocks razed. What few animals grazed on the common land have cropped the grass and bushes clean and moved on, driven by their Northman captors to new grazing grounds westwards into Suthrige.

'I *know* this land', Odd stands in his stirrups, hands cupping his eyes. 'Over there, in the lee of that wood is a drover's rest where we could rest for a while'. He points ahead but there is nothing to see from where we are, not that we would know where to look. However, as we ride on around a thick beech wood the shelter can be seen in the lee of dense woodland. This will be a useful hideout for us for long enough to catch up on much-needed sleep.

We will not have to break cover for some time on our long ride back to Lunden, so there should be little risk of falling into the clutches of Odo.

'They should not see the smoke from our fire', Odd points back the way we rode, toward Haestingas. Steep hills and deep dales lie between us and the Northmen on the coast. We seem to be safe for the time being. I feel happier now than I have for days.

In no time at all dry kindling has been found and laid within a ring of charred stones left by countless drovers.

The ground has been hard-scorched all around the head-sized stones, leaving a black rim where they have been moved inward for smaller fires. Whilst Saeward, Odd and Wulfmaer busy themselves putting together our first meal of the day, Theorvard, Theodolf and I look inside the shelter. These hardy drovers rested on the bare earth in their sleeping bags. The tight-pressed and flattened wicker door of hazel strips looks southward, and the inside of the shelter is fairly dry.

Made of a crumbling wattle and daub, the walls have seen better days. On the outside the hazel strips have been interwoven and covered with a mixed thick layer of daub and clay, and the wet weather from the west and north-west has not been too unkind to the shelter. These drovers knew how to make themselves feel at home!

'*The food is ready!*' Saeward soon calls and we waste no time seating ourselves on the earth around the fire with our cloaks wrapped around us to keep out the damp. We eat listening to birdcalls, taking swigs of apple ale from skins filled from the kegs. Not having eaten since last night, and then only little, the apple ale makes me feel drowsy, but I cannot bow to my need for rest, not yet. First there are the watches to agree on. We come to an agreement that we must rest during the day and ride by night until we are well away from this neighbourhood.

At some time during the next night's ride Odd will put us on the right road before leaving us to ride east.

Dark clouds pass from the east, over towering woodland beeches. Much as I would like, sheltered as we are from the wind, we cannot stay out here for long before the rain comes. If we are lucky, when we go inside none of it will come through the dense thatch of the roof.

Theorvard shakes me awake to share an early evening watch. A new rush-light is kindled to mark the time before we too can catch up on well-earned sleep. Thankfully nothing happens to shatter the peace of the evening after the rain, so we take in the smells of the woodland. We also take in the sickly sweet smell of the dung based daub, released by the dampness drawn from the woodland behind us.

We eat again before we leave. Odd bullies us into letting him say a prayer before we partake of God's bounty, as he puts it. He has to be humoured, but whilst his eyes are tightly shut Theodolf twists his mouth, aping Odd, to set us off laughing. Odd opens his eyes again, frowns, and shuts them tightly again, finishing his prayer with an almost barked '*Amen*'.

The bread is finished before it goes stale or mouldy, salted meat wrapped again before everything is bagged.

As the others mount I take a quick look back at Haestingas and, seeing nothing untoward, swing myself into Braenda's saddle. Last into his saddle as always is Wulfmaer, Theodolf watching him labour up onto his horse. He looks heavenward, as if in prayer. Knowing Theodolf, his thoughts are more likely puppish than ungodly. He is young yet, and the young always look upon their elders as dead-weights.

With Wulfmaer once more in his saddle, we set off on the first leg of the ride back to Eadgar. My thoughts on how he might go about cutting off Willelm's supplies take shape as I ride.

We have a long night ahead of us. Odd tells me, his throat still plainly giving him some trouble, about the road he will take when we reach Centland,

'Where I leave you will be Hafochaesten and your road will take you north-westward by way of Tonabrycg'.

'Take your time', I tell him. 'There is no hurry'.

'You should be in Lunden within two days'. He winces, pained by the effort.

'I think the riding will be a little harder than that, my friend', I tell Odd, 'King Harold took a week to reach Eoferwic!'

Odd stares in disbelief, so I tell him to ask Saeward,

'He came with us, so he should recall it well'.

'What was that?' Saeward cannot have been eavesdropping, as he usually does when bored.

'I said we took a week in reaching Eoferwic in September, is that not so?' I call across to him.

'God – aye, you are right! For the last few miles I sat on a cart because my backside was sore from riding. There were masses – what was that?!'

'What was what?' Saeward sits upright in his saddle, straining to hear something.

I stiffen and look to where Saeward stares.

'I heard rustling in the trees, but it was not the wind blowing!' Something has startled Saeward. Theorvard urges his shying horse toward the trees where Saeward points.

'*There it was again!*' Saeward shouts.

I think Theodolf heard it that time, too. He dismounts quickly and then freezes in his tracks. A great boar pushes through the undergrowth, out into the thwait ahead of us and, unafraid, stands his ground. Another comes out from behind him and stands almost shoulder to shoulder with the first.

'*Throw me my bow!*' Theodolf calls to Theorvard, who leans over to Theodolf's horse and draws the lance from its socket.

'I have thought of something else', Theorvard tells Theodolf and tosses the lance to him with the point upward. 'Use this, but be quick.

That one is sizing you up. Besides, I *like* boar meat!'

Theodolf protests,

'Give me my *bow*, Theorvard! An *arrow* would be quicker and better, *believe me!*'

Odd gives a yelp like a pup to warn Theodolf the boar is coming threateningly toward him. All he can do is fend off the animal with what he has. The first boar makes a sudden move at him and Theodolf grips the lance as if he were holding an axe.

'Hold it *point down!*' I yell as he changes his grip on the lance and thrusts it at the boar.

Somehow he misses, and the boar turns in at him under the shaft. The second boar makes for Saeward's horse. Seeing the move, Saeward brings down his lance point and casts the weapon onto the animal's neck. The boar drops dead, as if its legs had been chopped from under it!

I dismount, axe in hand, and cut down onto the first boar's back. He drops onto his belly with a high-pitched squeal.

As I slither on the boar's blood in my bid to get to Theodolf's side, Saeward is there before me and wrestles the lad's hauberk up to his chest to see to his wounds. Theodolf's waist is bloodied from the boar's sharp right tusk although, luckily, he has not been badly gored through the chain mail. The leather belt may have taken some of the creature's thrust.

'That will need looking at, *now!*' Saeward curses and looks up at me, as if the attack were my fault.

Theodolf looks down at his wound and up at Saeward, who stands over him. He nods and shakes his head at his own foolishness. I can guess he is thinking right now of what his father might have said, bloodied as he was near to where Harold was last seen. Hrothulf would have given his son some stern words, but he would not have been too rough on the lad. He would have spoken to him as he did to me when we tackled the bear.

Saeward peers closely at the cuts in the poor light, his head jerking from side to side in order to see better,

'I will have to make a potion with any herbs I can find here in the woods, and I shall have to tie it to your wound with a strip of fine cloth from my bag', he tells Theodolf. He likes the lad for all his youthful carelessness. Theodolf has spirit, but if he does this sort of thing again, that is all he will be, and *then* what do I tell Aethel?

These two work well together with their shared esteem for one another's skills – Saeward for Theodolf's skill with the bow, Theodolf for Saeward's skill in healing, and axe-throwing. I hope to have them both around me for some time to come, even when I am too old for the shieldwall!

Saeward gives Odd a folded piece of fine woollen cloth to hold against Theodolf's wound whilst he goes to forage for herbs in the darkness. He seems to know just where to look for what he needs and I leave him to it after he tells me,

'Ivar I am happy looking for what I need on my own', he waives any fears I have for his safety with a deft flick of his hand, 'Do you think there were no boars near Wealtham when I went with the brothers looking for herbs for the infirmary, that they did not grow themselves?'

'If you think – 'I begin.

'Trust me. I know what I am doing', he calls back to me as he wanders off into the pitch darkness.

'That *is* weird! No matter how long have you have known him, he *still* leaves you in the dark! Well, young Theodolf, I hope you know how much trouble he is going to for you!' He squints into the darkness, trying to follow Saeward with his eyes and resses a hand on the lad's shoulder, earning himself a scowl from Odd.

He ignores the young Suth Seaxan and turns to have a few words with me,

'This one fusses like a woman, Ivar. Do you think he is – well, *all there?*'

'Do I think he is what – oh, you mean an *over-mothered one?*' I know what he means, but if Odd knows how to help with the wounded, I see no grounds to scoff at his shortcomings as a man.

'Do you think we will get to Hafochaesten tonight, or whatever name the burh goes by?' Theorvard asks me.

'Not knowing its whereabouts, I cannot tell', I have to answer truthfully. He dearly wants to see the back of Odd. The fellow must make Theorvard crawl in his skin, but I have to say he earns his keep. One day the likes of Theorvard and me will be needed less, but Odd and his kind will find themselves wanted in greater numbers.

'It will not take too long', Odd has been listening in to our talking but says nothing of Theorvard's rating of him, 'once Saeward has gathered his herbs and the dressing has been fastened tight to the wound, we should be away'.

Odd takes another close look at Theodolf's wound,

'Your friend is very brave, for all the pain he must be in. He should be good for the ride to Lunden, but keep him clear of trouble!'

'Do you hear that, Theodolf, my fine fellow? You are a great *warrior!* The young women will flock to you, to look at your wound. Moreover, if they know you are a king's huscarl, you will *never* be lonely!'

Wulfmaer jokes and Theodolf grins broadly, but has to grit his teeth with the pain of looking up at Wulfmaer.

'*Keep still,* Theodolf!' Odd hisses, fussing over the lad, his hand still on the bunched cloth Saeward told him to hold against Theodolf's wound.

Wulfmaer laughs and sits down on the ground by Theodolf,

'God, this is damp!' he curses and jumps up, almost knocking against Odd. Although saying nothing, the young fellow's mouth twists downward in an ugly scowl.

Saeward shows again as the moon creeps out from behind thick cloud bearing a mixed bundle of leaves for the dressing. Rolling some together, he adds more, and then the rest is put in with the green mess that he shows me in an open palm. Most of the herb names I would never know again if I lived to a ripe old age, but one strikes me as an odd name,

'Feverfew, what is *that?*' I ask in awe of his knowledge of these things.

'I forget its proper name, but it keeps fever at bay', Saeward smilingly tells me.

This is another side of him I know little of. He is indeed a man to have around you when you are *sore-tested!* We do not have long to wait. Theodolf, still wearing the hauberk, is helped onto his saddle by Saeward and Theorvard. He wears the hauberk because, as he says, carrying it on the saddle would be even more awkward.

Odd leads the way again, northward along old, long-forgotten tracks. We see little of the land with the cloud-laden sky above us. Every now and then the moon shows through, affording glimpses of the hilly land around us, but it is all soon hidden from sight again as the moon is overtaken in its long ride across the night sky by the clouds. Onceover we would have said it is Jormungand wrapping himself around Midgard.

We have to ride slower because of Theodolf's wound. He puts a brave face on it. He *has* the makings of a huscarl, and I think he should one day rise to thegn but first he must live to tell the tale of his fight with the tusker that tore into his side!

Saeward sings out loudly, oddly enough in good humour, and plainly wishing to cheer us. Stopping his horse, he looks over one shoulder at me and almost shouts,

'When we are clear of these woods and Odd has put us on the right track, out of reach of these Northmen, we can start to sing. Singing will lift our spirits, Theorvard, *and keep us awake!*'

I see the young giant nodding as he rides, and laugh when he jerks his head around to grin sheepishly back at me.

'I was thinking of the young women I shall take to my bed when we are back in Lunden', Theorvard lies and grins again, turning to look ahead.

No-one says anything else until Odd reins in and looks at me. We all rein in and listen as he tells of which tracks or roads to follow,

'This track leads me east to Medestan. I must tell Dunstan's woman of his death. Then I on to Sceapig', Odd tells me.

'Do you have kin there?' I ask, hoping to sound friendly.

It is not as if I am prying into his life, but he has said nothing before about riding on to Sceapig. These past few days this young fellow has had to put up with my small band of men. They have been fighting Northmen, on and off, for weeks and his mild-mannered ways have been tested well. Being with us has cost him a dear friend.

'Aye Ivar, I have an old aunt who lives there. She will help me forget my ordeals with prayer', Odd tells me, looking me in the eye.

'She will, Odd, she will. Well, we all wish you luck, and give Gerda our deepest sympathies for her loss. Dunstan must have been a fine husband to her', I reach a hand out to Odd in friendship.

He looks at me for some time before taking my hand limply, and turns his horse away north-eastward without turning to look back.

'I thought he was riding east', Theorvard muses as we watch Odd vanish into the night.

'Who knows how his way bends, this way or that', I answer and turn Braenda to head north-westward, the way Odd said our track to Tonabrycg will take us.

Wulfmaer turns his head to look after the now almost unseen Odd. Shaking his head he presses his mount on after us. We are on our own now. Three of us can still fight, should the need arise. Theodolf needs rest but we must keep riding to reach the safety of Lunden. I think Aethel would understand that, although Theodolf is all she has from her years with Hrothulf.

I think of how Aethel might fare in company with Eadweard's widow Eadgytha, whether she is happy or whether she would sooner be at home in her steading. When we return to Thorney I will try to find time to see her. Eadgar's sisters Agatha and Christina will soon join Eadgytha, unless they have already left Thorney. Our new king may need us to safeguard them on their long ride west.

'When we see Eadgar again, Theodolf, I will ask him for time to go to Wintunceaster', I tell the lad, hoping to take his thoughts away from his wounds.

'Why would *we* want to go there, wherever that is?' Theodolf asks.

'Is it far from Lunden?'

'It is where Aethel went with King Eadweard's widow, Eadgytha, and is a day's ride west of Thorney', I tell him.

'Do we *have* to see Aethel?' Why would Theodolf suddenly fight shy of meeting her?

'I thought you were fond of Aethel', I have to know from him what is behind his sudden dislike of her.

'If you recall, I told Hrothulf she was once Copsig's woman', he recalls. 'They were not talking from then onward'.

'That is not true and you know it!' I have to rebuke him. 'Before they parted they kissed and, bear in mind, you were watching – *you recall?*'

Theodolf turns away, perhaps because he fears showing his feelings, or because he is trying to block out the pain.

'There is no need to be ashamed', Saeward tells him, but the lad gives him no answer for his troubles. Theodolf must know he deeply wounded his father, telling him of Aethel's time with Copsig.

We fall silent again and no more is said of Aethel until near Tonabrycg, where Theodolf turns in his saddle and asks me,

'Why do *you* wish to seek out Aethel?'

I know Theorvard's and Saeward's eyes are on me. They both know her, having met at different times. Both know her as Hrothulf's woman and would like to know where my wish to see her stems from. I have no ready answer to give them.

'Were you not tied up with that Braenda, the hwicce woman?' Theorvard is ahead of me, 'You know, the one that showed amid the trees when you were fighting Brand'.

'She did not show herself to us, but to Brand', I try to put him right, not knowing otherwise.

'*I* saw her in the woods when I was trying to get away from one of Brand's men', Theodolf recalls.

'So you said', I am glad to be given a way out. 'When I think on it, she must have been following me then, and since'.

'How so, why do you say that?' Theorvard looks up from thinking about what Theodolf has told me again.

'Do you recall the old woman at the 'The Eel Trap', where we stayed near Lunden Brycg? She told us of the red-haired woman staying there the week before we did?' I ask him.

'You mean Ymme - ?' Theorvard thinks back, scratching his beard.

Wulfmaer looks up at the moon, to jolt his own memory,

'Aye, the same', he recalls.

'Well, she told us of a Wealsh brooch that this red-headed woman

185

left behind', I am glad Braenda's name has been raised. It would be hard for me to justify wanting to see Aethel, 'Wynstan's wife Aelfthryth showed it to me'.

'This still does not tell me why you want to see Aethel', Theodolf leads me back awkwardly, and grins at my unease. All eyes are on me again.

'We had best not miss our road', I try to stall.

'Not before we pass Tonabrycg'. Theorvard knows this is a ploy to get out of answering and puts the question to me again with a sly grin. He must think there is something between us, '*Why* do you want to see Aethel?'

'I need to know if we have her say-so to stay at her steading when we go to Jorvik', I lie.

It is Theodolf's turn to lie now,

'You need not ask her. I would be with you when we do go north. It was Hrothulf's steading as much as it was Aethel's. She said that to us a long time ago, when I think on it'.

'Hrothulf told me that night we met he knew of a steading where we could buy horses for the ride to Lunden',

'That was just his way. *You should know that!*' With that Theodolf defends his right to a share of Aethel's steading. 'I thought you and he had been huscarls together in Tostig's household. You ought to know how he thinks'.

A stony silence falls on us all again.

'You were one of *Tostig's* men?' Theorvard asks after what seems like a lifetime of silence.

'Until when we all went to deal the Wealsh aetheling Griffith a bloody nose, aye I was', I answer, not without some pride. After all, Tostig had been looked up to in those days by many in the Danelaw as well as in Northanhymbra. Much of the Danelaw, as far south as North-anhamtun, was part of Tostig's earldom. 'Earl Harold, as he was then, asked me to join *his* household'.

I can see distaste in the way Saeward looks at me. Wulfmaer, how-ever, is not worried by Theodolf's unwelcome tidings. He merely shrugs and looks at Saeward.

'You did not tell *me* this!' Saeward spits his bitterness for all to hear.

'Why *would* I?' I am taken aback. I turn to Theodolf, who holds my stare, 'You have this talent for raising unwelcome matters. By and by we all learn each others' past, and take one another for what we are – or have been'.

'First before the slaughter at Caldbec Beorg you tell Hrothulf Aethel was Copsig's woman. Now you tell everyone I was one of Tostig's huscarls. What do you hope to gain from this?'

'My father Tofig was one of Tostig's huscarls', Theorvard now tells us. 'He was given a house in Aedwaltun by the earl'.

'They *all* seem to be crawling out from the woodwork these days!' Saeward calls out to the heavens.

'In his time Tostig was a good earl!' Theorvard burns with sudden anger. 'I do not know what, or how much you have been told, but his law was good. Copsig's grasping ways led to Tostig being thrown out of his earldom and Morkere - that fool son of Aelfgar - being allowed to take his seat at the Earlsburh!'

'Neither of them was any good. Waltheof should have been made earl when Siward died', Saeward protests his ignorance in the matter.

Theorvard shouts Saeward down before he thinks about where we are, and drops his voice,

'Fool, you should keep your thoughts to yourself on matters of which you know nothing! Earl Waltheof is little older than *Theodolf!*' Theorvard shouts Saeward down.

'I think this has all gone too far, Theodolf', I warn the lad.

'However good your fighting skills and whatever my friendship for your father, if you cannot keep your bad tidings to yourself we will have to go our own way when we reach Lunden'.

An angry hush cloaks us again until we reach Tonabrycg. Theorvard calls out from ahead as we give the burh a wide berth,

'It will be daylight soon, Ivar. We should make camp so as not to be seen by Odo's men'.

'I think so, too. We are all tired from all this riding. Saeward will look at your wound dressing, Theodolf', I tell him. 'Hopefully, if needed, there will be enough herbs for another dressing'.

I try to be friendly toward Theodolf, but find it a strain. Both he and Burhred have tested our friendships to breaking during this past week.

'I am sorry, Ivar', Theodolf tries to atone for speaking out of turn. 'I spoke without thinking. As you say we will have to go our own ways when we reach Lunden. We are not good for one another over a long time. Nevertheless you are always welcome to our steading, you know that'.

'Theodolf, we have had a trying time these past few weeks. I know no better man to have with me. Rest well, have your wounds seen to properly. We have all earned a reward!'

He is right that we should go our own way, at least for a short time. We do not know one another well enough to spend long days together. Even his father did not know him very well. Although she is not his mother, Aethel knows the lad and can read his thoughts – only too well. One day, if I ever have a son, I doubt I will understand him well enough to spend a long time with him without wishing harm on him. Menfolk can be like that, even toward our own blood.

We come across a thwait that we can use for a camp. Here we will hopefully be safe from prying eyes. The smoke from the home fires of Tonabrycg is blown uphill toward us by a freshening, cold easterly wind. We can warm ourselves and cook without the smoke being seen or smelled. As Saeward kicks out the grass in order to lay the fire, Wulfmaer and Theodolf fill it with kindling and Theorvard looks for some dry grass to set alight.

The dew lies heavy on the grass, but under and amid the oaks there are tufts that grow around their roots. I dig into one of the bags and draw a large, tightly bound bundle that smells like salted meat of some sort. In undoing it a lump falls out. It is covered in a greenish sheen.

'God, *this meat has gone off!*' I throw the meat to one side.

Theorvard picks up the bundle and holds it up to the light.

'*Fox bait!*' he laughs and calls out, tossing it to the ground. 'Hopefully there is something else in there that *can* be eaten!'

I rummage around the bottom of the bag blindly and pull out another bundle, smell and undo it, dropping the string onto the grass.

'We should pick up the string, in case someone comes by here and raises the hue and cry', Saeward looks at me as though he were chiding a child. In my haste to eat I have overlooked that likelihood, and stand there with my mouth tightly closed, ashamed of myself.

'Best burn it all and then we have nothing to fear. When the fire is burnt out, kick it over, throw some grass onto it and no-one will be any the wiser', Theorvard tells Saeward. 'When we were following Ivar and Hrothulf through the Danelaw, we tracked them by what they left of their fires'.

He looks at me and laughs,

'You have never had to hide your tracks before, have you, Ivar?'

'You are right. I cannot argue with you', I agree, 'When we chased Gruffyd we wanted his folk to *know* that we were on his trail, but when we were on our way to Eoferwic last month we stayed well to the west of the Norsemen. It did not matter about the ashes as they were unlikely to ride west of the Hvarfe or Ose'.

I have to admit I did not think of it. As to Brand finding us by following the pits of our fires, I think it was more likely to have been the Patzinak, the one Brand named Willelm, who found us.

We find food we can eat, washing it down with the now stale apple ale, but we will not be able to live for long on these mean rations. There will be homesteads or hamlets further north that have not been emptied of their freemen and ceorls.

10

As darkness closes again I hear my stomach grumbling. Theorvard and I are keeping the last watch again. He casts me a knowing smile, prompting my asking him,

'What gives, friend?'

'I was just thinking, if we do not get away from here soon, the Northmen will hear your stomach growling and come and get us!'

I can only muster a feeble grin in answer to his wit. Our search for food will have to begin anew when we leave here. If we head steadfastly north-westward, Odd told me, we should find some friendly souls nearer Egensford.

From what he told me, that is more or less a few hours' riding by night from here. By then Odo will only have to listen out for the rumblings from our bellies to find us!

Saeward has already burnt the string and the bundles. The foxes can have the mouldy meat. Between them, Wulfmaer, Saeward and Theodolf kick over the ashes of the fire. Grass and leaves are spread about on the earth to hide our fire and we mount.

'How is Theodolf's wound, Saeward?' I ask, wondering whether he made sure the dressing was kept clean. He stares long and hard at me as though I should keep to what I know, answering at long last,

'He is fine. A long scar will draw the young women, I think, when he feels fit enough to put himself about. Two scars will make them think he is a great warrior. Theodolf will live, *and well!*' Saeward looks at the lad and tells me, 'I looked at the wound during the night, when it was our turn to keep watch. Trust me, Ivar. He is *fine!*'

Theodolf in turn nods gravely, holding my gaze. He jerks his head away to look ahead to where we are going, so we ride on. I hope Egensford is not far away.

'Does anyone mind if we have deer meat again?' Theorvard suddenly asks.

'Why, can you see one to kill?' I ask, looking around.

He crooks a finger to our right,

'There he is, see, a fine hart. He looks to be past his prime, so the meat will be as tough as we ate the other night, but his rival will not worry overmuch'.

I can just make him out, cropping what few shoots there are on the smaller trees close by. A stiff breeze blows toward us, so he will neither smell nor hear us before Theorvard can cut him down. He reaches for

Theodolf's bow, draws an arrow from Hrothulf's old leather bag and sets it across the bow.

Before loosing off the arrow he licks a finger, holds it up into the wind, aims a touch down from east and lets fly the arrow. The animal goes down and Theorvard knees his horse to our right. Theodolf follows and together they let their mounts walk forward to the dead hart. They dismount a few paces away and bend down to lift it between them.

'There are *two* arrows in this animal!' Theorvard calls back to us, straightens and looks around before nodding to Wulfmaer to lift the shoulders as he bends down to take its hindquarters. They are about to heave the dead animal onto the front of his saddle when another arrow thuds into the saddle, almost hitting Wulfmaer's left hand. The carcase falls back onto the leaf-strewn woodland floor and we all look to see whether the Northmen are about to swoop on us.

'We seem to make a habit of bumping into one other like this'. Burhred shows bow in hand, another arrow already across it. 'I think this one is mine - *again*'.

Theorvard claims the carcase for us,

'How you can say that, Burhred? You can see that is my arrow in his neck!'

'Do you want to argue this one out, Theorvard? Feel free!' Burhred dares him, raising the bow.

'How far do you think you will get with it on your own, *eh*, numbskull?!' Theorvard points to us and prods a thumb at his own chest.

Burhred looks over at us, nods with a ready smile and makes a grab for the carcase now that he is closer, on the other side of Theorvard's horse where the animal dropped. Theorvard dives under the horse, grabs his right arm and clasps it tightly, bringing a yelp of pain from Burhred.

'Let go of the carcase', Theorvard snarls, 'else I shall have to break your arm! You would not want *that*, would you?'

Burhred, still defiant, calls to me,

'We can *share* it, then! Is that not so, Ivar?' He lets go of the carcase only to put Theorvard off guard.

As quickly as Burhred let go, he reaches for it again and Theorvard brings his right fist up onto Burhred's jaw. Burhred falls to the forest floor and Saeward makes to run to his side but is stopped by Wulfmaer.

'*Leave* him - I should have done that long ago!' Theorvard growls at Saeward.

'I must see how he is!' Saeward protests, and looks to me for help.

I shrug and have to agree with Theorvard, adding,

'We will not leave him here for the Northmen to find, fear not, even though I would say Odo would have fun dealing with a man who killed the wearer of that hauberk'.

'Where is his horse?' Theodolf asks. He looks all around, as do the rest of us. We see no sign of the animal.

'Perhaps he has eaten it?' Wulfmaer muses aloud. None of us laughs and he clamps his mouth shut as might a told-off child.

Some hours later, when Burhred has come to and the best meat from the carcase has been shared out, we sit watching him, waiting for him to tell us something. What I would like to hear is him saying he is sorry for his foolishness, to give me grounds for not leaving him bound to a tree for their scouts to take him to Odo in the hauberk.

As I see it, he followed us here but has done no harm - yet. I have to say that for him. He may have guarded against us being found.

'You are waiting for me to grovel, is that *it?*' Burhred finally speaks out. 'Then you are sorely mistaken. I have no wish to beg for bones like a thrall!'

'None of us wishes you to beg', I answer for us all, 'because it would make *us* squirm as much as it would you. Begging is not what we are thinking of. No, Burhred, a simple *'sorry'* would be enough. I am willing to allow you to ride with us back to Lunden. You could go back to Saewardstanbyrig if you so wished'.

'What would I do *there?*' Burhred answers sullenly. 'There is nothing for me there any more'.

'Eadgar might give you Thorfinn's land', Saeward tells him.

'I *hardly* think so!' Burhred snaps, 'He does not know me from Adam'.

'Why would he not give you a thegndom that you have earned with your sword on Lunden Brycg?' Saeward asks Burhred and turns to me, 'Would the king not give Burhred another man's thegndom, Ivar?'

'Aye, if he can be vouchsafed by an earl such as Waltheof'.

Choosing my words carefully I add, looking at Burhred,

'I can tell Eadgar you had a hand in dealing with the foe - and that you fought well'.

'I do not see why not!' Wulfmaer joins in now. Is he humouring Burhred, or can he see himself as a thegn? From miller to thegn in weeks, it would be a first – *ever.*

'You see *yourself* as a *thegn?*' Theorvard thumps Wulfmaer on the back.

'*I can if you can!* Who do you think *you* are, *for the love of God?!* You are just a man like me, albeit more gifted in fighting. We may still only be Eadgar's household men after this, but I for one shall be well

192

out of a life in the mill. I have killed men for the king, as have you and these others, Burhred notwithstanding!'

'Then every single fyrdman should be made a thegn!' Theodolf croaks, rising quickly to his feet. He gives out a yell of pain and holds his right side, the corners of his mouth downturned.

'Sit down, *both of you!*' I glare at them in turn, 'Behaving like children! Theodolf you need rest, and the rest of us should draw lots for watches'.

'I will share a watch with Saeward, if you and Wulfmaer would like to take the first watch', Theorvard tells me.

'What about Burhred and Theodolf?' Wulfmaer demands.

'If you do not trust Burhred, then perhaps you will offer to take *his* watch as well?' Theorvard asks. 'Anyway, with his wounds, Theodolf is in need of rest. He might fall asleep on watch and we could be ringed by laughing Northmen, wondering how it is we let ourselves be caught out so easily!'

'I *would* trust Burhred, if he shared a watch with one of *you* whom I trust more', like a child Wulfmaer earnestly pulls on Theorvard's sleeve.

We all laugh. Even Burhred laughs at Wulfmaer's foolishness.

'Why are you all laughing?' Wulfmaer cannot see he has openly admitted his distrust in Burhred.

'Before you go to sleep, think on what you have just said', still laughing, I push him toward where he will rest before taking his watch.

Wulfmaer stands, mouth wide open, scratching his head for the answer. I add, before we begin talking over other matters,

'For now, as you are still on your feet you can pull me up and we will keep our eyes and ears open',

Theodolf sits again, his back to his saddle. He nods to sleep.

Theorvard and Saeward make themselves as comfortable as they can on their saddle blankets, with their saddles to rest their backs on, as Theodolf has done.

'Where is your horse?' I ask Burhred.

'Do you trust me to go and fetch him?' Burhred smiles back at me. He knows what answer I will give him even before I open my mouth, and sets off into the woods before I can give him leave to do so. I watch him blend with the mist that has thankfully rolled over the land through the woods from the east.

'*Do* you trust him not to bring the Northmen down on us?' Theorvard almost echoes Burhred's words to me before he went.

'I think I would have to just let him do what he wishes. Whatever he does we will take him back into our number again because we have little leeway'.

I *have* given the matter some thought. His being here with us would mean Theodolf being better looked after by Saeward. If he were to be found by Odo's men, they would not be taken in by his tale that he was in these parts on his own, unless they took him for an outlaw. But outlaws do not have weapons made by master craftsmen. His sword was given to him by Thorfinn, and the axe was crafted by Asmund. They have the marks of a master weaponsmith.

'You might tell him to make his own way back to Lunden', Wulfmaer has been listening in and adds his own weight to Theorvard's outlook.

'He may be useful to us. While he is with us, Saeward can tend to Theodolf', is all I can bring myself to say on his behalf.

'What if he is more use to the Northmen?' Theodolf suddenly asks, 'Have you thought of that? I mean, he has had enough time away from us to set a trap. He could right now spring the trap, to save his own miserable neck!'

I have given thought to that, and in answering Theodolf lay open my trust in Burhred to each of them here,

'I hardly think he would sink a low as that, having fought alongside us, and killed as many as you have, Theorvard. Why would he suddenly turn? God knows, Odo would never truly put his faith in a man who turned as easily as that'.

'Again, what if he and Odd met somewhere after we parted?' Theodolf asks.

'They do not know one another well enough. Anyway, I do not think Odd was any more friendly toward the Northmen than Burhred', I answer again, to laughter from Theorvard. As much as Theodolf has me thinking hard, I dismiss it knowing they had little dealing with one another in our sight after we met Dunstan's friend.

Burhred helped take Odd down from the tree, and we all thought the lad to be dead until he came to.

Burhred comes back through the curtain of mist leading a horse. I do not recall the animal. Is it one of the spare mounts we held onto?

I ask Theorvard as Burhred slowly nears us,

'Is that the horse he took the other night?'

'Theodolf knows better than I. Is it one we had?' Theorvard in turn asks Theodolf, who nods sombrely.

'If you are wondering about this horse – 'Burhred begins.

'I was', I know what he is about to tell me, 'and these two tell me it is the self-same mount you were allowed to take after that attack on me'.

194

'I did not know it was *you* until you shouted. By then I knew you were no foe, but you were in no mood to listen', Burhred tries to tell me a different story now.

'That same night you tried to say your attack on me was in jest!' I shout fit to burst my lungs.

'*Quiet, Ivar!*' Theorvard tells me, 'The mist will count for nothing if you give us away shouting at him. Leave be and we will part company when we are closer to Lunden'.

'How do *you* feel about Burhred riding with us into Lunden?' I ask Theodolf, Saeward and Wulfmaer.

Theodolf looks away from Burhred and nods to me,

'If needs must', he adds with a sigh, and turns away again.

Arms folded, Saeward and Wulfmaer nod wearily first at Burhred and then at me. The matter is settled. Burhred may understand Theodolf's aloofness toward him, but he cannot fathom Theorvard's change of heart. He gives Theorvard a curt nod and keeps his own counsel. Only time will tell whether these two can really stand one another's company for the ride back from our errand.

Only days – *hours* ago Theorvard would willingly have torn Burhred limb from limb without a second thought. Now he gives him leave to ride back with us.

'I think it time we mounted', I tell Theorvard and signal the others to do likewise.

'Aye, this mist will make our ride easier as long as we stay on these grassy tracks. Were we to ride on earth they could follow us. We must be fairly close to Odo's limit by now', Theorvard agrees, 'and once beyond that they will not wish to waste their time.

Saeward and Wulfmaer watch us closely, to see what we are about.

Wulfmaer clambers up into his saddle, still as clumsily as ever but a little quicker. Saeward has mastered the art of stirrup-aided mounting and makes it look easier. Theodolf has to take his time, the pus from his wound still seeping into the dressing Saeward made for him when we broke our ride this morning.

Theorvard gives Theodolf a helping hand up into the saddle, and grins when the lad almost tips over onto the other side of his horse,

'Will you believe me if I say I am sorry?' Theorvard asks.

'Little do you know your own strength', Theodolf laughs and winces. It still hurts, but he keeps his smiles and quips, 'Next time you will send me over so hard I will land on the other side with my head buried in the road!'

He sucks in his cheeks with the pain and raps on Theorvard's helm to show that he has not taken the giant's help amiss, but I cannot help thinking he would sooner not have been helped. Saeward looks worriedly at Theodolf but says nothing.

'I can stand the pain', Theodolf scowls. 'What I cannot stand is your fussing!'

'He only has your welfare at heart, Theodolf. He has kept you alive with his dressings, so the least you can do is show your thanks'. Were I Saeward I would have rebuked the lad.

'Theodolf must be in great pain', Saeward allows for Theodolf's lack of manners.

'Aye, but he must also be mindful of the feelings of others!' Theorvard hisses, his deep-set blue eyes flashing angrily beneath a pair of beetling eyebrows, 'Do you not think so, Ivar?!'

'Leave the lad alone, Theorvard. As Saeward says, he must be in great pain. When we are closer to Lunden we will slow the horses to a trot to afford him a less painful ride', I press Braenda to a trot and we set off.

Willelm has pushed much further west in his bid to outflank Eadgar, and has stretched his supply lines thinly. How far has he gone since his men were seen by Wigmund a week or ten days ago? Odo will have to hold his men back if he does not want to risk Willelm's wrath with a northward push of his own, the strengthening of his defences at Hrofesceaster notwithstanding.

How have Thegn Aelfwold and his friend Brihtwig fared since we left them - are they still free, with their small band of dispossessed ceorls and freemen? The likelihood of their staying out of the Northmen's clutches will be smaller by the day if Odo goes on tightening his hold on the northern Centish shore.

We must be close to Watling Straet. I think back to when I saw the low hills that seemed to roll westward to Suthrige. When I saw them last from this side Theodolf's fine show of bowmanship had left Oslac and young Sigegar stirred. It will not be long before we come over the brow of the hill behind Grenewic again, hopefully with another half day's riding.

Although the mist has lifted we slacken our horses' stride for Theodolf's sake. The land is open all around and there is no sign of Odo's scouts.

Save for a huddle of Centishfolk coming toward us, there are no others sharing this track. They close on us slowly, a few hopeful-looking ceorls and their kindred trudging way we came. Whips are flicked at lumbering oxen, small carts piled high with belongings rumbling behind them over this tightly packed clay track.

Children stand gawping at us, pointing. Fathers chide, mothers cluck at their offspring and clutch at small hands for them to follow. We ride on. Someone must have put it about that it is safe to go home. Perhaps Odo has drawn in his horns for now.

'The Northmen must be further back than we thought', Theorvard calls out to me, turning in his saddle. He has put himself on point, over to our right since coming up onto the open land. 'I should say we *can* take our ease now'.

I nod, rein in Braenda and stand in my stirrups to look around. Happy in the thought that there are no signs of Northman patrols hereabouts, I wave everyone on.

'Look over there', Saeward points to the west, 'I wonder what that settlement is. Does anyone live there, do you think?'

There are dwellings clustered around a taller, longer building, a thegn's hall perhaps. And then I see them, between two buildings that lie closest to a small patch of woodland. A small company of horsemen, perhaps a dozen all told, lances pointing upward, pennons fluttering in the stiffening breeze that cleared this morning's mist.

'God, where did *they* come from?' I almost shout, taken aback with seeing them so suddenly.

'*What?*' Theorvard looks around and where Saeward points them out for him. 'Oh *Christ*, we have to outrun them now, and what with Theodolf in need of a rest!'

'No, we do not *outrun* them', I tell him.

'What then, do we go *at* them? Think about it - they are more than twice our number', Theorvard talks to me as if I were mad.

'Do *you* think they have seen us yet?' I ask Saeward.

'It is hard to say, but I think no. They would have begun to ride toward us, surely', he answers, still watching them.

'I think they are watching something - over there, on the ground'.

'Then we make a turn for the hamlet', I say.

'Are we taking our fight to them?' Burhred grins as he sees what I am about.

'You want to get us all killed, so close to home?' Wulfmaer thinks that I have lost my wits. 'We are outnumbered!'

'How are you with that bow, Wulfmaer?' I ask him quickly. I want to hear an 'aye'. 'Do you think you could have an arrow ready across it by the time we are within a hundred paces from them?

'Well, I suppose so', he answers hesitatingly.

'Can you, or *not?*' I demand, still watching the Northmen. A riderless horse prances at the end of the line, its reins held loosely by one of the mounted men.

'Aye, all right then, *I can!*' he snaps and pulls his bow up over his head.

Theorvard asks Burhred for his bow.

'You have the lance', Burhred tells him. 'Your shoulder may not be up to the strain of drawing a bow yet'.

'Give me the bow!' growls Theorvard.

Burhred meekly hands over the bow, pulls down on the helm nose-piece and rests the lance under his right arm in the manner of a North-man. He looks so much like one of them they will not know the three of us, Burhred, Saeward and I for not being Northmen until too late.

By then they will be too shaken to fight well.

I pull on my own helm and take hold of the lance. There is little to choose between one of our huscarl's helms and a Northman's. My axe rests in the socket just behind the saddle that is meant for the lance. Saeward, too, is ready to ride now.

We must look like Northmen, with Theorvard and Wulfmaer behind us, because even at a hundred paces they have not looked up. One man turns, peers at us and turns back. We are merely another troop seeking spoils. Theodolf rides behind me, in the middle of our short line.

'What do *I* do?' Theodolf calls out from behind.

'*You stay alive!*' I answer. On hearing no more from him I urge Braenda into a canter.

The Northmen are still watching what is going on in front of them when we bear down on them. Some wheel their horses around, but they have no room within their ring to wield their lances before ours tear into them. The others scatter to left and right.

What they were watching was one of their leaders raping a young woman.

Theorvard and Wulfmaer let fly their arrows, Saeward catches a Northman with his axe, scything into the fellow's midriff, spraying blood everywhere. Burhred breaks his lance trying to catch a second foe, throws it down onto the ground away from the woman, and hurls himself onto the leader before the man can pull up his breeks. Burhred brings down his sword once, like a meat cleaver onto the Northman's shoulder. When one of the others tries to attack him from behind, I stab my lance into his chest, pulling him off his horse when I draw back the head.

One yells behind me and I narrowly miss being skewered. Bare-handed Wulfmaer pulls the offender from his horse and rips upward into the man's belly with his hunting knife as he does so.

When I look up, three Northmen have fled eastward for the safety of Hrofesceaster. Theorvard draws Burhred's bow and brings down one of them, then groans and drops the weapon. Burhred's look says, 'I told you so', but he holds back the words. Theodolf looks awe-struck at Theorvard's skill with the bow, his mouth open as if he were choking. Saeward claps Theorvard on his other shoulder and shouts gleefully,

'Well *done* – even *wounded* your bowmanship is great!'

'I hope this damned shoulder heals soon!' Theorvard groans, nursing his wound.

'What do we do about *her?*' Saeward asks'.

'What *can* we do?' I ask out aloud and dismount. I make my way over to her between the bodies and kneel down on one knee. She cowers away from me with my helm on, so I doff it and ask her name.

'Why give you my name if you are going to do the same as he wanted to do?!' she smirks.

'Do I sound like a Northman?' I ask her.

'You *look* like one', she snaps, and whether you are Northmen or their friends, you are as bad *however* you talk!'

'We have been spying on them in the *south*', I answer, still on one knee, our eyes almost level, 'and we have had to kill a few to get their war gear. When you are few you can but try to look like them. You have to dress in their war gear if you need to get food from them. As it is, my helm is the one given to me by King Harold'.

The woman sniffles and wipes her nose on a sleeve. Her suffering is still plain to see, her cheeks wet from the tears of torment. She buries her head in her hands for a few moments, then looks up at me,

'I am Aelfhild', she tells me slowly, 'I live here'.

'Is there no-one else here? You cannot stay here on your own', Saeward asks, standing next to me.

'My folk will be back', Aelfhild looks up at Saeward, smiling. 'Are you sure you are not Northmen?'

'As God is my witness –', Saeward begins.

'No, we are *not* Northmen, Aelfhild', I tell her again, my hand on my heart. 'Trust me. I give you my word on that. Are you sure your folk will be back? We saw some along the track going south a short time ago'.

'They must have been from elsewhere. My folk will have left for the woods', she answers, a wavering finger pointing westward.

'Leaving you behind', Burhred is now standing behind me.

'I did not know they had gone before the Northmen came. I had been gathering kindling for the fire and they would have thought I was still in the woods', Aelfhild sniffs again and spits on one of the dead lying close to her with a long tear in his hauberk and a gash across his chest. 'I came out of the woods just as they entered the hamlet'.

'Where is your thegn?' I ask, waving idly at the longhouse.

'He was killed along with our fyrdmen when King Harold fought the Northmen', Aelfhild stares at each one of us in turn.

'Where were *you* then?'

'Apart from Wulfmaer and Saeward here, we also fought the Northmen on Caldbec Beorg', I tell her, trying to smile.

'Where is *that?*' she asks.

'It is where King Harold sought to halt Duke Willelm on his way to Lunden', I answer, 'above Haestingas, in the Andredes Leag'.

'You have a funny way of talking. I have never heard anyone talk the way you do! Where are you *from?*' Aelfhild wrinkles her nose in a manner of laughing, having forgotten her plight.

'My name is Ivar, and I am a kinsman of King Harold', I tell her. 'If you are sure about your folk coming back soon we will have to leave you here-'

'Hey what are you *doing,* threatening my wife?' I feel my sword arm being wrenched sharply back.

A fellow pushes between Theorvard and Saeward, and threatens me with a hoe. He almost tramples Aelfhild and Theorvard pulls him out of the way before he does her harm.

'I said *who* are you?!' the grating voice comes again.

I am being threatened by a stocky young man with a knife in his hand, ready to thrust at my chest as if I were likely to let him.

'*Ecgberht,* you fool, these good men saved my life!' Aelfhild jumps to her feet and thumps the young fellow's chest before one of us gives him a lesson in manners. 'If you had wanted to be a great warrior *you* should have threatened the Northman who tried to rape me!'

Ecgberht turns and stares dully at us, unable to understand what it is his wife has told him - but he is trying. The fellow is slow-witted and I wonder how it is Aelfhild could not find any better in her neighbour-hood, unless in the time-honoured way of finding a wife, threatening her father was the only way he could win her.

However, Ecgberht soon sees what has gone on here,

'The Northmen caught you – *how?*'

'I came back from the woods with kindling and all of you had gone...vanished. No sooner had I turned in my tracks to look for you, when the outlanders rode in. They were looking for sport', Aelfhild tells him.

She is almost his height, rich dark hair tumbles over her shoulders and down her back. Straight of limb and with a finely-shaped face with icy blue eyes, Aelfhild is a woman he could never hope to win with his lack of wiles. Ecgberht is of middle height, doe-eyed, slightly stooped, as are many who work the land, and roughly drawn.

Hard work throughout a ceorl's life will do this to a man, but what he has hewn from the earth is his, after his tithes have been paid. None of the men with him is much for the women to choose from, not that any of *them* are much better looking. Only one other woman is equal to Aelfhild. We will soon know who is worth knowing before we go.

'Are you hungry?' Ecgberht asks me, brightening with the knowledge that we are on his side, and offers the only reward he can give. It is the only reward we would take for doing our duty by our Lord and master Eadgar.

'We would gladly take as much as you can offer without you and your fellows going hungry yourselves', I answer honestly. I know I could eat a whole roasted bullock on my own, never mind what my friends' sharpened appetites would allow them.

'There is not a lot. *They* took most of our harvest. We have a drinkable ale, fruit, bread and salted meat', Ecgberht offers happily.

Theorvard and the others all nod quickly. Burhred walks to his horse and pulls out a bag, one taken from the Northmen to carry bread or root vegetables,

'As we are within a day's ride of Lunden, we had best finish the deer meat before it goes off! Here, help yourselves. There should be enough for everyone', Burhred drops the bag on the grass.

Aelfhild squats, showing smooth white thighs through her torn smock, opens the bag and pulls out some of the meat,

'We have never had this meat other than at feasts, when Thegn Cynrig told us we could', she stands again with a piece of the shoulder, the bone showing where Theorvard chopped it neatly.

Her neighbours and their wives busy themselves bringing food from their homes for everyone. They all want a feast to forget the coming of the Northmen. Some of the menfolk help Ecgberht and four of us drag the dead Northmen into the trees, away from their settlement.

Theodolf stands talking to one of the young women, who moons up at him like a love-stricken cow. His self-esteem needs a boost after this gruelling week! She stares at his wounds as he shows them, worshipping him and every word he says. Theorvard looks his way and shakes his head,

'That takes me back to when I was first taken into Thegn Eadmund's household. There was a young woman who always looked at me like that when we came back from teaching the fyrdmen. One day, when I had not yet pulled my shirt back on after swilling my chest in cold water, she saw me and keeled over'.

He laughs at the thought of a woman fainting with longing for him and recalls,

'For a whole week she could not do her work. She was still in a day-dream over seeing my bare chest! The other women were peeing themselves laughing at her, but she was in love – or so she thought'.

'What happened after that? Did you plough her furrow?' Wulfmaer has just finished dragging one big Northman into the bushes and has stopped to listen in.

'You have a way with words that fills me with awe, miller. Go and stuff yourself!' He turns to me and asks – or is he telling me? - 'How is it you cannot have a good talk these days without someone bringing it down to tilling the land or digging turnips or some such?!'

Theorvard puts on a look of mock disgust with Wulfmaer.

'What *did* happen, then?' I ask him with a wink.

'I ploughed her furrow, as he said', Theorvard grins and walks away, laughing aloud, across the grass to join Theodolf.

Burhred passes just then and looks at me with a gleam in his eye,

'You are happy suddenly, *how so?*' he asks. 'Has she offered you something for after your food? You will have to watch out for her man, though' Burhred catches my arm and looks into my eyes. 'Aye, you have taken a shine to this Aelfhild, I can tell'.

'Theorvard is right, worthwhile talk is becoming rare these days!' I say out aloud and make my way over to where Theodolf still holds the young woman enthralled with tales of bravery and warring.

'Well, Theodolf, have you told her about that dragon you slew yesterday?' I look at her as I say this.

Her eyes open wide and her hands reach to her mouth, knuckles white between rows of even, whiter teeth. The lad knows how to draw a fair maiden into his net, but I do not mind giving him a helping hand, 'And tell her about the bear'.

Theodolf gives me a knowing wink. He has grown to manhood since I first laid eyes on him not so long ago.

'I was just getting to that'.

It looks as if Theodolf is playing her along. He needs no help from me! I walk on to where Aelfhild and Ecgberht are getting out beakers for our ale. They are talking quietly together, smiling.

'How is it going?' I ask, burning with envy, but it looks as though I shall have to wait until I am under one roof again with Aelfthryth!

Aelfhild looks up from standing the beakers on the table. Ecgberht goes on putting out beakers without even peering sideways at me.

'You can bring your friends over now', Aelfhild tells me stiffly. I take it this is for Ecgberhrt's sake, so I keep the smile and make a half turn to Theorvard, who is already walking across the wet grass to me.

'Aye, Ivar, I heard', Theorvard answers and turns, cupping his hands

202

to his mouth, shouting loud enough even for Wulfmaer to hear from where he stands at the end of the hamlet. 'All right, now get over *here* lads!'

Theodolf looks over his admirer's head and waves, then puts his right hand on her shoulder and turns her. He is about to lead her over when we hear an unearthly bellowing noise, as if a bull had worked loose from his tethers. The young woman looks around, startled, and hides behind Theodolf as a heavily-built fellow lopes across the grass and lays bodily into the lad, knocking him backward. It is all we can do to pull him off as he kicks my friend in his ribs.

'*Fool*, Ealhstan! *Get off him!*' Ecgberht wades in between Theorvard and me and throws his neighbour head over heels backward. 'I said get *off* him, Ealhstan!'

'Ecgberht, *he was mauling my woman!*' Ealhstan whines bitterly.

'*No* he was *not!* He was only *talking* to her', I take my hands from Ealhstan's bull-like shoulders and stare into his eyes.

'I would not allow one of my friends to mistreat a woman. Theodolf was being friendly'.

'That is *not* how it looked to *me!*' Ealhstan howls, trying to get at Theodolf between Theorvard and Ecgberht.

'I only touched her shoulder to follow me to the feast', Theodolf, sprawled on the grass, winces with pain.

Ealhstan snorts, eyebrows low over a furrowed nose, like a bull shielding a cow. We stand, ringing him, waiting for him to calm down.

Aelfhild comes and squares up to him in a way that reminds me of the tale of David and Goliath that Harold told me once. Holding his wrists she looks up at Ealhstan and hisses,

'Why not put a chain around Aethelgyfu's neck and lead her, so that you can keep your eye on her at all times!' She adds, for good measure, 'I do not know what she sees in you, but perhaps one day she will tell me what hold you have over her. *Get a hold on yourself man,* or leave here if you cannot behave!'

'But he was going to *steal her* from me!' Ealhstan trumpets, near to weeping.

Ecgberht snaps, tired of Ealhstan's childishness,

'Aethelgyfu would *not* let anyone take her, believe me!'

Ecgberht tells him now,

'Yet perhaps she should, sooner than put up with you!'

Ealhstan the 'bull' is being tamed. This is a show no man should miss if he wishes to learn of the power a woman can have over a man, whatever size he is! He sinks to his knees and weeps, hands over his eyes to shield his misery.

'He is like this every time anyone talks to her', Aelfhild begs our forgiveness on his behalf. 'I am afraid your friend will have to stay clear of her until you go again.'

'By all means', I assure her and nod at Theodolf to stand up.

'*Not until the troll leaves!*' Theodolf waves his arm at Ealhstan.

I can see his meaning. The strength of the young fellow can be felt just by gripping his powerful arms.

Ecgberht leads Ealhstan away, followed closely by Aethelgyfu and Aelfhild.

'What was the name your friend gave Ealhstan?' Aelfhild asks me later as we finish off the food and ale. She pours me another measure of ale and awaits my answer.

'Grendel was the troll killed by Beowulf in the tale of the Geat warrior. Do you know the story of Beowulf?' I ask her.

Ecgberht stands behind her, crunching an apple as he listens to me telling of the killing of Grendel, his mother and later death of Beowulf himself after the slaying of the fire breathing fiend, the guardian of Hygelac's treasure.

By this time everyone gathers closely to listen to me by the crackling fire, hushed. When I have finished the telling, Theorvard taps me on my shoulder and says I should have had a lyre to play whilst telling. Everyone laughs and claps their hands. As I seat myself on a fallen tree trunk Aelfhild joins me, Ecgberht not far behind, as if on a leash.

'These long, dark nights are made for the telling of tales, of fetches, goblins - beings who crawl from their holes in the winter time to threaten our worldly lives', Aelfhild's eyes are wide as she looks upward at the blanket of twinkling lights. 'Do you know the names of these pricks of light in the heavens, Ivar?'

After some head-scratching I have to allow that, broadly speaking, I am at a loss about these things,

'I know of some that we use to steer by, such as the Great Bear and the North Star. Other than them... I am afraid I would be at a great loss to name'.

She points out the lines of the mighty hunter, and to the North Star that I knew already,

'...And *there* is the plough, that line of bright stars over there to the east', she finishes and smiles up at the tiny pinpricks of light, some brighter than the others.

'Who told you all this?' I ask. If her man were not close by I would have made a pass at her by now, but such is the enthralment of men by women that Ecgberht would have me stretched out on the grass awaiting my maker. *He* is the luckiest man here.

'My father was lately a fisherman, cutting through the folds of God's watery fastness, harvesting the plentiful shoals of herring before he took to harvesting the folds of the land around here. He passed on to me his love of the ways of the stars in the heavens'. She looks longingly upward and goes on to tell me of her wish to be a seafarer. 'If I had been a man I, too would gone to sea as he did', she shakes her head in regret and looks up at me, 'on which broad green-grey fastness did you steer your craft through the brine steepnesses, Ivar?'

The woman could reach into my chest and take out my heart, and I cannot see my way to losing myself to her when Braenda could slip into her body and ride me instead. I smile and keep my hands to myself. Perhaps because she knows I am holding myself back.

'Ecgberht will be sound asleep soon after emptying one of your skins of Northman apple ale on his own'.

As if to prove her right, Ecgberht yawns, stretches himself to his full height and turns to his wife to tell her,

'Aelfhild, I must be abed. The dawn will come soon enough to drag me from my slumbers'.

'Let me finish my drink first, dearest husband. I will be with you soon'. He hovers, unsure, until she shows him her half-empty beaker

Everyone has moved away and she wears a broad grin that tells me I may yet be lucky. I lean forward to kiss her and she holds back,

'*Not* here', Aelfhild points to the hall on our left, takes my hand and leads me across the leaf-strewn, damp grass. Something in this gives me a shiver down my back. Is it the tingle of taking a man's wife close enough to him to be sent to my maker if he senses she has not come to him?

I need not fear. No-one sees us enter Thegn Cynrig's hall.

'He took *all* his huscarls with him. The beds are still covered since the lady of the house left to stay with her father in Grenewic.

I might ask, 'How do you know this? Have you brought another lover here?' It would be foolish of me to risk her wrath. Instead I quietly follow her, up creaking steps into a darkened room.

Aelfhild lights candles mounted on an iron stand and turns back to look into my eyes,

'I have never before felt this way for a man since I was wed to Ecgberht', she stretches on her toes, kisses me and pushes me back with her lithe body toward a well-covered bed. 'Since seeing you today, I feel I do not want to let you go without feeling your warmth on my skin - and inside me'.

She unbuckles my sword belt slowly, dropping it to the floor by the bed, and helps me pull off the mailcoat. In the dim candlelight her ice-blue eyes burn. Her lips part as she pulls off my shirt and plants kisses on my chest, neck - up to my mouth. In the way Braenda did, Aelfhild climbs astride me and bends forward kissing my chest as she pulls back the belt from my breeks. I pull back her dark hair and hold it to the nape of her neck. When she looks up at me I find I am looking into Braenda's hazel eyes.

'Do you think I could live without you for so long, Ivar? *I ache for you with my whole body!*'

I am stunned by Braenda's showing suddenly like this,

'How – what have you *done* with -?' I begin to ask her.

'Aelfhild is asleep beside her man, as she should be – as I should be beside *you*, what else? Ivar, you have *me!* Fill me with your seed and give me a son I can raise for us to be *proud* of!'

'What was all that about your father being a seaman, and talking of the stars? Was it *you*, or Aelfhild?' I must be mad to ask, when I have a woman in the bed with me after what must be a week riding around Suth Seaxe and Centland, hiding from Northmen, fighting them and raiding their food stores as well as being hounded through woodlands.

'Who *cares* about that now? Let me make love to you and help you forget what has kept us apart!' I cup my hands around her full breasts and hear her purring like a cat that has licked the cream again.

'Who cares *indeed?*'I hear myself saying before losing myself in Braenda's warm, soft body.

11

I have no way of knowing what it is that awakes me from my deep slumbers. When I hear a door being slammed shut somewhere I sit bolt upright in the bed, alone. Another door slams elsewhere in Thegn Cynrig's hall. I leap from the bed and reach for my clothes. I almost have my mailcoat on when Theorvard bursts into the room, out of breath and red-cheeked from running.

'I was told you were here! Get ready, and be quick about it. Someone has seen Northmen, *riding this way!*'

'Are they many?' I ask as I pick up my sword belt.

'It hardly matters how many there are. There are more of them than there are of us. Now come on, buckle that on and be down as soon as you can! The horses are saddled and ready. It is almost daylight out there – who did you come here *with?*'

Theorvard looks slyly at me, grinning,

'It was Aelfhild who lured you up here. She will have hell to pay with her man if she did!'

I say nothing and thump down the creaking stairway after Theorvard, who takes the steps three at a time to the cavernous, still dark hall, almost knocking Wulfmaer from his feet as he rushes in,

'Come on, get mounted. Those damned Northmen are back, *and in strength!*' Wulfmaer yells, almost panic-stricken.

I yell back as Theorvard hustles me out through the door,

'*What about these folk from the hamlet -?*'

'They have all *gone*. Saeward saw the Northmen coming from afar and alerted everyone. My guess is they are most likely back in the woods'.

'*All of them?*' I ask again as I hoist myself onto Braenda.

'What did I *say?*' Wulfmaer turns to Theorvard as if I had gone deaf.

'Theorvard answers, waving an arm westward toward the woods and Wulfmaer nods gravely,

'*All* of them!'

'Right then, it is time we left too!' I wheel Braenda around and the others follow. We must make headway quickly if we are to outride the Northmen on their bigger mounts.

As we gain the open land to the north of the hamlet I look over my shoulder and see how many of Odo's men there are. A score of them chase after us across the fields. What would I not give for Oslac and

Sigeric to be here!

'Theodolf I promise you we will give you an easier ride just as soon as we lose our pursuers!' I call across to him. He does not seem to be able to hear me above the thunder of the hooves.

I put my head down and ride Braenda as hard as she can gallop. She can not keep up this speed for as long as their horses could. Nevertheless our horses are rested and we have to hope they tire their horses unduly. They will have ridden from Hrofesceaster, ten miles to the east. I would say we are as far from Lunden.

How close to Lunden would they risk riding? For at least a half hour the Northmen keep up with us, riding as far behind us as they were to begin with, hoping to tire our mounts.

Only three of us are riding stolen horses, many of the rest we set free before starting out on the homeward run. We have two spare mounts that Wulfmaer and Saeward are leading, but there is no time to change unless it can be done whilst riding. Both Theorvard's and Wulfmaer's horses are bigger than Braenda, so they will not tire as quickly. Wulfmaer is close behind me with Burhred bringing up the rear. Saeward is ahead, riding side by side with Theodolf should the lad show signs of wearying.

Theorvard is to my right, watching over his shoulder from time to time to see how we are faring against the 'hunters'. He sees me looking at him and shakes his head. Either that means the Northmen are gaining on us, or we are making their horses sweat. I have to push Braenda harder, hoping that she can hold her own against the bigger horses.

The miles hurtle by, the ground blurs. If *my* heart is thumping, I think Braenda's must be *pounding* like a smith's hammer on his anvil. She was bred for surefootedness, for crossing high hills in Wealas, not for headlong galloping. Her breathing is still steady but if I ride her too hard she will not make it to Suthgeweorce!

I drop back and wave down Wulfmaer,

'I need to change mounts whilst we are still riding!' I shout, 'But I cannot do that until we are on more even ground!'

He nods that he understands and slackens the reins on the spare mount for it to pass to my side behind his mount. When she is on my side we ride hard for a little longer.

'You can change mounts just a short way ahead!' Wulfmaer yells to me and points to where the going looks even.

I look back and see the gap between us and the Northmen is no greater, nor is it any less. I call out to Wulfmaer, who slackens his reins,

'Now, *change over!*' He reaches out his arm, passing the reins of the spare mount.

The two animals thunder across even, dry ground for some time side by side and I see it is time to change horses. Raising my left foot over the saddle, however, is hard enough at this speed. The land looks more uneven ahead, so I have to take the risk. I lift my right foot from the stirrup and lean forward, pull the other horse closer and stretch out my right leg to ready myself. Wulfmaer has come about behind me during this time. He draws closer on the other side of me and reaches out for Braenda's reins, catching them on the third attempt.

I reach for the other mount's saddle and heave myself over, almost falling over the other side. My feet find the stirrups and the two horses canter along together, gathering speed once more.

On looking behind again, I see our pursuers have gained. Theodolf, Saeward, Theorvard and Burhred have left me behind. Only Wulfmaer is with me. He reaches out to me with Braenda's reins and as I grab them from him we quicken our pace again. As we splash through a narrow ford men rush out from homes that flank a rubble-strewn track.

I hear shouting. Someone points at the pursuing Northmen. Men vanish into the darkness of their homes and show again with hunting bows. Theorvard reins in and jumps down from his horse, Saeward and Burhred join him in a dash back to the ford as the Northmen hurtle at the ford. The front rank splashes through the shallows, riding closer together through a gap in the trees. This is when several of the local men loose off arrows at them.

Theorvard, Wulfmaer and Burhred stand, bows at the ready and hold their arrows for a second arrow hail until our pursuers' first two ranks have drawn close enough together to make their arrows count. A second hail of arrows is unleashed heavenward, dropping onto the bunched riders, cutting many of them down.

Three of the Northmen try to cross the narrow river away from the ford. Their horses stumble on the wet, moss-covered rocks of the uneven riverbed. Some of the Centishmen splash through the ford and bring down the hapless riders still floundering in the shallows.

Cutting the saddle straps and pushing their knives between the links of their chain mail, they instil fear into the Northmen.

One of them screeches, having been brought down under the hooves of his panicking mount. The river churns and boils red between the legs of the screaming horses where their riders thrash, unhorsed, trying to flee their attackers. Whether one of the dead horsemen is one of their leaders, I do not know, but the men left behind on the far bank are suddenly no longer eager to close on us.

Seeing the foolishness of out-staying their welcome the rest of the horsemen turn about and thrash their mounts to outrun the hail of arrows that follows them. When they are far enough away, and look as though they will not be making a second attack the Centishmen stand and cheer loudly, for long enough to know the foe has heard them above the pounding of their horses' hooves.

'What is the name of this settlement, and who are you?' I ask the first man who nears with his arms outstretched in welcome.

'This is Egensford, and I am Swetman. Your men helped see off the Northmen, for which I am grateful! You are?'

'I am Ivar, huscarl of King Eadgar, and these are my comrades', I show Swetman to Theorvard, Saeward, Burhred, Theodolf and Wulfmaer in turn.

'They have each been of great worth to me in our errand for our new king'.

'I thought all the king's huscarls were killed with our thegn at Caldbec Beorg -' Swetman begins.

'Luckily many men outlived them. Lord Ansgar, King Harold's *stallari*, helped beat Duke Willelm's men at Suthgeweorce not so long since', I put in, but allow that he is not wrong. You are right inasmuch as many good men did die. But, as I said, enough of us lived through the slaughter to give Duke Willelm's men a bloody nose'.

Swetman peers at me as he asks, or rather tells me,

'And you were doubly one of the lucky ones', he smiles, 'because if we were not here the Northmen would have chased you all the way to Grenewic - if you had lasted that long'.

'Aye, you are right. We *were* doubly lucky', Theorvard answers from behind me. I do not know how long he has been listening in. Did he also gather what Swetman hinted at? If we *had* fallen to the Northmen, perhaps he would have thought more of us.

'Dead men cannot fight', I add.

I am given a friendly clap on the back from Theorvard as he passes behind me.

Someone offers ale. Everyone but Theodolf wanders over to where one of the older women fills the beakers that a younger woman hands out beside her. There is bread, cheese and salted lamb, offered by a fair haired child.

'Sigehild, take some food to the young man there', the young woman tells the child, pointing to Theodolf.

The child holds back. When I smile at her and take food from the platter she is to take to Theodolf, she looks fit to burst into tears.

'Let her bring it over', Theodolf calls and I smilingly put the food back on the platter for little Sigehild to take to him. He smiles and thanks her before she rushes back to hide behind her mother's apron.

'What is the matter with you today, Sigehild?' her mother chides.

'She does well', I laugh. 'I would never have gone anywhere *near* outsiders at her age!'

The young woman smiles and walks on with the beakers, leading her child slowly. Sigehild looks back over her shoulder at Theodolf and beams brightly.

'Aethelfrida is our thegn's widow', Swetman tells me. 'Sigehild is her only child'.

It is as if he could read my thoughts. When I came round after being hit on the head on Caldbec Beorg, my first wish was to be with the huscarls fighting around Harold. It took time for me to know I was of more use to him alive, to carry on the fight against Willelm. Not everyone thought that way, I know.

Luckily Theorvard, Burhred and Theodolf were also still alive, having lived through another clash. How much longer can they fail to curb us? Odo must be frantic with fury by now.

'You will have to leave soon... For our sakes', Swetman tells me.

'We will be leaving. I have tidings for King Eadgar', I tell him, 'and Theodolf's wounds must be seen to. Saeward can only do so much whilst we are underway. He must be well rested and fresh before he can be of further use to the king'.

'Is that the Eadgar who came with his father, the *aetheling* Eadweard nine years ago?' Swetman asks. 'We were at Dofnan when his ship docked. They had some rare-looking men on that ship, wonderfully clothed, but his woman was good looking, though, what was her name -?'

'Agatha, mother to Eadgar, Margareta and Christina was at Thorney when I saw her last. Her kinsman was Heanric, the Germans' king.

Swetman looks pained, as if I had given him too much to think about, then adds,

'I just wanted to say that I think the Northmen will be back again before long, that is all', he gives a shrug and walks away slowly, sipping his ale. I stride across the open ground to where Saeward is quietly munching on a chunk of bread, 'with many more men'.

'How goes it?' Saeward talks through the bread he is chewing when he sees me near.

I nod in answer. What I need to know most of all is whether Theodolf thinks he can bear the ride on to Lunden. Swetman is keen to be rid of us before the Northmen come again.

'Do you feel fit to ride, Theodolf?' I ask the lad, and make a half turn to speak to Saeward, 'I want to know if Theodolf's wound dressing

211

needs changing before we ride on'.

'I have looked at his dressing. His wounds look no worse, but he needs rest. Being kicked in the ribs by Ealhstan would have done him no good', Saeward tells me. What I told Swetman is no idle guess about Theodolf's health. I should have liked him to rest longer.

He looks at me as if to ask 'Is that all?' and goes on eating.

I look back at Theodolf before I leave them again to speak to Theorvard.

'I feel well enough to ride on to Lunden, if that is what your thoughts rest on', Theodolf tells me between mouthfuls of lamb.

I nod and make my way back to Theorvard. He is talking with Aethelfrida when I join him and looks up when I greet them,

'Is Theodolf well enough to ride yet?' he asks, taking care not to talk too loudly so that neither Theodolf nor Saeward overhear him.

'He seems to think so, and Saeward agrees with him. We ride as soon as we are ready'. On looking up at the clouds scudding over the trees from the east I finish, 'I think the rain will be with us again, too. That may help us clear this hundred without too much meddling from Odo's men'.

Theorvard finishes his ale and Aethelfrida takes his beaker. She nods to me, walking away slowly toward the older woman. I watch after her, telling the young giant,

'Saddle up when you are ready', I tell him. 'Where are Burhred and Wulfmaer?'

'Burhred went into one of the homes with a young woman', Theorvard grins. 'Wulfmaer is talking to one of their bowmen'.

'Find Burhred and bring him to his horse. Hopefully he has not given her something to think of him by!' I tell Theorvard, mindful that it is I who should be looking for him, but as he knows which dwelling Burhred entered, I would be wasting useful time.

'That is easily enough done', Theorvard answers breezily and shouts out,

'Burhred you diddling fool, get out here unless you want us to leave you for the Northmen!' he strides along the fronts of the dwellings, stops at one doorway and waves to me. I hasten to him, fearing the worst.

'Have you found him?' I ask when I am still some way away from him.

'In a way, I have. One of these good folk found him first, though'. Theorvard waits until I reach him, and nods at Burhred lying sprawled on his back on the earthen floor of the dwelling, naked in a pool of his own blood. In his right hand he clasps a piece of cloth. I would guess that was ripped from the clothing of the man who killed him, or from the shift of the woman he bedded when he thought no-one was looking. In death, as in life, his mouth is twisted in a foolish grin. Where countless Northmen could not bring him to book, he has picked a bedmate unwisely and fallen foul of an unknown husband. His weakness for womanly flesh has seen him cut down in his prime.

'They can deal with him, Theorvard, *we must be away!*'

I pull my young friend away from the doorway, almost running back to where our horses await us and throw myself onto Braenda's saddle. Unsteadied by my hasty mounting of her, she takes a few steps backward. I lean forward and pat her neck, '*Sorry*, Braenda!'

When Theorvard is back in his saddle we set off, only ahead of our new pursuers. More Northmen ride in again from the east.

'*Make for the woods!*' I shout, waving away from Egensford.

The trees have shed most of their leaves, enabling anyone to see further into the woods, but soon it will be too dark to follow us. The crisp red of the afteryear sunset matches the deep reds of the leaves that carpet the ground here. A bank of bluish-grey clouds coming in from the west threatens the restful outlook. We should be able to sit here and take in the way these hues blend, but instead we have to flee Odo's underlings, angered like hornets out to sting their comrades' killers. We can only hope their horses will tire after hurtling over this uneven land. We could soon outrun them.

Saeward looks back at to where Theorvard and I had come from, as if to ask the whereabouts of Burhred.

'*Burhred has met his match!*' I shout over the pounding of hooves on the dry, open grassland.

When I look over one shoulder I see our pursuers are riding hard, the pennons on their lances dancing furiously in the freshening wind. They must dearly want to catch up with us after the bloodying we gave them, but I sense that their horses are already slowing with the weight of their hauberks, their weaponry and heavy saddles.

Saeward looks back again.

'Ride, Saeward! *Ride hard for the woods!*' I yell to him, throwing away the kite-shaped shield I have been carrying for the past few days since we slew the bearers.

'Let one of their horses *stumble* over it', I pray aloud, not looking back to see it does happen. I can only hope they are watching helplessly as we leave them behind, their horses panting, tired out from being pushed heedlessly from Hrofesceaster. We *have* gained ground away from them, *I can feel it!* The beating on the earth behind us lessens, their horses' snorting carried away by the wind. The woods offer shelter and darkness, where we will soon be able to slacken our pace.

Suddenly Wulfmaer's horse goes down! I rein Braenda in and make a half turn but he waves me on,

'Go, Ivar. *I will be with you!*'

I pull Braenda back, almost to a trot, but he waves me on again. Underway again, I look back at him over one shoulder.

Still struggling to get out from under his horse, he has had to let go of the reins of the spare mount he was leading, the one I changed over to this morning to give Braenda a rest. Now she prances out of reach as he reaches for her bridle. He sees me holding back again and waves me on, shouting something I cannot hear.

The Northmen are gaining again and Theorvard shouts, pointing behind me. It would not be helpful to Wulfmaer by going back for him, and I would only put the others at risk by doing so. In my anger at the way wyrd meddles with us I do something now that I have never done before. When I dig my heels into Braenda's flanks she give a start with a high-pitched whinny. On catching up with Theorvard, Saeward and Theodolf I turn to Theorvard and call out,

'What were you trying to tell me?'

'You did it anyway, Ivar. I shouted for you to leave him', Theorvard answers. 'You would have helped no-one staying with Wulfmaer'.

None of us says anything for the rest of our ride to Lunden. We regain Watling Straet again shortly before riding over the hill into Grenewic and reach Suthgeweorce when the sun begins its daily climb over the wooded hills behind us.

One of Ansgar's huscarls challenges us as we near the bridge,

'Who are you?' he calls out to me.

The morning sun is in his eyes. Even with one hand over his eyes, to him we are dark outlines against the glare.

'I am Ivar Ulfsson, and these are King Eadgar's men, you saw us leave a week or so ago for Centland', I answer.

'Some of you wear Northman war gear!' he stabs the air at Saeward and Theodolf. 'Your friends also ride Northman war horses – why is *that?*'

'It is a long story, and I will first tell it to King Eadgar when we reach Thorney. For now I need to find somewhere to leave one of my men', I point to Theodolf, 'to see to his wounds'.

'He will have to ride with you to Thorney. There is nowhere closer', the huscarl tells me glumly, 'unless you stop off at an inn'.

Theorvard has a thought,

'*We* could go back to the 'Eel Trap'. Aelfthryth could look after him, and you may as well ride on to Thorney'.

Saeward agrees readily, showing me a dark red stain on Theodolf's side where his knife tore away the padding to see his wounds.

'She will have clean cloths and fresh water to bathe his wounds with. Not having had to pay for our keep, we still have silver for his upkeep whilst you ride to Thorney and speak with the king'.

'Do *you* wish to ride with me?' I ask Theorvard, who nods. 'Very well then, what are we waiting here for?'

'You had more men with you when you last rode out', the huscarl recalls.

'Aye we lost two to the Northmen, both of them yesterday on the way back', I tell him as Theorvard and I ride on over the bridge.

'It is a shame to lose good men so close to home', Theorvard agrees, 'when they have gone through so much and been kept from harm so many times before'.

The huscarl nods gravely and allows us past over Lunden Brycg once more. Osgod awaits us at the northern end of the bridge.

'Eadwin and Morkere are still at Thorney?' I ask him.

'Aye, they are, *somewhere*', Osgod nods and asks, tongue-in-cheek, 'were you hoping they might have gone by now?'

'I wonder that they *are* still here. Are there tidings of Duke Willelm? We have seen the Northmen's supply stores on the coast. The king only needs to send the best of his butsecarls in a few ships from Lunden – 'I begin to tell Osgod.

'You had best tell him yourself, Ivar. I will ride with you to Thorney because I think Morkere may be missing me. I have been waiting for you here since *last night!*'

He casts his eyes over the remainder of my friends,

'You are missing some of your men?'

'We lost Burhred and Wulfmaer', I tell him of the ride from Egensford, where Wulfmaer's horse stumbled under the noses of our hunters, and lie about the loss of Burhred, saying he lost his life fighting at the bridge.

Theorvard winces when I tell of how Burhred died bravely, lanced in his chest, his killing avenged by Theodolf. Thankfully Osgod does not look Theorvard's way when he clears his throat noisily.

'Whilst we ride on to Thorney, Saeward needs to take Theodolf to the 'Eel Trap' on Billinges Gata to have his wounds seen to by Aelfthryth', I tell Osgod and turn Braenda to the left, ready to ride that way.

'I would have taken him to the infirmary at the West Mynster. They have a very good name for healing around these parts', Osgod turns his horse ready to ride westward.

Theodolf looks at me, wondering what I might say to that.

'Would you sooner ride on to the West Mynster?' I ask him, hoping that he would sooner be looked after at the 'Eel Trap'. 'It is after all closer to the road north'.

Theodolf knows he will be in good hands with Saeward, and turns his mount to follow our East Seaxan friend. Osgod senses that his counsel has fallen on deaf ears and says nothing further about the brothers tending to Theodolf's wounds. One of Osgod's men is told to ride ahead with news of my reaching Lunden alive again.

'Tell King Eadgar that I have a wounded man who needs tending, and that he has been taken to be looked after by a good woman', I ask the rider to add, a bemused Osgod giving me sideways looks.

Theorvard and Saeward grin as we part company. As I nudge Braenda rightward, to head for Thorney Osgod tells me,

'Ivar, I have to give you Aethel's fondest greetings. She asked me to tell you when I next saw you. The Lady Eadgytha saw fit to take her to Wintunceaster with the rest of her household. It seems that King Eadweard's widow deems it a proper way for her to live, rather than raising horses in the woods by Tadceaster!'

'Did she say anything about who should take over her steading?' I ask on Theodolf's behalf.

He looks askance at me, looks down at the ground and scratches his neatly trimmed beard before answering vaguely,

'No, there was nothing of that'.

'The steading must be Theodolf's to look after until she rejoins him', I tell Theorvard, then joke, 'Meanwhile Braenda will watch over it with her all-seeing eyes'.

He gives me a blank stare and clicks his tongue to hasten his mount and Saeward vanishes behind the houses at the end of Billinges Gata. Theorvard rides side-by-side with me and asks me earnestly,

'Do you think it is wise to joke about your hwicce woman?'

He may gather from my grin that I am not afraid of Braenda. Within me burns the nagging worry that I have already overstepped the mark with her in wishing to see Aelfthryth, perhaps even meaning to bed her again. Or *did* I bed Aelfthryth? The chilling memory floods back that it was Braenda who took me to Thegn Cynrig's bed in the guise of Aelfhild. It must have been her when I thought I was bedding Aelfthryth in her sons' room. I am beginning to feel awkward about going to the 'Eel Trap' now, but as I have told everyone we are going there, I have to go through with it. Could I own up to fear of a woman, be she ever as powerful as Braenda?

Before we have gone too far along the road toward the church of

Saint Paul I rein in and call out to Osgod ahead of me,

'I shall come to Thorney later, Osgod. Theorvard we should follow Saeward and Theodolf, I have something I need to see to before we ride to see King Eadgar'.

'If that is your wish, Ivar, we shall meet again soon', he looks puzzled at me, not knowing what he should tell the king when he shows without me. My wish to stop at 'The Eel Trap' rather than giving my news to Eadgar may jar with him. Nevertheless, I am putting the well-being of my men before my duty to my king – the delay should speak well for me.

When we come to the inn there is no sign of either Theodolf or Saeward. I take it they have handed over their horses to Wynstan. He is washing down a horse when we push open the door to his yard.

'Welcome Lord Ivar, welcome indeed!' he shouts as if we were still halfway along the road from the bridge. He walks slowly to us with the horse cloth in his left hand, the right outstretched to greet me,

'You will have Cyneweard's room this time, as you are my honoured guest!'

Gudheard passes with another horse and smiles at me.

'Gudheard, be a good fellow and finish washing down this mount when you have put that one in its stall. Ivar leave your horses in the yard here, they will not go any-',

He looks at Theodolf's and Saeward's mounts and gives a low whistle,

'Where did *these* beautiful animals come from? Look at them, Gudheard!' Wynstan blows through missing teeth as he looks the two horses up and down that we have brought back.

What would Wynstan have said if we had been able to bring the others? Gudheard's eyes seem to pop from their sockets. They both stand there, gaping at our prizes.

I laugh as I tell him,

'We borrowed them from some Northman fellows!'

Wynstan beams up at me and reaches a hand out again in greeting.

'After we had given them our usual greeting they did not seem to want them any more', I add. 'They ride their horses into the fight and we borrow them after we have sent the riders to their makers. We would have had a string of them if we had kept all the riderless horses, but we had to let them go again. There were too many for us to handle!' I add, telling Wynstan, 'By the way, we brought Theodolf back here to the 'Eel Trap' for Aelfthryth and Ymme to look after his wounds'.

'I know, Ivar. I saw him with Saeward just now. They await you in the main room'.

He lets me dismount and hand him the reins before adding,

'You might have some luck with Ymme', Wynstan laughs hollowly. 'She will be here in the morning. As for Aelfthryth, she has moved to her friend's alehouse. We had what you might call a 'parting of the ways'. She now lives at the 'Crooked Billet' with Gunnhild and Inwaer'.

I try not to let it show how put out I am, but Theorvard laughs out loudly,

'Have I said something funny?!' Wynstan is not cowed by Theorvard's size and turns on him, 'Or is it so widely known that she beds anything in sight with two legs and a big enough piece of meat hanging between them?'

Saeward almost walks into the door post laughing.

Theorvard doubles up. Rarely has he seen Saeward show such worldly wisdom. Only Theodolf seems not to share in the laughter, but then the pain of laughing may be too much for him. I grin for Wynstan's sake. If he is unbowed by Theorvard he would surely not hold back from berating me for bedding Aelfthryth if he knew. Moreover, he could tell us we are no longer welcome at his inn. I shall drop soon if I do not get a bed to lie in for at least a few hours.

'Perhaps now you will sleep better', I tell him. There is no need to cheer him up. He beams, happier now than when we last saw him.

Theorvard cackles, whether at my unease or at Wynstan's unbelievable cheer at losing his wife I shall never know.

'You have an odd sort of wit in the Danelaw, and that is all I can say!' Wynstan rumbles gleefully, breaking into a broad smile when he sees Saeward in pain from laughing, 'I am glad *someone* can see the funny side of it all. For all I know, she may be bedding Inwaer with Gunnhild looking on, going mad with hatred. It would serve *her* right!'

'No, friend, we were not laughing at your bad luck, although you do not seem to see the loss of your good wife that way', Theorvard tells Wynstan when he takes a grip on his mirth at last.

'*That* would be a first!' Wynstan grins, then bursts out laughing at the thought of his wife wronging Gunnhild with the greatly overweight Inwaer. 'Fear not. I am not in the least worried. I should think we will see Aelfthryth shortly, perhaps even before this day is over'.

'I had not thought you would want to see her again', I join in now, oddly cheered by the thought of his wife being back so soon. If he can find no use for her, I have no doubt I could.

'The thought of seeing her so soon does *not* cheer me Ivar'. Wynstan times his answer well. Theorvard begins to guffaw before the innkeeper can finish.

'It is of Gunnhild throwing out one of her own cronies that is the funny part! I have often thought about it ever happening, and it makes me happy to think of my wife outstaying her welcome with that fool Inwaer. It would be a treat for me to see Aelfthryth trudging back with her tail between her legs, so to speak-'

'Is there an Ivar Ulfsson here?' someone else shows in the inn yard.

'I am he', I answer, and ask in turn, 'what do you want from me?'

'Some Northmen came by at the Suthgeweorce end of Lunden Brycg and the bodies of two men were dropped from their horses!' the fellow looks fretful. 'Thegn Osgod thinks you might know who they are'.

'I will be there shortly', I assure the fellow and offer to pay him silver for his trouble.

'No, Lord. I have been paid by Thegn Osgod. He says you are to come now. One of the riders has word for you. He says you must hasten before they tire of waiting'.

'*Who* says I must hasten?' I ask, walking to the doorway. I wonder why he and other Aenglishmen, including Saeward, call me 'Lord', when I have never even been made a thegn in this land.

Osgod's messenger steps back, fearful of me doing *him* harm.

'*Who* says I must hasten?' I ask again, my right fist balled in anger.

'One of the Northmen who brought the bodies says so', he steps back out into the street as I close on him, 'and Thegn Osgod wants you to come back to the bridge with me to hear the Northman for yourself.

'I shall bring a friend', I tell him and beckon to Theorvard. He steps up to me and ushers me forward. *He* wants to know whose bodies the Northmen have brought, fearful – as I am – that one of them may be Wulfmaer's.

The messenger shrugs,

'As you wish, Lord Ivar', he bows, mounts his horse and awaits us before making his way back to the bridge with Theorvard and me in tow on foot. We hasten after Osgod's messenger until we reach the north end of Lunden Brycg.

'Better not to look too eager to them. They might think of themselves as more worthy than we would allow', I tell Theorvard. He nods and we walk the rest in measured strides. When we reach the southern end of the bridge Osgod nears us and stops us from going any further,

'One of these Northmen speaks our tongue well. However, I would counsel you to go nowhere with them now, whatever *he* says', Osgod beckons one of the riders to him. 'You might be riding into a trap once you pass between the houses over there, and you would then be beyond our help. As you see I do not have many of Ansgar's men with me here, and none of Morkere's'.

'I will listen to what he says, Osgod', I offer, and make myself smile to show that I am unafraid. As I pass behind him I put a hand on his shoulder to assure him I will do nothing foolish, 'Fear not. I will not ride *anywhere* with them. I have things to do before I can leave this burh'.

Osgod and Theorvard walk a few steps behind me. When I stop and bend down to look at the corpses and pull away the canvas sheet that has been laid over them both by Osgod's men, I see they are both clad only in their undergarments. In turning them over I make a show that I know neither of them, and lay their heads carefully back on the road.

One of the corpses is Burhred's. Why someone bothered to clothe him in his undergarments I cannot think. He was naked when I saw him last. The other one looks as if someone had beaten him to death. His eyes are swollen, his nose broken and mouth bloodied. I *had* thought that one of them might have been Burhred and the second Wulfmaer.

Perhaps thinking I would pull back on seeing who these men were, or because he wonders why Odo bothers so much with me, he stares balefully at me. Before he passes on his lord's veiled threat I ask,

'You are Odo's men?' I ask, staring up at him, taking care not to betray any feeling.

To his slow nodding I ask further,

'What have you to tell me?'

Unblinking, he passes on Odo's words,

'My Lord Odo, the Bishop of Bayeux gives leave to tell that he has captive a woman, name of Aelfhild. She says she knows you. My Lord Bishop says you should come to Hrofesceaster now, with us', he leaves the worst news for last. 'If you fail to show, she will be hanged together with all the other captives from their hamlet'.

He points to the dead men by my feet and I turn to look at Osgod and Theorvard. Their faces show nothing because they too have doubts about my safety and suspect a trap.

I turn back to the Northman.

'What proof do you have of this?' I demand.

In answer I am thrown a strip of someone's bloodied woollen undershirt.

'*This* is a piece of blood-soaked clothing', I chide, waving the cloth in the chill evening air. 'It shows me nothing you could not get merely by bending and ripping a strip of cloth from anyone's shirt or shift. You will have to do better than *this* to make me believe what you have told me, or what you are about to tell me!'

The Northman weighs me for some time. Whether he is cursing his master for not sending better proof I cannot tell. He fumbles in his saddle pack and holds up a bag with drawstrings, from which he draws a small pouch. Is the bag one of those they found in Aelfhild's home? If so, she was foolish to keep them.

'The bag was found in the woman's home. It is a bag we put foodstuffs in that have been shipped from Northmandige. Her husband was beaten into owning up to taking food stolen from us. We found this, and another bag in which was still a half cheese. There was also found in their hovel a flask of cidre that they said was given by you or one of your men. Do you know anything about that?'

The pouch is Aelfhild's. She carried it around her neck when she put out the food on the rough wooden boards that she and her neighbours brought from their homes.

'*Do* you know the pouch?' Osgod asks. He looks from me to Theorvard, who nods, worried now.

'Open the pouch and show me what is within', he says.

'I know she showed me a garnet-inlaid bright silver brooch that she put back in there. She told me her father gave her it as a gift from when he sailed to Bornholm'.

The Northman takes off one mailed glove and hooks out the selfsame brooch with his fingers. He hands it down to me,

'Do you believe me now?' he asks, fat lips twisted in a smug grin that tells me I have been caught out.

'I can see *you* have it. I also know that you captured another friend of ours, Wulfmaer. You yourself could have picked up the pouch from one of their dwellings and showed it to him to ask if he knew of it'. He has lost the smug grin and clamps his jaw tightly. 'He knew who it belonged to, because he was standing next to Theorvard when she told him about it'.

His brow is now arched in anger at my stubborn refusal to believe him.

'Is Wulfmaer the old fool whose horse stumbled in the chase?' the Northman asks, barely hiding another smug grin. I would cheerfully knock it from him, but in doing so might make life harder for Aelfhild.

'He is no more foolish than you take *me* to be!' I berate him. 'Aye, I recall he called out to me to leave him behind and not to try to save him. He is a brave man!'

'He was *foolish* in his bravery. One of my men lanced him in the throat when he stood defiantly in front of us with his axe. That was before we found the woman and her friends', his answer takes me aback but I still feel he is lying to me. It is likely Odo has told him to get me back at all costs, however many lies it takes to do so.

'Why did you bring these bodies *here?*' I ask, looking down at the bloodied corpse of a man I have never set eyes on before. Burhred looks emptily heavenward with the half-grin he wore when I last saw him.

'We thought you would bury them as the great warriors they were', comes the tart answer.

Theorvard snorts and throws his head back.

'Is that a reason for laughing?!' Osgod scolds Theorvard. The Northman looks askance at the young giant, as if he himself had been offended.

'You are right. I *am* sorry', Theorvard stretches to his full height to look the Northman in the eye as he answers Osgod. 'I *was* touched with grief at the loss of another of my friends. You know how it is. We either laugh at our wyrd or die wretchedly'.

Theorvard bears in mind that we agreed to tell of Burhred as being a warrior to the end when we returned to speak to Eadgar.

'*So we do!*' I echo the feeling.

'We found one of our hauberks and other *equipement* by the body of this fellow - why?' the Northman demands, pointing at Burhred. They must have found it on the bed under his naked corpse.

'It may have been a trophy', I lie. 'You, too have trophies. I have seen Northmen such as you with weapons taken from dead Aenglishmen. You are wearing a thegn's badge of office around your neck!'

'*Give that badge to me!* You see none of us wearing Northman insignia', Osgod orders, but the Northman turns his horse before my friend can reach him.

'Are you coming back with me?!' the Northman demands again before he leaves and his horse stamps a hoof as if wanting to be away again. 'You have until the early morning to save the woman and her friends!'

'I will *follow* you', I tell him. Theorvard groans and Osgod shakes his head in disbelief. To them I merely add, 'I must'.

'Theorvard can you bring Braenda?' I ask. He must know I would ask him.

'*We* have a horse for you to ride', the Northman snaps his fingers. One of the Northmen draws on the reins of a chestnut mare.

They both glare at me, slighted that I wish to ride my own horse, trying to bully me into mounting theirs.

'If it is all the same to you, I will ride my own mare', I smile, 'unless you have good grounds for wanting me to ride yours. If I am to be taken into captivity at the end of this ride, at least give me the right of one last ride my own horse'.

The Aenglish-speaking one can only sigh and waves his hand at Theorvard,

'If you must - go ahead, bring his horse'. He plainly wants to be away from here and must be at the end of his tether, being made to wait so close to sworn foes.

Theorvard looks back at me and I nod, the smile still frozen on my lips. He grins and strides back to the 'Eel Trap' for Braenda. Whilst I await his return I study these Northmen in the failing light. The one who brought forward their horse for me looks haplessly at his surroundings, bored by waiting – or afraid. The Aenglish-speaking one looks at Osgod, as though trying to recall him from somewhere else. I doubt these two could ever have seen one another; as far as I know, Osgod had never seen a Northman before our fight on the bridge.

My stomach begins to growl. I should have eaten by now.

'Have I seen you before?' the Northman asks Osgod.

Not knowing he is being spoken to he looks across the river to where Theorvard rides back to us leading Braenda.

'It looks as though your friend Theorvard means to keep you company Ivar', Osgod sounds taken aback. I feel dismayed on the one hand, yet glad to have a friend with the likelihood of a threat to my life.

Saeward also shows at the end of the bridge on a borrowed mount, leaving the horse he took from the dead Northman with Wynstan. The three horses clatter noisily over the bridge boards toward us and my escorts begin to look worried.

'We were to bring only you on your own', I am told.

'*Why be so fearful?*' I smile crookedly, pointing southward at the still ruined houses near the bridge. 'Surely you need not worry if there are just three of us. There are six of you, *with lances*. I can see others skulking in the shadows by that ruined dwelling. Odo will be as happy with the three of us as with only me, I should think'.

'You will only need to find a few more feet of rope', Osgod jokes darkly.

The huscarls have something to tell their friends now, of how three armed Aenglishmen were escorted east into captivity to Hrofesceaster by six Northmen.

'I could not let the pair of you ride alone', Saeward shouts when he is halfway over the bridge.

'We would not be on our own, him and me!' Theorvard leans across to stop Saeward.

Our East Seaxan friend is set on riding with us and sharing our wyrd. He nudges his horse past Theorvard's to show he will brook no hindrance, not that either of us would dream of stopping him. I have made some good, true friends lately, I tell myself. Few men could count on such loyalty.

When I am mounted I turn to Theorvard and Saeward on either side of me,

'It will be a good day to look down our foes' lances again!' I laugh and bring Braenda about. To the Northman I add, 'Lead on, *friend*'.

As we ride away from the bridge Osgod grins and takes my hand in bidding me farewell. Will I set eyes on him again? Ansgar's huscarls raise their swords in salute and we let our horses canter on between the Northmen, away from Lunden, away from the safety of our friends, trusting our wyrds to luck. In my thoughts I see Aelfthryth. I shall miss the warmth I would have felt in meeting her again, out of sight of Wynstan.

12

Darkness greets us as we climb the hill behind Grenewic, into Centland beyond. My stomach growls again.

'I have not eaten since early this morning. Have you any food with you?' I ask the Northman.

'We do not carry food, but there is an inn along the way'. He warily looks back at Theorvard and Saeward as he answers, and smirks at me. 'You can have something to eat there'.

'We have not eaten, either', Saeward speaks on behalf of himself and Theorvard. 'A good cooked meal would not go amiss, but at this time of the day who will cook food for *us?*'

'There is always a way to coax food from unwilling hostellers', the Northman smirks again, no doubt full of himself, having his whims being obeyed of late. .

'Well then' Theorvard shouts cheerfully, 'we can be sure of a *warm* welcome from these Centish innkeepers, can we not - who could say no to friendly fellows such as you?'

The smirk turns to a scowl and in turn back to a smile, no doubt at the thought of us ending our days in one of his master's cells,

'Who could refuse a fellow his last meal on earth?' he smirks.

'The last will be the *best!* Think of the Lord's last supper, Ivar'. Saeward calls out cheerily. 'As Saint Peter welcomes us into heaven he will ask if the Centishmen can cook well enough to satisfy an East Seaxan!'

Theorvard laughs as he asks,

'What do you think your answer will be, East Seaxan?'

'Why, I hope my answer will be 'aye'!' Saeward ruffles his mare's mane and looks at me, grinning. 'And I very much hope their ale will be as good as their food!'

'Like fools, you Aenglishmen are always cheerful', the Northman gives us an insight into *his* wit.

'Perhaps being aware that we are fools is better when your land is trodden underfoot by a foe who does not know *he* is the fool!' Theorvard quips, earning himself a scowl.

One of the other Northmen says something in his own tongue to his leader.

'My friend Ralf asks me why Aenglishmen talk so much', I am treated to more stilted wit.

'What would your answer *be* – what is your name?' I ask.

'My answer would have to be along the lines of 'fools chatter aim-lessly when their lives hang on the thread. My own name is Walter'.

'Well, Walter, your answer tells me as much about you as I could ever wish to know', I show him the measure of my scorn.

Walter's smirk fades fast and he wears a look of anguish as sudden-ly the tip of an arrowhead shows between his ribs. He looks down at the tip, eyes rolling upward in their sockets, and then he falls sideways from his saddle toward me with his right foot still jammed in the stir-rup. His underling Ralf is ahead of us in the darkness with the other four of his landsmen, and does not know the fate that has befallen Wal-ter. We ride further and Ralf himself suddenly jerks about wildly. In falling from his horse without a sound, his left foot catches the stirrup and his head bumps along on the hard road.

Saeward, Theorvard and I rein in our mounts. No other sound is made until someone calls from the darkness,

'I know that horse – could my friend Ivar be in Centland so soon again?'

The other four Northmen are still ahead of us and only know some-thing is wrong when one of them calls out for Ralf. On hearing no an-swer he turns in his saddle. He barks something to his comrades and they haul on their reins, looking back at us. They look about in the dark for Walter and one of them turns his mount to seek him out in the moonless gloom. He stares long and hard, sees we are too many for the four of them and kicks his mount into a gallop. The other three follow, vanishing into the darkness towards Hrofesceaster and safety.

I hear someone say again in the darkness,

'I would know that horse anywhere'.

'Who is there?' I ask before any more arrows are loosed off, but be-fore he answers I know him, 'Oslac, are you here again in time to save our worthless hides?'

'It is only days since we last spoke to you, *or* Theodolf. Where is he, by the way?'

First Oslac shows and then we see Sigegar pushing through the un-dergrowth by the roadside to our left.

'Cyneweard has the other one's horse safe', Oslac looks ahead past me along the track. Sigegar looks up at me and grins.

Wynstan's son brings Ralf's horse back, the Northman's head still bumping on the inset stones on the old road. He pats the horse on the nose to calm it and Sigegar pulls the fellow's left foot from the stirrup. Ralf's battered body slumps like a half-filled sack of oats onto the muddy road, his short-cropped, helmless head spattered, battered and torn from the hard road.

'Theodolf is wounded', I answer Oslac. I have in turn a question for him, 'Do you know Cyneweard?'

'Cyneweard and I know one another from our many times at the 'Eel Trap'. His mother and I shared many delights on her bed when Wynstan's back was turned! Has she ever let *you* sample her wares?'

Still not sure whether it was Aelfthryth or Braenda in my bed I can only share a knowing smile. They will have their thoughts on that, no doubt. Cyneweard grins, the gaps between his teeth partly filled by blackened stumps. He feels no loyalty toward either his mother or his father, but then he knows them a lot better than I.

'What are you doing here? I thought you dwelt eastward from here, closer to Medestan', I look to Oslac for an answer, but I would not press for it.

'Our homes were forfeit when we left for Lunden. By the time we came back our wives, children and kinfolk had left before they could be dragged away to Hrofesceaster to build the Northmen's stronghold for them, and we do not know which way they went because *everyone* in eastern Centland has been uprooted'.

'Now you are here, do you want to come with us to Hrofesceaster to see if a certain woman Aelfhild is really captive –'

'Or whether they only tried to lure you there for their own ends?' Oslac finishes my words. 'Of course we *will* come with you, but you must take your time. If you get there too early they will be awaiting you'.

'Get there too late and we could watch her, and whoever else, hang in front of a throng of onlookers who will be as powerless as we', I try to tell him.

'The time to get there is dawn', Oslac assures me. 'They will be bored waiting for a foolish night raid, and half asleep from being kept from their beds all night'.

'How long do we have before they are ready for us?' Theorvard looks at me for an answer.

'Before who are all ready – you mean the Northmen?' I answer. From what I have seen, they are often still half-asleep even after the hangings.

They carry them out to cow the local folk, so that they do the Northmen's bidding without ado. If these folk were to witness us snatching the captives, they would rebel and run riot', Oslac answers Theorvard, warming to the task of teaching Odo's men a lesson they will not forget.

'How would *you* set about it, Oslac?' I ask him. 'I ask as you yourself may have witnessed the hangings'.

'Were I you, I would lie low somewhere near the burh –', he begins. It is my turn to break in.

'I was thinking more about having something to eat along the way, resting awhile and then going into the burh',

As I tell him my thoughts he smiles,

'Have you thought this through?' Oslac asks me.

I look around at the dark shapes of trees blurred in the moonless light as I tell him and ask,

'Are there many more of you?'

'You mean besides Sigegar and me? Aye, we have Swetman from Egensford, Ecgberht with dark rims under his eyes, and Ealhstan from Scealfing... oh, and not forgetting Wulfric of Oteford', Oslac did not need to tell us the names of the first four. They step forward out of the darkness of the trees to let themselves be seen.

There are others who follow behind Wulfric that we do not know by name. Ealhstan no longer glowers, looking instead to be bridled. Perhaps the Northmen do have his woman. Swetman eyes me warily, as if we had led the Northmen to his settlement. Perhaps we did, unwittingly.

Whatever, Ecgberht does not look as though he thinks we are blameworthy. His lips are still puffed up and bloody, heavy rings under his eyes where he was beaten. There are rope burns on his hands where he would have struggled with his bindings when the Northmen caught him.

'Is it true the Northmen have your woman?' I ask Ecgberht.

'*Who told you that?*' he asks, taken aback.

'The Northman with the arrow in his back told me when he came to take us from Lunden. That is why we are back here so soon'. I look into the eyes of the astounded Ecgberht and add, 'He told us that Aelfhild and some others would hang in the morning if I did not yield to Odo', I tell him as much as I have been told.

'Did he tell you your friend was alive?' Swetman asks.

'He told me he was speared and left for dead', I answer.

'He would, the lying *toad!*' Swetman swears, hawking and spitting bile on the Northman's forehead.

'He did not tell you that they had tormented your friend for sport after they caught up with him? I thought one of them *had* speared him, but he was still on his feet, being led away eastward when I ushered my folk away to safety', Swetman's brow furrows deeply when he is angered, his dark eyes almost hidden by bushy brows.

'You think he is still alive?' I ask, hopefully. If we can free him as well as their Centish captives, then our day will be well won! I suddenly recall I have an empty stomach, 'Lead the way to the inn and we can hatch a plan whilst we sink one of their good ales with a dish of hot food!'

I am looking forward to showing Odo who is master of this land. The last time I saw him he wore a scowl dark enough to frighten a lesser man. I only wish Thorfinn were still alive. He would have relished this raid on the whoring bishop to free the hostages!

Our ride to the inn is quiet, and from time to time the moon shows blotchy between banks of clouds. Oslac tells me what we should find around the bishop's stronghold whilst we make our way in the darkness. From what he tells me there must be hundreds of poor souls encamped within an outer palisade, and an inner one has been built on a man-made hill. Atop the highest point is a solid, tall, wooden tower with a bridge that can be drawn to ward off attackers. They take no risks with their strongholds, these Northmen.

At long last a pinprick of light shows through the trees, to let us know where the inn stands set back from the straight road we know as Watling Straet.

'You will soon have food set before you Ivar', Oslac smiles. 'However you *will* need to offer silver for his pains. You will not begrudge yourself the outlay, though. Lyfing's wife makes the best wild hare stew in the whole of East Centland!'

'I have no fear of parting with silver for a good meal, Oslac. It has been some time since I sat with friends to a good meal. We will have *earned* this food by morning!' I can already taste the stew before I put a spoon to my mouth, so good is the smell of cooking!

When we have tasted Astrith's noted wild hare stew, downed some of Lyfing's best ale, and talked about what has happened lately, Oslac, Theorvard and I sit by a crackling fire to set out our thoughts. Raiding Odo's stronghold will tax all our wiles.

'We will show them it can be done!' Wulfric thumps the table with his balled fist, 'The good folk of East Centland will rise and bring such a blow on these Northmen that they will run with their tails between their legs back to Dofnan and beyond!'

'Sit down and finish your ale, lad! We will talk about how to make them shit in their breeks in Hrofesceaster', Oslac grins sideways at me.

'Believe me the stuff will be running down their legs by the time we are done! And now, as to our attack -'

He sits bolt upright on the bench and begins to pour forth his thoughts. We all listen closely except for Wulfric, who has passed out with the ale he has downed. Oslac tells us,

'*Fire is the key!*'

The way he looks at me I would say the thought has come to him like a bolt out of the blue.

'These Northmen are going to let us burn down their stronghold!' Theorvard laughs, 'What about their captives? They will be held within, surely'.

'We wait until they bring them out', Oslac looks sharply at Theorvard, shaking his head at him. 'The gibbet will be within the outer wall because they do not trust the Centish folk any closer to the tower where Odo lives. Some have to be able to get closer to the gibbet, which will be built on a wooden scaffold. It will not be a single gibbet, but long enough to hang a number of poor souls at once', Oslac tells me. He must have seen how the stronghold is built, although from how near I would not know until I see it for myself.

'Who do you see as being near the scaffold?' I ask. Saeward looks closely at him too. Perhaps he has thought of the same answer as I have.

'Three should go in dressed as ceorls, with long winter coats over their swords. One could be in a habit. Do any of you know how a brother or priest would behave?' Oslac looks from me to Theorvard, and to Saeward, '*Do you?*'

'I *was* a layman at Wealtham. I thought you knew that'. Saeward turns to me and asks, 'Did you not tell Oslac?'

I shrug sooner than lie.

'Do you know the words a priest would say for someone about to be punished?' Oslac asks Saeward, 'This matters greatly, because if you use the wrong words they will hang *you* – and us - with the others and use a proper priest to give you your last rites!'

'I know the words in *Aenglish!*' Saeward answers tersely.

'Would an Aenglish priest or monk say the words in Aenglish?' Oslac asks me.

'I recall when Odo tried to have Thorfinn and me hanged, the priest mumbled in a tongue unlike that used in the great church in Rouen', I answer. 'He could mumble a few words to them that would sound to the Northmen as words of comfort, and those words could be a warning to you bowmen to be ready to loose off your fire arrows'.

'That is something I had *not* thought of!' Oslac's eyes widen in wonder.

'You could tell them what is to happen and none of Odo's men would be any the wiser', I offer. 'Then we listen out for our watchword! You raise your right hand as if you are about to bless them and Wulfric passes on the signal to us outside'.

'Have you any other bowmen?' Theorvard asks him.

'Leave that to me, my lad', Oslac lifts his beaker of ale. 'Us folk from Lindcylne are not as foolish as you in Snotingaham perhaps think we are. I can lay my hands on as many bowmen as you have fingers on your hands. Meanwhile, I drink to your health, Ivar'.

'If you are as sure as that, then by all means', Theorvard already has his ale beaker in his hand.

'I drink to you and yours. You did not say before that you were from Lindcylne, Oslac, only that you were from the Danelaw. My uncle came from Gaegnesburh, do you know the burh?'

'Well enough, lad. Well enough!' Oslac laughs and downs the rest of his ale.

'We need at least a few hours' sleep', I tell my friends.

'We do. We have a long, hard day ahead!' Theorvard looks across the table at Oslac, 'You will wake us before you go, Oslac?'

'Why should I not leave you slumbering here whilst *we* do all the fighting?' Oslac grunts, offended by Theorvard's slight.

'There you go again. Talk to me as if I were a fool, or a child! I *will* rouse you in time for you to stuff some porridge into your bellies. We would not be able to stop here on our way back, so the next time you eat would in Lunden'.

Theorvard's mouth twists down at the corners on Oslac's warning. Oslac smiles at him and adds to me,

'We will have enough horses and more than enough spare mounts, should there be more captives than we bargained for. Some very trustworthy folk will watch over them when we are there. We shall then have to fight our way away as we run for dear life!' There is a stark warning that he leaves to finish with, 'Not only will our lives hang on our getting back to our horses in good time, but if the Northmen see the men looking after our horses before we reach them, then *their* lives will be worth nothing'.

'You have thought of everything', I smile and doze off.

Someone kicks my boots and I awake with a start.

'Time to go, Ivar', Theorvard tells me. 'We tried to raise you earlier but you were sound asleep. You are harder to awaken these days, *old man!* There is porridge on the table and we will see you outside shortly to ready your horse'.

He wears an old coat drawn across his byrnie, a loose cloth cap covers his fiery locks and his sword is well hidden from sight. Saeward wears a well-worn, almost threadbare brown habit over his mailcoat, his sword hidden in the folds. He will have to pull the thing up over his scabbard when he needs to draw it. With luck he will not need to draw the sword hastily.

'Oslac says to wear that thick plaid coat over your mailcoat', Saeward shows me a dirty-looking rag heaped on the other end of the long table that I am sat at.

'It has a hood that you can pull down over your eyes as you get near Odo's stronghold, should there be anyone who knows you', Theorvard tells me as he lifts the latch on the creaking, leather-covered, studded door.

'I shall be out soon enough', I taste the porridge. It is no longer hot, but I cannot quibble. It may be the last I eat for some time. I shall have to make the best of it and look forward to Ymme's cooking, and the warmth of Aelfthryth's naked body against mine.

The taste of last night's hare stew is still on my tongue as I shovel the porridge into my mouth and pull on the old coat. The garment has seen better days, but it is warm and for that I have Oslac to thank. The sky is finely streaked with grey in the east when I stride out through the door on this chill morning.

'It is a fine morning for killing!' Oslac greets me as I ease my sore seat onto Braenda's saddle once again.

'It is a fine morning indeed. Shall we go and share Odo's gathering?' I bring Braenda around and my heart nearly stops.

There are Northman horsemen all around me, grinning at a prize they have been given on a plate.

'Odo will be indeed pleased to see you again, Aenglishman!' one of them smiles. I cannot put a name to him, but he sounds like someone I know.

'Who in Christ's name has *betrayed us?!*' I shout fit to burst and reach into the coat to unsheathe my sword. Saeward clasps my arm and shakes his head. His broad grin tells me I am safe.

'Put your sword back, Ivar', one of them pulls off his helm so that I can see who I have been fooled by.

'Theodolf, I thought you were meant to be resting in the 'Eel Trap'!' I urge Braenda forward towards him and grip his hands when our horses are side by side. 'You fool. You should be resting! What happens if your wound opens again?'

'I have Saeward here to tend to me', Theodolf tells me calmly.

'How did you come here?' I ask. 'Did someone bring you?'

'Cyneweard sent for me. Although we rode here through the night I feel well enough to be able to handle a bow. The pennons on these lances belong to Bishop Odo's household, I am told'. He throws one of his winning, maiden-stunning smiles at me and laughs,

'If we fooled you, think how the Northmen will feel when they think that their own comrades are attacking them!'

232

'They will be foxed, Theodolf! We are friends again, then?'

'We are... You will have to forgive me, Ivar. I was tired, and what with the lack of proper food - I have tasted what you had last night, so my temper is even again – and now I am *ready* to fight!'

'That gladdens me', I reach over to give him a friendly slap on the back.

'It does not gladden me to feel your hand slap me on my back, not right now. I shall be able to get through this well enough otherwise, thank you', Theodolf grins sheepishly and we ride east to deliver our greetings to Odo.

The stronghold, built under Northman overseers by Suth Seaxan and Centish captives, rises from the earth like a wooden hill, the tower standing upright like an attacking serpent. We shall give it *fire* to breathe!

His men are everywhere, hawkishly watching everything that passes Our horses have been left not far away in an orchard to the west of the burh, away from this stronghold that has taken shape with Aenglish sweat and tears. No doubt there is Aenglish blood in here too!

I am on my own, Theorvard, Saeward and Wulfric having walked on ahead through the outer main gate. Theodolf and his 'Northmen' are beyond the stronghold's thick, twin-timbered walls Oslac, Sigegar and six other bowmen have gone to the western end of the stronghold to await Saeward's signal.

I have to make sure that when I watch the Northmen, none of them sees me doing so. They are eyeing anyone whom they think could be a threat. As I do not want to be seen, I walk slowly with a put on limp as the mass of slowly trudging men, women and older children shuffles ahead of us. Their younger siblings are carried by their fathers as *everyone* has been called from their homes to watch their new masters humble their fellow landsmen.

Theorvard joins me and nudges,

'Ivar, *look to your right!*' he hisses behind his left hand. He nods that way so as not to be seen pointing.

I ask, unsure about what he wants me to look at,

'What - *who* am I looking at?'

'In the black coat, ten paces ahead', he hisses again.

I take my time looking for a black coat and find myself looking at Odd. I thought he went to Medestan and on to Sceapig.

Theorvard gives me a worried look. Odd knows us well. If he has anything to do with the Northmen here and sees us, our aims would be thwarted. In slowing our stride we allow others to pass. There are now more heads bobbing about in between us. Some curse us for getting in their way and I bow my head, nodding mutely.

Saeward and Wulfric are some way ahead of us. They keep looking up as they climb the bank toward the scaffold, taking care to hold their heads bowed. I hope they are not caught looking straight at any of the Northman guards. Should they catch any of us looking at them, they may feel threatened and challenge any one of us.

There is no sign of Odo yet. Nor is there anyone else of high standing. Only younger Northman nobles can be seen, from time to time slapping mailed gloves onto saddles when the throng looks as if it might be moving too slowly or stopping needlessly.

'Allez, *allez!*' someone shouts at the slowly-moving mass.

Saeward stands by the scaffold, almost hidden by a Northman's giant frame as he watches the slope above.

I reach my hand to Theorvard's elbow to catch his eye. He looks quickly back at me and then at the upper gate. And then something begins to stir. Men scurry to line up along the ramp from the tower. High-ranking nobles ride down from the tower toward us, flanked by horsemen with lances and full-length shields. Odo is easy to pick out by his girth, even with his helm pulled down low. Half naked as he was when Thorfinn and I saw him in the inn, what I noted about him then was his barrel-shaped chest, the full belly and the drinker's nose. The hauberk and broad cape make him look markedly bigger, fatter – not so much a cleric as a tormenter.

Behind them a dozen or so captives with their hands tied behind their backs are pushed down the ramp by guards who carry shields only as a show of strength rather than from fear of being attacked. It makes no odds, if amongst the masses of men here there are those who have weapons hidden under their clothes. Shields can be splintered by hacking. There is no sign of brooding threat, though. Everyone seems calm, as if they are here only to hear a shire reeve reading out new laws.

As Odo and his party gather behind the scaffold the captives are led up the steps onto the scaffold platform by their guards. Everyone surges forward to hear what is being said by a young nobleman standing square to us, in front of both Wulfmaer and Aelfhild.

The others line up on either side, heads bowed.

The young Northman calls out louder now,

'Is there one amongst you', he looks around and finishes his question, 'who knows the last rites, so that they can be given in your own tongue?'

Saeward steps forward, looking the part in his habit,

'I know the words, my Lord', he flatters the young Northman.

There is stirring as Saeward threads his way through those standing closest to the scaffold, up to the steps and onto the platform to be shepherded behind the young noble who begins to call again on all of us here,

'These men and women here', he says in fair Aenglish, 'are accused of killing Northmen'.

Everyone hears him out quietly. Not even a babe-in-arms whimpers as he begins again,

'My Lord Odo, the *venerable* Bishop of Bayeux was hoping that a certain Aenglishman would be here to stand in their place', he pauses again.

There is stirring in the throng. Murmuring and head shaking follow but no-one knows who he means, even after the he begins afresh,

'We are told his name is Ivar Ulfsson, a kinsman of King Harold. If you are here, Ivar, *show* yourself', he looks around, over the heads of the gathered Centish folk and up at his master. To all around him he adds, 'You seem to have forsaken your friends here'.

He does not wait long before turning to the hangman standing at one end of the line of the condemned, telling him something behind his hand as though we might understand. As the hangman tests the nooses along the line of the condemned, the Northman tells Saeward,

'Say your words, priest'.

Saeward walks a little way behind the hangman, giving his blessings. The hangman leads, putting the noose around each neck. Wulfmaer brightens. He must know Saeward by his speech and tries hard not to look too happy, but can barely hide his glee. I cannot hear what he tells his fellow East Seaxan before Saeward passes on to Aelfhild without breaking his stride. Luckily the young Northman does not understand Saeward and watches the masses before him, their upward-turned eyes taking in the gruesome rite.

Aelfhild must know Saeward by his speech, too, because she bends her head to peer under his cowl. The young noble has seen nothing untoward, however, and leaves the platform by the steps to stand in front of Wulfric.

Theorvard, standing close beside me keeps his head bowed but the Northman moves away without so much as a stare.

Before Saeward moves on to the man next to Aelfhild, he raises his right arm as if in blessing. He makes the signal again before striding on, should Oslac's lookout have missed his cue. Burning arrows soar high over the wooden walls of Odo's stronghold onto the slope where the bishop and his friends are gathered.

There are screams as the women and children try to flee. Their menfolk scream too, with hatred, as they hack at the hapless guards around them with whatever weapons they have brought. Panic strikes hard at Odo's unsteadied men, who are being picked off all around. Some rally and begin hacking back at their assailants.

Theorvard has brought his bow with him and looses arrows off into the horsemen as they bear down at us, lowering their lances as they close on him. As if mowing in a field of grass I scythe at the first rider, catching him on his right leg as he tries to turn away. Wulfric also has his bow and shares Theorvard's store of arrows, plucking them from the earth whilst Saeward brings down his sword on the shocked hangman's outstretched right arm as he draws a noose over Aelfhild's head.

Centishmen leap up onto the scaffold, lift the nooses from the bared necks of the hostages and untie their bindings.

Saeward, Theorvard and Wulfric lay into the advancing row of kite-shields with their long-handled axes, the loud splintering clear in the early morning air despite the clamour. My axe is busy, too, singing through the air and sending our foes to join the ranks of their forebears.

Steel clashes on steel, the slashing of blade on chain mail hisses, adding to the din of fighting. Swords and axes hack at shields, the dull thud of blade on wood echoing around the stronghold's walls. Odo rides down at us and lays about him with his staff. One of the Centishmen wrenches the useless bauble from his hand and knocks him from his horse. He cowers, arm over head, but the fellow who unhorsed him is beset by Odo's men, pushed back unharmed onto the men behind.

I turn my head briefly toward the scaffold to see everyone is clear before we pull back to the horses. The platform is clear but for the dead hangman, hanging limply through one of the trap holes. His right arm severed at the elbow where he tried to fend off Saeward's sword blows.

It is time to leave. Beyond the burning wooden walls a horn sounds, high-pitched above the noise of slaughter. Aelfhild, Wulfmaer and the others are safe. Theorvard still scythes at any and all Northmen who come near him as he backs toward to me. Saeward and Wulfric are already by my side.

Beyond the palisade Theodolf pulls his bow over his shoulders and slashes with his sword. Around us Northmen and Centishmen alike lie dead on the still bare earth where they fell. There will be many more grieving widows and mothers today. Drawing back to the outer gates, and dragging our wounded with us we threaten our attackers with sword and axe. However, one of the Northmen has a crossbow and uses it on the thronging men drawing back with us.

Luckily few in number, his bolts flash silently into our ranks. He has to draw each bolt back, giving us time to pull back through the gate and out into the street beyond. One bolt hisses by my right cheek and hits someone behind me. On hearing a loud yell of pain I turn quickly to see it is Theorvard who is hit. The bolt has taken him on his left shoulder and is buried deep in his flesh.

'Go – be *quick!*' I shout at Theodolf and Saeward. Wulfric is about to turn and flee when another bolt cuts into his throat. He falls silently. The crossbowman has another of his comrades with him now, and together they threaten our withdrawal.

I take Theorvard's right arm over my shoulder, Saeward takes his left. Between us we drag the young giant along the street back to our waiting horses.

The Northmen have spilled out onto the street through the gate. Arrows and bolts follow over our lowered heads and at last we are safe around the corner of a stone-built house.

'We will have that bolt from your shoulder very soon, Theorvard', Saeward tells him breathlessly and is answered by a feeble groan. We try to stand Theorvard against a wall of the house so as not to cause him undue pain. He cannot stand for long, however. Another bolt had lodged itself in the small of his back as we withdrew and he is now deathly grey, but breathing yet.

'*Saeward,* we have to get him back to his horse!' I yell.

Saeward answers testily, pointing at our friend,

'He will not be able to *ride* her. Look'.

I can see why when I look again at Theorvard. Tiny red bubbles run from the corners of his mouth in driblets. He coughs and sags, coughs again and drops to his knees.

'He will be dead before we get him to his horse, you know that', Saeward tells me. I do not want to leave Theorvard for Odo to show off as a prize.

I can only nod. With the last of my Danelaw friends dead a numbing sadness overcomes me. He chose to follow me, fought beside me for Harold and Eadgar, and now we have to take him and bury him in a Centish field. *I might as well have killed him with my own hands!*

Saeward sweats like a bull dragging Theorvard's lifeless body with me. He has been fighting like a madman and now he snorts with the strain of dragging our friend. Theodolf cannot help us lift him because he is still nursing his shoulder; nevertheless he manfully hacks with his sword at any Northmen who come too close.

Oslac looks around a corner ahead of us to see if we are near. He dashes toward us, comes around us behind me, and lifts Theorvard's feet, enabling us to run. As I turn the next corner a bolt scrapes my neck and hits a stone wall, showering me with splinters. I feel one has scratched my right cheek but my task is to help take Theorvard to his

237

last rest. The Northmen are closer behind us than I would like to have thought! We must gain on them otherwise we will have no time to mount our horses safely.

'Where is Cyneweard, Theodolf?' I ask as I hand him my axe to carry. He looks around and shrugs in answer.

Sigegar awaits us at the next corner, bow at the ready. Oslac turns to him as he passes and yells,

'They are close behind. Two with crossbows have already killed Wulfric, and Theorvard is dead too!'

'Where is *Wulfric's* body?' Sigegar jerks his head around the corner, quickly pulling it back again. There is no way we can reach Wulfric without being riddled with crossbow bolts.

He readies an arrow and looks around the corner again. On seeing us still there, getting our breath back he yells,

'*Go on,* will you?!' Get to the horses, I shall stop at least *one* of them!'

We need no second bidding. Saeward takes Theorvard's left arm again and we drag him to the horses. Cyneweard is there, holding one of the horses steady for Aelfhild to mount.

'What is happening back there?' Ecgberht asks and fumes when he sees Theorvard. '*Let me go back and help Sigegar!*'

'Go back and help him but do not outstay your welcome', I warn. 'These Northmen have crossbows. Their bolts can shatter shields, just as they shattered many a shield where King Harold was killed'.

Swetman and Ealhstan stand with the horses when we reach them, sweating with the weight of Theorvard over our shoulders. As Oslac sets the young giant's feet on the grassy bank Swetman strides over to us,

'What has happened?' he asks wide-eyed.

When I catch my breath again I ask,

'Help Sigegar hold back the Northmen whilst hoist Theorvard's body onto his horse. Try not to get yourself killed'.

'Watch out for their crossbow bolts', Oslac warns. 'They are too good with them for the likes of us. Perhaps *we* should have some'.

'*Crossbows,* what are *they?*' Swetman asks, but does not wait for an answer and runs to where Sigegar leans back against the stone building with his bow at the ready. Cyneweard follows with his bow but the Centishman shakes his head at him to tell him that he is not needed.

Swetman pokes his head around the corner and is almost skewered. He pulls back quickly.

'Keep your head back and do what I do', Sigegar tells him.

'*Now* you tell me', Swetman sucks in his cheeks and looks back to me grinning at him. He looks back at Sigegar at the corner, edging forward to take a look.

Sigegar suddenly pulls up his bow, draws it, looses off an arrow without taking aim and pulls back again as quickly. Another of the short, thick bolts flies past his head as he thumps his back onto the wall, but his wide grin tells me he has found a target. He looks at me and yells out in triumph,

'There will be less of those weird-looking arrows coming our way'. Sigegar looks around the corner and pulls back as another of the bolts flies past him. He has an arrow ready across his bow when he steps out and takes aim again.

This time he falls back, a bolt in his chest. They must have brought up another crossbowman to strengthen their number! Swetman sets an arrow across his bow, stands on the corner and lets loose at a foe I doubt even he saw for long enough to mark his target.

'*Another one is gone!*' he shouts with glee. He looks down at Sigegar and swears, 'By Christ, I shall stay here until you are avenged, little Sigegar!'

Ecgberht and Ealhstan join him at the corner and the three of them hold back the Northmen between them, punching the air each time another is felled.

Aelfhild tries to help lift Theorvard over his saddle but gives in and allows Saeward and Cyneweard to finish pulling him over from their side. We have nothing to drape over him, and secure him so he does not fall off when we are riding. Saeward says a silent prayer for him and we all bow our heads.

'Come *on*, get mounted!' Oslac shouts and calls back our three bowmen.

'If only there had been more bowmen like you on the hill, we would not have had to fight Odo here', I tell Oslac.

'We were on our way, believe me', he looks sadly at me and shakes his head slowly. He raises his arms and lets them drop at his side, shrugging as he does so.

'Our thegn took all the horses with him when he rode with the others of our fyrd. He never came back, nor did half the others and we were still in Centland when the first of you came streaming through, you know that!' he shows the sadness that he must have felt with the loss of so many friends. He has lost another here, 'Now I have to tell Sigegar's woman'.

Although the daylight is still strong, Odo's men call off the hunt short of a hamlet Oslac tells us is Hanehest.

'We can bury your friend there', he says quietly, 'by a small wooden church. The priest will ready him for the afterlife'.

'It looks a calm sort of hamlet for a man to be buried', Saeward agrees.

I nod, looking around at the dwellings bereft of their owners. Cattle roaming freely over the grazing land beyond the trees do not seem to belong here, as if these folk have lost their rights over their animals. No geese or hounds warn of our coming. Not a soul is about.

'I was getting to like the fellow and he has to go and get himself killed', Theodolf smiles bleakly, patting the dead Theorvard.

They might have been friends from childhood, the way this youth strokes Theorvard's limp, lank hair. He adds, staring into thin air,

'The world is becoming unsafe for the likes of us'.

Aelfhild, Ecgberht, Ealhstan and Oslac dismount and lead their horses along the track between the dwellings. Swetman carries on riding a little further, beside me. Cyneweard rides some way to our right, watching for straying Northmen. We did not want to run into an eastward bound patrol on Watling Straet and took this way instead. Cyneweard need not worry. What there is in this hamlet will be of no use to them.

Trees line the track that leads past a few homes before we call a halt outside a small, solid, square-looking stave church. I dismount and lead Theorvard's horse, stopping in front of a low wicker gate that anyone could simply stride over. Swetman dismounts and waits with the others at the side of the track

'Father Leofsige, *you have visitors!*' Oslac calls out. There is no answer and Oslac calls again, 'Father Leofsige we need you to bury a brave *warrior!*'

I hear the hollow rattling of bolts being drawn. Iron hinges creak and a narrow door opens close to where I stand.

'Who wants me?' a man answers from behind the door.

'It is I, Oslac'.

'Do I *know* an Oslac?'

'I should hope you *do* know me. I was here to help bury my wife's father, Osric last summer. You know, Leofsige, the one who was butted by his ram'. Oslac is forbearing, but this might not last for long if he is tried too hard. 'I gave you some silver for your help. Now my friend needs you'.

'Who is your friend?' Father Leofsige asks from behind the partly opened door.

'I am Ivar Ulfsson', I answer, looking up at thick cobwebs in the top corners of the doorway, 'and I have a good friend who needs your help

240

to ease him into the company of his forefathers'.

'Is that the Ivar Ulfsson who was a huscarl of Earl Harold God-winson?'

An elderly, stooped fellow opens the door wider. Behind him in the half darkness is his fearful flock, staring wide-eyed at us from the depths of this small church.

'You have the better of me, Father Leofsige. Forgive me if I say I do not recall you, *but where do you know me from?'*

'I too was once of Earl Harold's household, given land as a king's thegn until I gave up worldly things to minister to this flock'.

Leofsige smiles broadly at me, his broad jaw lifting and I try to see him the way he paints himself in his younger years,

'Think about me with golden, reddish hair, gingery whiskers around my chin, not this wispy grey flax that you see now'.

He must have been around ten years older than I when he bethought his fighting ways to follow the teachings of the church, as odd as it may have seemed at the time. I see him now as he was then, an ever grin-ning, fiery copper-haired fellow, apt to wearing a waist-length byrnie in the way of the Suth Seaxans. Belts crossed his chest bearing the weight of his sheathed long sword and short sword on either hip.

There was a scramaseaxe for close fighting tucked into his waist belt. He looked odd beside Harold's other huscarls, who wore the long-er, calf-length straight-hemmed Danish style of mailcoat, much like the ones the Northmen wear.

'It comes back to me now, Leofsige. Aye, I *do* recall you – *well in-deed!* Have I altered so little over these last few years', I ask him. 'You know me so readily even after this time?'

'A *few* years, you say? I think it must have been more, but you are right. It is my memory that tricks me. I have been a priest for over half those years – I think. *It does sometimes seem like more!'*

Leofsige laughs. His teeth show clean and even still behind a full grey beard. The tasks of tending to his flock must weigh heavily on his shoulders. However, his eyes light up as he laughs, making it easier for me to think of him as he was then, tall, well built and always well turned out with gleaming weaponry. We thought then that he dressed beyond his standing, but Harold was happy with him and one day we saw Eadward nod when asked to raise him to the king's thegnhood.

Leofsige played the fool in Harold's household, but cross him or come up against him in a fight and you soon found he was no fool!

'The cares of the world have been heaped upon my old bones, my friend', Leofsige points with a thumb over one shoulder to his flock that still cowers within the shelter of the church. 'I shall take care of your friend, Ivar Ulfsson. Tell me his name and I will see that he has something that will mark his passing well'.

'His name is Theorvard', I tell my one-time comrade-in-arms.

'He lives on in you, Ivar, I know. I can see that you hold him as a brother in your heart', Leofsige rests a comforting hand on my right shoulder. 'We have lost many friends over the years, you and I, Ivar'.

He senses I am unable to say anything, suddenly struck dumb. He adds to put me at my ease,

'I too, am haunted by the faces of the dead and dying. That is why I took the cloth. The losses saddened me so, but I am now haunted by the deaths of folk who cannot rightly *afford* to be buried'. Leofsige takes his hand from me and goes to Theorvard, telling me over one shoulder, 'Put down *your* sword soon before the burden crushes you'.

He mumbles a short prayer and makes the sign of the cross over the slumped giant.

'Take your farewell of your friend and I shall have Theorvard's worldly remains wound in cloth before entrusting him to God's love'.

Leofsige stands back as I, followed in turn by Saeward, Wulfmaer and Theodolf each pay our last respects with a kiss on Theorvard's broad young forehead. He looks rested now since we fought Odo's men. Aelfhild comes forward to kiss him on his bearded cheeks as a show of thanks for a fallen warrior who went to her rescue although the odds were well-stacked against us outliving our visit to Odo's stronghold.

She looks up at me, her eyes welling with tears,

'I have never known a man so ready to lay down his life for folk he was neither kin to nor knew', Aelfhild weeps and hugs me, Ecgberht standing behind her wipes his eyes and, together with Swetman and Ealhstan are last to pay their respects to Theorvard.

Upon kissing him on the forehead as we had done, they walk slowly up to me and take my hand. Oslac asks Leofsige to say a prayer for the souls of his friends Sigegar and Wulfric, whose bodies we were unable to bring with us and turns to me,

'This is where we go our own ways again, Ivar. One day we will meet again, fighting the same foe, losing more friends and – hopefully - learning our lessons well', he gives me a bear hug as if we were old friends and wipes away a tear. It is not for us to call the Norns to task if they do not weave our wyrds to our liking.

Oslac then hugs Theodolf, Wulfmaer and Saeward in turn. To Theodolf he laughs ruefully,

'I should have liked to have known you sooner than I did. I would warrant that you would soon be a lot better bowman than you are now...

a *true champion!'*

'Thank you, Oslac. I shall tell that to my father when I join him one day', Theodolf laughs too, mindful that Oslac means what he has said as deeply-felt praise for his skill with the bow. He clutches his bow tightly and waves it as a salute to our leaving friends.

'And you, Cyneweard, what will you do?' I ask.

He shuffles, looking down at his feet briefly before looking up at me, grabs at my outstretched hand in parting and mounts together with Oslac,

'I will stay with Oslac for a time. If my father speaks of me, tell him I fought with you against the Northmen. He may think better of me one day'.

'I envy you, my friend. Look after him. One day he will be a warrior to be reckoned with!' I call after Oslac, who raises his brows and smiles ruefully.

'He had *better*, if he wishes to stay with *me* for any length of time!'

Aelfhild, Ecgberht and their neighbour Ealhstan leave for the south. Swetman lingers before he too mounts and swings his horse around to ride back to Egensford. I wonder if it will be safe for them to go back to their own settlements. He must have been reading my thoughts because he halts and half turns in his saddle to speak to me,

'We will each have to settle elsewhere. It would be wrong of us to go back to our homes and think life will go on as before. The Northmen would take out their spite on everyone else who lives around us'. He sits there, astride his mount, thinking a little longer,

'Ealhstan will go back to Scealfing for his woman and take her to his kinfolk in Suthrige. Aelfhild and Ecgberht will go west to Healdinges where he has kinfolk', he brightens, 'out of reach of Odo, I hope!'

'And you, Swetman, where will you go?' I ask.

'I shall ride back to Egensford, gather my wife and a few of my kin and ride to the heartland of West Seaxe. Who knows, one day our paths may cross again', Swetman smiles, turns his horse and rides away.

13

We are on our own again, Theodolf, Saeward, Wulfmaer and I. My thoughts turn to when we rode from Saewardstanbyrig, ten of us eager to fight for my kinsman - our king. We have gained two, but we have lost as many friends as I have fingers, more when I add Sigegar and Wulfric.

Of us all who rode south through Lunden nearly a month ago, only Theodolf and I are left. Saeward was lucky he was held in Jorvik, or he may have been killed with Thorfinn.

Leofsige is right, in that we are losing too many friends in this struggle, but we must take our leave of him and mount again. Wulfmaer has his new lease of life and Theodolf his wounds to nurse in Lunden. Saeward will think on whether he still wants to ride with us, or whether he should follow his other path at Wealtham again.

Killing – even our sworn foes – still sits heavily with him, but if he wants to stay with me he will have to take the killing in his stride. I will abide no man who sobs for the souls of the dead that he sends to their maker with a vengeance!

The night draws in as we leave the shelter of Hanehest for the Lunden road, dark, angry clouds ushered across the early evening sky from the north east. A freshening wind from seaward threatens colder weather to come. There is an iron edge to the wind that tells me snow is on the way.

We ride down into the hamlet of Grenewic from the last ridge on Watling Straet, the wind blowing across my right shoulder, pulling my lengthening hair across my jaw. With it comes the first sleet of the year. To the north, across the Temese, nothing can be seen beyond the slanting, cold, white mass that will soon engulf the burh of Lunden.

No-one is about as we make our way through Suthgeweorce in the cold wetness. I should like a good meal at the 'Eel Trap', and a good night's sleep before riding on to Thorney. The sound of my belly rumbling sounds to me like a rock fall, yet I still hear Saeward mumble something behind me.

'What is it, Saeward?' I turn in my saddle and look at the poor fellow, his face coated glistening white.

'It is nothing Ivar, nothing that a good seat by the fireside *and* a hot broth cannot cure!' Saeward pulls his cloak tightly around his chest and sets his jaw to stop his teeth chattering.

'We will soon be in the inn, friend! I myself am looking forward to some hot broth. I feel the meat juices running in my mouth as I speak', I tell him with what I hope looks like an assuring grin.

Braenda trots dutifully along the wettened road as if she too senses the end of our long ride. She has earned her keep many times over and I cannot think how much she must have endured bearing me through the south. It seems to me that each time we come to the end of a hard ride, we have to be away again. I lean forward and give her a rub along her neck. Near the bridge I see a start has been made on rebuilding some of the charred dwellings. The sleet gives the new timbers a thick white rime that glows in the torchlight from the southern end of Lunden Brycg.

'Halt! Who goes there?' one of Ansgar's men hails before we cross the bridge.

'Ivar Ulfsson and the few men I have left after saving some of the Centish folk from Odo's rope', I answer dully. My whole body aches with the need for food and rest, nothing more.

'Thegn Osgod asked me to tell you the aetheling Eadgar will see you in the morning', I hear him tell me.

'Surely you mean *King* Eadgar?' I stare down at him in disbelief. He could not have made a slip of the tongue, could he?

'*No* my Lord, I mean the *aetheling* Eadgar. You will learn more in the morning when he speaks to you. I have been told to tell you that much, nothing more, because there is much more that Thegn Osgod himself can tell you here in the morning', the huscarl cannot even summon a smile to show that everything is well.

'Thank you, my good fellow', I give a salute and wave my friends on across the bridge.

Wynstan and Gudheard are busy in the yard of the 'Eel Trap', helping a local smith calm a frisky colt.

'Ivar, you are back - *again!*' Wynstan shouts gleefully at seeing me again after Theorvard brought our horses. When Wulfmaer and Saeward left afterward he must have thought his custom was leaving him. I hate to think what his feelings were when Theodolf left his sick bed to follow on.

He looks over my right shoulder, sizing up Wulfmaer, Saeward and Theodolf, and sees one of us is missing,

'Where is *Theorvard?*' Wynstan stands agape, unable to understand that the young giant might be dead. None of us could have foreseen that happening at the time. It seemed he would be with us forever. When I look down at the stone-set yard as I dismount he understands.

'He was a true warrior to the end', Wulfmaer tells Wynstan, 'a man whose worth could never be bested!'

My friends dismount after me and we walk wearily into the inn. I follow them after resting a hand on Wynstan's shoulder to comfort him. He had grown fond of my friend from the Danelaw, since Theorvard won back Saeward's silver from Inwaer in the drinking bout at the 'Crooked Billet'.

The main room is warm from the great fire that crackles in the hearth. Only Ymme waits to hear what I and my friends wish to eat.

When she sees me looking around the room she guesses that I am missing Aelfthryth.

'Aelfthryth is ill in her room', Ymme tells me. 'She is suffering with a bad rash'.

Saeward looks up and asks if anyone is treating her.

'There is an old woman who came yesterday, when Aelfthryth had only been back a day. She said Aelfthryth should be left to rest until she came again', Ymme answers. Whether she told him that to keep any of us from seeking out Aelfthryth or whether she really has a rash is a moot point.

'What we need is some good hot meat broth', I tell her. 'Have you any?'

'I can soon get Gerda to put something in the pot', Ymme brightens at being the lady of the house. She calls out loudly, 'Gerda, come in here and set out some bowls of broth for our guests!'

A wan looking young woman enters the room with a child trailing, hanging onto her apron strings. I cannot tell if it is a boy or girl at that age.

'That child should be in its cot, fast asleep by now, surely', Theodolf tells her.

Gerda whimpers softly,

'He will not sleep on his own because he misses his father. The child has become fretful'. To look at her size she herself is not long out of childhood. 'We were to come together in Medestan at my mother's home, but he failed to show and we narrowly escaped the Northmen to come here'.

'Where was his father when you last saw him?' I ask.

'He was near Pefense, in hiding because he had stolen some of their food. We were left alone on our way east, but I do not think we would have been safe for much longer'.

I think I know the outcome of this tale, but I hear her out.

'My husband sent us on to my kin in Medestan whilst he took their eyes off us by stealing a horse as well. Whilst he led them a merry dance we slipped away. But the Northmen were already in Medestan too, and I was helped by kind folk my mother knows in Centland to come to Lunden'.

'Would your husband's name be Dunstan?' I think back on when he said his woman's name was Gerda.

Her eyes widen, taken aback at my knowing him,

'You *know* him?' She stands agape.

'I *knew* him. He was a brave man. You and your son should be proud of him. He did not flinch from death'.

I cannot hide her from the truth, as much as it grieves me to tell her of his dying. 'He and his friend Odd were helping us with our task'.

Gerda stands forlorn on the flagstone floor, a dish in her hand, dazed from hearing my tidings. She lets the dish fall to the floor, shattering into tiny shards and buries her head in her hands. The child looks at me, mouth pursed, ready to join his mother in crying. But it is likely he understands nothing about what I have told his mother. Ymme takes her in her arms and comforts the shaking young mother, turning angrily on me,

'Are you sure you are both speaking of the same man? Otherwise you are just being needlessly cruel, telling her of her husband's death. Better you kept your own counsel and let her think *one* day they would be together again!'

'He is right, Ymme', Gerda's sobs from the depths of the folds of the old woman's loose apron bosom, 'I would be forever thinking that he is alive, waiting for him in vain to come back to me'.

Ymme lets go of the young woman and wipes around her eyes with the apron. Gerda pulls away, thanks Ymme and turns to me,

'This way I can look for a father for my little Brihtwin. Perhaps I will find a man as forthright and honest as your good self'.

I am flattered by the way Gerda paints me, but Saeward looks sideways at her, as if to question her wisdom. Theodolf is blind to everything happening around him, watching Gerda open-mouthed as she turns to a small table piled high with parsnips, turnips, different meats and offal. He asks cheekily with a winsome smile,

'You could toss me one of the parsnips, Gerda. It would give me something to chew on until that broth is ready'.

Gerda turns to look at me, as if I were her master. I shrug, give a curt nod and she does as bidden. Theodolf catches the parsnip and breaks it in half, offering the lower half first to Wulfmaer, who shakes his head wearily in reply, and then to Saeward.

Upon seeing Saeward shake his head, the lad offers it to me. I cup my hands and he happily flicks it to me,

'Never say I give you *nothing!*' he quips and smiles at Gerda. They must be almost of an age, the young woman being a little older, I would guess.

Gerda answers his smile with a giggle and goes back to chopping when she catches Ymme scowling at her. We all fall silent again, watching the fire in the hearth, thinking. Theodolf and I gnaw at our half parsnips, Saeward and Wulfmaer nurse beakers of ale. Wynstan enters, beams at us all and asks with a mock frown,

'Why are you all so quiet?'

He calls from the doorway on his way out again,

'Theorvard would not have wanted you to be so distraught!'

None of us answers straight away, so Wynstan comes back to me and asks,

'No-one *else* has died have they, aside from Theorvard?'

'None you would know of, Wynstan', I answer.

He looks at Saeward, who gives him the full story,

'Gerda has heard she is now a widow. Her husband fought bravely alongside us against the Northmen in Suth Seaxe'. He swallows some of the ale, licks his lips and adds,

'Mostly we are not as cheerful as we might be because we are tired and hungry. We will be our cheerful selves tomorrow, when we have rested. God will thank you for your kind thoughts'.

Wynstan looks at each of us in turn, from one to another, shakes his head and leaves the room. All we hear then is Gerda's chopping of parsnips, turnips and meat for the broth, and of Wulfmaer slurping his ale. Later, when we have eaten and finished our ale, Ymme comes to tell us where our rooms are,

'...As there are fewer of you this time, you can all have a room to yourselves'.

We follow her wearily to the rooms that she has made ready for us, and I shut the door of mine after she has lit a rush light for me. She wishes us each a good night and shuffles off to a room she now shares with Gerda.

'I wish you a good night, too, Ymme', I call loudly after her fading footfalls, and sink onto a cot bed.

Theodolf has been deemed fit by Saeward to sleep on his own. His wounds have been looked at and he has been passed to be 'as well as any man could be, who had been speared by a Northman and slashed by a boar's tusk'.

Gerda made round eyes at Theodolf on hearing of his wounds and trials, allowing the lad to bask in some sort of warrior-worship. Wulfmaer told her with a crafty smirk that he had hurt himself more often in the mill at Saewardstan when he was a lad.

'No doubt, if you drank as much then as you do now', Saeward not-

248

ed drily, shutting off the poor fellow with few words, and earning himself a wry grin from each of us for his wit.

In the room next to mine are Saeward and Wulfmaer, who have chosen to share a room. There is not even the usual banter of two men readying themselves for a night's sleep. We will soon hear Wulfmaer's snoring, and Saeward will curse himself for sharing a room with the miller instead of taking a room of his own.

'What is to happen today?' Theodolf asks me after he has wolfed down the porridge set down by Ymme almost under his nose on the table. Saeward is seated at another table across the small room to his right, a knife in his left hand, cutting bread to eat with the platter of crumbled cheese that Ymme has put on the table for him.

'*I* must ride to Thorney to speak to King - I mean the *aetheling* Eadgar - and ask him why he is no longer king. Lord Ansgar may be there, too, so. I may hear what is afoot', I tell him although I am not sure Ansgar would be able to shed any light on the matter.

'If we are no longer a king's huscarls, why do you need to see him?' Saeward asks, nursing an empty beaker. Setting down his beaker on the table next to Theodolf's empty bowl, he turns to me.

'We would still be *his* huscarls', I tell Saeward. 'He is still our lord. It is to *him* we gave our oath, not to a crown'.

'*You* gave our oaths *for* us', Saeward puts me right. He asks further, 'Who will be *king?*'

All eyes are on me. I wish I had an answer and tell them so,

'That *I* cannot tell you – unless our lords have given up the struggle without our knowing', I hazard an answer. 'I would not wonder it were either Eadwin or Morkere – or *both*'.

'Which means that the Northman bastard is king? The Witan have sold him out for their *own ends!*' Wulfmaer swears, making Ymme turn in her steps. She gives him a look as frosty as it is outside on the street, but she knows he would pay her no heed were she to say anything. She keeps her scolding to herself – for now. Wulfmaer rumbles on,

'After all the bother we went to, all that way to the coast and everything - we could have saved ourselves the trouble!'

Brihtwin has been playing on the floor near our table and looks up. He beams at Gerda and shouts, over and over again, 'Bastard, *bastard!*' until Ymme hushes him up with her hand over his mouth.

'*Now,* do you hear what you have done?' Ymme yells at Wulfmaer over Theodolf's laughter. 'The poor mother does not want this on top of all her *other* ills!'

Saeward tries to calm the old woman,

'Hush woman! The child does not know its meaning. Let him

screech it from the rooftops and he will forget it soon enough. Make too much of it and he *will* keep on shouting it, for a lot longer!'

'When the inn is full of Northmen, perhaps?' Ymme challenges.

'Perhaps when you have guests who have more feelings about children shouting oaths than we have', I tell her, 'you could take him to another room. We need to *talk* here and Wulfmaer is given to swearing when he is aroused'.

Ymme scowls darkly, gathers up her things and marches from the room with Gerda in tow leading her young son. The door slams hard enough for dust and cobwebs to fall from the lintel in a cloud.

'Do some dusting, woman, instead of *fussing!*' Wulfmaer calls after her. We hear her stumping heavily up the wooden stairs to the guest rooms, I would guess to grudgingly air our beds.

'How long will we be staying here?' Theodolf asks. He has been eyeing up Gerda since he first saw her yesterday. I see from the way he follows her everywhere with his eyes when she is in the same room that he would dearly like to know her better.

'It would all hang on the answers Eadgar gives me', I answer. 'Broadly speaking, we could be here a few days longer, or a week even'.

'That is an open-ended answer if ever there was one!' Saeward puts in again. 'Can you do no better than that?'

'No I can not', I tell him bluntly. I *would* give a better answer. 'But I think at least two of you should come with me'.

'Why?' Theodolf asks warily. 'You will be coming back here, surely?'

'I hope I will, believe me, but each of you may have seen things along the way that I missed', I give him a bland answer.

'You mean such as when we doubted your leadership, and that you nearly killed Burhred - or having to save those Centish folk from Odo, losing good men such as Theorvard and Sigeric?' Theodolf drips words like venom over my friendship toward him. 'Perhaps you mean getting Dunstan killed helping us on our worthless errand?' He rises from the bench and stands square to me. I stay seated, my fists clenched, should he make to strike me. We glare at one another.

'I knew you were not worth *dying* for', Theodolf sits again and pours scorn over my friendship with his father and lies, 'I told Hrothulf before we left Aethel's steading, but he could only think back to when you fought side-by-side. He would not see Tostig had others he would reward better, such as *Copsig!* Still, Tostig was given his comeuppance at Staenfordes Bridge and you dealt with Copsig yourself, the 'grey wolf'. Now Aethel is the handmaiden of an ageing widow and

Hrothulf is dead, his bones licked clean by the crows'

'Why did you come *with* us?' Saeward demands loyally on my behalf. 'Answer that, *if* you can!'

'I was hoping that one of you would take your rightful place as leader in his stead!' Theodolf almost spits his loathing for me at Saeward and Wulfmaer. 'Like you, Saeward'.

'It may be that I am happy with Ivar as leader, that Wulfmaer and I trust him, and think he was doing his best for us. No doubt Theorvard thought so', Saeward answers for them both, plainly rattled at the way Theodolf seems to have turned against me. Whilst Theodolf carries on running me down Saeward rises, his arms folded, and walks slowly across the floor to stand close to him. Theodolf looks up at him but, thinking Saeward has crossed the room to stand by the hearth he goes further – too far,

'Wulfmaer spoke of his distrust for Ivar, as did Burhred. You both know that!' Theodolf's gripe against me is in vain, but does not know how far he can push the loyal Saeward. 'Theorvard would have followed Ivar to the ends of the earth, but he was that kind of man. I think he would have followed *any* man with all his limbs and as much if not more between his ears than he himself had!'

Saeward bends and takes Theodolf's collar in both hands. He draws the lad's head forward so he can stare into his eyes until he yields, tightening his grip as Theodolf tries to worm free,

'That is where you are wrong, Theodolf. You know that in your heart. Ivar did not lead them to their deaths for any selfish thoughts of his own gain! He may have had his own grounds for keeping faith with King Harold, and for winning Eadgar's trust, but we could have told him at any time before we left Lunden for Haestingas that he was chasing a lost cause', Saeward does not look once at me whilst he lays out to Theodolf his trust in my leadership.

Theodolf glares at me past Saeward, trying to break their trust in me.

'Did he try to stop Osgod taking you to Eoferwic, Saeward?'

Theodolf's mouth twists in a hideous grin. I see Braenda suddenly instead of Theodolf, looking coldly at me. Is this for my faithlessness in thinking of bedding Aelfthryth, and then in my thinking that I had bedded Aelfhild? Perhaps it is only I who can see Braenda and I struggle to keep my wits. Is Theodolf challenging my leadership, or is Braenda acting through him to unsettle me?

'Satan is within you, Theodolf, I am sure!' Saeward cannot see Braenda, surely?

'*Why* do you say *that?*' Theodolf suddenly stands. He looks dazed as if waking from a dream. He stares around him in the half-dark and blinks, seeing suddenly where he is,

'*What is happening?* Why are we like this, glaring at one another? All I know is that I was giving Gerda the glad eye until she left the room. I feel as though a great dark cloud came down over me, and then left as suddenly!'

Saeward and Wulfmaer stare at one another, and at me. Theodolf sits down heavily on the bench and puts his head in his hands. A look of grief has come over him where there was earlier a look of hatred.

'As I said', I go on, ignoring what has gone before for Theodolf's sake, 'we must hear what answers Eadgar and Ansgar have for us. We need to know if there is anything further that we can do for our lord. When you are ready we can saddle the horses'.

Wynstan has come into the room and without saying a word leaves again. I look from Theodolf to Saeward and Wulfmaer to hear if they have anything they would like to share with me on the matter,

'They will be well fed and rested by now', Saeward agrees, his thoughts on our mounts now.

'Aye, they should be', Wulfmaer agrees, stands and looks down at Theodolf on the bench and makes his way to the yard with Saeward behind him. At the door Saeward looks back and I nod for him to follow Wulfmaer out to the stable.

I stand by Theodolf, put a firm hand on his left shoulder and make for the door to follow the other two. Before I walk out into the yard he looks up and asks,

'Who did you see just now when you were staring at me?'

'What do you mean - who do *you* think I saw?' I answer, looking away from him to the door. I leave the door open for him should he want to follow me into the yard.

This may happen again. I hope not, but that would be a forlorn hope. Knowing Braenda better now, she can break into my life as and how she wishes. I have given in to her before and will do so again because I fear what might happen to me otherwise. I also like being with her, however and whenever she shows herself.

Eadgar is seated alone by his hearth. He looks to be thinking about something, perhaps musing over his wyrd, when I am ushered in to his room

'Ivar, it is good to see you again. I had despaired of setting eyes on you again when you came back to Lunden and then left again for Centland. Osgod told me you were given word from Odo to ride to Hrofesceaster. You have heard the worst?' He waves me to a chair.

'I had heard something about you being king no longer, my Lord. Is that so?' I lean forward in the chair and take a beaker of ale offered by his discthegn.

'Archbishop Ealdred and the earls have sold me out for fear of losing their titles and land to Willelm's followers, as has Stigand. A priest called Lanfranc, I hear, is to be Archbishop in his stead. He is still in Northmandige but Duke Willelm awaits him in the New Year. I will laugh if Stigand loses Cantuareburh to this Lanfranc, despite his toadying! What am I *saying?* He *will* lose his seat'. Eadgar plays with the soft hairs on his chin, smiles ruefully and adds, 'Everywhere in Christendom Stigand is known to be stained with the shame of taking the seat of Cantuareburh from Harold whilst he still holds Wintunceaster. Can you *believe that?!* I offered to uphold his claim for the pallium to the Holy Father, but he had to go running with his tail between his legs to Beorh-hamstede for fear of being trampled in the mud when the others stampeded. The earls Eadwin and Morkere followed, foreseeably, and Ansgar was almost flat on his face on the cold stony floor. Ivar you can understand how I felt like retching over these spineless buzzards?'

He looks at me as I struggle, trying to think of Ansgar grovelling. I shake my head because it is beyond me to think of a man made up to Shire Reeve of Middil Seaxe by Harold as being worthy of such a base act, selling out his true king to the bastard Duke.

'I know it is hard to see it', Eadgar can easily read me and laughs. 'I would have been hard put to see it myself. The best is yet to come'.

I take a mouthful of his sweet ale to take away the burning dryness from my mouth and sit awaiting further bad tidings.

'I am to be treated like a hall hound. They think I should sit at Willelm's feet when he becomes king – 'he begins.

'*When* he becomes king?' I break in, forgetting myself, and screw my eyes shut thinking of the outcome of Willelm's crowning.

I shall have to lie low when he hears that I am still about, and can be only a matter of time now. He would have gathered from Odo sooner or later that I am a thorn in his side again.

'Aye, *when* he becomes king', Eadgar stares at me, rightly irked at my breaking the flow of his thoughts. 'I shall be given an allowance of as many shillings as there are days in the year! Picture that if you will, me – like a *hall hound!* What will *you* do then?'

What will *I* do? If Eadgar must be at Willelm's side then we his household warriors will be cast loose - like as not we will have a reward on our heads, alive or dead. Odo would like nothing better than to have me with a rope around my neck. I had best stay clear of Thorney, or wherever the duke stays until he is crowned.

'Duke Willelm knows you, does he not?' Eadgar may have been told Thorfinn and I were almost hanged by Odo and only saved from the noose by Willelm's showing at his Falaise stronghold with Harold. Had my kinsman not been there, I might well have swung from the gallows anyway.

I think Odo has a close kinship with his rope maker. Having put paid to this love of theirs twice, he will be only too happy to catch me a third time! Third time lucky, they say. I answer with a hollow laugh,

'He knows *me* well enough! I was warned by him not to set foot in his duchy again and will soon hear if he thinks this kingdom is part of that duchy'.

'From what I know of him, he harbours grudges. I will not tell him that you were in my pay when you went to the coast for me', Eadgar offers, 'to spy on his supply havens'.

'It might count against you if you *did* tell him. For your own sake do not own to knowing me', I warn him. His standing is already weak, having been let down by his Witan for their own gains. 'What of Eadwin and Morkere? Are they assured of their titles?'

'He must seek the counsel of his own nobles before he can make offers, but I think he wants to keep them on their toes, guessing what will come to them', Eadgar muses with a wry smile.

'*His* nobles will do what he wants them to once he is king. He will have his hands on the title deeds in the scriptorium here at West Mynster. Waltheof is no better off. His earldom is small enough as it is, but he has widespread lands in Deira. However he can be cut to size quicker than they. What do you think, Ivar?'

'We will have to look outward soon, to the Wealsh or to the Scots. Or we may need to ask my kinsman, Svein for help', I take a mouthful of ale to take away the bad taste in my mouth, whilst Eadgar mulls over what I have put to him to think over.

'They would want to see something by way of reward for helping us. I know your Danish kinfolk would do nothing for my sake from the kindness of their hearts', Eadgar answers, watching me closely. 'They would first offer help to Harold's kindred, surely?'

'That is true', my answer is met with a tired smile. I empty my beaker which Eadgar rises to refill, having sent his discthegn from the room. 'No-one ever said we Danes were saints when it came to helping folk. When Svein Haraldsson came with Knut they helped themselves to what they thought was their just reward for not attacking your great grandfather, Aethelred. When his coffers ran dry Svein set out to take the kingdom but died suddenly at Gaegnesburh –'

'I know all that, Ivar. Do not think I hold it against you', Eadgar looks away from me and stares into the embers of his fire.

'Knut would have seen my father and my uncle Eadmund done

away with. They were taken by their teacher and guide Gaimar to Anund Jakob, the Svear king whose sister was my grandmother. He had them sent on to Novgorod for their own safety. No, I think we would not be wrong to seek help from King Maelcolm, possibly also Gruffyd's son Llewellyn. Even Diarmuid, the king of Dyflin might help if he were offered enough reward. But Maelcolm should be asked first, as he wishes to have my sister Margarethe for his queen'.

'The Erse king of Dublin gave Harold and Leofwin men to help Godwin regain his earldom in the years before you came with your father', I offer Eadgar hope for help.

He mocks me with quiet laughter and hands me my replenished beaker,

'You seem to forget that Godwin was at odds with my great uncle, Eadweard. And let us not forget what happened to the old king's brother Aelfred. Of course I will not forget that Diarmuid may offer help in return for booty. After all, if when the Northmen feel at home here and they begin to cast their eyes on nearby prizes, the Erse kingdoms will be the next they see beyond Wealas or Maelcolm's kingdom', Eadgar shows me that he can see beyond our own turmoil.

'They will understand your plight, my Lord', I offer.

'Ivar, do not take this amiss but I am not your Lord'.

He sits heavily on Eadward's great chair and takes a long draught of his own ale before pleading with me to speak to him as if he were a brother,

'I am Eadgar, no longer even an *aetheling* for as long as Duke Willelm has heirs, and I will *never* rule my grandfather's kingdom. My given name will be enough for me until mightier men than you can help rid me of Willelm', Eadgar smiles as he tells me, but I sense that he feels he pain of his hopelessness. 'I must also release you from the oath you made to uphold my claim. You would be hindered in your duties by Willelm's and Odo's hatred for you'.

Eadgar rises from his chair again and looks down at me,

'Go with your friends and if our paths cross again, and *if* I should come to my due throne, I will gladly offer you the standing of your choice within the kingdom'.

He reaches out his right hand and I move to kneel and kiss his ring finger.

'No, Ivar, stand and give me a greeting fit for a brother!' Eadgar chides and takes my right hand in both his. 'I wish you farewell and good luck in your forthcoming undertakings!'

I can see his eyes brimming and take my leave before he unburdens himself on me. Beyond the door my friends stand talking with Osgod and I make my way across the hall towards them.

Osgod sees me and breaks off from the small talk. He takes my hand and pumps it whilst greeting me as if I were an old friend,

'Ivar, it is good to see you again, and you live to tell the tale of your fight with Odo's men in his own stronghold!' I feel he did not think he would see me again.

'It is good to see you again, too, Osgod', I lie, smiling.

'Theodolf told me you lost more men in Centland', Osgod tries to look friendly but he is only talking to pass the time of day. 'The young giant Theorvard *and* Thorfinn's friend, Burhred - they will be sorely missed I would warrant'. As he knew neither he can only make a show of mourning their passing.

'*Indeed*, they will be missed. I looked upon them as if they were my brothers. We had lived and fought together, and in their turn both men had saved my skin more than once'. I miss them even as I speak. A lump comes to my throat and I have to swallow as if I had tasted some foul-tasting morsel. Saeward comes to my aid, sensing further questioning might move me to tears.

'Our friends fought as great warriors. Burhred was slain on the day we were on our way back to Lunden from the coast', Saeward lies, or perhaps he did not see the way his fellow East Seaxan was spread-eagled on the bed, 'and Theorvard died trying to shield us from the Northmen's crossbow bolts at Hrofesceaster'.

'You have lost too many friends Ivar, I think, since I first saw you in Eoferwic', Osgod winces at talk of crossbows and looks earnestly at me. 'I can understand, since I have lost many of my own friends fighting Tostig and Harald Sigurdsson'.

Perhaps his kindness is real, after all.

'Where *are* the young earls?' I ask when able to talk again.

'Morkere and Eadwin are hunting in the west. They will be leaving for the north again soon, but have to be back to witness Willelm being crowned, whenever that may be'. Osgod grins wryly, adding, 'I do not know where Waltheof is. He may have found himself a woman - perhaps that woman Aelfthryth at the 'Eel Trap'?'

'She is much too old for him, married with a son, Cyneweard. Her husband Wynstan could wrap his hands around Waltheof's scrawny neck without too much trouble! More, Aelfthryth is ailing in bed, so her housemaid Ymme tells me'.

I hear myself scoff at Waltheof, but deep within me I think it may be so. Aelfthryth would not be the first woman to feel pride at being paid court by a younger man. Inwardly I feel bitter. If he were paying court to her, Ymme may have been fending me off by telling me her mistress was suffering from a rash. I would not have been happy to find her with Waltheof.

'And Ansgar, where is he?' I ask after the shire reeve.

'Most likely seeing to his lands, assured by Willelm's Aenglish monk that his standing is safe for now. Whether he sized the fellow up and found him lacking, I do not know. It may be he knew of Ansgar being in Harold's shieldwall, therefore he already had his eyes on a Northman to take over Ansgar's tasks'.

Osgod does not seem to think that Ansgar would be missed, even after seeing him lead his fyrdmen at Lunden Brycg.

'Ansgar is an able fellow', I feel I have to speak up for him, but could have to fight him one day.

'That may be so, but I do not think Willelm trusts Ansgar, and that must be for our good'.

Osgod turns from me to a young fellow who has shown in the yard dressed for war, his hauberk chest ventail done up and helm nose piece down and almost hiding his eyes.

'What can I do for you, friend?' Osgod takes the newcomer to task.

'I bring word for the ears of the aetheling Eadgar only', we hear the fellow tell Osgod.

'Do *you* need to give it to him, or can I get his discthegn to pass on your words?'

Not understanding Osgod he looks to me,

'What my friend asked is – 'I begin.

'I *know* what a discthegn is! I paid court here when the old king asked for me', the fellow answers haughtily. 'Is your friend of this household or do I need to speak to someone who *can* take me to Eadgar?'

Osgod snaps at the uncouth young Northman,

'Who do you think you are, and why can you not understand that a household discthegn is as able to pass on your words as anyone else? As it is I am a *thegn* -'

'I am Gilbert de Warenne', the Northman breaks in, 'and I wish to give the child Eadgar a spoken command from my liege Lord, Willelm of Northmandige. Kindly lead me to him and stay with us to attest that I have told him!'

Osgod nods to me. I take the Northman to Eadgar's door and knock briskly.

'*Enter!*' Eadgar calls out and when I open the door delightedly addresses me, 'Ivar, *you are back so soon!*'

'I have a Gilbert de Warenne to speak to you. He has word for you from his Lord, Willelm', I tell Eadgar to raised eyebrows from de

Warenne.

'*You* are Ivar Ulfsson?' asks de Warenne, eyeing me warily.

'I am', I answer without asking why he needs to know. I have a name with these Northmen for foiling their well-laid plans and he wants to make sure that I do not pass through their clutches again.

'You are the Ivar Ulfsson who has crossed Bishop Odo more than once?'

'I am the same', I answer calmly, slowly.

'Then my words are for you, too', he turns from me to tell Eadgar whatever it is Willelm wishes him to know,

'You should speak to the aetheling Eadgar as is his due, Gilbert de Warenne', I tell the Northman to his horror. De Warenne gives me a pained look and turns again to deliver his master's words as if I had not spoken,

'My Lord Duke Willelm kindly wishes you to attend a meeting this evening in the Deanery office of Bearrucing with your earls Eadwin, Morkere and Waltheof, and Ansgar the shire reeve of Middil Seaxe. He bade me to assure you of your safety, that you need not bring your men-at-arms', he nods at me to let me know that this is not as much a wish as a command.

'I have no men-at-arms', Eadgar answers flatly. 'The fellow here who brought you in here is not of my household. I have no leave to command huscarls, you should know'.

De Warenne is awkwardly silent, nonplussed by Eadgar's answer. Eadgar goes on,

'Ivar is a free man, and can make his own choices. Do you wish to attend this meeting, Ivar?' Eadgar shakes his head behind the Northman whilst de Warenne's eyes are on me.

'We would gladly escort the aetheling but we are needed elsewhere in the land', I take Eadgar's cue and make my way to the door. De Warenne reaches out with his left hand and grabs for the hauberk I am wearing.

'I *would* counsel attending!' de Warenne shouts. He is mistaken in trying to order me. Osgod rushes into the room, closely followed by Saeward and Wulfmaer, who stand on either side of the door whilst Osgod strides up to the young nobleman. He reaches with his sword hand for the pommel of his sword to unsheathe it.

'My Lord Aetheling, I thought you were being threatened!' Osgod stares down de Warenne.

'No, Osgod, nothing untoward has happened. Ivar wishes to leave with his men. Can you see that he leaves safely without hindrance?'

'I have men outside!' de Warenne hisses.

'And *I* have men inside *and* out', counters Osgod.

'There are more of them than you have. You had best bring *more* the next time you come to show your lack of manners! Ivar you can go'.

Osgod bars de Warenne's way as he makes to grab for me again, and unsheathes his sword to back his threat. Saeward and Wulfmaer follow me out of the room. I turn at the door before leaving and give him my heartfelt thanks,

'I wish you well, my Lord Eadgar. I hope our paths cross again one day!' I take my farewell again.

'God go with you, *Lord* Ivar', Eadgar stresses the 'Lord' for de Warenne's sake, grins and gives a saluting wave. Osgod follows me out of the room with Sacward close behind. Theodolf, having waited beyond the door for us joins us with Wulfmaer.

'Make sure the Northman does not leave here before Ivar and his friends', Osgod tells his huscarls, three of whom follow us to the yard.

More of Morkere's and Eadwin's huscarls have squared up to de Warenne's few horsemen, axes at the ready. They make way for us to leave and close on the hapless Northmen, who can only look on as we make our escape.

Morkere will have words with Eadgar and Osgod about taking my side and weakening his standing with Willelm.

'We need to ride back to the 'Eel Trap' for our belongings first', I tell my friends before we press our horses into a gallop away from Thorney. The land between here and the River Fleot is open heathland, and we can be seen for miles.

Along the road between the scattered hamlets are few men who might try to stop any Northman horsemen from riding down fellow Aenglishmen. We should stay clear of this road. Osgod will not be able to hold them back for long if Eadwin and Morkere come back from their hunting, but the other tracks will slow us down.

'I have nothing to go back for', Wulfmaer tells me under his breath. 'I do not think Saeward has, either'.

'Theodolf, do you have anything you need to go back to the 'Eel Trap' for, aside from taking your leave of Gerda?' I ask the lad.

'I asked her to come with me', he tells me offhandedly.

'You did *what?!*' Saeward is more shaken than I am.

'You could have told me that you were going to ask her', I shake my head at his foolishness.

Theodolf answers,

'They will not be looking for tradesmen'. He has plainly thought this through since he first learned she was a widow. 'We can go north on a borrowed cart with my horse pulling'.

'We could be craftsmen, riding together', Wulfmaer offers, what trade do you think we should say we follow if we are stopped?'

'Why did we not think of that, Ivar? You, Wulfmaer, Theodolf and I could be millers' Saeward laughs at the ease at which the thought came to Wulfmaer.

'We could wear something over our chain mail, hide our weapons under flour sacks', Wulfmaer adds, laughing 'and get food at Saeward-stan to last a few days, into the midlands'.

'I was not thinking of going any further than Wealtham for the time being', I tell them, 'but you could be right. We need to see if there is anyone else around who wishes to come with us. Were you thinking of going back to Aethel's steading?'

In looking back at Theodolf I see him nod at me.

'It is a shame. I could use a good bowman, such as you are', I look down at the ground, thinking as our horses canter along, and then at him again and try to humour him and ask. 'You could teach others your bowmanship skills here and we could go on to Eoferwic after the snows have gone in the fore-year. Will you not think again and stay in East Seaxe until such time as we know better what is happening? Besides, at this time of the year it would be folly to take a slow cart that far north, with a woman and a small child to take care of'.

'Outlaws abound on that road, you know that. A woman and child could count against you if you were to be stopped by any. With four of us together you would be safer', Saeward warns, thinking of Gerda and Brihtwin.

'He is right, Theodolf. You could stay in one of the empty homes near Wealtham and make yourself enough arrows to hunt with during the winter, perhaps more to arm yourself. Dean Wulfwin would take the Northmen's thoughts from us by feasting them. A man is less sharp when he is full of wine or ale', Wulfmaer agrees Enlivened now, he tells us, 'Aye, there are enough empty homes to hide us, where the man of the house was killed fighting'.

I know what he is leading to.

'The three of us could make out that we are millworkers', Saeward agrees. Our arms could be hidden until they are needed and Theodolf could be a woodsman'.

'How does that sound to you?' I ask Theodolf.

He screws up his eyes, nods and answers,

'I will think about it until we reach the 'Eel Trap. 'I am promising nothing!' he finishes, fighting a smile. We mean something to one another after having lost so many friends lately, despite his turn this morning. We press on for Lunden burh.

13

Wynstan and Gudheard are helping a smith shoe horses when we enter the yard, and Ymme is crossing the yard carrying a basket of clothes to be washed.

'You are back so soon? What did the *aetheling* Eadgar have to say?' Wynstan asks.

'We are our own men', I tell the innkeeper.

'Speaking of own men, some more came whilst you sought out the aetheling. One said his name was Oslac, the other I know already. I do not know what you did at Hrofesceaster, but you made a man of my son. Cyneweard wants to ride with *you*, wherever it is you are going'. Wynstan looks happier, now that his son has fulfilled his hopes.

'I think they will have to listen to what I tell them, before they think about what they want to do with their lives', I tell him. 'Are they in the main room?'

Wynstan follows us into the inn on his way to the kitchen,

'Aye, they are eating. They have only just got here. Go in, do *you* want something to eat? The night is drawing in again and you must be cold and hungry after your ride'.

Oslac and Cyneweard are talking. Cyneweard, his mouth full, sprays food as he laughs at something Oslac has told him.

Oslac sees us enter and stands,

'*Ivar*, how good to see you again!'

'Aye, and it is good to see *you* so soon too, Oslac!' I greet them in turn. 'Cyneweard, you are well? Wynstan has told me you wish to join us again'.

Once we are all seated, and Oslac begins eating after being chided by Ymme for letting his meat cool, I outline our thoughts on going on to Wealtham dressed as tradesmen. Ymme seems to have put her washing basket away and shuffles into the room with Brihtwin trailing. Wynstan tells her to make something for the three of us to eat whilst we talk. As I listen to Wulfmaer my eyes stray to two fellows seated at a table in the half-darkness at the far side of the room.

Oslac and Cyneweard slowly pick out the small bones from wildfowl they are eating as they listen to me. Cyneweard downs his ale and asks for more from his father. He relishes being a guest at the inn in which he toiled before. His father now waits on him hand and foot since hearing of his part in the fight at Hrofesceaster.

'Should all stay close together at Wealtham?' Oslac asks.

'We could be scattered, but not so much that we lose touch with one another', I put to him. Wulfmaer nods his agreement.

'Aye, we can be spread between Saewardstan and Wealtham. Some of the older children can take word between us, as the two settlements are only a couple of miles apart. I know a number of women whose men were killed when Tostig landed on the coast before he joined up with the Norsemen. They would be glad of a good pair of strong hands about the place', Wulfmaer laughs.

'They might show how grateful they are in a number of ways?' Oslac grins at Cyneweard, who responds with a playful punch on Oslac's right shoulder before setting about finishing his food.

With an eye on Cyneweard's platter, Oslac asks me,

'When are we riding from here?'

He leans over, tears off part of a wing and fights off the annoyed Cyneweard with a belly laugh and a belch.

'We leave when we have all eaten. Duke Willelm's men came for us when we were at Thorney. Whilst I was speaking with Eadgar some fool named Gilbert de Warenne threatened to take us to his lord with his bodyguard', I tell him, trying not to laugh at his antics. 'Earl Morkere's thegn Osgod and his huscarls held them until we were well on our way here. They may be looking for us right now'.

'They would have to comb many inns for you', Oslac answers drily. 'Take your time. We can have the horses saddled, ready to go'.

'Will you still need that cart that you asked for, Theodolf?' Wynstan asks the lad, and on a nod tells the old woman, 'Ymme go and tell Gerda to be ready soon! I will have Gudheard help with saddling your horses and harnessing your horse to put between the shafts, Theodolf'.

'I can tell her myself, Wynstan. Ymme needs to finish getting our food ready, I am starving!' As Theodolf makes for the kitchen, Wynstan shrugs, and then vanishes into the yard.

Whilst everyone is busy, I hasten to fetch my few belongings from my room. Loud banging on the inn door is answered by a flustered Ymme,

'What is all this noise about?' she yells above the banging as she pulls up the iron bar from inside the door.

'I have word for Wynstan. There are some Northmen looking for his guests, and they are only a mile away at Lud Gata!' a high-pitched woman's voice calls out.

'God, where is Ivar?' Wynstan calls out, 'Ivar, there is no time for you to eat here! Theodolf get that young woman and her child out of here if you are taking them!'

'Theodolf, come quickly! We will have to wait until we reach

Saewardstanbyrig at least before we can eat now!' Saeward shouts above the din.

'Ivar – oh, there you are!' Wynstan fusses. 'Where is Theodolf?'

I turn to speak to Wynstan as Theodolf clatters down the wooden steps into the inn room with Brihtwin in his arms,

'I thought you were harnessing the horse for the cart –'

Wynstan shouts his answer as if we were still upstairs in our rooms,

'Theodolf, the draw bar of the cart is rotten. You will both have to ride!'

'Get a hold on yourself, Wynstan!' I tell him, 'We will leave as soon as the horses are saddled. Have you another horse for Gerda?'

'No, we have no more horses!' Wynstan holds his hands up to his face.

'Whose horse was that your friend was shoeing when we came back from Thorney?' I ask.

'That horse is mine', says one of the fellows I spied earlier. A tall fellow, clothed in the manner of a nobleman, he strides forward from the shadows at the back of the room and stands, arms folded, next to the demented Wynstan.

'Are you going to need her before the morning?' I ask.

Pulling silver from my purse and laying it on the table next to a boggle-eyed Wynstan, I tell the fellow 'I can pay well'.

'My horse is as dear to me as that Wealsh mountain horse is to you, the one you call Braenda', he answers. He has still not told me his name and am at odds to know who he is. How does he know me?

'You know me, but who are *you?*'

I reach for my sword but Saeward pushes my hand back before I can raise the pommel. The fellow gives a smile and tells me his name at last,

'I do not wonder you do not recall me, Ivar. It is years since we last met. I was a mere stripling! I am Eadmund, Harold's son', he tells me. 'Bondig's spare horse is yours, for your friend's woman'.

I stare at Eadmund for so long he becomes troubled and Saeward chides me,

'Thank the fellow for his offer, Ivar and let us be off!'

'*Eadmund*, where were you when we needed you?!' I roar, unable to hold in my anger, 'Where were Godwin and Magnus?!'

'We were at King Maelcolm's court. Believe me, if we had known that we were needed, we would have *been* there. Father did *not* send for us!'

Eadmund has grown since I last saw him and his brothers. He has his mother Eadgytha's fine, dark red hair and high colour, where his brothers are fair-haired like Harold and the other sons of Godwin. He wears a full beard, unlike the trimmed, groomed beard his father was so proud of. He is also taller than his father was, by the breadth of a hand at the very least.

'*My* understanding is that a rider was sent from Eoferwic', Eadmund tells me. 'But he was waylaid by men of the woods in Beornica. Had traders riding to Beruwic not found him bound and gagged, stripped near naked on the heath near Dunelm, he would have died! We were told of Duke Willem's landing only when father had already left for Lunden'.

'But that was weeks ago! Where have you been *since* then?'

I stare into his eyes, searching for something that will tell me he did not forsake his father. If what he tells me is true, they were only at the northern head of the old Great North Road, after all. It is not as if they were overseas, out of reach of riders who could let their father know they were on their way!

'Ivar, we must *ride!*' Theodolf pulls at my sleeve like a child. 'We have a woman and child to look after!'

'*Ride, then!* I know where you will be going, go now. Saeward and Wulfmaer will help you find your way to Wealtham!'

Theodolf winces at my answer but Saeward steers him away and they leave the room for the yard together, Theodolf holding Brihtwin in his arms as if he were the child's father.

'Had you not best follow them?' Eadmund asks, 'Godwin and Magnus await me at Leagatun. We can ride together and talk about what has happened!' He looks crestfallen suddenly, '*Understand,* Ivar, we are deeply saddened by father's killing. He was our staff and main stave, after all'.

'As am I, Eadmund', I agree as I look at my young kinsman. 'Aye, as am *I.* We shall all miss him sorely'.

'My brothers and I mean to ride soon to see mother. Grandmother has awaited her since she took father's body to Wealtham. Bondig come, we are riding back to Leagatun with Ivar!'

The squat, spry weasel-faced Bondig I have never set eyes on before eases himself from the booth and follows after us into the yard. If I were one of Harold's sons I would not trust him with my life, with so many Northmen about. I could be *wrong.* I tend to see a threat easily in these fraught times. He may well be a worthy fellow, as any man of Eadmund's standing should have riding with him.

Wynstan opens the creaking yard doors and looks to left and right, listening for the sound of hooves on the stone-set street.

'*Go with God!* Look after Gerda and Brihtwin, Theodolf!'

'Theodolf is almost like the little lad's father already!' I shout and urge Braenda onto the moist stones in Billinges Gata.

Everyone else's mount slips on the mist-greased thoroughfare - all but the firm-footed Braenda. The night is cold and damp. Our breath hangs on the air in white clouds around us and Gerda pulls Brihtwin's thick woollen cap down over his nose to keep the cold from him. The child sits quietly, cradled in her arms for safety. Only the echo of distant hoofbeats can be heard coming from somewhere to the west. I would guess the Northmen Gilbert de Warenne to be closing on us. We ride eastward, eager to gain headway on them.

'There is grass by the road not far from here, beyond Eald Gata. We can ride for Stibenhede and strike north from there', Eadmund counsels, 'the hoofbeats of our horses will not be heard there'.

He makes sense. Once we are beyond the burh walls, the Northmen will not be as bold as in daylight. There may be men lurking near the marshes beyond the Cambrycg heath road, waiting for such a prize as Gilbert de Warenne to ransom. Even with six men on horseback to help him, he would be understandably wary of outlaws, bowmen who can deal death so quietly that he would not know his men were no longer with him until too late.

We keep to the shadows as much as we can until we come to the old wall.

'Who is here who wants to leave the burh so rashly?' an elderly fellow calls out to us when we are under the looming shadow of the Eald Gata gatehouse.

'Good evening, friend', I call out. 'I recall you were the gatekeeper when we rode into the burh from Thorney not so long ago, were you not?'

'I know *you!* Pass friend, and to hell with the Northman duke who *now* pays me!' comes the greeting. Two men show from the darkness of the guardhouse and pull back the heavy, groaning, iron bolt-studded oak gates. One of them, a tall stout old fellow waves us on in the flickering light of a wall-mounted torch. Eadmund pats the gatekeeper on the shoulder as he passes and the old man beams up at him.

'I shall reward you well one day soon, mark my words, Eadmund thanks him and leads us out into the blackness of Middil Seaxe beyond.

Hoofbeats can be heard from within the gates, and yelling. Gilbert de Warenne calls on the gatekeepers to open up again, but no-one is there any more. Our friend would have seen that he and his younger companion will have crossed their new master and left.

Eadmund turns to me and points back over one shoulder. De Warenne must be demented at losing me again from the way his shouting echoes around the walls of Eald Gata,

'Is that who you are escaping from?'

The sound of his yelling fades as we ride out along the Colneceaster road.

'*Anglaises imbeciles!*' de Warenne yells on last time at the top of his voice, almost screeching like a fishwife and we laugh loudly, mockingly, but we are well down along the road, too far for him to hear us – *more is the pity!*

A break in the clouds allows the moonlight through onto the road we are following, letting us see further. Where the Cambrycg road leaves the old Colneceaster road there are horsemen riding toward us. They must be more of Duke Willelm's men on their way to take up their duties.

'Hopefully they have not seen us yet. We can hide behind these buildings!' Wulfmaer waves at a number of dwellings that sit close together by the wide road and we follow him into the darkness.

A hound barks and is hushed by his owner. Nothing or no-one else stirs in the blackness between the few fruit trees that cover the open land behind the dwellings.

We are safe between barns and animal sheds. Soon the steady drumming of hooves can be heard on the roadway as the riders pass by on the road. The smell of sweat from the horses is carried by the chill breeze from the marshes. I would guess they must have been ridden hard from a camp beyond Straetford.

Muffled talking can be heard between the riders as they make their way westward at a trot. The snorting of the horses on the road hides the low snorting from Gerda's horse as she stamps angrily in the inky blackness now that the moon has gone back behind the clouds.

Eadmund casts a wary look over one shoulder at Gerda's horse and Theodolf lays a calming hand on the beast's neck to quieten him. He would not have been heard anyway over the clatter of hooves on the stone-set road. We wait a little longer to allow them to pass out of hearing and take to the road again in single file.

'Bondig's horse is skittish', Eadmund frets.

'Their own mounts were making too much noise for them to be able to hear one animal snorting out here. Besides, we are between animal sheds. You would hear *some* creature making noises in the night', Theodolf assures him and pats Bondig's horse on the neck.

'You are good with horses, lad' Eadmund asks Theodolf.

'Have you had much to do with them?'

'Aye, my Lord, you *could* say that', Theodolf smiles.

Eadmund looks askance at me, so I feel I should enlighten him,

'My friend Theodolf grew up with horses. His step-mother, Aethel bred them at a steading near Tadceaster before she came south with Theodolf's father', I tell him.

Theodolf grins at Eadmund and edges his horse close to Gerda on Bondig's horse,

'Is he asleep?' he asks about Brihtwin.

'I think he is resting his eyes', Gerda smiles back up at Theodolf. I wonder if she thinks of Dunstan in some way when she looks at our young friend. Her husband was a head shorter, yet burly.

'What did you say the woman's name was?' Eadmund asks.

'Her name is Gerda, my Lord –'I begin to answer.

Eadmund breaks in,

'I am not 'my Lord' to you, Ivar. You are kin!'

'Lately I have been dealing with so many men of high standing who are *not* kin to me.

He looks hard at me and laughs,

'You should rest, Ivar. Stay with us at father's hunting lodge before you go on to Wealtham. Godwin and Magnus would like to see you again, I am sure', Eadmund reminds me. 'We can talk of old times, of when we used to hunt boar and stag near Naesinga, and when we were still at one with Tostig. You can tell us of his end at Staenfordes Bridge. I hope he died nobly, as he should have'.

'Aye, Eadmund I will tell you all these things. But for now we must have our wits about us. If these Northmen were riding westward on the Colneceaster road, there must be others on their way', I turn in my saddle to see where Saeward and Wulfmaer are riding in eerie silence.

When Saeward waves and smiles to show all is well with them, I look ahead again. We are at the road fork, where the road leads on to Cambrycg beyond Eanefelde. I say road, but it is really a well-worn track, broken and crumbling at its edge. Countless men have ridden it over the years since Harold first came this way with his father as Earl of East Aengla.

'You are thinking of the old days when we rode this way?' Eadmund asks as our horses canter briskly northward now.

I see the road as it was then, when I first came this way to live with Earl Godwin and my aunt, Gytha.

'Your father said he often took this road with your grandfather before I came to Aengla Land. He told me that they would laugh and boast about the boar they would ride down', I do not tell him what Eadgar told me about Svein's killing of my half-brother, Beorn. 'I was told that your grandfather a good hunter then, before they fell out with King Eadweard over your uncle Svein'.

'You must tell us everything that you can think of, Ivar', he asks, '*everything* that happened'.

However close I am to them, I must choose my words with care. I should be glad of the ale, and give away nothing that may offend Eadmund and his brothers. Soon we are at the banks of the river Leag, at Hakon's eyot again, where we last crossed the river before riding south through Lunden burh. I am mindful that of all of us who crossed from east to west, only Theodolf and I still live.

The darkness hides my grief at the loss of so many good friends, old and new, Hrothulf, Theorvard, Karl and Ubbi from the Danelaw. Ubbi, whose charmed axe I used in fighting Brand, had known that I would win. Yet he could not foretell his own wyrd.

Thorfinn, and Burhred – even he, for all the trouble he caused us later – Aelfwin and Aelfwig from Saewardstanbyrig, who joined us along our way, they all became firm friends before Urd tore them from life's roots.

Theorvard, the loyal giant was the latest to be wrested from our company by a Northman crossbow arrow. I would hope not to lose more friends, but even now Urd could be toying with them - or me.

Our horses clatter over the wooden bridge in the blackness of this clouded night. Though we are still six weeks from the Yule Feast, I sense snow on the wind that whips the cold into our bones from across the marshes. We have already had sleet, always a harbinger of worse weather to come here!

I wipe my eyes with the palm of my hand and hope no-one sees how sharply my grief cuts at my soul. Should anyone look closely at me, I can say the easterly wind has whipped across my eyes.

'The wind cuts into your eyes too, Ivar?' Saeward has caught up with me on my left. Wulfmaer rides a little further behind on my right.

'Do *you* think it will snow?' I ask him, glad that he thinks I am wiping my eyes from the biting wind.

'It feels that way, aye', he wipes his nose on his sleeve. 'At Wealtham they will feel winter's cruel blade tear through their clothing in the morning', Saeward has been reading of the skald's art in Wulfwin's books.

'Not long now', Eadmund assures Gerda. Brihtwin whimpers like a small pup in the cold.

'Hush now, we will soon be there', she tells the child.

Harold's hunting lodge looms dark against a blanket of sudden driving whiteness. Snowflakes even settle on the shoulders of my wet cloak. Did my asking about snow bring it on?

'It will be like this near Tadceaster now', I tell Theodolf.

'*Worse. Much* worse, I assure you!' Theodolf's rough snow-covered cloak gives him the look of a snow bear.

When I think of it, the winters we had on Sjaelland were as hard as those I knew during my years in Tostig's Northanhymbra. Nothing ever happened in winter, no-one did anything out of doors save to chop wood or to take household waste to a midden near the river.

Bondig has ridden ahead to tell Burhwold we are close by, to be ready with hot food. He has also to tell him we have a woman and child with us, tired, hungry and ready for sleep.

'God, my bones *ache!*' Wulfmaer groans out aloud.

'The life you lead is for *younger* men!' Eadmund laughs, 'Old man, why is it you wear chain mail? You should be abed by now, surely?'

'My Lord, there is a long story to that, and it begins with my being a simple fyrdman who happened into the wrong company!' Wulfmaer wryly elbows Saeward as he tells Eadmund his woes.

Eadmund looks at me, winks and agrees with Wulfmaer,

'You have made your point well. What is your calling?' he asks as he hands the reins of his horse to Bondig.

'My Lord I am simple miller', Wulfmaer looks up at the thickening snow, 'from Saewardstan'.

Eadmund gives him a look, as if to say, 'In telling me that, perhaps you think *I* am simple'.

Instead he merely waves his hand broadly toward Wealtham and tells him,

'You are nearer to home now. By morning you will think back on your past weeks, as if they were a bad dream'.

'*I* think Ivar has more in store for me!' Wulfmaer growls, causing us all to laugh, thus waking Brihtwin again and making him whimper.

'*Hush, child, you will be abed soon!*' Gerda tries to comfort the child and looks darkly at Wulfmaer.

'Now look what you have done!' Saeward playfully chides and brings more laughter, '*Sorry, Gerda!*'

Gerda tries to scowl at him but merely raises her eyebrows to hold back a smile. She rubs Brihtwin's back to warm him, fighting a laugh.

Burhwold comes to us through the flurrying snow and takes Brihtwin from a cold and tired Gerda.

'He is a fair child! What is his name?' he asks her.

'His name is Brihtwin', Gerda smiles wearily.

Burhwold seems to foster a feeling of kinship in everyone he meets. He cradles the child and takes him indoors to where his wife Winflaed fusses over both Gerda and Brihtwin as if she were the child's grandmother. I have to give Harold his due, in choosing Burhwold as his discthegn he showed himself to be a master at reading a man.

'The child is well named', Burhwold hugs Brihtwin.

Magnus is first to see me within. Since we last met he has grown his light brown hair longer, and unlike Eadmund Magnus sports trimmed, reddish bristle on his upper lip.

He wears a mailcoat, although he has never fought in earnest. Like his brothers, he learned some weapon skills from Harold's huscarls and I taught them some tricks with sword and axe in the past, but so far they have not had to use their skills to save their lives.

That will change, and all too soon. I will have to help them to sharpen their skills in the shieldwall before we take on the Northmen.

'Is that *Ivar?* My *God*, your hair has taken on a grey look, like an old wolf!' he calls, summoning his elder brother Godwin with a delighted shout. 'Here, brother, see how Ivar has *changed* in these past months!'

'Ivar is *here?*' Godwin roars from the main room.

The wooden floor boards shake as the eldest brother storms to the door to greet me and grips me in a tight hug, like a bear with a beehive

'Ivar I am so glad to see you are still *alive!* We did not know what had become of you. I had nightmares of you falling beside father, Gyrth and Leofwin!' Godwin is not the tallest, but the broadest and most like his father. He rushes to greet me.

'You have been eating well, I see', I chide, thumping him lightly on his stomach as we stand shaking hands. He hugs me as if hanging on for dear life.

'There is nothing I can *do*. Everyone keeps feeding me as if I were starving!' Godwin stands back and laughs as Magnus, too gives me a strong hug to show me how much I have been missed.

For now we are happy in one another's company. When I begin to take their weapons teaching to where we can best Willelm's men, they may not be as happy to be in my company. Still, that is to come. First food and drink must pass my lips before I can become my kinsmen's best friend again. I have had too little of either these past weeks and I would like to be able to make up for the lack of sleep!

In the morning much of the snow has gone when I make my way to the stable. Braenda is happy to make inroads on the hay that Burhwold's stable hand put out for our horses. Magnus joins me in the yard before I make my way back to the lodge for my morning meal.

'I was hoping for the snow to stay', Magnus casts a weather eye on the clouds now being driven by a north-westerly wind across the marshes and turns back to me. 'It can be bitter out here in winter before the snows finally settle'.

'It may well come back', I steer him by his left shoulder back to the door and inside. I have more pressing things to think of, such as filling my belly. Talking about whether it will snow or not can be left for after the morning meal.

'How did our father die?' Magnus asks suddenly.

'He died bravely', I turn to look him in the eye. 'There was nothing he could do against three men on horseback after he had been wounded in the eye, and I was too far away to reach him in time before I was brought low by a Northman's cudgel'.

'Mother told me of an arrowhead lodged in his skull', Magnus' mouth curls downward at the thought of his father being brought low.

'Although a brother bathed the wound, he was unable to draw the arrowhead where father's right eye was skewered. He was so badly mauled when she found him amongst his huscarls, no-one knew him but she, by a birthmark on his hip'. He draws air through his teeth and stands, arms folded looking at me as he asks, 'How is it that you are still alive?'

'I had been on the hillside and was hit over the head by one of the Northmen. When I came to your father was being set on by three of their nobles on horseback. Many of his huscarls lay dead around him'.

I can see the laughing horsemen now, around Harold, hacking at him with their swords. I was laid out again from behind by another rider before I thought then I had breathed my last. When I opened my eyes some time later the dark was on us and Willelm's men walked about the hilltop, spearing our wounded'.

Magnus looks askance at me as I go on,

'When I made my way off the hillside I was taken for a Northman by a Suth Seaxan fyrdman and when led away I came across the few of my friends who were still alive in the gully to the west of the hilltop'.

He says nothing still, although he is right to wonder why one of his father's huscarls outlived the others, and allows me to finish telling of our flight,

'Horsemen were sent to stop us finding our way off the hill, but Theodolf and some of his friends sent them fleeing with well-aimed arrows that parted their leaders from their lives and horses. Early in the fighting your father asked me to join Ansgar's Middil Seaxans, to bolster them, strengthen their shieldwall. Then, when Leofwin was cut down, Ansgar sent me with some of my friends to stem the gap in the line as some of Leofwin's best huscarls had been killed with him. When I was struck on the head it was the second time in days that had happened to me. I do not know how long I lay there'.

Magnus stands, his head in his hands, grief-stricken. His older brothers stand downcast, trying to comfort him. My fists clench and unclench in anger at the way Willelm's men dealt with their father, my kinsman.

It is as painful for me as it is for them, being asked to relive Harold's death. I do not know how often I can do that.

'When your father was struck by the arrow I was below, on the other side of the hill. I wanted to die with your father, believe me!'

Godwin drops his hands to his sides and looks up into the grey sky, still listening, saying nothing.

'Harold was my *kinsman* and ring-giver'. I am upsetting myself in reliving the hour of their father's death, tears of anger well in the corners of my eyes. The anger is not at Magnus, nor even at Duke Willelm, but at my *wyrd.*

'I am sorry if I have hurt you, Ivar'. Godwin smiles wanly and asks, 'Forgive my distrust'.

I put a hand on his shoulder and assure him he need not fear offending me,

'You are right', I grant, 'insofar as a kinsman and huscarl of your father's household I should have fought until overcome'.

He looks away as I tell him,

'We will throw back the Northmen into the sea'.

'What are you going to do now?' he moves on.

'We would live amongst the poorer folk of Wealtham', I answer, 'live as they do, teach your men the ways we can crush Duke Willelm and take him and his ilk unawares'.

'That might be a way for many men, to lower themselves into a life amongst the folk on the land', Magnus smiles. 'Are you sure it is the way for *you?*'

'When I was young I was fostered on a poor fellow and his wife, as is the custom amongst Danish nobles. I can be as one of them again when needs be. Think, Godwin, that when the time comes you should call upon us in Wealtham and we will follow you', I follow him to the door of the main room.

'For the time being, however, you need to eat. I think I understand now, Ivar', he grins, relieved of grief for his father, and pushes the door open for me to enter.

We walk into the main room, where Eadmund and Magnus await us. They stand when I walk to their table, and Eadmund is first to take my hand and wish me a good morning,

'I am glad to see you again, kinsman. If you had felt offended you would have left. I can only say how deeply I feel about our meeting again'.

'Godwin only asked me what I had asked myself after the slaughter. My friend Theorvard told me that I was still alive to carry on the fight, to throw out the Northmen and to put Eadgar on the throne'.

'Where is this good friend of yours now, Ivar?' Godwin's eyes open wide as he asks me to show him to my wise young friend. 'I must thank him for saving you from yourself. There are some of us who have some sense, at least'.

'He was killed the other day by one of Bishop Odo's crossbowmen. We had gone to free hostages he was to hang before the folk in the burh', I have to tell him.

The corners of Godwin's mouth drop, his smile freezes. One hand grips his cup tightly, and with the other he thumps the great oak table in his disgust.

'*For shame,* the way our great warriors fall! We are losing too many good men this way! At least you yourself are lucky. Tell me, Ivar, what are these crossbows that you speak of, and who is Odo? He sounds a foul sort of fellow. Seat yourself, but tell me first, what had these folk done to warrant Odo wishing to hang them?'

I tell them about our errand for Eadgar after our win at Lunden Brycg, and of how we went to see Willelm's supply lines, of how we stole food from his camps.

Godwin and his brothers sit rapt as I tell about our running fights in Centland and Suth Seaxe, and of how we outran the Northmen more than once. They listen closely to my telling of the fight at Egensford, of how the men there turned on the Northmen to help us as we rode through the ford.

'I hope one day we can do something to reward these folk!' Magnus brings down his palms flat on the table, shaking the beakers and ale pitchers.

'*And* we shall have to rid the land of the likes of *Odo!*' Godwin fumes, his fists balled, ready to take on the first Northman to come through the lodge doors.

'Aye, we must rid the land of Odo and his ilk!' Eadmund echoes. 'Who does he think he is, putting the Centishfolk to work for him? We shall burn their buildings to the ground and show them how we deal with outlanders who wish to break us!'

Everyone in the room thumps the table to wring another speech from Eadmund, but he rests a hand on my right shoulder and tells them all to be silent,

'If I found out one thing in life, it is to go to war to send our foes packing'. He breaks from talking and takes a draught of ale to wet his throat, and thumps the beaker down before speaking again,

'*However* - making proud speeches here may be good for the soul, but being ready for the fight will be better. In the New Year, after the Yuletide feast, we will begin our work. Before that there are things to do, men to teach their fighting skills and our numbers must be strengthened many times over'.

Godwin rises from his father's chair and calmly puts down his cup on the table. Everyone falls silent and he begins to outline his thoughts on how we should make ready – or as much as we should be told without giving anything away to eavesdroppers,

'In the fore-year we must ride to West Seaxe, to be with our mother and sisters. There we will bar the way for Duke Willelm and his followers to one of the main burhs'. Godwin grips the table tightly before going on. 'Whether the burh be Exanceaster or Wintunceaster, there is still a following among the bishops, thegns and all the good folk who once rallied to our grandfather's banners. I, Godwin Haroldson will lead any and all, and together we shall shove the Bastard's underlings back into the sea, *out* of this kingdom!'

'We shall make him plead for his own safety, to bring back Wulfnoth Godwinson himself with all due haste!'

Magnus earns himself loud cheers with this, the shortest of speeches, followed by more thumping on the table.

'Let us not be too hasty here!' another speaker raises his voice so that he can be heard above the din. 'In taking on Duke Willelm we shall need to make sure that we have more men than he or his underlings has – *at any time*. We must do again and again what we did at Lunden Brycg, and we will need to muster a greater number of bowmen'.

Hakon stands to show himself. The scars on his brow and arms bear witness to the part he played among Harold's defenders to try and keep his uncle and king from harm. He beckons me to stand and points to me,

'Let us see you, kinsman', Hakon bids me stand. 'I saw that man there – on his own, mind - hold back more than a few horsemen! Had it not been for one of them bringing down his cudgel on Ivar's helm, they would have lost more... *many more!* We all did it again, together with Ansgar and the young aetheling Eadgar on Lunden Brycg. Now, all of you rise and raise your cups to a man Duke Willelm and his ilk would like to see in chains!'

'How do you know this, Hakon?' I ask, taken aback by his praise. He was as beset as I was both on the hill and at the bridge.

'Thorfinn and you were seen by the duke, I know'. Hakon raises his beaker to drink to me, turns to look at Godwin and bids he and his brothers join him in thanking me,

'*You* were lucky to get away with your hide in one piece, Ivar. I was lying under corpses when I came to. I think the same Northman must have sent us both tumbling. I could hear the Duke speak of you to both Odo and to Count Rodberht. He saw you standing close to Thorfinn and had been looking for you amongst the dead. When spearing the wounded, one of his men narrowly missed me. I had to wait until they had all gone to their feasting before I could make away. After having seen me bearing arms against him, who knows *what* he would have done with me if we had lost at Suthgeweorce! *I* for one was damned glad to see you again when you came to Thorney!'

'Hakon speaks their tongue, of course. He would know'. Magnus nods and taps one side of his nose. He smiles at the thought of his kinsman eluding his erstwhile host.

I cannot find the words to give voice to my feelings at hearing his telling about seeing me fighting on Caldbec Beorg, and then finding me alive again when I sought out Eadgar at Thorney. Only Theodolf can know how we feel, being another of the few lucky enough to outlive Harold. Hakon tells me with a little laugh and a weak smile,

'You had best seat yourself and eat. You will need your strength in the coming weeks'.

'When did you get here?' I ask.

'I came here after the earls and bishops sold out Eadgar. It was the only sanctuary I knew of, where Morkere or Eadwin would not think to come looking for me to betray me to Willelm. I learned of your return to Hrofesceaster from one of Ansgar's thegns who came to speak to Godwin here', Hakon sips ale from his beaker and looks thoughtfully at me as he swallows.

'Eadgar told me of you leaving on your errand and I was saddened. I should have liked to have gone with you, as I would have been useful to you with my knowledge of the Frankish tongue! Before your return, Willelm and his men had already reached Lunden from the west, from Beorh-hamstede. We were told to yield there, and it was Archbishop Ealdred's shameful crawling that assured Willelm of a crowning, robbing Eadgar of his right. Ealdred was not the only one, however. Stigand's belly scraped the stone floor like a snake's, almost *begging* not to be shorn of his lands and wealth. Eadwin and Morkere were no better –'

'You can finish telling Ivar about their toadying when he has had some food', Hakon is stopped by Godwin.

'I can listen whilst I eat', I tell Godwin.

I want to hear the rest of what Hakon has to say but Godwin frowns and shakes his head at his kinsman.

He should have been allowed to finish without Godwin breaking in.

'Fear not, Ivar, it will keep', Hakon smiles and puts a hand on Godwin's back, to the relief of us all.

'When Ivar has finished eating, he can tell us', Eadmund smiles broadly. 'His friends must have words to add, I am sure. Then we must talk about what we should do about bringing men here.

'Aye, I want to know everything that is afoot', Hakon agrees.

I nod, and set to attacking what has been put before me with a sharpened knife and even sharper hunger. Theodolf looks around at the nobility gathered around the table, not knowing who many of them are, mouth agape. Eadmund is seated to one side of him, Magnus on the other.

We begin eating before Saeward can say a prayer. Godwin laughs and slaps Saeward's left shoulder,

'You had best begin eating whilst there is still food on the table for you to eat. As I see it, Ivar may start on yours before long!'

Burhwold brings in a pitcher of ale and sets it down in front of me. Saeward lifts it and fills his beaker before I have my hand on the handle. Everyone laughs at the look of dismay I wear.

'Your friend learns quickly', Magnus holds out a beaker for Saeward to fill and laughs when the East Seaxan gives him a look of disbelief,

'Go on, Saeward, you can spare a few drops for a man from East Aengla!'

'Try to get on my good side, eh?' Saeward's testy challenge brings us all to tears of laughter. That is the Saeward I recall from our march north!

On finishing our morning meal the table is cleared. A young woman catches my eye as she takes out some of the platters and bowls. She smiles openly and brushes past me on her way out to the kitchen. When she comes back to the table, she brushes past me again and I turn to watch as she gathers a few of the boards with food still on them.

I look up and give her a friendly smile as she passes again.

'*Oh-ho*, Ivar, has Ingigerd has caught your eye?' Magnus beams broadly and laughs, 'Do not let Healfdan catch you eyeing her!'

'There is someone with a claim on her?' I ask as if Ingigerd could be the ugliest woman on God's earth.

'A good-looking woman such as she is will always find a man willing to fight for her', Magnus says ruefully.

'Have you never shown your hand for her?' I ask Magnus with a wink.

'She has never looked twice at *me!*' he grumbles, fingering the brown bristle on his upper lip.

'*What,* I do not believe a son of Harold's could not draw any woman worth her salt. A good-looking fellow such as you should have a woman on either arm. You do not have two heads, nor do you have ugly warts on your face. *What is wrong with you?*' I tease him and give him a playful thump on his shoulder.

'I *have* a woman', he tells me coyly.

'Is that all... one woman?' I laugh, 'I am sorry, kinsman. I just cannot believe you. They should be lining up outside your room at night!'

'Magnus is much too humble, or else too blind to see them', Godwin grins at me, pulls at the short hairs on Magnus' top lip and winks,

'I see them fainting at the sight of this bristle'.

'He is every inch the Aenglish nobleman! I think you are both much too envious', Eadmund comes over and stands behind his still-seated brother.

'I was saying Magnus should have a woman on each arm', I lean back and look up at Harold's eldest son.

Godwin looks down at me and smiles,

'He needs no-one to egg him on there, so his woman tells me. She often sees them mooning after him'.

He steps back in mock surprise when Magnus turns in his chair and takes a swipe at his eldest brother with his right hand. He raises his voice to sound like a woman's, 'Oh, *Magnus!*'

Everyone in the room turns to watch as Magnus rises to his feet and chases Godwin around the room. They put on a mock fight, their playacting taking me back to their boyhood games. Magnus seats himself again and Godwin tells me what is behind this show of brotherly rivalry,

'We both gave the same woman the eye. Godgifu took to Magnus more than she did to me, so I took a step back – as older brothers sometimes do - and then she came chasing after me! When Magnus began showering her with gifts she lost sight of me – '

'*That is only because you are an old skinflint!*'

Eadmund ruffles Godwin's hair and is in turn chased around the room.

Beakers whipped in Eadmund's flight fly from the table onto the floor to hold up his brother, ale slops everywhere and Godwin slips, almost skidding into the door.

'I thought we were to talk over the ride to West Seaxe!' Hakon shouts, and the chasing ends.

Ingigerd enters the room again to clear our table, only to find beakers lying on the floor amid spilt ale and crumbs. She stands there with her hands on her hips and shouts at the brothers,

'You are like foolish little children, you three! Now someone has to come in and clean up after you!'

The brothers laugh wildly with Saeward, Theodolf and Wulfmaer staring disbelievingly at them. Hakon sits, arms folded, shaking his head. All I can do is sit and grin sheepishly, my kinsmen showing that for all their noble upbringing they are the same as all other young men who have grown up together.

15

Gerda comes in to clean up the mess with mop and pail. Theodolf stands open-mouthed as she mops up the ale from the stone-flagged floor.

'Why are *you* doing this?' Theodolf draws all eyes on her.

'I told them I wanted to be useful here'. She carries on mopping, not looking at him.

'But we are *guests* here. Where is Brihtwin?' Theodolf behaves as if they are married and draws knowing smiles from everyone else in the room.

'He is being cared for by Ealhswith', Gerda answers flatly, not looking at him. She finishes, picks up the pail and leaves.

Theodolf looks at me, at Saeward and finally at Godwin, who shrugs and offers the only counsel even I could think of,

'You are a lucky young fellow. Go on, marry her before another man catches her. From what I know of women – and I admit that is little enough in Ivar's eyes – they come like her, and like Ingigerd. You would not want Ingigerd for a wife because you would never sleep for watching your rivals. I would guess that Healfdan always sleeps with one eye open. He has to watch her, in case she runs off with the next man who catches her eye. *Ivar, mark my words!*'

'Why would I need to mark *your* words if I did not want to cross this Healfdan?' I laugh, not wanting to cross Braenda. 'I have come through more strife than you ever shaken a spear at!'

Godwin grins at me and looks longingly at Ingigerd. She in turn seems to be sizing me up.

But that might just be wishful thinking on my part. I should try to gain more sleep instead of thinking of bedding every woman who looks at me twice.

'These thoughts of yours, about what you mean to do after the Yule feast – can we talk about them now?' I ask him to begin laying out what he thinks we should do next, after the coming winter.

'I am not the only one who put them together. We each thought them out, Magnus, Eadmund and I. We will have to wait until the fore-year before we can ride for West Seaxe', Godwin looks up. Eadmund plays with his beard and Magnus fingers his upper lip. To see them now, I would not have thought them able to talk together on any matter, still less on how anyone else would act on it.

'Why do we have to wait until the *fore-year* before we go?' I hear myself asking Godwin. Sitting here, talking to Harold's sons seems unreal. I have had this feeling since rising this morning, and I am likely still to feel this way when I leave here to ride to Wealtham – *if* I ever get there at this rate.

'Have you tried to make your way through the hills and moors of West Seaxe in the winter?' Godwin asks earnestly.

'The snow hides the dale sides so that you do not know whether you are on firm ground, or likely to sink in to the horses' bellies and die in the cold!'

'It is the same everywhere, kinsman', I play with my empty beaker and ask further, 'but we *could* be on our way before then, surely?'

'What about teaching fyrdmen how to fight before then?' Magnus asks. 'To show them the skills we need from our huscarls? We need at least three score men to take with us'.

'There will be men *there*', I try to reason with Magnus. 'Fyrdmen are everywhere. They only need a little sharpening, like good axes. I have heard that the West Seaxan fyrdmen are stern in their resolve when tested in the shieldwall'.

'What Magnus means is that we should have our own huscarls', Eadmund feels he needs to be his older brother's spokesman.

'I think I know what Magnus means', I answer and turn to look up at Eadmund, 'but huscarls are men who have been taught over many years'.

'Hopefully they will be men who grew with you, as were your father's. Skalpi, Gauti and Tofig had been with him since he was a youth. They had land hereabouts, and taught the East Seaxan fyrd during the winter, tending to their lands and honing their skills during the rest of the year. Now they are dead it will take a lot for any man to stand in their shoes. Have you thought of anyone to teach your own huscarls?'

'I thought *you* might', Godwin looks at me. He smiles kindly, but I do not for one moment think he is *asking* me.

'You want *me* to teach your men the fighting skills that they will need to face the Northmen?' I ask to eager nodding from my kinsmen. Godwin awaits much from me. I warn him not to want too much from the fyrdmen I am to teach. I have to add,

'They will need more than mere skill. *Luck* plays a great part, but if you do not believe me, then you should ask Saeward, or Wulfmaer, or Theodolf. We have lost many friends we *thought* had lady luck with them, only to find she is fickle and walks hand-in-hand with Urd'.

Godwin's steel-blue eyes seem to bore through me. He throws up his hands and sighs heavily, but says nothing about my speaking of the old ones,

281

'What more than skill can anyone *need*, surely? To teach him how to stand against men on horseback, to know how to lock shields is as much as a man needs. I agree, about luck, too. You make the task sound truly like scaling a sheer wall!'

'But that is where *you* have the insight?' Eadmund shows how easily pleased he would be as a leader of men. 'It is *you* who will pick the best from the hundred we bring here and give us perhaps three score to take west'.

'Unless you have iron in your blood, when the Northmen ride at you with their lances your blood freezes at the sight of them bearing down on you. You need to stiffen yourself to the sure death they will bring, unless your skills come to the fore to save you and help you bring down your foe', I tell him. 'Oh, and you need thicker shields to stop their crossbow bolts splitting them and striking you'.

'*You* are still alive', Godwin tells me with a disarming smile. 'What makes you different from the others?'

'Again, more by good luck than skill, I think', I have to admit. 'I had good men around me. Most are now dead, having fallen trying to keep us alive', I find myself looking at Theodolf.

'Have you learned to *fear* the Northmen, or to be wary of their fighting skills?' Eadmund asks me.

'I do not *fear* them as such. We have killed enough of them to know that they are flesh and blood, as we are', I look up at him as he strides back and forth across the floor, plainly trying to think of something I will agree with.

'But *they* also have skills we need'.

'Do you trust in our being able to throw them back into the sea, whence they came?' Magnus asks me now.

'I think we will do that only by mastering skills they have. They build wooden strongholds, but these can be wrought useless by fire –'

Eadmund holds up his hand to stop me, and begins again,

'You stopped Duke Willelm at Lunden Brycg without fighting the way they do, am I right?'

'Aye, we did', I agree, but only to a point. 'But then *they* had only horsemen and no bowmen, or men on foot. Willelm had hoped to be met by willing earls and nobles who would yield to him without a fight'.

'They could not have broken our line on Caldbec Beorg if we had more bowmen, and if the fyrdmen we had did as they were bidden', Theodolf speaks up and all eyes are on him.

'You think that if we had more bowmen the Northmen would not have won?' Godwin asks. He is taken by my friend's insight.

'I do think so my Lord, aye', Theodolf nods gravely.

'Could *you* show men how to use the war bow so that we might break the Northmen's mounted attacks?' Godwin asks. 'Think carefully, my friend. We have an Aenglish king whom the Witan have spurned, twice within a year. If we could set the crown on his head by next year, then we need not fear Duke Willelm'.

'You will to be ready before the fore-year', I break in and tell Godwin. 'Archbishop Ealdred means to crown Duke Willelm before the year is out'.

Now all eyes are on me again.

'We will have a Northman king by the end of this year?'

Godwin's words come slowly as he tries to understand the weight of what I have told him.

'The aetheling Eadgar has given in to it taking place', I add. The plainness of my words stumps Godwin.

'*He* told you that?' Magnus asks and turns to his brothers, wondering if he has not been taken on a lost cause. The three of them look glumly at one another and then at me for hope.

'As sons of our late king, does one of *you* not foster a claim for the kingship?' I ask in turn.

'Ealdgyth has a son, also called Harold', Godwin answers. 'She might one day put him forward to be king, if he has our father's strengths. That, though, is a far cry. We need a king *now* to stand behind. Eadgar *has* won one fight against Duke Willelm and he *should* be our king, despite what the churchmen say'.

'What about the Witan?' I ask testily.

'By that you mean Eadwin and Morkere, who wish to keep their lands and income with a Northman on the throne?' Godwin sneers as he says their names. To the grandson of Earl Godwin, the grandsons of Earl Leofric *are* almost as foes. Mistrust of Leofric's brood still brings the blood to boil amongst Harold's clan.

'We do not need to fear trampling on their feelings, as they have already done that to Eadgar. As you know, Ivar, there is no love lost between Earl Leofric's offspring and those of our grandfather. I feel sorry about Waltheof, though, being lumped in with the likes of *them!* I think we may have to do without their help if they have already become Willelm's men to safeguard their lands and titles'.

Magnus is as disgusted as Godwin at Eadwin and Morkere yielding so easily. Eadmund takes it all in his stride, folds his arms and looks more openly at the matter,

'Still, we must not discount them altogether. We *may* need their help'.

'What do you say, Eadmund? You think the old weasel's grandsons will become useful to *us?* They may when frost-rime coats the walls of hell! Perhaps Waltheof might yet, but I doubt that somehow. I have heard that he ducked out of fighting the Northmen when father was killed', Godwin is taken aback that his brother should ever think of the young earls as ever being of use against Willelm. He goes on, 'Ansgar was unhappy about Waltheof leaving Harold's side, even though he showed his mettle fighting Duke Willelm's men at Lunden Brycg'. Godwin is scathing about each of the young earls.

'Who knows *who* we will need', Eadmund sits looking at his hands. He then stares up at his brother briefly and finishes,

'Nevertheless Godwin, as you say, we cannot seek their help too much, or too often. Willelm will want to keep them close to make sure their underlings do not get out of hand. He will have to go back to Northmandige to see to his lands and underlings there'. Eadmund lets everyone think about that briefly before closing, 'He *will* have to go back there because that is where his wife is, and his kin. His eldest son Rodberht is the same age as Eadgar, but he will never take his father's titles because he was born out of wedlock. He may be a friend to us'.

Godwin looks at Magnus and tries to keep himself from laughing. Everyone but Eadmund breaks into laughter after Godwin finds he can no longer hold his back.

'What is so funny?!' Eadmund demands, unaware of the sour look Magnus gave him from behind as he talked. He only sees what we are all laughing at when Godwin points across the table. The look of scorn Eadmund wears at the sight of his younger brother mimicking him turns to a broad grin,

'Well, there you have it! You know what I speak of', Eadmund ruffles Magnus' hair and sits back with a look of mock horror when his brother moves to do the same to him.

'Come on you two, I thought this was meant to be earnest talk about what we need to do about our fyrdmen'.

Godwin fights his laughter again, looks around the table until we have all taken a hold on ourselves and asks me,

'Ivar, you know Duke Willelm -'

'I do, but not that well', I have to stop him before he asks for some answer I cannot give him. 'Hakon must know the way the man thinks. Unluckily, those others who know him best are not our friends to seek counsel from'. This earns me a wry smile from Godwin.

'I was going to ask you that when he goes back – as he surely will – are Odo and Rodberht of Mortain likely to go back with him?'

'They *might* leave with him', I answer, 'but who knows? He may tell them to stay here and watch over his new kingdom whilst he takes the young earls with him to Falaise'.

'He may well do that'. Hakon twiddles his thumbs, and adds, 'Perhaps he will bring Wulfnoth back with him'

Godwin might recall his uncle, whereas Eadmund and Magnus were only small when Archbishop Rodberht took Hakon and Wulfnoth to Northmandige with him.

'I should like to see him here again, poor fellow', Hakon sniffs. 'That fool monk Aethelweard will turn Wulfnoth into something like himself if he has him there for much longer'.

'We can only hope he does come back soon. I have almost forgotten what my uncle looks like', Godwin mulls. I dare say even with him the memory of Wulfnoth is only hazy.

'Even if Willelm left Odo and Count Rodberht to look after the kingdom, they cannot be everywhere. We would have free rein until, or even after Willelm comes back', Eadmund brings us all back to what we were talking about.

'When we have enough men to keep us from unwelcome Northman prying, we can ride to Wintunceaster and think about where we shall go from there', I offer.

'How many would you say is *enough?*' Godwin looks at me squarely across the table, 'This brings us back to what I was talking about earlier. You say we could teach the West Seaxan fyrd when we get there. I think we need perhaps at least two score that we can make huscarls of before we go'.

'All the men I had around me who were huscarls are dead. Theodolf, Saeward and Wulfmaer have been thrown into the fighting and have learnt their skills the hard way. Oslac and Cyneweard have chosen to come with us and have skills of their own honed in fighting the Northmen, sometimes alongside ours. They could teach others their skills wherever they went, each of them'.

Godwin is happy with what he hears from me,

'Then they can ride with us and teach the best of the East Aenglan and East Seaxe fyrdmen'.

He needs to learn much himself. One skill is leadership. Harold had his father from whom to seek counsel in his youth, Godwin has us. Although I have fought alongside Harold and Tostig during their many years of warring, I would not say that I am as skilled as a leader of many, even though I was born to it.

We have a cunning and ruthless foe in Willelm, who has lived through many years in the saddle, and with some of the best of his father's men to learn from. Who knows, perhaps one day Godwin might gain the skills that Willelm now has. This is a time when Tostig will be dearly missed.

'It is such a shame that Tostig is no longer with us', Eadmund echoes my thoughts to grunts of agreement around the table. Only Saeward and Theodolf stay silent.

'Put word about the eastern shires', Godwin tells Eadmund. 'That we want their best fyrdmen. Take Ivar with you and talk over the best way forward with the thegns'.

Eadmund nods and beckons me to leave the table with him. When we are outside in the cold, Eadmund turns to me and asks,

'Ivar, as you are the only man here with a spark of leadership skill, we must start somewhere. Are we agreed?'

'You know I will give you my best', I bite my lower lip and nod. I almost feel as if I were talking to their father. 'I have faith in my friends that they will do their utmost for you. We have two good bowmen in Theodolf and Oslac, who will also make good teachers. Saeward is an axe thrower of proven skill. He gave a good show for Eadgar at Thorney before we left for Centland and Suth Seaxe. Wulfmaer and Cyneweard will show your men how to stand steady in the shield wall. Before we ride for the west we will have your three score of well-taught men. Whether they could be thought of as huscarls remains to be seen. Should we have to fight the Northmen before then, so much the better, because then your men will be given the trial of their lives and that should stand you in good stead'.

'That is as much as we want from you!' Eadmund smiles and gives me a bear hug. 'It is perhaps more than we could ask'.

The afternoon is spent walking along the eastern bank of the River Leag, talking about ruses, shield walls and bowmanship. He listens closely to my telling of Duke Willelm's running of the fight against Harold, of how Odo, Count Rodberht and Alan Fergant hurled their men at us. I tell him also of how Willelm had two horses killed from under him and still came back leading from the front - and how he drew our fyrdmen from the shieldwall.

'We have a strong foe in Duke Willelm', Eadmund agrees. 'How much would you say he differs from my father?'

'In many ways your father was better. He took risks, but this time he was drawn headlong by his wyrd'. I look back on what Gyrth and Leofwin told me before we fought Willelm, how they felt betrayed about not being asked. 'Your father was unlucky this time, but we – Gyrth, Leofwin, Ansgar – were at one in that he answered too quickly to the Northman threat. He wanted to free the folk in Suth Seaxe from their burden and lost sight of his goal for long enough to be robbed of the prize', I tell Eadmund. 'He did not lead in his usual manner when he took the field. We do not know why, only God knows what thoughts flooded through him because we can no longer ask him'.

Eadmund falls silent, nods and tells me,

'Now we must take Duke Willelm to task for robbing us all of a good king and father. We must also seek the Witan's goodwill for Godwin to be made king. Ealdred may quake in his boots when he learns his lands could be forfeit for selling out to Willelm. Deserving men would be glad of some of Ealdred's good land by the river outside Eoferwic!'

'Godwin wants the crown for himself?' I ask. As the son of the dead king, he may see himself as the true heir to the kingship.

'Eadgar may have showed his mettle at Lunden Brycg, but we feel Godwin should be made king', Eadmund tells me stiffly.

Flushed with brotherly pride Eadmund looks at me, and goes on without waiting for my answer.

'You should be given the earldom of Northanhymbra, as would befit a high-born man such as you'.

'It is something that has never arisen before, when I spoke to others, but would you follow *me* if I claimed the crown?' I jokingly ask Eadmund, for which I am treated to dark looks.

'Do not take the kingship so lightly!' he rebuts my jest and comes back to what he was talking about. 'I would be given the earldom of West Seaxe and Magnus East Aengla. You would be a good earl for Northanhymbra, I am sure. It is your right as the brother of a king, do you not think so?'

I smile wearily and sigh aloud,

'I recall the Northanhymbran nobles chose Morkere over Tostig because he was not one of Godwin's clan, and because Eadgytha had Orm Gamalson murdered to further her brother's land claims', I try to make Eadmund mindful of what led to Tostig's downfall. Morkere's followers would be angered if a West Seaxan king tried to thrust an earl upon them who had no blood tie to the earldom. Waltheof might be seen by me as 'tainted' for the way he forsook Harold, but he has the blood of Baebbanburh through his mother.

'However, I would say if the good folk of the north knew their earls had sold out their rightful king to the Northman bastard, they would not be as forgiving as you think they are, Aunt Eadgytha's sins notwithstanding!'

Eadmund's outburst has startled the birds and put me off my stride. I did not know he had this much feeling for Godwin's kingship.

'The northern earls wanted Eadgar as king', I try to tell him. 'They were unhappy about your father taking the crown almost as Eadweard breathed his last-'

I am halted in mid-flow by my young kinsman.

'*And* they sold out to Duke Willelm, as soon as the Northmen began to look as though they might take their lands, the *poor wretches!* They had no stomach for a fight, as was borne out by our father having to thrash Harald Sigurdsson's men after Morkere and Eadwin ran scared back to Eoferwic. It is a pity Tostig put himself on the wrong side by raiding around the coast, allying himself with the West Norse king', Eadmund might have read my thoughts. 'He should have waited and fought *alongside* father against our foes; once we had won and the Miercan brothers been made to look foolish the earldom may have come his way again'.

He breaks off to let me take in his meaning, and goes on,

'Harald Sigurdsson would have come anyway, feeling that the pact between his nephew Magnus and Harthaknut ought to be fulfilled. The Northanhymbrans might have asked Tostig back as their earl when they saw Morkere as unworthy of the earldom. After all, Tostig had been earl for ten years before Eadwin and Morkere levered him out. His mistake was in trusting Copsig!'

'Have the three of you spoken of Godwin becoming king, or is it just you who sees yourself as the leading earl of Aengla Land?' I ask, still feeling wrong-footed by this sudden show of zeal. But he has not finished.

'This duke, Willelm may have wedded his Flemish bride, but he himself is still unwarranted as king. Unlike where the church did not see father and mother as wedded, they were in the eyes of the law. Harold 'Harefoot' was made king when Harthaknut was unable to claim the crown of this half of his father's kingdom, his claim upheld by the northern earls', Eadmund tries his best to sell Godwin's kingship to me. 'Father's marriage was not acknowledged in the eyes of the Church. In the same way Knut's betrothal to Aelfgifu of Northanhamtun was looked on as unholy. Our father's namesake and his older brother Svein were the issue of the one, as are we and young Ulf the issue of the other. It all fits, can you not see it?!'

I can see his point, but there is a barrier to Godwin's kingship.

'I would want nothing more! But we live in another age. There is an *aetheling* from the line of Cerdic and they have forsaken him in fear of losing what they have', I watch him closely as I tell him my misgivings. Whereas he has been hitherto forbearing with me, I see his temper shortening. Yet suddenly he pulls me to him, hugs me tightly and then steps back as if taken aback by this outburst. He puts his hands on my shoulders. Taller than his father, the tallest of the three grown sons, he is able to look me straight in the eye. What I see there is depth of feeling, as if I were as close to him as Godwin or Magnus.

'Ivar, just say you will help us!' He grips my hands and offers me Tostig's earldom on Godwin's behalf, 'Northanhymbra is yours for the asking!'

So they *have* spoken about it amongst themselves. There is nothing more for me but to burst out laughing,

'I *will* help you, and God help you if you cannot deliver!' I agree to go forward with him and his brothers. We stand there, the pair of us laughing like children on the snow-covered meadow, hands gripped tightly.

He calls out his oath for the world to hear, loudly, making me wince,

'And I will hold *you* to *your* oath, Ivar!'

I must suddenly look as though I do not believe him, because he reaches his right hand out to take mine,

'Godwin *will* honour the deal, fear not. He will honour your earldom because *I* shall make him do so. Think on that Ivar!' he shouts into the wind.

The world seems lighter on this dull, overcast afternoon, even though as we turn back to the lodge, the snow begins to fall again.

'Duke Willelm will not send his men out now', Eadmund holds the door open for me, 'as before long the whole land will be under a covering of snow and the Yule feast will follow soon. There are but, what, four or five more weeks until the feasting begins. His men will not be able to think straight until well into the New Year'.

I warn him as we return to the warmth of a roaring fire,

'Do not be mistaken, Willelm and his half-brothers will be able to push their men into anything whilst they are still hungry for land and wealth. I wish to go to the West Mynster to see the rite for myself'.

'You wish to go to the *West Mynster* - to watch Willem being made king?!' Godwin splutters, and wipes ale from his mouth with the back of his hand.

'I hope I hear you right, because otherwise I need my hearing tested', Saeward stands next to me, staring disbelievingly.

'Why do you want to do that when you risk being hanged? At worst they will make you feel so *worthless* before they kill you!' Saeward pinches his forefingers almost together to show me how he thinks Willelm will try to render me before they put me out of my misery. He may be right, but I have to follow my wyrd.

'Aye, why do you want to risk life and limb on such a useless errand?' Eadmund gapes. 'When I listen to you now I cannot help but think back to when you laid out your thoughts about teaching the fyrdmen your skills. This now sounds so hollow! *What could you gain from it?*'

'To fulfil my wyrd, I will see the liars who swore an oath to your father', I tell him. 'I wish to see the earls and bishops swearing their false oaths to Willelm, and know them for who they are when you are crowned king, Godwin'.

I do not want to lie to my kinsman, but the *Aetheling* needs to know his kingship will slip from his hands even if Willelm *is* thrown out, unless he shows himself to be the master of his kingdom. I swore to *him* I would uphold his kingdom, after all, when I offered myself and my friends to stand by him as his huscarls.

'That is all very well for you to say', Godwin snarls,

'Who do you think you are, putting your life, and ours, at risk from Willelm's grasping kinsmen and underlings?'

He is right, of course. Should I be taken, Odo would like nothing more than have whatever I know torn from me in the bloodiest way he can think of. My kinsmen would have to uproot themselves and their followers and find shelter elsewhere before they are ready. They would have to give Lunden a wide berth, taking a much more northerly road than they would need to stay out of Willelm's clutches, all because of my foolishness.

'Why are you so stubborn? Is it inborn in *us*, too?' Godwin shakes his head and, wearily asks the more helpful question, 'How will you steer clear of making yourself known to them?'

'I will be a brother', I answer.

'What do *you* know about being a brother?' Saeward demands, adding, 'You will need to have the back of your head shaven'.

'Not if I keep my hood up. Anyway, I can ask *you* how he thinks I should look and act', I chew my lip, knowing that I am digging myself deeper into a pit of my own making. 'And you will show me how a brother behaves at a crowning'.

'I have not the faintest inkling of what a brother does at a crowning', Saeward is taken aback that I should bring him into this.

'Nor would I ever have known that brothers *do* anything, or even *be* at crownings at all. Were there brothers at King Harold's crowning?'

Of course the thought is foolish and, so Godwin must think, is my lack of thought for their safety. If I were followed to Leagatun, Harold's sons would be taken hostage. There *is* a likelihood I will be taken alive and be made to curse the day I was born. But if they do not know to look for me why should I *fear?* Who would tell them I am there? Odo must hope I have left the kingdom, and Willelm will have much more to think of. Their hatred of me would only show itself on my making a mistake and letting myself be caught.

'The West Mynster is home to brothers of the Order of Saint Benedict, I know that much', I tell my friend, 'as are the brothers who help the sick at Wealtham, although the teaching is done by canons'.

'Dean Wulfwin may help you with a brown habit', Eadmund bows to the likelihood of me undertaking my errand despite their misgivings. 'Will you go there unarmed, or will you carry a weapon under the habit?'

'On the grounds that the Northmen would not search a man of the cloth for weapons, I should carry a weapon', I agree with Eadmund, 'should I have to fight my way out of the abbey'.

Saeward adds a warning,

'Do you not think that they would still be looking for you after Gilbert de Warenne lost you?' It is a reminder that I may not be altogether forgotten by the young noble who was unlucky in losing me.

Having warned me of what the likes of Odo would do with me if I were found anywhere near Willelm on the greatest day of his life, Saeward may not relish the thought of being taken captive along with me.

'What do you fear most, Ivar being killed or never seeing him again?' Wulfmaer throws him a trick question.

'They amount to the same', Saeward looks sternly at the miller. 'I am only warning him that he may yet be known at the West Mynster'.

'You sound fearful for my kinsman', Eadmund does not admonish Saeward for trying to put me off going, 'but if you went with him, then perhaps the likelihood of him doing the wrong thing would be greatly lessened. What do you say, Saeward?'

Saeward looks around from one of us to the other. He looks crestfallen that he has been caught out,

'You think that I should go with him to guide him in the ways of the brothers? Still, we might not stand out so much'. His cheeks are flushed now at the thrill of my gamble.

'The brothers will be paired to go in, as everywhere'.

'Well, there you *are!* Life is not as bleak as you first thought, and you will be within sight of each other to pass on warnings', Eadmund smiles wickedly. 'That means that our kinsman's life is in your hands. Bring him back safely, Saeward'. We all laugh in the way of young lads when one has been caught in a trap of his own making.

Saeward arches his eyebrows. He groans long and loudly and Godwin slaps him on the back to wish him good luck,

'You can still wriggle out of your trap if you wish. You are *both* free to call off this madness, as it *is* of your own making. None of us would want you to put yourself at risk if you felt you were unable to see it through. However, if you go through with it, and you both come away from it unharmed, who knows we might all do the same sort of thing again to a better end. Ivar has a good friend in you, from what I have heard. *Keep an eye on your temper and you could go far!'*

Saeward nods and makes a mock bow to acknowledge the thumping of hands on the long table.

'All the same, I still think Ivar's errand to see Willelm being crowned is a waste of time, when he could be helping us teach these men to fight the Northmen', Godwin eyes me closely.

He stands there smiling, hoping I will put off what they all think of as foolishness. Propping himself against the long table, waiting for me to start, his right hand rests idly on his sword pommel. When there is no change of heart forthcoming, he changes his bearing, raps on the table with his knuckles and looks at Magnus,

'How do things look in the way of food, brother? These men will need to eat well to keep up their strength'. With that Godwin has drawn talk of us watching Willelm's enthronement to a close.

'Dean Wulfwin has told me that there is enough for our household from his barn and meat stores, as long as we do not hope for a nightly feast until we leave for the west. We have been asked to join him at the feast of Christ's birth, by the way', Magnus tells his eldest brother.

'*All* of us, the fyrdmen outside as well?' Godwin teases Magnus.

'No, *only us*', Magnus answers, then adds with a smirk, grinning at Saeward and Wulfmaer. 'Ask a foolish question! You Saeward, and you too Wulfmaer will be looked after here, as will everyone else'.

'Where is Theodolf?' Eadmund asks me suddenly, reminding me I had forgotten about him. When he goes on to talk about something else, I suddenly think back,

'He is with his bowmen', I turn his way, still grinning at Magnus' wit.

'Godwin needs to speak to him, when he is free, can you tell him as soon as you are able?'

I nod and look around for food,

'Is there something to eat? I am famished, what with putting your men through their paces, showing them how to fight with an axe!'

'Soon, Ivar - we will all be eating soon. Burhwold will call us when all is ready. I can offer ale for now, and bread, if you are happy with that?' Eadmund wipes his beard and smiles. 'I wish you would tell us why it is you need to risk your life watching their duke being crowned. I should not wonder everything will prove so boring you will forget yourself and yawn'.

'Is that your only fear?' I follow Eadmund through the great room, where Burhwold and Winflaed help Ingigerd set the table, 'You should see the gaping mouths at Wealtham when some of the older brothers have to listen to long talks!'

Seeing us standing, watching, Burhwold stops on his way with a plate of cut meats and tells his young master,

'The food is not yet ready, my Lord Eadmund'.

'Have you ale and bread for my kinsman, Ivar?' Eadmund asks, smiling longingly at Ingigerd when she brushes past him on her way to the other end of the long table.

She shows us both that she is not taken with us and bustles with her back to us. Burhwold leaves and starts for where a vat stands against the wall, across the floor from the table. He pours a beaker and makes his way back to us.

'Would you pour me one?' Eadmund asks the old fellow when he is halfway back.

Burhwold nods gravely and turns, puts my beaker on the bench alongside the vat and takes another beaker. Whilst he pours Eadmund's ale, the young man follows Ingigerd around the room with his eyes. On coming back, old Burhwold forgets my beaker and Eadmund laughs, pointing,

'Would you bring Ivar's ale with you, Ingigerd?'

He watches, grinning foolishly as she slows, and then stops. She looks at Eadmund, and across the room to where my beaker sits on the bench, and then back at Eadmund. She says nothing, darkens with anger at my kinsman and brings her small clenched fist up to her waist. With measured strides Ingigerd crosses the room, gathers up my beaker and brings me my ale, looking up into my face as she holds it up to me, mutely.

Having delivered my drink to me, she strides away again to finish what she had been doing. Eadmund laughs, long and loud. The hand that holds his beaker shakes and ale spills on the stone floor. Eadmund laughs louder and bangs his beaker on the table, slopping more ale onto the floor.

'Are you drunk, brother?' Godwin has followed us into the main room and stands there with his hands at his waist, 'Look at the mess you are making, what loutish manner is that you are showing the household?'

Eadmund laughs again, but not as loudly as before, trying to rein in his mirth. Godwin stands in front of him, mouth set in grim distaste.

'God, man get a grip on yourself, will you? We need you to lead the

293

West Seaxan fyrd, and look at the state you are in!'

'He is not drunk, Godwin', I answer for Eadmund. 'I think he is trying to hide his fears for me. He has only come to know me again and he fears he will have seen the last of me'.

'You *think* so? We must avenge our father's death and wrest the crown from Willelm, and to do that we must keep our wits about us! Brother, I hope Ivar is right. When we have thrown the Northmen out of our land and I am king, then we shall have time to give ourselves up to some merrymaking!'

'You have to let them rest before then, too, Godwin', I warn Harold's eldest son. 'Otherwise everyone will be overwrought. We need to be well rested to meet Willelm's men on a war footing'.

'We will have to see that he does', Godwin lightens and gently punches his brother's chin in jest.

'Eadmund will do well for you when the time comes, believe me', I speak for him, and chide Eadmund. 'Drink up and come outside for a breath of fresh air'.

'See that you *are* ready, Eadmund. See that you *are* ready!' Godwin has lost the faint smile and stares balefully at his brother and at me, and leaves the room.

Eadmund shrugs and picks up his beaker, drains it in one gulp, slams it upside down on the table and belches.

'I thank you, kinsman. Godwin drives us all'.

'You can rest assured, I know you are not drunk now, but do you ever drink too much?' I ask Eadmund.

'From time to time I have been known to drain a tun by myself. I heard that Svein drank well and hard, is that right?' he answers, setting me a question in turn. On seeing me staring askance at him, he adds, 'Father's eldest brother. He never said much of him, but Tostig told me that he was always ready for ale... apart from whoring'.

Eadmund grins lopsidedly as Ingigerd passes again.

'He was known for overdoing things, aye', I agree, 'but then I have had the odd skinful and whored with the best of them'.

'More than that...'

Eadmund may wish to stir old ashes, but I will have nothing to do with it,

'Let Svein be. His deeds were foolish, to say the least, but nothing is attained in bringing all that up now. Let us not speak ill of the dead, but ensure that men will speak well of *us* when we are no longer here on the earth'.

I hope I have laid Svein's ghost to rest with that, wherever his bones may rest. Eadmund takes my meaning and nods. Burhwold smiles at me. He barely knew Svein when Harold brought him here to hunt. Svein was not as bad as Eadweard's Witan made him out to be. Earl Aelfgar's own foolishness drew Eadweard's wrath when he joined in Gruffyd's raids on Herefordshire, on Svein's lands, yet he was forgiven and took his father, Leofric's earldom shortly before he himself died.

Svein's deeds lay heavily on his own heart, and his search for forgiveness led to death at the hands of robbers on his way home from the Holy Land because he went unarmed. Willelm's father Duke Rodberht met the same fate.

My father told me when I was very young, that whoever speaks ill of the dead brings down the wrath of his fellows upon himself, and muddies the waters of Urd's well.

Whilst we await our evening meal Eadmund and I leave the warmth of the great room to stand at the doorway and take in the bracing, cold air. From here to the River Leag is a broad meadow onto which wild animals often stray. On this grey winter's evening, before the unseen sun sets over the river, a doe picks her way through the deep snow to the river to drink from where the ice has been broken, leaving her trail to be seen plainly.

In winter wolves can be seen here too. With little food at this time of the year, emboldened by hunger they will kill close to the lodge even. A swan can be a fitting kill if nothing else shows itself for the taking. A doe would make a better meal for a small pack, and I can see dark grey shapes against the leafless trees to the north and east.

On her own in the snow the doe senses the threat. She is not yet heavy, but I can see that she will be soon. There will be a fawn at her side in the fore-year, if she lives that long.

To a wolf this is an added gain, more meat, two hearts to fight over and another, more tender liver to gorge on.

My breath hangs on the air as I walk into the doorway,

'Theodolf, bring your bow', I call, one hand cupped to the side of my mouth to lessen the sound.

Theodolf has been playing with the growing Brihtwin, teaching the child how to creep up on a foe without being seen. He looks out through the open doorway, sees the doe and nods.

'Not her, the wolves... over there', I point across to the trees, 'look'.

'You want me to get one of the *wolves*, from *here?*' he asks, stunned at my belief in his bowmanship.

'*She* will not come this way unless the wolves panic her into running this way because at this time of the year they are not afraid of us. The doe will try to run away from us, and past the pack', I reason. 'She might try to leap over them to get away'.

'You *think* so?' Theodolf looks sideways at me, one eye on the wolves.

Brihtwin looks out of the doorway and jumps with glee at seeing the doe.

'Brihtwin, go inside and play with Ingigerd', Theodolf tells the child before he gives us away.

'Want to look at *deer!*' Brihtwin screeches, frightening the doe. She wobbles by the river, unsure.

'Come in here, Brihtwin. Look what *I* have for you', Gerda calls for her son, knowing I have asked Theodolf to carry out this hard task.

'Go see what mama has for you', Theodolf pushes the child to the door with one hand on his back.

Just then the wolves close on the doe from the north side and she stands shivering with fear, as if frozen to the ground. The haze of her breath hangs in the still air. She is as terrified of us as she is of the wolves, with good reason. We could just as easily claim her for our table.

Theodolf lays an arrow across his bow and stands ready, watching as the wolves mark the doe's gait when she makes for the open land. There is a blur as a big male runs at her and the arrow finds its mark. The wolf drops lifelessly onto the thick snow. Some of the other wolves dart away again, shaken by the sudden killing of their pack leader. The others set hungrily on the dead wolf. Meat is meat, after all. The doe is well away, almost out of sight before I catch sight of her again.

'We missed some good tender meat there', Magnus has joined us outside.

'We did not. An older hart would be the best for meat. She will give birth soon, if she stays clear of the wolves'.

I turn and lay a hand on his shoulder before heading back to the table. 'One day perhaps, when she is older, or too old to bear young, we may find her on our table'.

'You have an answer for everything', Magnus smiles and I follow him into the warmth.

Before I get beyond the doorway I glance over my shoulder at the wolves tearing at the dead male. A new pack leader will take over, and life will roll on pitilessly. How alike we are to *them*. In some ways we are not. We draw the line at eating our own kind.

'Magnus tells me that Theodolf brought down a wolf', Eadmund sees me in the doorway with Theodolf behind, knocking the snow from his feet.

Theodolf grins. It is a shame the fyrdmen did not see this art. I am reminded of Arngrim. He too was brought down in mid-flight not so

296

long ago, on my horse. My young Northanhymbran friend goes from strength to strength with his prowess. I only wish Oslac had seen this.

He would have been overjoyed, but he has o be with the men in Wealtham, as is Cyneweard. It was Godwin who sought to break up the learning groups, should the Northmen come prying. We only number a score here now, together with Harold's sons and our fyrdmen.

After the Yulefeast Wulfmaer and Saeward will be going to Saewardstan to take over teaching the fyrdmen there, leaving Theodolf and me with the rest. Soon there will be less, when we have picked the best from them.

16

The Yule Feast is almost upon us, and Duke Willelm will soon be king, hopefully not for much longer. We have heard nothing from Eadgar or the young earls. *They* may have been allowed to go north until recalled to witness the crowning at the West Mynster.

Osgod will no longer be at Thorney. He may have already have gone north to Jorvik because his duties lie with his earl. He has been losing respect for a lord few men would stomach knowing Morkere went on his knees with his brother Eadwin to their new Northman over-lord. I dare say Morkere would have taken a dim view of Osgod's hold-ing back the Northman Gilbert de Warenne to aid my flight.

'Dean Wulfwin will send your habit with Cyneweard and Oslac', Eadmund tells me quietly. He must have come around behind me whilst I was deep in thought.

'I thank you', is as much as I can think of by way of an answer. My thoughts are awry now. Have Cyneweard and Oslac been sent back to Leagatun because of me, to ride with me to the West Mynster, to look after me? Could it be Godwin wants me to go after all and see for my-self who gives himself under oath to Willelm?

It would be useful for Godwin to know who to trust for when the crown is set on *his* head. I say when because I want to believe a kins-man to sit on the throne of this kingdom. Even so, I have nagging doubts on that score.

'Godwin is the one to thank, Ivar. For the life of me I cannot think *what* ails you', Eadmund scoffs, still hoping to put me off what he thinks to be a fool's errand. 'To want to go there, when you could be caught sounds frighteningly foolish'.

Magnus shakes his head,

'I would never have believed it of you that you would risk so much to see the 'Bastard' having that trinket dumped on his red thatch by Ea-dred. They would throw you to the wolves, you know'. He tries to hide his fear with wit, dismayed at the thought of losing a kinsman that he has only just come to know again.

'Much as King Aella of Northanhymbra had Ragnar Lothbrok, 'Leather Breeks', thrown into a pit of vipers', I joke.

'Is that so?' Eadmund says off-handedly. He may never have heard the tale, or else does not see the link I made. Ragnar was taken captive after a raid on Baebbanburh, and I may be taken spying on Willelm. I would not have thought Eadmund could have missed my point.

Harold had much to do at the time his sons were growing. Many of the tales of times gone by may not have been passed on.

'I will be back, fear not', I pat him on the back as he leaves me to join Godwin in the great room.

'I want to believe you, Ivar, I really *do*', he mutters as he passes through the door.

He will believe his eyes when I ride back to the lodge in a day or two, cock-a-hoop and ready to tell them all what I witnessed, who paid their respects to Willelm. And he will listen to me telling of sneaking by the Northman guards, under their noses, to take part in the brothers' chant, watch Eadred 'dump the trinket on Willelm's red thatch', as he put it. Yet he does not show his fears for my safety. He has some of his uncle, Tostig in him. He may have learned more than to hide his inner-most thoughts from his fellows, and in the fullness of time I shall see how much.

'Magnus, how goes it?' I greet the youngest of the three, who has been outside again. He goes out of his way to cross the floor to shake my hand. 'Do you think there will be more snow before Yuletide?'

'I fear so', Magnus says little, but looks worried as he takes my out-stretched hand. He too has misgivings about my wanting to watch Wil-lelm's crowning, 'Although it is perhaps better to have the snow than a gnawing cold frost'.

Theodolf enters the lodge and lifts Brihtwin. Gerda must have set the child down again, having seen the threat from the wolves had gone. The child gurgles with glee as Theodolf rubs his belly, and throws his head back to make it last.

'So it is set then, Ivar. You go tomorrow?' Theodolf asks.

'Aye, my friend, I do. Will you come, too?' I ask and laugh at the way his twists his mouth.

'You are on your own this time', he swings Brihtwin around as he answers. Whatever he says after that is lost in the child's high-pitched laughter that fills the fore-house.

'Have a good rest, then, Theodolf. You have earned it after all the fighting I have dragged you through these past two months', I pat his shoulder and walk into the great room after Magnus, leaving him with his newly-found kin.

'You have made ready for your ride to the West Mynster?' Godwin asks as I seat myself on the other side of the table from him, next to Magnus. He asks further, 'Which way are you taking?'

'When Oslac brings the habit from Dean Wulfwin I shall ride north to Eanefelde, and then around to the western side of Thorney. I shall take the same way back. If the Northmen follow us from the West

Mynster they will think we are riding north to Mierca'.

'You think they would fall for that ruse?' Eadmund asks, raising his left eyebrow, the look of hopelessness written across his brow that tells me he has almost given me up for lost.

'Cheer up, Eadmund', Godwin chides, 'Ivar is not even *there* yet!'

'Kinsman, you will be eating here on Yule eve!' Magnus puts on a brave show for my sake. Nevertheless I gather he too thinks I will not be back. 'Shall we put some silver on that, brother?'

Godwin raises his ale to me,

'Come let us drink to Ivar for his sheer cheek! Let us wish for his sake his horse does not tire too fast'.

'If he aims to make such a roundabout ride, he should put wings on his horse!' Eadmund laughs, to which we all raise our beakers and give a full-throated roar, 'To Braenda's wings!'

We down our ale in one mouthful, laugh foolishly, and hold out the beakers for Ingigerd to fill again.

'Let us wish, too, that Eadweard's crown falls over Willelm's big nose!' Magnus' has us all laughing again as Ingigerd refills our beakers and some of Eadmund's slops on the floor.

She stands behind him, looking on scornfully as he drains his beaker again,

'Fill your own!' she scolds, and thumps the pitcher down hard enough to spill across the table. Eadmund looks up at her, wide-eyed, taken aback. As she strides away to the kitchen he can only muster a girlish giggle.

'You have done yourself proud, brother! You had best go after her and tell her that you are ashamed of yourself at your own sloth. You never know you might endear yourself to her, with Healfdan away at Wealtham', Godwin sits back in his father's high-backed chair and tries to hold back a wide grin.

Eadmund heeds his brother's counsel and chases after Ingigerd, followed by gales of laughter. Whatever happens between them is unknown to us, but we hear Ingigerd screech and he comes back nursing his right cheek.

'I would wager you grabbed her backside out there!' Magnus tries to stop himself from choking with laughter.

'You have a glow on your face that does not come from healthy living!' I raise my beaker to the unseen maid. 'Here is to the brave Ingigerd, and long may she teach manners to the young men of this world!'

'Amen to that!' Godwin and Magnus raise their beakers to Ingigerd as Eadmund sheepishly pulls out his chair and seats himself at the table again just as Burhwold brings in food.

Theodolf follows him in with Brihtwin on his shoulders. Gerda brings up the rear with more platters of food and smiles up at her son whilst she sets out brightly painted wooden platters in front of us.

'Theodolf seat yourself', Godwin welcomes my young friend and beckons him to a chair next to his, 'and tell me about the doe that you saved from the wolves out there'.

Oslac and Cyneweard come early in the morning looking like a pair of frost elves. The snow, hurried by a following easterly wind, still falls as I open the door for them.

'Which way do you think the weather will turn tomorrow, Burhwold?' Godwin asks the old man, all eyes on me trying on the habit sent with Oslac by Wulfwin. Saeward has come with them to accompany me to the Mynster church, leaving Wulfmaer on his own at Saewardstan.

No-one will be learning to master their weapon skills over the Yuletide, most men drinking themselves foolish.

'I think what snow falls now will settle and the rest of the day should be fine, if a little crusty with hardened snow. There will be a frost in the night', Burhwold answers slowly and painstakingly, 'and I think there will be more on the way tomorrow, perhaps in the late afternoon. The wind has come about more from the north-east in the last half day or so, bringing snow soon across East Aengla from the sea'.

'Would you agree with that, Oslac?' I ask my friend.

'He could very well be right. In northern Centland the winds are fairly much like those around here in East Seaxe. By my thinking, Hrofesceaster will be under several inches of snow by now, if not a full foot as it is between Saewardstan and Wealtham', Oslac nods sagely. 'I would say, going by Wealtham, the whole of East Seaxe must be like this'.

Oslac waves his hand toward the drifting snow in the meadow, where the bones of the wolf killed by Theodolf yesterday have been given a good covering.

'My horse tripped on animal bones out there, just beyond where the doe stands now', Cyneweard nods at the doe, shivering in the snow in the middle of the meadow.

Why is she not in the woods where the wind is not nearly as strong as out on the meadowland? She could rest among the fallen trees near one of the woodland springs, unseen by wolves.

Having learned from their old pack leader's mistake, the wolves are not risking coming close enough to pick off another of their number.

'The doe is back, Theodolf', I point her out to him and earn myself a grunt of acknowledgement.

Godwin looks out from the doorway and tells me dourly,

'Oslac and Cyneweard are to go with you, Ivar'.

'I do not need them!' I do not wish to take any more with me than Saeward. 'Four of us will stand out!'

'We will not be with you all of the time', Oslac assures me. 'Cyneweard and I will ride some way behind you into the back of Thorney. He knows the way'.

'Leave your horses a way north of the minster church, you and Saeward', Godwin tells me. 'Oslac and Cyneweard can look after them, and see they are ready for the ride back. They can hold any Northmen at bay whilst you mount and make your way back'.

'You have given this some thought, Godwin ', I laud his foresight and he reddens.

'Eadmund and Magnus had a hand in it', Godwin hastens to grant them their due worth for what he has just outlined to me. 'We sat and mulled it over last night, long after you went to bed'.

He has the makings of a good leader, one who holds the loyalty of his men and gets the best from them, as his father did before him. Eadmund stands grinning, as if willing to take his due for it on his own. He is surer than Godwin in many ways, more like his father than either of his brothers. Yet in some ways he is also much like Tostig, as in his gift for keeping his thoughts to himself until called upon to share them.

'You had best be off', Godwin tells us. To Saeward he adds, 'Make sure he looks right, at least with things like sandals on bare feet'.

'I am to go in *bare feet*, with *sandals?!*' The thought alone makes me shiver.

'Only when you have dismounted, not before', Eadmund grins roguishly, 'and not after you start back'.

'Mark my words, kinsman. That *alone* will be long enough!'

Saeward laughs. I can feel myself going a shade of plum with cold at the thought of wearing sandals on bare feet for any length of time in this winter.

Still, he would know about that sort of thing from his time at Wealtham. Beorhtwulf wore sandals when he came north with us, for all he had not taken vows.

'Were you not wearing boots when you came with us to Eoferwic?' I cast my thoughts back.

'Ah, I have never *had* to wear sandals. You know I was only ever a *lay* brother. Anyway, I will be doing the same as you tomorrow in the West Mynster, so I shall be going blue with the cold with you!'

The thought of his suffering along with me cheers me up. I shall not be the only one glad to pull on my fleece-lined boots after being out in the snow with my toes sticking out from beneath the habit!

'We will not need to fold up our breeks, either. As you can see, the habit is long enough. Only the toes will be seen', Saeward cheers me further with the only good news. 'It is how many of the Brothers cheat'.

Eadmund scratches the bristle around his cheeks, leans toward Oslac and laughs,

'These two handsome fellows will show up the brothers!'

Oslac says nothing. He has no need of words.

He merely brightens at the sight of me in the worn habit. Having seen me in my Danish war gear, in Northman war gear, and in an old ceorl's coat, I have now changed the way I look again. It looks as though it is a struggle for him to recall how many new outfits he has seen me wearing, as well as what I am no longer wearing. I have on a fur cap brought back from my seafaring days to the Vistula, and my chin has been shaved. Saeward tells me bearded Brothers are rare in the south, more so amongst the teaching brothers of Wealtham and the West Mynster.

Saeward himself still wears the ceorl's woollen cap he was given to work the fields. Together we must be a sight to behold, but hopefully will not draw unwarranted stares on our way. It will be different waiting to go into the church with the brothers.

'You look the handsome devil you always did!' Theodolf laughs and points at me for Brihtwin to take in. As is the way of a small child, without my beard he does not know me. He is wide-eyed and open-mouthed with wonder.

Gerda and Ingigerd smile sideways at us both with our hoods over our heads and hands clasped within the roomy sleeves. The farewells ring in our ears long after we have passed northward, out of hearing and soon out of sight in the thick slowly-falling snow. I hope Burhwold is right about the snow easing off during the day.

On our way to Eanefelde the wind drives the snow into our eyes at a slant, the cold keenly felt on my cheeks without the hair. I shall see to growing it back before the week is out.

A heavy blanket of snow covers everywhere, and Cyneweard has trouble picking out way markers to guide us on our way. This is a part of East Seaxe I have never knowingly crossed, and Saeward only knows the land to the east beyond Cingheford. In all this whiteness it is hard enough to see, let alone find landmarks, so our fates hang on Cyneweard's keen eyesight and knowledge of the land.

'I know where I am now'. Cyneweard breathes out and lets us know after walking his horse. He mounts again and points ahead. 'We need to cross the river at a ford just along here, then ride northward to Eane-felde by way of Aethelmentun'.

'Lead the way, Cyneweard', I tell him. These places are all just names to me. The only parts of Middil Seaxe known to me are on the western side, near Ceolsey and Thorney, where King Eadweard chose to hunt.

Harold and I rode with Eadweard, along with a number of my kins-man's huscarls to shield him against the many outlaws in those parts.

'Why are we riding to Eanefelde anyway?' Oslac asks Cyneweard. 'I am asking only out of interest, mind, not wishing to question your wisdom in choosing that way to ride to Thorney'.

'Lord Godwin has asked me to take word to Lord Ansgar', Cyne-weard looks over his shoulder. Oslac nods his understanding and we all fall silent. The wind drives the snow so thickly across the land that Cyneweard misses the ford beyond the thicket we almost passed.

'With this damned freezing fog, it is hard enough to know where the ford is without the snow adding to our woes!' Cyneweard pulls hard to his left on the reins to bring his horse about. He looks to where we must ford the Leag and then stands in his stirrups to stare at the swollen river,

'God, *look* at this river! Where does all the water come from?'

'I am guessing that all this water stems from those hills in East Se-axe and Heortesford scir', I take a long, hard look at the river and rate the likelihood of our crossing without coming out sodden onto the other bank as being slender.

'Are we going in or not?' Oslac nudges his mount on.

'The sooner we get through it, the sooner we reach Eanefelde and warm ourselves by Ansgar's fire', he chides.

'Very well then – *you go first!*' Cyneweard snaps back at Oslac and urges his horse after him into the icy water.

I follow, with Saeward bringing up the rear. The heavy weight of the habit trailing on either side of my saddle makes the fording harder, as the raw, icy cold water rushes around Braenda's flanks to my right. No doubt Saeward curses me under his breath for being brought into this gamble of mine.

Cyneweard's mare misses her footing when we are halfway across, but he steadies her before she shies and dunks him into the fast flowing water. Fording any river in winter is nothing short of foolish, but our next crossing would be well to the north of Eanefelde, which would mean us having to come back on ourselves, and that would not be any easier. Going the other way would bring us to Hakon's island, much too close to where the Northmen are now billeted, and too far south of any useful road to Ansgar's hall.

On reaching the Aethelmentun side of the river we halt until Saeward and Cyneweard catch up. Cyneweard waves his hand forward to show that we need not stop for him. Saeward's horse is not happy scaling the bank, however, and backs down toward the icy water.

'Give her a few smacks on the rump, like this!' Cyneweard hits Saeward's horse with the flat of his hand and she scrambles awkwardly up to the crest of the bank, almost losing her rider. Cyneweard's horse follows closely behind, struggling as she reaches the crest. Saeward reaches out for the bridle but is waved on,

'No, by Christ, do you want to unhorse me?!' Cyneweard bends low in the saddle to make the climb easier over the last few feet. On coming onto level ground he rests a hand on Saeward's shoulder and pats it in friendship.

Saeward shrugs and clicks his tongue at his horse.

'I am sorry, Saeward. I did not want to sound ungrateful, but you would have had me off her. Am I forgiven?' Cyneweard pleads.

Saeward nods quietly. He understands, but stares bitterly at the lad's back when he thinks he is not being watched.

'He is right, you know', I tell Saeward. 'Had he fallen under his horse into the bargain, he might have been kicked and drowned. You need to think a little longer, but your heart is set right'.

He brightens a little as we set off again for Ansgar's hall, still a long way through the snow. I wipe my eyebrows, and try to pull the hood of the habit away from my right cheek, to no end. It is wet with hard-driven snow from the north east.

At least, when we leave Eanefelde our backs will be to the weather. From Aethelmentun it is only a short ride to find Ansgar seated for a meal as we enter his hall. As we kick the snow from our boots by the doorway he calls to me,

'Ivar, how wonderful it is that you come to seek me out!' Ansgar rises from his table and greets me enthusiastically. 'The snow will melt from your boots by the hearth, fear not. See, one of my hounds is licking the snow off before it melts, even!'

He wrings my right hand, slaps the shoulder and turns to see who I have with me. He greets Oslac. It must be the first time they have met again since we all fought side by side at Lunden Brycg. Although the shire reeve is under a cloud owing to the way he yielded to Willelm, he is overjoyed to meet one man who sees him for what he is, a leader of worth,

'You have with you one of the *best* bowman of the kingdom! Where are the other two?' Ansgar is overjoyed at meeting Oslac again. He looks Cyneweard up and down closely and asks, pointing to Saeward and Cyneweard, 'Do I do know who you have with you? I do know this one – from the 'Eel Trap', surely?

'I think you do', I smile wryly at Ansgar. 'Cyneweard may also have fought at the bridge – did you?'

'I *was* there', Cyneweard grins sheepishly, *'somewhere'*.

'Saeward was on his way from Wealtham at about the time we saw off the duke and his men. We met him near the 'Eel Trap' after the fighting. You saw him at Thorney, throwing axes at the target to show his skills to Eadgar', I tell Ansgar.

'I think I made up for not being at the bridge when we rode to the south coast', Saeward assures Ansgar, breaking into a laugh.

'I am sure you *did!*' Ansgar slaps Saeward on the back and turns to me, *'Did* he?'

'He surely did - well and truly. Indeed he more than made up for his lateness in Lunden burh, my Lord', I grin at Saeward and slap him on the back. 'He has been doing so ever since, teaching fyrdmen his axe-throwing skills'.

'What do I owe the honour of your band of friends?' Ansgar turns back to me, laughs and shakes his head in disbelief when he sees the way I am clothed, 'God, Ivar, you have shaved your beard - and wearing a habit, too! Have you taken holy orders?'

I chuckle and scratch my chin, even though it does not itch, and look sideways at my friend.

'No I have not, Lord Ansgar. I was told by Saeward to do so for my errand. I must look right to watch Ealdred crowning Willelm'. I scratch my chin again and add, 'Saeward tells me he knows of few bearded brothers and I need to be like the others'.

I draw Cyneweard forward and tell him he has word from Godwin. Ansgar looks bewildered at me, shakes his head and turns from me to Cyneweard,

'What did Godwin tell you for me, Cyneweard?' he asks gravely.

'Lord Godwin asks that you stop by in Leagatun to talk about joining him in the west', Cyneweard falteringly passes on Godwin's words. 'He asks also that you give your answer through me on my way back'.

'Where are you going now?' Ansgar asks Cyneweard, having misheard what I told him.

Cyneweard looks to me to give Ansgar the answer and I tell him again what I told him moments ago,

'We are riding to Thorney so that I can witness the crowning of Willelm in the West Mynster'.

Ansgar takes a long look at me. He betrays no feeling when he tells me levelly after deep thought,

'You are a *fool,* Ivar. I know you are a marked man'.

'I may be', I answer with a lopsided grin. I add, 'Yet I wish to see who gives their oath to Willelm, and to whom we must show our disdain unless they see the error of their ways'.

'I am to attend the crowning', Ansgar drops his eyes to the floor as he tells me of his duty to the new king as shire reeve, 'and Godwin can have my answer now'.

I feel my heart sink even before I hear his answer,

'I wish him luck with all my heart, but I must stand behind Willelm. Neither I nor my men will raise arms against your kinsmen, I swear'.

Half smiling I finish his answer for him,

'But nor will you raise arms *for* him. Cyneweard, now you have it. We need not ride back this way for Lord Ansgar's answer'.

Ansgar looks crestfallen at me and tries to make amends,

'You may rest here for the day, even for the night if you wish. I still value your friendship, Ivar. Eat, drink, and dry yourself by the fire. I will not betray you to the Northmen, fear not, but understand this, nor can I help you if you are caught and handed over to Willelm'.

Oslac, Cyneweard and Saeward look thoughtfully at me, holding their breath, wondering if I will grant them time to dry out and rest in Ansgar's hall. I nod and they breathe out with relief. Ansgar smiles and tries to steer talk away from that which would drive a wedge between us after fighting side-by-side at Lunden Brycg,

'I have some good ale that you should try whilst you are my guests. Do not abandon your errand, but put it aside for now. Go, by all means, but share my hospitality first!' In wordlessly agreeing to his hospitality I grip his hand tightly, so tightly he winces, but he bears the pain with a brave smile. He will not betray us!

Early next morning we lead our horses out into the pallisaded yard of Ansgar's hall. He himself is not to be seen, the pain of his calling being at odds with mine. We are given food to put in our saddle bags and mount in the half darkness.

No-one bids farewell, so we turn out from Eanefelde westward in a sober mood. The snow has stopped falling, but the wind still blows from the north east, blowing from behind as we take a road westward through Middil Seaxe.

Everywhere I look the land has taken on a blueish hue. The low hills to the north are bleak and threatening before the sun rises behind us. There are still no signs that the Northmen have pushed northward out of Lunden. They may be biding their time until the fore-year, when they can strike out and try to bully everyone in the south before taking on the rest of the kingdom. How many more of the Northmen and their friends there are in the kingdom since we last fought them I do not know, but they will need many more to catch us.

They may be like spiders, waiting for some poor fly to alight on their web. Some think – and the higher churchmen are chief among them - that Willelm will only need the strength of the crown to win over the nobility of this fair land, and we may yet find Aenglishmen fighting one another. Even if that *were* the case, he must first show he is next to God in his love for his new underlings.

He must let them know this by a show of sorrow for the deeds his men have enacted in the southern shires. Willelm would have to rebuke his brother Odo in front of his Aenglish lords. That, in the eyes of his Northmen and Bretlanders would not work well for him.

I am still deep in thought when Saeward tells me quietly,

'There are Northmen on the road ahead, Ivar'. A company of horsemen nears from the west.

'Where are we, Cyneweard? This is another part of Middil Seaxe unknown to me', I turn to Wynstan's son beside me.

He stands in his stirrups, looks around in the half light, rubs his lips together deep in thought, and finally answers,

'I think we must be near Cyngesbyrig. We must ride south from here to the river at Ceolsey, and then eastward into Thorney. If you say we must ride wide around Lunden burh, this is the best way'.

My eyes are on the horsemen, who do not seem to be in any haste to find out who we are. The wind drives the drifting snow across their path, and as they have to keep their heads down out of the biting wind they can not have seen us yet.

'Who do you think they are?' Oslac asks me.

'They look as if they must be Northmen'. I still have to strain my eyes to see them against the low hills and woodland.

Oslac's hand goes to his bow, and his breathing quickens but does not raise the weapon lest he alerts them.

'Hold your bow down at your side until it is needed', I tell him. 'They will find it hard enough to keep the wind out of their eyes. As Saeward and I wear habits, they may think that you are our guardians against robbers'.

Oslac eases, his breathing slower again and draws his bow from the leather bag that he keeps it in, holding it low on my side, out of sight of the riders nearing us. They *are* Northmen, as I thought they were, but other than the first rider they do not look at us. He nods, and then lowers his head again to shield his eyes until they pass.

When they are some way behind us, Oslac looks over his shoulder at the quickly vanishing riders, puts his bow away again and looks sideways at me,

'Well, *they* were no threat!'

'Like as not they looked at us and thought the same', I laugh. There is no need for me to see if they are out of harm's way, Oslac has done that for me. I trust to his watchfulness.

'Why did Theodolf not come?' he asks.

'I think perhaps because Godwin did not deem we needed more than two to ride with us poor Brothers', I tell him with a half smile.

'As we do not bear gifts for the new king, even if singing his praises were thought to be noble, there will be many there whose company will be more highly prized!' Saeward adds wryly.

His wit brings a wry smile to Oslac's lips and I raise my eyebrows at the thought of my untried singing jarring on someone's ears. Saeward laughs out loud, as if reading my thoughts,

'Something tells me *your* singing will not be missed if the bastard never hears it!'

I rise above the slight and keep my eyes peeled for more Northmen on the road ahead.

'*Your* talents lie elsewhere, Ivar', Saeward kindly smoothes my ruffed feathers. 'The Lord bestows his gifts on men in his own unfathomable manner. You could have been more like Odd '.

'Aye, God *forbid!*' I spit on the ground, 'I think I would have been cast to the wolves, had I been born like him!'

I wonder what he was doing in Hrofesceaster, so close to Odo's stronghold. It was too *uncanny,* him being there when Wulfmaer was to have been hanged. He did not know Aelfhild because we met her after parting company with him. It may have been he who drew the Northmen to Dunstan's hideout, not Burhred. Trying to hang himself may have been from guilt at the betrayal of his friend Dunstan. Once Dunstan was dead, Odd could have felt nothing in leading the Northmen to us.

We reach the forlorn hamlet of Ceolsey without any further sightings of Northman patrols. The snow had begun falling again, but has died down to flurries. Nevertheless the wind still whips at our backs. Now we have to ride almost into the wind again, north of eastward on our ride east to Thorney. The road leaves the riverside here and leads across the heath.

I know where I am now, and look for landmarks that will guide me to where the Tyborna forks to the north of the hunting lodge and abbey. There are no Northmen about here, yet I would have thought that they would be out looking for the likes of us. In their eyes we would be up to no good and should not be here at this time of Willelm's honouring. Perhaps they will be out in greater numbers when we close on the West Mynster itself.

'You know this part of the shire well, Ivar?' Cyneweard asks and leans over to me to be able to hear my answer in the squall.

'I do. The old king liked his hunting. When he could no longer ride far in the last year before his death, we would bring him out onto the heath to watch the hunt. Eadweard still liked to see others on the hunt he once led'.

'Eadgytha, his queen watched over Harold's younger brother. They were both saddened that Earl Leofric's grandsons were able to oust Tostig without too much hindrance, yet they never thought of Harold having to set aside his own feelings to hold off a war within the kingdom', it seems funny, my telling of my kinsmen's shared bitterness.

'Fighting between the earls would only make it easier for an outsider to break the kingdom asunder. That was why he married their sister Ealdgyth, to keep the peace, not because he wished to be rid of Eadgytha Svaneshals', I have time to outline the background to all our present troubles until the landmarks show me when to leave this road.

Saeward puts an awkward question to me,

'When you became a huscarl in Harold's household, did Tostig feel you had betrayed him? Was he aware his brother wanted to save you from what might happen to you one day in Eoferwic?'

'I joined Harold after fighting the Wealsh prince Gruffyd with Tostig's blessings. It was two years later, when Tostig was a guest of King Eadweard that tidings of his households being burnt down were brought by riders from Eoferwic. Then we heard the same tidings from Northanhamtun too. When I last saw him at Thorney, he greeted me with a kind of brotherly love he had always felt for me. We *were* still kinsmen for all that!'

I have been sworn to keep the knowledge to myself about Tostig being alive, and although Harold is dead, I feel my oath is still binding. Careless talk could threaten Tostig's wellbeing.

All is quiet again whilst we take a track that leads to where we might take off our boots and pull on the sandals. From there to the abbey will be a brisk walk in an icy mist that will hide us from prying eyes.

On looking back to the road through the trees I see we picked the best time to leave the road then. A troop of horsemen rides westward out from Thorney. This near to the church we would have been stopped and searched for weapons. Men of the church have been known to bear swords. Some abbots fought beside Harold, but the Northmen might not

310

understand that. The wind has thankfully driven the snow across our tracks, as none of them raises the hue and cry that would have led to the scouring of the heath for us. That would have been the end of us.

Once I have made sure that the Northmen have ridden beyond where we left the road, I turn Braenda to follow the others to where the tangle of trees and bushes screens us from the road. The thickening mist gives us further cover. As we ride further the trees give way to marshy land, where we will be safe to make our way to the West Mynster on foot.

'You can wait for us here Oslac, Cyneweard. We must take off our boots and pray our feet will not freeze!' I laugh off the coldness and look at Saeward. He takes care not to look back at me and stares down at his boots as he undoes the strapping.

'It is all in a good cause, I tell myself', Saeward rumbles, and scowls, still without looking up. 'Tell, someone, before I forget. Who thought of it?'

'It was me, Saeward'. I try to cheer him up, 'If you want to curse me, do it now'.

'I might curse you on the way back to Leagatun, but I might let you off if you buy me enough food and ale to help me forget', Saeward stares, trying to fight a weary smile that pulls at the corners of his mouth.

'We will have to take the long way back again', I add, watching the scowl growing again.

'Then I *will* curse you on the way back'.

He tries to fight a grin, loses and slaps me on my back, telling me,

'We had best make our way to the abbey church quickly. The bell tolls and the brothers will be readying themselves, and I have to talk two of them into staying in their cells for us'.

'Will that be hard?' I ask as we hasten across the marshy ground from where the burn forks toward the Temese.

'I somehow doubt they will be looking forward to this, although it hangs on what the abbot has told them. If he thinks that crowning Willelm is the answer to all our prayers, they might be awkward. I have to be careful, and I will have to tell them who I am', he looks to left and right with me as we leave the shelter of the undergrowth and trees to slip through a side gate into the yard of Eadweard's abbey.

'*Why* do you have to tell them?' I ask, nonplussed at Saeward's need to be truthful, even though we are not meant to be here.

'I will tell them that I am a Brother from Wealtham', he turns his head to look at me, 'and that Dean Wulfwin would like to hear my telling of Willelm's crowning. What did you think I would say?' Saeward turns to me again as we await the brothers from their cells at the door to the great church.

'I thought you were going to tell them something –'

I have to finish as the sound of hard wood scraping on the stone paving echoes around the yard and signals the brothers' coming. Saeward puts himself before the leading pair.

17

'Brothers we greet you in the name of Dean Wulfwin of Wealtham', he holds his hands shoulder-high in greeting.

'Greetings, what do we owe the honour of your call here?' a tall, lightly bearded fellow answers on behalf of the others.

'My Lord, Dean Wulfwin has asked that we take part in this august rite to witness the crowning of Willelm, King Eadweard's kinsman, to be king over the Aenglish. He asks that we follow you there, so that we may look upon the rite of kingship and tell him what went before', Saeward's words, uttered in his deep voice sound right to me, but will they win over this monk, who threatens to be difficult.

It is understandable that he should be loth to giving way to men he does not know, even men in the habits of the Benedictine order that he belongs to.

'This is most uncommon Brother. Your dean, Wulfwin would have known weeks ago when Willelm's crowning was to be. He must have sent a letter to Abbot Eadwin, surely?'

'Word did not reach us at Wealtham until late, Brother -?' Saeward wants to know his name and is fraught, trying to talk him into this. I have dropped him into this and he is bravely doing his best for me. It would be easier on us all if I tell Saeward to forget about recklessly talking his way into the church on my behalf, but we have come this far -

'I am Brother Wicglaf', the fellow answers helpfully.

I know this man, surely?

'*Brother* Wicglaf?' I ask. He turns from Saeward to look more closely at me when I add, 'You have not long been with the Order of Saint Benedict, have you?'

'No, I was a huscarl in the household of Earl Gyrth until two years ago, when I sickened and was cured by a miracle sent by the Lord to show me the right path to honour his Grace', Wicglaf answers at length. He stares at me, trying to think of where he last saw me. 'You are Ivar, Lord Gyrth's kinsman. I did not know you without your beard. Have you too taken the path of righteousness?'

'Aye, friend, I am at Wealtham with Brother Saeward', I lie. 'We tend to the sick in the infirmary'

'It is good that you have seen the error of your ways, Brother Ivar, a put your sword down for the last time', Wicglaf smiles forbearingly at me, and takes my right hand in both his. 'What do you wish to glean from witnessing the rite?'

'We wish to witness– ', I nearly say the bastard's, 'the new king's crowning because we have heard he upholds the teachings of the Holy Father and his ministers'.

Saeward does his best to hide a smirk, and thankfully the witless Wicglaf misses my friend's disbelief, that I can dream up such a childish answer. Wicglaf looks hard at me, and at Saeward.

Plainly believing that I wish to do nothing more than gape at the rite, he turns to speak to his fellows,

'A pair of you may wish to spend time in prayer in your cells?' Luckily two look up, show their hands and begin the walk back through the yard to their cells.

'You can take the seats of Brother Aethelweard and Brother Eadstan', Wicglaf tells us as he files slowly past with the others. We follow them into the church.

Of all the men to test my new guise, Gilbert de Warenne stands at the door to the church with some of his men and eyes us idly as we file past him. Only ever having seen me once, he would hardly know me without a beard.

He looks more closely, up and down, at Wicglaf. With *his* well-trimmed beard, he looks much the way I did when Osgod kept him back to help us escape. De Warenne looks away from Wicglaf when his stare is met, and turns back to talk to one of his peers.

Once inside the church we seat ourselves either side of the throne, awaiting the duke, our hoods drawn down over our eyes. I am seated across the floor from Saeward to follow his lead. When Willelm comes through the great doors he will not see us. Only on passing his nobles and underlings, on his way to the throne could he even catch a glimpse of any of us. Once seated, he would be unable to see any of us.

The young earls are seated looking inward onto the main aisle, with Eadgar close beside Waltheof. Morkere and Eadwin are across from one another at the nearest end, closest to the throne. Stigand is there, amongst the higher church men on either side of Willelm. I can see Morkere just beyond him, but the light is too poor to see if I know anyone else beyond.

A few strides behind, and on either side of the throne stands a Northman armed with a lance held at arm's length away from him, the point at an angle above a red and gold pennant.

Trumpets blare suddenly, deafening me. I cannot think, was Harold crowned like this? The fanfare must be for Willelm.

All eyes turn to the west door to watch him enter. His shock of flame-red hair is lit like burnished copper by torches held high by his men. Behind are his half-brothers, Odo to his right and Rodberht on the left. This is the first time I have ever seen Count Rodberht without his helm. A little taller than either of them, he is dark, and barrel-chested like the other two.

Ealdred, with his following of bishops and priests awaits the Duke at the high altar. When Willelm is half way along the aisle and the last of his followers has passed into the church the great, iron studded door is drawn and closed with a loud, dull thud.

The bolts are rammed home and a hush overcomes us all, so that we quickly feel the dark eeriness of Eadweard's last resting place. Weak midwinter daylight glows beyond the high, painted glass windows and we are all closed in here until the rite draws to its end.

Trumpets blare again as Willelm nears the throne, almost vanishing from sight. It seems a long time before he seats himself at last at Ealdred's command. For some time now we will all be at the mercy of the elderly archbishop.

I find it hard to recall Harold's crowning. Aside from my being half asleep after our revels until the early hours - someone kept nudging me awake - we had already laid Eadweard to rest in the morning. That added greatly to the time spent in the church.

Darkness had cloaked Thorney by the time we left for the feasting in Eadweard's hunting lodge. The faces of those still there were lit in an eerie glow from the torches held by the unlucky huscarls who had drawn the short straws to stand watch at Eadweard's tomb.

Ealdred drones on, and rites are carried out that I would never have dreamed of. I see nodding heads. Only the fittest will last through Willelm's crowning without having to hide their drowsiness. He will be so drawn into the rites he will nothing else anyway. From time to time we are brought into the rite to chant, and to answer to the mystery of God's greatness, or something like that. I would say the churchmen around Willelm are unaware of what *anyone* else is doing. Saeward stifles a yawn more than once and is shaken awake to chant by an irate monk to his right.

Willelm's nobles are called upon to swear loyalty to their new king, beginning with Odo and Rodberht. Soon it is the turn of the Aenglish nobles and churchmen to do likewise. Eadgar, Eadwin and Morkere are followed by Waltheof, with Ansgar coming only before the thegns. Stigand does not relish giving his oath and for his mumbling he is chided by Ealdred. Each thegn nears the throne to put his hands between Willelm's, swears his oath and puts his life at the king's behest. I would guess there are many here more afraid of losing their lands than of crossing their fellows outside.

At long last the crown is set on Willelm's head, the sword put in his right hand, the orb out of sight in his left. Ealdred drones on at a higher pitch, his forehead shiny with sweat from wearing the heavy robes. The church is chill, teeth chatter amongst those seated around me.

The sword in Willelm's right hand shakes as he holds it point upward. Those around him would sooner not see their new king shaking like a leaf and look away. Harold did not behave in this way when he was crowned almost a year ago. Odo looks worried but keeps his own counsel, as does Rodberht of Mortain.

Suddenly the Aenglish churchmen and nobles stand and shout out,

'*Vivat, Vivat, Vivat!*' They all raise their clenched right fists in salute to Willelm. Odo and Rodberht must be the only other Northmen who know of this part of the rite as the others first look afraid at one another, but soon see the shouting as part of the rite.

Beyond the door is scuffling, yet no-one leaves the church to see what the ruck is about. Have his men taken the cries as an attack on their lord? I peer across in the gloom at Saeward, who shakes his head, looks down at the stone floor of the chantry and clasps his hands as if in prayer. I sit back and do likewise. We must bide our time and await our turn to leave the church, without mishap.

Brother Wicglaf eventually looks up from his prayers, hands still clasped under the folds of his sleeves, and nods. We all rise and make our way to the door. When one of the Brothers opens the door we see De Warenne standing in the yard, weighing the blade of his sword in his left hand as though he might be ready to use it on one of us.

'What was happening in there?' he demands. His men stand around the doorway, swords unsheathed, threatening.

'Kindly put up your weapons!' Wicglaf growls scornfully. 'Nothing happened in there that should not have happened. The Aenglish lords and churchmen have acknowledged your duke as our king. What did you *think* happened?'

Gilbert de Warenne glares at us as we file past him. This upsets one of the brothers, who gives a start and misses his footing. The poor fellow trips over his cord and falls back onto me.

He treads on my toes with his right heel and I wince. The Northmen stand back and laugh. It is as much as I can do to make sure my sword scabbard does not drop clattering onto the stone floor of the yard. They would not be so happy if they thought that their lord had been under any threat. Odo would like nothing better than to bring to bear his new found might on me with Willelm's followers looking on. Pity would be seen as weakness by our new overlords.

'Ecgfrith, *steady yourself!*' Wicglaf snaps as if he were showing his lord's fyrdmen how to hold an axe and de Warenne steps toward him, sword at the ready to deal someone a death blow.

'*Steady*, my friend. What you are about to do may leave you sorry for a lifetime!' Wicglaf stares down de Warenne.

The Northman unwillingly sheaths his sword. He does not argue. Wicglaf must be given the benefit of the doubt on pain of drawing his master's wrath. The burden of the killing of a brother in the shadow of Eadweard's church would hang heavily around Willelm's shoulders and de Warenne's own life would be forfeit. I think he could see that himself.

As we are about to pass through the yard to the Brothers' cells, another Northman noble shows, his sword half drawn. De Warenne strides toward him with his hands held high, palms forward to halt the newcomer in his tracks.

He tells him something in his own tongue, earning himself rebuke and an angry stare from the fellow who stands a head taller than him. The newcomer looks over his friend's shoulders at us and frowns again. He says nothing loud enough for us to hear, were we even able to understand what it is he murmurs behind his mailed glove.

'Are we free to leave?' Wicglaf asks de Warenne loudly.

'The Brothers have their devotions to attend to before they can eat, and we have been in there for some time, you understand?' The young Northman turns toward us, at a loss about what he should do and looks back to his friend. They stand close together, talking. The older man stares at us from time to time and then shrugs.

'By all means', de Warenne waves us on.

Before we get very far yet another of Willelm's nobles bursts into the yard and halts us, flapping his arms about. He yells something that sounds more like the barking of a mad hound and De Warenne and his friend look askance at us. Their men begin to shepherd us back into the church, but Wicglaf stands firm and stubbornly refuses to go anywhere. We stand behind him, eager to leave.

'You must go back in there', de Warenne tries to urge Wicglaf back into the church. 'My Lord Rodberht de Bruis has told me not to allow *anyone* to leave before the king has left safely. If you please, will you go *back in there?*'

Wicglaf solemnly looks over one shoulder at us and raises his eyebrows. He lifts his arms in despair, turns back to de Warenne, and points to Saeward and me, asking as he does so,

'I have two Brothers who came this morning from Wealtham', Wicglaf beckons us to step forward.

'Dean Wulfwin will be worried. Wolves are about'.

'Do they have to go back *today?*' de Warenne groans. He would sooner not be bothered and speaks to his lord in hushed tones.

When they have finished talking, de Bruis looks witheringly at de Warenne and tells him something under his breath that shakes the underling into yielding. De Warenne comes back to us and gives Wicglaf his lord's commands.

'My Lord says he does not care *how* far they must go. No-one leaves before the king! I am sorry, please go back into the church', de Warenne's men push us back with the staffs of their spears.

The Brothers stare dully at the Northmen and turn back to the great door that leads into the church. Wicglaf wearily nods and turns back to the door. Saeward glances fearfully at me, saying nothing and I make my way back after Wicglaf. The half light of dusk gives way to the darkness. Oslac and Cyneweard will be cursing under their breath as they wait in the cold. They may have gone to find a hostelry, as lighting a fire would give away their whereabouts to the Northmen.

We take our seats in the creeping coldness of the church. Saeward sits, his jaw set, folded hands hidden by the great sleeves of his habit. I think he too will be silently cursing me for the foolishness of my errand, yet he keeps his fears well hidden.

One of the Northmen looks into the chantry through the open door, turns his back on us and leaves us to our thoughts. At least they do not mistrust *us* yet. Nor have we been locked in, so when we can, Saeward and I will slip away. I begin to feel ill suddenly. A long time has passed since I last relieved myself by the road from Eanefelde.

There is a lot of noise outside again. Shouting echoes in the yard and men's boots thump on the stone setts on the road outside. Some of de Bruis' men pass our door back and forth, and leave the abbey by a side gate.

'What can be happening out there?' Wicglaf asks, looking first at one of his friends and then at me. Neither of us can no more than shrug. After all, what can we see from in *here?*

Willelm and his nobles have not yet left the church. I can see him beyond the throne, passing along the aisle to the west door. On either side of him his Aenglish and Northman nobles and churchmen bow, some awe-struck, I will warrant. Eadgar, however, will see him and his heirs as another stumbling block to the throne. I feel sorry for Eadweard's young kinsman, having been passed over twice because of his youth and lack of following. The Witan was looking for a proven warrior leader to step onto the old king's throne. Eadweard's true heir had been brushed aside again, no doubt wishing his father had never left the east.

When Aelfred became king because each of his older brothers was slain, there were no others to take the crown of West Seaxe. Aelfred was allowed to prove himself, as Eadgar has probably read and heard countless times. The only Seaxan king we Danes ever acknowledged as being 'Great'. What is to become of the fledgling Eadgar, now that he has become too big for the nest?

Saeward stealthily makes his way to the doorway and looks warily beyond the half open door. He edges further into the doorway and I look down along the aisle again to see what is happening.

Willelm and his half-brothers have drawn level with Eadgar now and the lad gives him a curt nod. The new king acknowledges him and moves along, past Morkere and Eadwin, Waltheof gives a deeper bow and Willelm bids him lift his head. He shows no dislike for the three young earls or our would-be king, I would say because they did not fight at Harold's side.

He knows, however, that they fought against him at the bridge. Perhaps he thought they *would* have stood by Harold if bidden. He passes Ansgar without so much as a brief glance at him. Does he know Ansgar fought alongside us in Suth Seaxe? He still has some way to go before he reaches the great west door.

'*Ivar, they have gone from the yard!*' Saeward hisses at me from behind. He has the door wide open and stands, beckoning.

Wicglaf sits bolt upright, looking straight at the Brother who sits across from him in the chantry. He may be unaware of what is happening around him, or perhaps he does not care to know. I pass him on my way out and he makes stares ahead without acknowledging my leaving.

In the yard again we look both ways before Saeward leads to the side door through which we entered earlier. There is a lot of shouting from the street, and the smell of burning.

'Ivar, the Northmen are burning the houses! In heaven's name why are they doing that?' Saeward looks pleadingly at me, as if to go out and attack Willelm's men. He would never dream of asking me to, but for the blink of an eye I saw that flicker in his eyes.

'What has caused them to attack the folk around here?'

'I would like to see, but my first thought is to be rid of these', I point to my footwear. 'Whoever laid down the rules for the way the Benedictine Brothers dress, had meant to slow them down'.

Saeward nods and raises his eyes heavenward,

'Saint Benedict did not think his brothers should have to run, *whatever*'. He grins ruefully, shrugging, 'why *should* they?'

There has been more snow since we came this way in the morning. Hopefully none of the Northmen will come looking for us.

Our footprints would make their search too easy.

In the gathering darkness I can hear talking ahead. They are Northmen, coming toward us and there are no bushes to hide behind.

'What do we do?' Saeward asks, echoing my own thoughts. He looks into the darkness and begins to hoist his habit, ready to unsheathe his sword.

'No, do not draw your sword. Look as though you are praying, and pray they do not think our being out here is odd or else we will have to make a fight of it!' I stay his hand and he lets the habit fall again to cover his breeks.

Out of the darkness three Northmen come on horseback, dressed for fighting. The first sees us standing in the open, our heads bowed in prayer, hands clasped.

'Do not fear, Brothers, we do not kill men of the church, unlike some of your Aenglish friends!' he tells us and laughs hoarsely at what he thinks passes for wit. His comrades laugh with him, whether they understand or not. What he said is nothing to me, I just hope they will ride on and leave us to make our way back to Oslac and Cyneweard. Before vanishing into the darkness he calls again, 'Say a prayer for our new king, and the Aenglishmen we have killed back there!'

Saeward stares at me in horror. I can only shake my head in disbelief. Why would Oslac and Cyneweard allow themselves to be seen, let alone killed, by these fools?

'We still have to go back there as soon as they have passed, to see what has become of them. There is a long walk back to Leagatun ahead of us unless we can find horses to carry us. I am not walking all that way in these', I point at the sandals and he looks glumly at me. 'My toes will freeze off!'

A little further on, where we think we left our friends, we see several corpses. The bodies of four men lie slumped on the snow-laden ground where they would have fallen. Bloody islands in a sea of white, a thin, fresh coating of snow coats their backs over slash marks from longsword and lance.

Saeward and I each turn over two of the corpses. We know none of them, nor were they armed.

'Who are they?' he is the first to ask.

'They are the poor unlucky ones who came running across the open marshland here with three Northmen hard on their heels', Oslac answers from behind us.

My heart leaps to my mouth where I thought we were beset by more of Willelm's men. Saeward spins in his heels to see Oslac and Cyneweard striding through the frost-rimed, leafless trees.

They had not been seen in the half-light through the screen of bushes and bare saplings in their grey cloaks. Behind them Braenda raises her head at the sight of me and is about to neigh when Oslac puts his hand over her muzzle. When I come abreast of her I give her a welcoming rub with the flat of my right hand over her nostrils. She licks my left hand, the warmth of her long tongue a welcome feeling in this still, raw coldness.

'What happened here?' I ask Oslac. Braenda nuzzles me still and he grins at the sight.

'She missed you', he says, then goes on to tell me very briefly what went before. He plainly feels sorry that he and Cyneweard were unable to help the fleeing Seaxans, 'These fellows just came running across the snow as we came back from the inn'.

'We would not have been able to do much', Cyneweard adds, 'no time to draw our bows before the bastard Northmen hacked down at their backs. We could have loosed off some arrows, but that would not have helped *us*, would it? Before we had our second arrows ready we might have died too'.

'No, you are right, you did well keeping yourselves hidden. You could not have known when we would be back. Nor could you know whether there were others with them. They ride in *sixes*. Where is this inn you came back from?' I wish I had known about this inn.

'We went back along the track towards Ceolsey and saw pale woodsmoke rising from the trees, away from the hamlet', Cyneweard tells me with a happy smile. 'We rode that way and saw an inn amongst the trees. If you like, when you have pulled on your boots again we can go back there'.

'No, I feel fine now. My feet can warm up by the fire first. They sell good ale there, I hope?' I feel cheered about not having to ride all the way back to Leagatun before I have taken some food and drink.

'The woman who owns the inn said to bring our friends when we came the next time', Cyneweard tells me with a broad grin.

'It seems to me the next time will be sooner than we thought. That is fine by me', Oslac laughs. Something he has just thought of raises another laugh, 'Oh, by the way, she was quite taken with your horse, Ivar. They seemed to know one another'.

It may be that I am too tired and hungry to think about what he has just told me. Or perhaps I did not hear him right. Whatever, I try not to think about how cold my toes feel as I trudge through the deepened snow with Braenda walking behind me to where the earth is firmer and swing myself up into the saddle. I ruffle her mane and nudge her with my left knee to turn behind Oslac and Cyneweard.

Saeward heaves himself into his saddle in his usual clumsy way and slaps the withers on his horse to catch up with us. His horse shoots forward and passes us at a quick trot, with him hanging on for dear life.

'Fool, you only need to nudge her with your knee!' Oslac calls after him, laughing. 'Come on, Cyneweard, we have to catch him up before he gets there and empties the ale vats on his own!'

Cyneweard and I laugh. Still, however unlikely that might be, we have to keep up with the other two, urging on our mounts to catch up with Saeward before he draws the eyes of other Northmen returning to Thorney.

'*Hold fast!*' Oslac hisses at Saeward when he draws level and pulls the reins hard for him. The deep snow has thankfully muffled the drumming of our hoofbeats. We come to a stop at the edge of a line of bushes and bare trees to allow another patrol to pass on their way east, laughing and talking blissfully unaware of us.

Once they have been blanketed again by the thick mist that has crept across the meadow from the river and leave the cover of the trees. Oslac leads to the inn's heavy door.

'Not long now before we can sit before a crackling fire, warm our hands and fill our bellies!' Oslac looks grins back at me. 'You two will be looking forward to getting your boots back on, eh?'

'Aye, make no mistake about that!' Saeward answers for us both. My feet will be going a deep blue by now, but in my thoughts I already feel the flames licking at them as I sit by the hearth with a pot of mulled ale.

'Well, we will soon be warm and cosy!'

'What is the name of this inn?' I ask.

'I do not rightly know...Who cares what this place is called! Come on, last one to sit down spreads his silver!' Oslac almost leaps through the door when it opens.

'What about our mounts? Is there anyone to look after them?'

'Aeldhelm will see to them', Cyneweard assures me as an elderly fellow leaves the warmth of the inn to see to our horses.

'You are Aeldhelm?' I turn to him.

'Aye, father, I am', he bows and touches his forehead with a withered hand, 'enter and be seated. Your needs will be met by the lady of the house'.

Oslac grins at me and says nothing. What harm is there in being taken for men of the cloth? If Aeldhelm thinks I am a priest or Brother it may help me. Should any of Willelm's men come chasing after us, they will not punish him for thinking us men of the church.

We enter the inn behind Saeward, who earns a bow or a nod here and there from those sober enough to be aware of us. I also find myself nodding blessings at those who stand for me by the fire. Some North-men also stand for me and move over to a table a little further away from the fire. The three of them start talking again once the maid has topped up their drinks from an earthenware jug and comes toward us.

'Can I bring you something, Father?' she asks me. A crooked smile spreads across her face when I look up into her hazel eyes. She seems to know who I am, but how? I look nonplussed at Saeward, who looks up at her, and then back at me, saying nothing. However, he cannot help grinning to himself.

Oslac gives me an odd look. He knows that there is something afoot here, but he too keeps own counsel. Only Cyneweard seems not to see anything beyond what his eyes tell him.

One of the Northmen eyes me, as if searching for a name. He shakes his head and goes back to listening to his comrades. They look odd, these three with their hair shaved short amongst the longer-haired Se-axans around us. I do not know how it was they took to wearing their hair in the Frankish style of helm cut. They look odd with their hair shaved high on their necks. Their shields are propped up against the wall near the door, lest they be called upon to leave hurriedly.

We talk amongst ourselves as if they were not there, although I doubt they could understand whatever we say.

'You could bring some mulled ales for us', I answer after what I think must be an age since she asked.

She has been standing looking down at me all that time, one hand resting on her hip, the jug in her other hand, her forehead framed by a white cloth bonnet that hides most of her hair. She has been taking me in for all that time, her hazel eyes all but eating me. The crooked smile comes back and I am still at odds to know why.

'You shall have whatever you wish - *Father*', she leaves us through a door at the back of the inn.

'She seems to know you', Oslac observes under his breath to me, making me feel uneasy. 'Do you recall I said she and your horse seemed to know one another?'

'Dimly, aye, but –'I begin.

'That is her. She is the one who knows your horse', Oslac finishes.

I promise him I will speak to her, but I am tired from sitting in a cold, draughty chantry.

'I shall ask if she knows me or my horse. All will come clear'.

Oslac says no more and warms his hands over the fire.

'Best we get our boots back on', Saeward leans over and whispers hoarsely, 'I for one think my feet will *never* get warm!'

'Not now, Saeward', I answer and nod toward the Northmen.

He looks at them over one shoulder and shakes his head,

'I doubt they would see'.

He reaches for the haversack with his boots in, nevertheless does not pull them out. A chill wind blows through the inn as another two Northmen enter.

'Slam that damned door behind you, will you?' one of the Seaxans calls from the back of the room at the newcomers without looking up to see who they are. 'You are letting in the cold air!'

One of the Northmen strides across the stone floor and sweeps the fellow's cup from the small table, spilling the contents on the burly Seaxan and over everyone around him. As tall as he is, the Seaxan's knees are bent upward to his chest where he sits, but he does not dare stand with the Northman standing over him.

'You *said* something?' the Northman demands, casting his eyes over all in the room, daring us. His Aenglish is fair. Was he one of King Eadweard's standing guests in days gone by?

From under the rim of my hood I take him in. He is thickset, dark-haired and I see he is not shaven-headed like the three seated by the door when he removes his helm.

From his finely chiselled face and greying temples, I would say that he is about my age, older perhaps. From the way he stands, swaying, I would say he has already raised a few cupfuls to his lord's crowning and now he wants to be lord over *us*.

The fellow who came in with him looks around the room to see whether his friend is under threat from anyone. Having taken in the shocked looks of those Seaxans in the room, and the worried looks of his Northman comrades seated behind us, he seats himself beside his friend and puts his hand on the other Northman's shoulder, saying something under his breath. The first one turns to him, laughs and says something that I cannot hear properly. For our sakes he speaks to his friend in Aenglish,

'Is it any wonder we had to show these Seaxan *curs* how to fight?!' he roars with laughter.

Oslac looks at me and shakes his head.

'You, Seaxan, did you *say* something?' the Northman shouts at him.

'I said nothing', Oslac answers.

'What about *him*, did *he* say anything?' he prods the air at me with a crooked finger. '*Did* you say anything, Brother?'

'I said nothing, either', I do not look up at the fellow from under the rim of my hood, yet I know now to whom I am talking.

Standing over the cowering Seaxan ceorl is Eustace, the Count of Boulogne, who married Eadweard's sister Godgifu. It was he who started a riot in Dofnan fifteen years since. *He* had the other guests thrown out of an inn near the old haven, so that he and his retinue could rest overnight before their return by ship to his lands.

Because Harold's father, Earl Godwin would not punish the folk of Dofnan for their 'sins' against Eadweard's kinsman, there was almost a war within the kingdom between the northern earls and Godwin's kin. Now Eustace wishes to do something like that again. This time there is no Earl Godwin or King Harold to speak on anyone's behalf.

Eustace begins to yell, almost screaming at me,

'You speak to me as if you were my equal, *Brother!* Come and grovel at my feet before I throw you out!'

I stay seated. The Northmen at their table nearby rise and warily edge toward Eustace and his friend, should trouble arise.

'*Come here!*' Eustace bellows, reddening deeply with rage.

His friend tries to calm him and stands between us, but Eustace pushes him aside. The door behind Eustace opens and the Northman spins around, thinking to find a foe standing behind him. He looks instead at a woman so comely he is taken aback by her gaze.

She walks slowly, steadily toward him, her full, red lips moving without making a sound. Her eyes light up and he backs away from her, his eyes tightly closed, hands shielding his forehead. We are all blind to whatever *he* can see, but I am sure it is terrifying for him.

He bends, still trying to shield himself, clasping his hands tightly as if in feverish prayer, and drops to his knees. Eustace's friend plainly cannot see either what he is afraid of and slaps him across his right cheek to bring him round. Eustace opens his eyes wide with fear.

He howls something none of us can understand, rises shakily to his feet, totters to the door and wrestles it open. He flees the inn with a sudden, frightened yelp, his friend following him. The three who were sitting by the fire when we entered look once up at Braenda, snatch their shields and helms and hasten after the others. We will never know what it was Eustace saw before he fled, but he plainly feared for his life. The men still in the inn laugh and jeer after the Northmen, thumping their tables gleefully.

Uncannily Braenda almost glides to stand before me,

'You have taken holy orders, Ivar?' She smiles and when I stand to greet her she asks, 'Tell me, who was it shaved off your handsome beard?'

'It needed to be done', I answer sagely. The least said the better, but I feel I must tell her, 'It will take little time to grow my beard back, and keep it trimmed as I had it before'.

The feeling of welcome returns to the inn. Everyone else sits and begins to talk again, as if nothing had happened. Oslac, Saeward and Cyneweard look at Braenda, and at me. Somehow Oslac takes my nod as an answer to an unasked question,

'Is there something between you?'

'I must see to the mulled ale!' Braenda turns and leaves the room again as suddenly as she showed behind Eustace.

Oslac asks once he is sure she is no longer within hearing,

'Is she the spay-wife Theodolf spoke of in the 'Eel Trap'?'

When he sees my nod all he says is, 'Ah!'

A little later when I am at ease again, when roasting my feet by the hearth, I feel a tap on my left shoulder.

'If I had known you would be settling down to sleep, I would not have made you this mulled ale and bowl of lamb stew', Braenda's seems hurt when I look up at her and her tone alters,

'Do you think perhaps a little later there might be a reward forthcoming, for ridding you of your Northman friends? I wonder what would the new king say if he were offered that Ivar Ulfsson as a hostage?'

'A little rest would be useful before the numbness leaves me and I can think straight again', I answer. 'In the morning we must make our way back to Harold's sons. Until then I am yours'.

Saeward glances sidelong at me and smirks. I stare blankly back at him and smile up at Braenda before she leaves us again. For help such as that, I think a reward *is* in order. For now I can dream of what she has in store for me. Somehow I do not think I will be far wrong in my guess.

18

At last the inn is clear of all guests but us. Saeward has fallen asleep on his back on one of the benches near the fire, his habit pulled tightly around him; as my feet are now hot, so must he be sweating in that thick cloth that enfolds him.

Oslac plays Nine Men's Morris with Cyneweard, allowing him to win a few times. The game is little known amongst the Seaxans. Oslac being from the Danelaw is steeped in the Norse lore, but good-naturedly smiles when Cyneweard beats him once without Oslac being aware of what he was building up to. I am watching them, warming my hands on my mulled ale when Aeldhelm asks,

'Are you Ivar?' On seeing me nod he tells me he will show me to my room. I shall not be sleeping throughout the night, Braenda will see to that.

There are few rooms in this inn. Only two other doors besides mine stand open along the dark gangway upstairs. A famed snorer, I daresay Saeward will have a room to himself. My guess is that Oslac will allow Cyneweard another win to keep him happy. The lad will not have much rest before the morning.

I seat myself on a wide bed, feel the softness of the wool sheets and almost fall asleep with my feet still on the floor before Braenda enters and stands before me.

'This is not the time to fall asleep, Ivar'. She bends forward, rests her hands on mine and plants a kiss on my upturned mouth, 'Not when there is a reward due'.

She kneels before me and rests her hands on my hunched shoulders, telling me,

'I dreamt once, not long ago, of making love to a man of the cloth'. Braenda kisses me on my mouth. Her long, sweet, warm kisses take me back to the few hours we spent together in each others' arms. She throws back her fiery mane and looks long and hard down at me,

'You are hopeless, Ivar. I think you know that', she whispers and kisses my neck.

'*Oh*, why do you say that?' I ask, making out I know nothing of what she means.

'Not only will I have to help you take off your mailcoat and breeks, but you have a habit over them. Are you not hot in that?'

'You have not been out in that snow and mist for very long today have you?' I raise my eyebrows as if I were talking to a child. 'I needed that habit, but I have nothing against your pulling it off me'.

She laughs and shakes her head, letting her red hair dance in the feeble light of the single candle by the bed head. She chides,

'You have not changed, have you?' I throw my hands up and she slowly pulls the heavy brown lode habit over my head. When she drops it to the floor she sighs and gives me a knowing look, scolding me affably, '*You* are a lazy lover, Ivar. Even Sigurd used to undress himself. Why is it you think of yourself as so out of the ordinary?'

'*Am I not?*' I act as though my pride has been pricked and cast my eyes to the roof beams. 'If I am to reward you for seeing Count Eustace on his way, the least you can do is to help me out of my clothes'.

'You know him? *Get up!*' Braenda laughs and moves her hands slowly over the front of my breeks to undo the belt, caressing me, giving me a foretaste of what I can look forward to.

On undoing the belt she draws my mailcoat up over my woollen shirt, pulls it over my head and throws it across the room,

'You can pick that up yourself in the morning', she tells me with a look that says I will have other things to think of between now and then. She orders me to sit back with my legs outstretched, my arms taking the weight of my upper body, 'Sit up! I want you to watch as I unwrap myself for you. Think of me as your Yuletide gift'.

Braenda kneels on the bed in front of me and very slowly draws her shift over her head, allowing her full breasts to lift and drop as she lets her shift fall to the floor.

'Do not tell me that you have not longed for me these past few days, Ivar. I can read you as I would read a book'. She tells me of her dream world, the one she entered to follow me through the southern shires. I watch her flex her thighs. She stares into my eyes, watching me longing to be at one with her again, '... When I saw you fighting I wanted to be at your side, to deal them the death blow that would free you of your fears'.

I sit staring at her, wondering what is to come next.

'I sent you help-'

'You sent *help?*' I suddenly sit up, aware for the first time that those times we were beset by Odo's men, the Centishmen coming to our aid were not wholly our wyrd. 'You mean Dunstan and Oslac?'

'Not altogether, no', her soft skin shines in the dim golden glow of the rush light, 'but I summoned their spirit-masters to bring you help'.

'Could you not have summoned Dunstan's, Theorvard's and Burhred's spirit masters, to tell them to keep them *alive?*'

I feel angered now, sitting forward, cross-legged, my brow in my hands, trying to think why I had been spared when my friends' lives had been made forfeit. She leans forward and nurses my head on her breasts.

'My love, I could do nothing about the Northmen capturing Aelfhild and Wulfmaer. There is a dark, wandering shadow abroad in eastern Centland. His strength is greater than mine. He is one of the old ones, from before the Jutes came. His anger at my meddling in his realm on your behalf manifested itself in your friends being killed'.

With her long, slender fingers she draws my mouth close to hers. She tells me softly to belay my anger, all the time pleading for me to believe her with her soft hazel eyes,

'That was why I had you brought from Hrofesceaster quickly with the help of Swetman, Ecgberht and Ealhstan. Your friends Theodolf, Cyneweard, Oslac and Saeward are still alive. They look to you for leadership, despite what Theodolf says. There is nothing *I* have done there for you. That is *your* own doing, trust me'.

I stare at her long enough for her to wince. She pulls me to her and kisses me tenderly on my mouth,

'I would no nothing to hurt you, Ivar, *do you understand?*' She pleads, begging me to take her, but she first needs me to believe her, to set my thoughts at rest - to be at one with her.

'The Centish warlock, Ifon killed Theorvard, Wulfric and Sigegar, their life spirits crushed by his hatred for an outsider – me, not the Northmen', Braenda tells me and kisses me again on my mouth and neck, pushing me back to the head of the bed, 'and he likes Odo. Look, Ivar, forget what is gone. I want you to give me a son'.

I feel the hairs on the back of my neck stand stiffly. However, my willpower weakening, I yield to her otherworldly strength. Straddling me now, Braenda tells me as she rises and falls,

'I want you to give me a son, Ivar'. As her hands slowly stroke the matted, greying hairs on my chest, she arches her back and shudders. Spent, she lies half over me, whispering as she nibbles and kisses my right ear, 'When you leave to meet with Harold's sons again your seed will be planted in me. Next year, when the winds begin to bend the trees and scatter their leaves you will be a father'.

Her mouth widens with a broad, vixenish smile, eyes tightly closed with the joy of knowing she has what she wants.

Morning comes and Braenda has gone again. Someone knocks on the door of my room. When I pull the door open, Saeward stands there, with Oslac and Cyneweard close behind.

'What does a man have to do to get a morning meal these days?' Saeward asks, bewildered. 'The old man is gone, the woman nowhere to be seen and the fire looks as though it has not been lit in an age!'

'Have *you* seen her?' Oslac's eyes search mine, as though he knows the answer anyway and is merely testing me.

'Not since last night', I answer truthfully.

'Not since last night?' Cyneweard grins slyly, echoing me.

He knows something odd is going on.

'Aye, as I said, I have not seen her since last night', I tell them truthfully, finishing. 'And I want to get up to wash and clothe myself for the day. We can look for another inn between here and Leagatun, or stop at Eanefelde again on our way back'.

'I warn you the water is icy', Oslac smirks. 'Do you think we will be as welcome there as we were when we came this way?' Oslac asks. He does not know Ansgar well enough. The shire reeve will still be open-handed toward us.

'*Ansgar* would not hand us over to the Northmen', I assure Oslac, shaking my head. 'We fought side by side on Caldbec Beorg, he and I. Now let me dress, will you? We have to take these habits back to Wulfwin, is that not so, Saeward? I think he would thank us for our forethought'.

'Meaning one of his *household* might?' Oslac's eyes narrow, speaking of Ansgar again, raising his eyebrows. 'We had best not go back that way as no doubt someone else would, on his behalf'.

Saeward nods quietly and turns away behind Oslac, who stands there, still looking me up and down as if he did not know me. I gaze back at him, raise my eyebrows and ask,

'Be a good friend and close the door on your way back down the stairs'.

I signal that I wish to clothe myself without onlookers and he suddenly sees that he has been standing there eyeing me as if I were likely to vanish like Braenda. He takes his leave and I can hear the stairs creaking as they go down together.

When I step onto the cold stone floor from the bottom step I feel just how cold the floor is.

As Oslac said, it is as though the fire downstairs had not been lit in a long time. We come to the stables, where our horses stand patiently munching on hay that someone has left for them.

'Your horses are fed and watered', we are told by a fellow half-hidden in the darkness at the back of the stable. 'I was wondering who could have left them here. You must have been cold last night. How did you sleep without a fire?'

'I know *I* slept well', I answer for myself.

I search the darkness of the stable to see the fellow. He steps forward, tall, full-bearded and long-haired. A thegn, I tell myself, thankful we have not been caught by Northmen back to see what frightened Eustace.

'There were *other* guest here last night', Oslac adds, 'and the fire *was* lit. By the time *I* went to bed I was roasted on one side! That fellow, what was his name, Aeldhelm? When he led us to our rooms the fire was still burning downstairs in the main room'.

'*Aeldhelm* led you to your rooms, you say?' the fellow smiles in a way that tells me he thinks Oslac is telling stories. '*He* died last year, before King Eadweard. Some would say King Eadweard died because his old friend Aeldhelm was no longer in this world'.

Oslac's jaw drops, Cyneweard shivers with fear and Saeward crosses himself, twice. I know what happened, I think.

'Who are you, friend?' I ask.

'I am Hereward, a thegn from Borna in the shire of Lindcylne. I came here when I was summoned by the old king to give account of myself and my deeds, and I saw the new king being crowned yesterday', he tells me.

'If you knew this inn was no longer in use, as you say, why did you come here?' I ask him, my right hand nursing the pommel of my sword.

'You need not fear', Hereward nods at me, seeing that I have become wary of him now. 'I came because I heard at the inn in Ceolsey that someone had seen smoke rising from the roof here. One of the Northmen, who came with me from the West Mynster back to the inn, told me odd things happened here last night. He was told by one of his fellows of Count Eustace fleeing in fear of his life'.

'Word gets about', Saeward stifles a laugh and looks levelly at Hereward, asking him, 'Do you believe in spirits?'

'I am apt to, aye, as well as elves and hobgoblins', Hereward shudders and laughs. He strokes Braenda on her nose and looks at me. 'She is your horse?'

'Aye, she is mine. I thank you for putting out hay for our horses, Hereward', I pat Braenda on her neck.

'That was not me – what is your name, friend?' he asks.

'I am Ivar', I tell him, my flesh creeping. The sooner we leave here, the better, whether or not I needed my woman. *My* woman, what am I *saying?* God, how did I ever come to need her so much?

'A kinsman of King Harold', Hereward smiles again, recalling my name, going on to tell me something I did not know before, 'I was told of a Dane by the name of Ivar, who was a huscarl King Eadweard thought that as a man of high birth should long ago have been given a thegn's lands. When Earl Harold became king there were those who thought that, being your kinsman he might raise you to being a thegn, if

331

not an earl. It is only hearsay, mind you'.

Hereward scratches his beard knowing he has told me something no-one had ever told me before, but ought to have, and turns back to my horse,

'She is a wonderful creature, is she not?' he admires her.

'Aye', I stroke her neck as Hereward walks around her, patting her and stroking her back. 'She has done me proud since my kinsman Harold bought her from a stockman in Wealas some years since'.

'When you rode from Eoferwic with Earl Tostig', he recalls, admiring Braenda, 'to deal Gruffyd his due fate. Earl Aelfgar asked me to join him when he befriended the Wealsh aetheling'.

'No, I understand you did *not* join him', I think back. I had never seen Hereward amongst Harold's number.

'No, *indeed* I did not! My oath was to King Eadweard, but I left for Flanderen soon afterward! I had worries of my own. Now I have given my oath to Willelm – although I cannot think *why*', Hereward sucks sharply through his teeth to show he treats any thought of fickleness with disdain. 'I must ride north to see my kinsman Abbot Brand and then ride to Borna to see my brothers. Abbot Brand had to pay Willelm a hundred pounds in silver from the abbey's funds because the king had wished to put a Northman over the monks of Burh on Abbot Leofric's death. Brand was chosen by the Brothers'.

'Surely they would have asked Archbishop Ealdred about choosing a new abbot for Burh?'

I wonder when it was the Witan had second thoughts about asking Eadgar to be king.

'Ealdred bowed to Willelm. He feared for his own lands on learning of Eadgar's grant to the Brothers of their named abbot. You understand Willelm was glad Ealdred yielded to him. Of course the whole Witan collapsed then - *even Stigand!*'

'Where do you go now Hereward?' I ask, sickened at the way everyone bowed to Willelm, having forgotten he told me already.

'I have to go back to Borna to take up my duties to this new king', he tells me wearily. As an afterthought he adds, 'Heaven help us when he learns everyone wants to ask in the Danes to help rid us of him! Yet I fear they, the Danes that is, will not help us from the warmth of their hearts'.

'Is that how things are in the Danelaw lands?' I raise my eyebrows in wonder and chuckle. Could this mean we will be rid of the Northmen after all? I feel hopeful again for the first time since I watched the Northmen being cut down at Suthgeweorce under the Middil Seaxans' hail of arrows.

'Does your way back to Borna go by Leagatun?' I ask.

'It did not when I came south, wherever Leagatun happens to be, but it can on my way back. Are there good grounds for your asking?' Hereward looks me fully in the eyes.

'I would like you to meet Harold's sons, to let them know of the groundswell of feeling in the Danelaw', I tell him.

He lowers his eyes and shrugs.

'There is little warmth in the north and east for Harold's kin since Morkere was made earl. I do not wish to offend you, Ivar, but no Danelaw thegn thinks of Harold or his kin. His following is in the south and south west, where Godwin should look. King Willelm wants to pull West Seaxe apart, to wipe Harold from the land'.

Hereward holds out his hand before leaving, gazing at me as I take it, as if I were a long-lost brother. There is nothing more for me to do but to show him I have taken his honesty for its own worth, and that I hold no ill will toward him. He has been open with me, and I thank him for that.

'*You* would have a following in the Danelaw, but only if you stood by *us'*, Hereward adds, patting me on my back before mounting. 'Although many thegns have given a sworn oath to Willelm at the West Mynster, he cannot really hope for us all to hold with him against our own kind. Should he ask for our swords against rebels that would surely turn us against our oath to him, would you not say?'

We walk to where his horse is tethered behind the stable. Once more we shake hands before he mounts and takes the road north. He waves back before he is lost in the greyness of the mist from the river and I stride back to my friends.

'You will see *him* again, I will warrant', Oslac foretells. The three of them are already mounted and move off as I swing myself onto Braenda. We head for the road back to Eanefelde, not to burden Ansgar with our company, but to take the best road back to the River Leag.

Ansgar would have to offer hospitality toward knights who may be foisted upon him. Our being there would irk this king.

Cyneweard asks when I catch up with them,

'Are we riding back by way of Eanefelde?'

'We are, but not for me to give our good wishes to Ansgar. We must find a way around there to Leagatun. Is there another way?' I look back at the ruined inn amongst the bushes and trees before it, too, is lost in the mist.

Cyneweard thinks for a short time and answers,

'We can go around the north of the burh, through Hamstede'.

'Will that be safe for us?' I ask, 'Hamstede is not far from the walls of the burh. There might be Northmen about, and we do not want to be followed back to the river Leag. It would take little thinking on their part to see where we are headed'.

'We could be riding for Cingheford', he argues.

'If we have to outride them, what happens if any of Godwin's men come to help us?' I ask, but I have to think long and hard about the way he offers,

'The road over the bridge is close to Leagatun, is it not?'

'That bridge is guarded by the Northmen now', Cyneweard kills any thoughts I may have for crossing by the bridge we used when we rode with Thorfinn.

'We ford the river again upriver of Leagatun, where there are trees and bushes to hide our crossing'.

'Very well then - if it has to be, so be it', I shiver at the thought of another cold river fording through icy water.

'We will be in the warmth of your kinsmen's hunting lodge before the coldness saps our strength. Some mulled ale will put us back to rights', Saeward laughs at my mawkishness on fording again.

'Aye, if we had gone back by way of Eanefelde we would have had to ford the river anyway', Oslac joins in.

'Well, we *will* be no dryer than when I was at sea'.

I laugh at myself and my friends laugh with me. Snow settles on our shoulders as we take a road that leads closer in to Lunden burh than we came by.

Saeward looks heavenward, smiles and calls out to me,

'At least Willelm's men will not see us so easily in this!'

'They might not be able to see you very well', Oslac laughs, 'But they will surely hear you. Your laughter sounds like thunder in this snow. Stop shouting, will you?'

'I am sorry. I did not know I was -!' Saeward's last words are muffled by Oslac's gloved hand over his mouth.

'Hush!' Oslac rasps on taking his hand away from Saeward's mouth and holds a finger to his own. With his other hand he points to our right.

I hear laughter and boasting from that side. These are not Aenglish voices, nor are they Northman. Are these Bretlanders, or even Franks? They could be speaking the same tongue, but do not sound the same.

'*Keep your heads down!* If they come much closer, look as if you had not seen them!' I tell my friends, not that either Oslac or Cyneweard need telling.

One of the newcomers asks haltingly,

'My friend can you tell ... how might we, er, come to Thorney?'

334

I make as if I had not heard him, but before he can ask again I lean forward and wipe the snow from my mouth as a few of the heavy flakes come to rest on my lower lip,

'You see the clump of trees atop the rise behind us?' I turn in my saddle to show the way.

'I do, is it that way?' he spurs his horse but draws hard on the reins when I raise my voice to add more.

'...When you reach the trees you will find a crossroad. Take the road to the left', I shield my eyes from the billowing snow with the heavy sleeve of my habit, 'The road leads to the river; where you will see the West Mynster across the river bend'.

I may have told him more than I needed, because his eyes narrow and he stares at me before he answers,

'I thank you, my friend. I know of King Eadweard's hunting lodge. I married his sister, Goda. I do not know my way around in the whiteness. God be with you, friend'. He nods curtly at each of us in turn. A thickset, lightly bearded fellow of roughly the same age as I, he is nevertheless friendlier than his Northman neighbours. His followers may be Franks or Bretlanders. They grudgingly nod their acknowledgement as they pass and we soon lose sight of them.

We have not long parted company when more riders come on the same road. One of them demands to know,

'Hey, did you see riders come this way just now?' He is a Northman, both in the way he dresses and by his overbearing manner.

'I did, aye', I answer, not wishing to tell him which way they went, hoping he rides around in the whiteness without knowing where he is bound. With luck he will lose his way.

'And... Which way did they go?' the rider is keen to catch up with his friends, if they are friends and not unwilling companions.

'They took the road to the west', I tell him, 'beyond the clump of trees on the hillock behind us'.

'Fools they were, to ride that way at the road fork there!' he barks and turns in his saddle to wave his men on.

It is only when they have gone a little further past us it strikes me I was speaking to Gilbert de Warenne. I stand in my stirrups and look back over my shoulder to see how far on they have ridden and turn to Oslac,

'We should put some miles between us and these last few. I know him, but he did not know me without my beard and with this heavy cloak on my back. Come, ride as fast as this deep snow will allow. He might yet know who it was he spoke to'.

'It sounds to me you are not the warmest of friends'. Oslac grins broadly, nudging his horse into a trot. We must cover enough ground for it to be unwise to want to chase us.

Besides, he must catch up with the count. They will not meet for some time yet, if de Warenne goes as far west as the count has followed the right road. I would hope they do not meet before nightfall. De Warenne will be unable to wriggle out of a tongue lashing from Willelm, before having to yield to Count Drogo's scorn as well! If we meet again he will rightly feel he has a score to settle with me, so I had best be on my guard.

Saeward knows de Warenne now, too. Sucking in his cheeks he looks cheerily heavenward to his maker,

'*He* will be no friendly soul if ever we meet again!' Saeward warns as if telling me off for sending de Warenne on a wild goose chase.

'With luck we *will* never meet again, although by the look of you, never will be too soon', I answer with a wink. Deep within me I feel de Warenne and I are fated to cross one another's paths more often than I would care to hope against. He will be looking out for me now that I have slipped his clutches twice.

'We are above Hamstede now', Cyneweard tells me from some way behind.

His horse seems to limp, and he has fallen back since taking an earlier lead to guide us around the lower hills to the north of Lunden burh.

'You know your way about, even with all this snow on the ground?' Saeward looks at the young fellow in wonderment.

'We learned about standing in the shieldwall with the Middil Seaxe fyrd a good few times under Lord Ansgar and Leofwin', Cyneweard enlightens us. 'We came this way in all weathers'.

I can see fires burning in iron baskets some way downhill on the burh walls, so that the watchmen can keep warm on a midwinter's day such as this. They have lit torches, too, to show the way for those who pass through the gateways on their daily rounds to and from the many markets.

Since Willelm was crowned yesterday the Northmen's grip will be tightening in the south and east of the land. It is for us to loosen it come the new fore-year, and to break it one day. Hopefully that day will come soon. With luck it will be Harold's son Godwin who wears the crown when the next Yuletide comes again. We shall see then how Eadwin and Morkere fare with their followers when this brood of Earl Godwin's grandsons makes its mark on the kingdom. They will want their earls to fight, as they should, not skulk in their halls fearing the onset of Willelm.

Our track rises and falls through woodlands well beyond the Northmen's hearing. All around trees shield us from prying eyes, giving ample shelter as we drop down from the heath behind Hamstede. Cyneweard keeps post on our right.

To ensure we are not taken unawares by a returning patrol, Oslac rides above us to our left. Saeward is ahead, watching for anyone out gathering kindling lest they see us and warn the Northmen.

'Someone stirs below'.

Cyneweard points to a lone man rummaging for kindling.

'Saeward, as you still have on your habit, can you ride down there to talk him into keeping quiet about seeing us', I ask, rather than tell him. With his new-found skill at talking, he could take the fellow's eyes from us. I would not want to have the fellow killed if I failed to win him over. Saeward pulls on his horse's reins to head her downhill.

'Good afternoon, my good fellow', I hear him hail the lone wood gatherer loudly. 'Can you tell me how I might best find the Wealtham road from here? My friends and I are lost, I think'.

'Aye, father, I think you *are* lost. Lost to the devil's brood, you are! Am I so stupid I would not see you have a sword under that habit?' the old fellow croaks. 'Go to the devil and take your Northman friends with you!'

'We are not Northmen, nor have we any Northman friends', Saeward answers mildly and urges his horse closer to the fellow. 'How can you say such a thing?'

'You do not frighten me, *I know who you are!*' the wood gatherer snarls and brandishes his curved coppicing knife. 'I dealt with the likes of you before, in Suthgeweorce, when we drove you off with heavy losses!'

'I do not seek to frighten you, and we are *not* Northmen', Saeward draws tightly on the reins to stop his horse from being carved up by this doughty fellow. 'My friends also fought there against Duke Willelm under King Eadgar and the young earls!'

'Tell them to come closer, if they are not Northmen! After all, what can I do with this against real weapons?' The wood gatherer holds his knife up in the air in his right hand, 'Come nearer, all of you, and let me see you if you are Aenglishmen'.

'Oslac, can you come here? We have to make ourselves known to our friend here', I call him to me.

When we are close enough for the fellow to see us, to know us for who we are he points up to Oslac and smiles broadly, showing gaps in his upper teeth,

'I saw *you* with your bow, what is your name?'

'My name is Oslac, and what is *yours,* my friend?' Oslac reaches down to shake the man's hand.

'I am Ealdsige. My home is on the hillside - there', Ealdsige stabs the still air with his knife at smoke rising above the bushes. 'Do you wish to take shelter until you take the road again?'

Ealdsige peers at Saeward through the thickening snowfall.

'*Are* you a Brother?'

'I was a *lay* brother at Wealtham, Ealdsige, ready to give my vow to the Lord. I think I have made a better bargain with this Lord, however', he nods toward me.

'He does not look like a lord. At least he does not look lordly, like Ansgar over at Eanefelde. I would say he is not even a Seaxan!' the old man screws his eyes up against the wind to look at me.

'You are right, Ealdsige, I am not a Seaxan. I am a Dane, kin to King Harold, his brothers and sons. I too was at Lunden Brycg, and before that with King Harold fighting the Northmen. I took you for a thrall gathering kindling'.

I lean forward over Braenda's neck and take his hand in friendship.

'You took me for a *thrall?*' Ealdsige wails and turns to Saeward. 'The cheek of it – he calls me a thrall! Who is the other one... the lad? I think I may have seen him somewhere else, too', Ealdsige nods at Cyneweard, who answers his acknowledgement with a cursory nod of his own.

'Unless you ever stopped off at the 'Eel Trap', you might not have seen him', Oslac slaps Cyneweard playfully on the arm.

'No, I do not mean I saw him in an inn. I saw him riding behind a Northman lord', Ealdsige creases his face in annoyance at Oslac's joke', I have no silver or pennies to go drinking at inns!'

'Riding behind a *Northman* lord?' Saeward looks from Ealdsige to Cyneweard, 'When was this?'

'When the Northman duke rode through Suthgeweorce', Ealdsige sneers at Cyneweard, 'I swear I saw him. Before he and his men fought Eadgar and Ansgar, he had men riding behind him who wore no chain mail. One was him'.

Ealdsige points at Cyneweard again, as if he thinks the lad will own up to the sin of riding with Willelm. Instead Cyneweard half draws his dagger from its sheath.

'That will change nothing', Saeward sees the lad clutching his dagger hilt from the corner of one eye and calmly counsels Cyneweard to put it away. 'I know what *will* change his way of thinking. If I tell Ealdsige that you fought with us in Hrofesceaster against Odo, and killed some of the Northmen, that will talk him into believing you'.

'Aye', I add, '*and* he helped put the dying Theorvard on his horse

338

when the Northmen were hard on our heels!'

'What do you say to *that?*' Oslac demands an answer from Ealdsige.

'He did not deny riding behind the Northman Duke, though, did he?' Ealdsige casts a sidelong long glance at Cyneweard.

I stare down at the fellow before answering,

'You may think he did not, but he was in the burh of Lunden with us when we drank to the health of King Eadgar at the 'Crooked Billet. *No-one* passed through our line at the end of the bridge that we did not know. How do you answer that?' I ask. 'He was on Billinges Gata when we came off the bridge'.

'I know what I saw', Ealdsige sneers, and eyes Cyneweard.

The lad merely purses his lips and looks from Ealdsige to me, watching as I weigh Ealdsige's words.

'Be that as it may, he rides with us, and I would vouch for him against any man's oath', I assure Cyneweard with a hand on his left shoulder.

Ealdsige, whatever his aim, has tried to sow the seeds of doubt in our hearts about Cyneweard. The lad can only hope to crush any doubts about him that Oslac may have about him with his ongoing, unwavering loyalty toward us.

Beyond that, his steadfastness toward Godwin Haroldson and his brothers will be repaid handsomely when we have achieved our goal. None of us will tell of Ealdsige's snide claim against Cyneweard to assure Godwin's goodwill toward him.

Ealdsige asks Saeward,

'Do you still wish to take up my offer of hospitality?' He turns back to the lad. 'Cyneweard, your friend here speaks well for you and that is good enough for me. My wife will give you something to eat that will make staying the night with us well worth it, I promise'.

'I am afraid I must risk offending you. I thank you, no', I smile at Ealdsige and wonder why he scowls.

Perhaps he had set great store on showing off his wife's cooking skills. My hope is to be back with Harold's sons at Leagatun before night sets in, but my friends think otherwise. Oslac shakes his head. Cyneweard sides with Oslac and Saeward nods at me.

'Are your years catching up with you?' Saeward teases Oslac.

'My hand will catch up with your ears yet, Saeward', Oslac growls. His threat earns laughing mockery from both Saeward and Cyneweard. He laughs back at them, so in the end no-one knows who is mocking whom.

'Very well, Ivar, we can bide a while to give the old man a well-earned rest from the cold', Saeward tells Cyneweard and grins at me, ducking a sideswipe from Oslac.

'There is no need. Not for my sake, believe me!' Oslac snaps, eyes flashing like hot coals.

'I think tiredness is catching up with all of us', I tell Ealdsige and wave him on. 'For all our sakes, we will all rest awhile with you and your wife. Come, fellow, we will ride behind you to your dwelling place'.

'By all means, Lord Ivar, be my guest', Ealdsige looks up askance at Saeward and shoulders an axe that had been leant against a small tree. He sets off to lead us down to his home, threading his way through the already deepening snow.

His dwelling is a lean-to against the side of the hill, a doorway opening to the west away from the snow. I wonder whether the thickness of the snowfall hides the true lie of the land.

There is a plentiful supply of kindling stacked against the front wall and I ask myself why he was up on the hillside with his axe.

'Bring your horses in here, Ivar', Ealdsige opens a door to show the inside of a low outbuilding that looks to be a stable.

There is one horse in there already, munching on hay pulled from a wooden rack on one wall. We dismount and lead our mounts single file into the outbuilding. Ealdsige pulls a rickety wicker door behind him as we lift our saddles off the horses onto a shoulder-high wooden wall that closes off the stabling from his hay bales. We are ready to follow him into his dwelling house.

When he opens the door again he leads across the snow-covered yard, through a more solid-looking door and into a warm, smoke-filled room.

A bed-closet takes up one corner of the room next to where his woman keeps her pots and cooking tools. In the middle of the room, in the hearth, a crackling fire lights everything close by and throws up dancing shadows onto the walls. A fire-charred table and benches stand close by the fire.

'Seat yourselves', Ealdsige bids us and shows us to the benches either side of the board, 'Godthryth will give you broth to be getting on with'.

'We thank you, Ealdsige', I nod to him and seat myself on the short bench at the table nearest the hearth.

Saeward sits across from me next to Cyneweard. Oslac stretches, almost touches the low rafters and looks around the room before seating himself by me.

'You have a friendly, warm homely dwelling here, my friend', Oslac lauds Ealdsige.

'I have Godthryth to thank for that', Ealdsige slaps his wife's rump. Godthryth is no goddess, being most likely the same age as her husband, and plump. He makes a fair living from whatever it is he does.

Most of her hair is covered by a shawl, what little I see pokes out from around the rim. She has greyed with age. Godthryth smiles uneasily. I would say she does not often feed those by-passers thrust upon her by her husband, and I begin to wonder why he has asked us in. It is not as if she were the best cook in Middil Seaxe. She ladles watery broth into small wooden bowls put before us on the table by Ealdsige. Still, I do not want to seem an ingrate and spoon the hot, steaming broth into my mouth slowly.

There is too much salt in the broth, and as I reach for the bread I see Godthryth has put a pitcher of ale onto the table.

19

'You must be thirsty', she smiles uneasily and withdraws to a chair on the far side of the hearth. She begins knitting, sitting with knees wide apart under her long, wide skirts to rest the wool.

'Eat. Eat my friends - there is more if you want it, more ale?' Ealdsige holds the pitcher ready to pour. The salt in the broth makes us thirsty. Soon we are quaffing ale and laughing. Ealdsige is not drinking, however. Oslac asks why,

'Ealdsige, what ails you? You are not drinking'.

'I had some of my wife's broth before I went out for the kindling, and as for the ale, I have been feeling out of sorts lately. I have a queasy stomach that needs taking care of', Ealdsige answers simply. He looked pained, drawn.

'The yeast and barley do me few favours in my old age, but do not fret. I have more for when my stomach settles. Feel free, drink heartily and I will be cheered by your lust for my ale!'

I thank him and we hold up our beakers to his better health, and drain them. He refills our beakers quickly.

'We drink to your good health, Ealdsige, *and to your wife!*' Cyneweard stands, beaker in hand and holds it up to the old man in salute to an open-handed host.

'This is *good* ale!' Saeward tells him. 'Do you brew your own, or have you a brewer in whom you trust?'

'This ale is my own', Ealdsige smiles, 'but sometimes I bring ale from Lord Ansgar for the odd deer or hare I kill for him'.

I was shown the art of brewing by one of the Brothers of Wealtham in thanks for a meal I gave him when he passed this way...'

Whatever else he says I do not know. My head feels heavy and I am suddenly overcome by drowsiness. Oslac is on his back on the floor next to the table, and Cyneweard sits at the board, resting his head on his hands, eyes heavy with sleep. Even Saeward seems far away and I rub my eyes in the sad hope of seeing better for it.

Everything seems to whirl around madly. Suddenly everything goes black and my head hits the table.

I awaken as if from some nightmare, a pounding headache grips me, my tongue feels as if it is swollen and there are men standing around, looking down at me. These men are wearing hauberks and helms, some standing over me with swords in their hands, talking amongst themselves.

Someone shoves me in the small of my back and I turn to see who it is has lost his manners. At first everything is still blurred. In looking up at the nearest man my eyes make no sense of what it is I am looking at. Like an awakening hound I shake my head hard, and my eyes begin to take in the tall fellow standing beside me. My blood freezes.

'Well, my friend, you are awake at last', he says coldly. 'There is no rush, the king told me. When your friends have come to we can be on our way to the king, who wants to speak to you about a small matter of killing. The killing of our fighting men is punishable, aside from in war', a calm, smiling Gilbert de Warenne smugly tells me. 'First I must finish dealing with your Seaxan friend, Ealdsige'.

Ealdsige shuffles awkwardly beyond the hearth. He looks though he awaits some sort of reward and is plainly suffering under Oslac's hot glare.

My sight is getting better now and, as I stare at the old man he looks away, down at the dying embers of the fire.

'Here are your forty pieces of silver, Seaxan', Gilbert de Warenne likens Ealdsige's deed to Christ's betrayer, and tosses a small bag onto the board by which his woman stands, her arms folded across her chest. In my still addled head I hear the dull chink of coins on wood. What was it Ealdsige put in that ale?

De Warenne turns to his men and, pointing at the door, barks an order to them. Ealdsige says nothing, nor does he go to the table to pick up his reward. He merely stares unseeing at the wall as we are herded out into bright, blinding sunshine.

Oslac and Cyneweard are bound, lifted in turn by two Northmen and carried out to the yard, where they are dumped like sacks of grain onto the dirtied snow. Oslac somehow raises himself onto his elbows, shakes his head and looks up at the Northmen standing by his feet and shoulders.

'What in hell's name is *happening* here?' he shouts and glares again at Ealdsige, who takes a step back and puts his arms around his woman's shoulders. Godthryth's eyes are wet and she pushes her husband away.

'*Satan's* brood, *you* are!' she hisses and rushes out into the yard, almost knocking down one of the Northmen.

'Godthryth, *I did it for you!* Can you not see?' Ealdsige groans and sits at the table whilst Saeward and I are led out.

Out in the yard where the sun shines brightly on the snow, I squint again, and close my eyes to stop the many shapes from swimming. When my eyes open again I see Oslac and Cyneweard with spearpoints pointing upward across them. Their hands have been bound and they too are still bleary-eyed.

Bright sunlight on the snow in the yard does not help either, when de Warenne orders his men to push us to our horses. He snaps at me to stand still when I am at the door of Ealdsige's stable.

'*You*, Dane, hold your hands together behind you, so that my men can tie them!'

'How do I mount my horse with my hands behind my back?' I demand to know.

'As your friends will be, you are to be lifted onto your saddle'. He turns away again to speak to one of his henchmen.

Our horses are brought out into the yard by Ealdsige, who cowers when Saeward makes a start at him. There is nothing he can do to harm the old fellow with his hands tied. De Warenne watches as two of his men pull Saeward back by the log that they have jammed behind his back to tighten the binding.

Sneering at Ealdsige, de Warenne tells him,

'*You* have no friends here, Seaxan!'

The old man hides behind his hands. He has sealed his wyrd with this betrayal and his life will be forfeit whenever the news reaches his neighbours. Nor will his woman shield him; that much I can guess. She stands staring at the front wall of the dwelling, bowed and shaking, her hands pushed up under her armpits in shame.

'You will hold your hands behind you!' De Warenne stares into my eyes and nods at the Northman standing behind me to begin tying my hands when I nod to do as his lord tells him. The young Northman noble I took to be a fool has now become a threat.

I will be handed over to Willelm or, worse still, left with Odo to deal with me as he will. He has doubtlessly been smarting since his brother belittled him in front of everyone at Falaise. I have been warned, as Willelm would no doubt cheerfully remind me. With Thorfinn now dead, Odo can channel all his hatred into me.

The snow has begun to fall again. Whilst our hands were being bound, our horses saddled and readied for the ride to wherever Willelm has been given rooms, short flurries of snow were being driven by the north-easterly wind that gnawed at our bones. With the air thick with snow again I can see only as far as the closest trees. I had thought of nudging Braenda headlong into the whiteness.

Our captors have already thought of that. A rope is fed through the halters of each of our horses to keep them together lest one of us should try to flee. When he thinks we are all ready, de Warenne gives a lazy wave with his right hand. All I understand is the name of where we are to go, to Bearrucing. We have a long ride ahead of us, beyond the bounds of southern Middil Seaxe, well into East Seaxe. I look at Oslac, then at Saeward and Cyneweard. As we have each made our mark on the Northmen's numbers, none of us will be spared. I can be sure of the greatest share of Willelm's wrath.

Our way ahead leads to the northern gates of Lunden burh, blanketed and unseen now through heavy snow flurries. De Warenne will risk nothing and takes the earliest road into the burh where he can strengthen his small company for the ride out past Eald Gata.

Our way into Lunden burh is through a much-mended Eadred's Gata. The old walls had been battered before King Aelfred had them strengthened. When Knut was made king after the death of Eadmund 'Ironside', there was no need for the Danes to attack Lunden, and the walls were left as they were. Now, after over thirty years they are beginning to look the worse for wear, no threat to an attacker. Doubtless this was where the Northmen entered the burh from Beorh-hamstede after the Witan yielded to Willelm.

It is early. Few doughty souls have ventured out on this cold, snow-heavy morning.

Some shopkeepers and market traders have only just set out their wares and bystanders gather, gaping at us on our way past. Some cross themselves, thankful it is we who are fated for the Northmen's punishment, not they.

Our horses step briskly through dirty snow where earlier incomers have already made tracks with their drays and horses, past the north side of the church of Saint Paul onto Ceapside. The market here bustles until we ride by. The traders and shoppers stop and stare, but the Northmen pay them no heed and keep up the brisk pace with the odd flick of a whip.

All we can do is try to look as proud as we can, trying not to fall from our horses and show we are not beaten. We might as well not bother. By the way they look at us, most of the bystanders have written us off already.

Our way takes us along the corn market, downhill past the church of Saint Edmund the Martyr, and on to Eald Gata Bar. Older dwellings have wooden rooms added where the stone ones were crumbling, or have had wooden lean-to workshops built onto them. This is where Danes from the days of Guthrum settled. Our horses are jerked to a halt at the gate house whilst de Warenne enters one of the few still whole stone buildings nearby. Our guards watch us closely whilst he is out of sight, making sure we do not try to flee our wyrd.

Some time passes before he shows again with more Northmen in tow, one of them being the fellow Saeberht and I now know as Rodberht de Bruis. He says something to de Warenne and nods toward me. De Warenne cockily walks over to me, looks up at me on Braenda with a look that tells me he would relish handing me over when we reach Bearrucing,

'My Lord tells me he recalls seeing you at the West Mynster. You were with the Brothers, wearing a habit and pretending to be a chorister at the crowning of our Lord King Willelm! What you were doing there will become clear when the king's priests question you.

Whoever you were with will also be questioned, as will the Brothers who entered the church with you. I hope you *all* have answers!'

I say nothing, keeping my thoughts to myself. Saeward looks at me sorrowfully and shakes his head. Cyneweard is plainly afraid. Only Oslac stays cheerful, winking at me when I catch his eye, nodding light-heartedly at Cyneweard beside him.

De Warenne mounts and waits for de Bruis and the others before waving his men on again. He turns in his saddle to sneer at me and tells me,

'You will not have to wait much longer to know your fate'. So saying, he spits on the slippery stone setts by the gatehouse.

De Bruis heads out through Eald Gata Bar on either side of us. Most of de Warenne's own men ride behind us. Two of his men lead our horses. One tugs sharply on the rope to bring our mounts into line. Braenda shakes her head and her eyes roll whenever her rope is pulled hard, but thankfully does not rear up. The snow has been turned to slush by the many horses that have passed through this way.

New building abounds along the old Colneceaster road where Willelm's fellow Northmen have begun to settle, their stone halls now stand close to Eald Gata Bar, the timbers of the Seaxans' homes strewn around where they were pulled down.

The new traders will be striving for the best sites for their shops, to seek gain from their fellows as they make their way out of Lunden burh.

De Bruis spurs his horse as we pass the Seaxans' shops and dwellings, closing on the road fork where the Cambrycg road leads north at Stibenhede. Bystanders begin to jeer at the Northmen on their prancing mounts, and look pityingly at us. They point us out to friends who run to the roadside to watch what is happening.

This is something new for them, the first time the Northmen have led captives this way to feel the wrath of a new king, who seemingly dares not dwell at Thorney because he fears for his life there. Men crowd the roadside, one coming too close for de Bruis' comfort.

He strikes out with his shield when the fellow comes near his mount.

'Strike a poor *blind* beggar, will you!' I hear the yell from where he has landed on his back, sprawled on the muddied snow. Now wary, the riders on either side of us are slowed by the pressing throng. A score or so of the bystanders pushes toward them.

De Bruis' mount turns skittish, testing his horsemanship skills to keep the animal from rearing. But that is only the beginning of his ills. Stones fly, crashing onto his raised shield, and onto those of his men.

Wheeling in panic, de Warenne's frightened mount backs into the horse ridden by the man who has Braenda's rope in his grasp. Fighting to raise his own shield and stop his own horse from rearing, my guard loses his hold on the rope. Fate will not be kind to him if he is thrown to the ground here, now. Aside from the wounds he would suffer if these Seaxans reached him before his comrades, he could be maimed if not killed outright.

The rest of our guards close tightly around us to stop anyone freeing us, one of them snatching the rope linking Saeward's horse with mine and some of the stones meant for them hit us.

'Stop throwing stones at them', someone shouts. 'You are hitting *our* men!'

Oslac's lips can be seen bleeding from a sharp stone aimed at the Northman riding closest to him. The bystanders drop their missiles meekly and when the Northmen see that the stones are no longer flying at them they lower their shields. An arrow strikes the Northman closest to me from behind, the tip showing through at his chest in the way I recall the Turk dying at Akeham.

I lower my head, fearful of another taking me from this life before I can be freed. Another arrow, from the other side now, lodges in the leg of a Northman flanking Saeward. His scream takes de Warenne's eyes from the Seaxan closing on him with a spear and he only sees the threat too late. The spear is thrust into his thigh as he turns to fight the man off

One of his men beats the fellow down with his mailed fist, but too late. De Warenne bellows like a bull and tries to turn his horse, snapping off the spear shaft as he bumps into one of his men, the pain showing as his jaw tightens.

Ahead, de Bruis has drawn his sword and brandishes it above his head. Someone laughs out aloud, a whip cracks and suddenly de Bruis' stallion hurtles headlong eastward along the road with its rider holding on for dear life. His men spur their horses to catch up with him, and to flee the mob that now closes on the four mounted Northmen still trapped around us, fighting for their lives.

The rider who held the rope tied to our horses is knocked from his horse. Two of his comrades somehow beat their way free from the mass of men and women who closed in on them.

De Warenne himself is still struggling to stay on his horse. He holds his wound with his left hand, his right holds his sword but he cannot keep the angry throng away any longer and gives up the fight.

'Let go of the ropes!' With his back to me, a tall, grey-haired bearded fellow threatens our last guard with an arrow aimed at the man's chest. They stare long and hard at one another, but the bowman's threat is greater. There is no way the Northman can leave alive without dropping the lead ropes.

Pity may be shown if he yields now, before it is too late for him. Warily he hands over the rope to the tall bowman, one hand held in the air. One by one as our bindings are cut we rub our wrists to let the blood flow again. Someone calls for de Warenne and his last horseman to be sent to their maker, but I call out for them to be freed,

'The one we should have caught has fled. He would have been the better catch as we might have made some silver from his neck. This one', I point to the sour de Warenne, 'is a sprat, to be thrown back into the water. Tie him to his horse, with his nose under the tail, so he can smell what his mount has eaten!'

I recall how we dealt with Brand, who proved more of a threat than I first took him for. However, I believe de Warenne will be no threat, nor of much use to draw in the likes of our new king. I must speak to the fellow who threatened his underling without having to lay hands on him. And I must find the bowman whose well-aimed arrows led to our being freed. I would be willing to lay a wager on him being Theodolf.

'Thor, it is you who brought the Northman to his senses!' I know the tall bowman straight away when he turns to look at me.

'Ivar, I should have liked to have seen you on a more even footing with the Northmen, not riding between them, hands bound behind your back!' he grins broadly and shakes me by my shoulders in greeting.

'What were you doing *here?*' I ask, 'Your workshop is away to the west. I am glad you *were* about. We were being taken to Bearrucing'.

'Why were they taking you on *this* road? Well, whatever - I was on my way to join Asmund with pig iron bought nearby to make a sword for some young noble, I forget his name. There was shouting, so I made my way here from the back street to see what for'. Thor looks around before adding, 'I met Theodolf and asked where you were. He pointed at the Northmen. I thought you had joined them –'

Thor does not finish what he was telling me.

'I might have known the bastards would get you without me around to keep you from harm!' Theodolf pushes past some young women, who ogle him as he stands talking up at me on Braenda.

I slide down from the saddle and greet Theodolf warmly, then punch him in the chest and swear,

'You young pup, *did you want me to get killed?'*

He gasps and stares wild-eyed at me as I chide him,

'Kindly let me know beforehand before you set out to cut down the Northmen with your arrows!'

He grins foolishly at me, ruffles my hair and laughs, yelling heavenward for all to hear,

'Could you be a little *less* grateful? If it had not been for an old fellow called Ealdsige and a young pup like me, you might have met a grisly end in East Seaxe!'

'I *am* glad to see you!' I grasp Theodolf's shoulders and, kiss him on the forehead. He screws up his mouth in mock loathing and pulls away.

'If you do not want to be given a great warrior's thanks, Theodolf, do not save them from their wyrd!' Thor slaps him on the back, pushing him back onto me.

'Well, Thor, I thank you again for your part in freeing us. Greet Asmund for me when you see him. We must be off, back to Leagatun to tell Godwin Haroldson of Willelm's crowning'.

'You went *there*, did you? Did you know that the bastard's men burned down the dwellings around the West Mynster?' Thor is suddenly angry, 'I cannot think why you would want to see him being *crowned!*'

'I wanted to see which of the earls and thegns gave their oaths to him. Godwin should know who he can trust, and who might give him away. What I learned from one thegn, who had been to the West Mynster and given his oath, was that his only real hope of a following was in the south and south west shires. The north and east would give him a harder time'.

Thor looks askance at me, as if doubting the wisdom of my errand, and then asks,

'What would you have done if you and Saeward had been captured at the West Mynster?' he berates me and points westward. 'You were lucky *here,* because there were all these good folk ready to help you. Over there things could have turned very ugly for you. Did no-one question your foolhardiness?'

'I think *everyone* did', Saeward laughs, nodding at me as we mount. 'You know these bone-headed Vikings!'

'And you *still* went ahead with your fool's errand?' Thor stares disbelievingly at me. 'You are without doubt a blundering fool, Ivar. Perhaps you *should* have been captured earlier!'

'I may be a fool, but I am a lucky fool!' I answer in the manner of a fool and I am upbraided by Thor,

'A real fool relies too much on the help of his friends'.

He scowls briefly and punches my chest playfully,

'Begone with you and try to *stay* lucky! Your utter foolishness may *catch up* with you one fine day'. Thor pumps my hand in friendship and then turns back through the throng. It would be foolish of me to call him back, to ask him to come with us. I feel in my bones that I will see him again.

In turning back to Theodolf and Oslac, I can see folk looking eastward, leaving hurriedly. This can mean only that more Northmen are on their way. I tell my friends to mount and make their way to the Cambrycg heath road,

'We must leave. I think de Bruis is coming back with more men', I tell my friends. 'Willelm does not want to let me slip from his grasp again. Have you your horse with you, Theodolf?'

'She is behind the houses, over there', Theodolf has already started back. 'Come, wake up Cyneweard, you look half asleep!'

Saeward slaps Cyneweard's bare arm.

'Wake up, lad. You might be taken to Bearrucing after all!' Cyneweard almost falls from his horse when a thoughtful bystander shoves him back upright on his saddle.

I nod and smile at the fellow, thanking him for his help,

'Many thanks, friend, although young Cyneweard is the one who should thank you'.

The fellow grins and answers with a twinkle in his eye,

'When I was his age I was as much in need of rest! Perhaps for the same reason, who knows?'

'I doubt it. None of us has had much sleep these last two days, nor has he had a woman', I laugh and climb into my saddle, suddenly overcome with a weariness that I cannot rightly understand.

'Best get away before you are taken again, then', he answers. 'We shall not be able to save you a second time. There will be more of them this time.

Back in the saddle again, I turn to bid the man farewell but he has gone, as if spirited away. I take my cue from him and nudge Braenda away. Oslac turns his horse, followed smartly by Saeward and a still yawning Cyneweard.

Sounds of a scuffle come from behind us, and as I look across over the heads of the milling townsfolk I see horsemen trying to push through the throng. Theodolf, now mounted, shows at the roadside and waves for us to head into one of the alleys.

'Follow him - follow *Theodolf!*' I yell at my friends and urge Braenda into a trot, to where the throng has thinned to let us through.

We can only be thankful for these shorter days. The light is fast fading and another snowfall threatens. I hear shouts and yelling from where our pursuers are still trying to push through. Our way now leads through darkening groves and alleyways behind the shops and dwellings. Soon we will be out of harm's way, on the road back to Leagatun, food and rest and, like as not, more ear-ache for me from Godwin when he hears how we were saved from de Warenne..

'This Ealdsige', I ask Theodolf when we are on our way, our horses trotting along the back roads, 'what did he look like, was he young, old, fat or thin?'

'He was an old man, older than *you!*' Theodolf laughs. He sees my scowl and becomes earnest, 'No, really he was old, and white-haired. A reedy old ceorl if ever there was one! He came out of breath from hard riding – well, hard for *him* anyway. I doubt his horse was any fitter than he was. Lord Godwin told me to see for myself if freeing you was a worthwhile risk.

'Godwin sent you on your own?' I am taken aback. Then again, he must have been sure of Theodolf's skill with the bow.

'I offered to come before he sent me. No-one else would leave the warmth of the hearth for *you*, my fine Danish friend', Theodolf guffaws.

Saeward looks at him angrily but says nothing. Oslac and Cyneweard are too far behind us to have heard him. I do not believe him anyway. Godwin and his Brothers are more likely to have been out hunting and may only have returned at dusk.

'You relish your freedom?' Magnus is the first to greet me. He thumps me on the back and offers a cup of his father's best ale.

Eadmund greets me next and tells me,

'When we came back from hunting Theodolf had gone. We asked everyone here where he was. Burhwold told Godwin that some old fellow had come in a state of despair, weeping about betraying you to the Northmen, and that you had been taken to Bearrucing under armed guard'.

'Is that where our new king dwells?' Magnus asks, wiping his upper lip bristle, laughing quietly 'Is he so afraid of being torn apart by the good folk of Middil Seaxe that he lives with a fellow Northman in a fortified abbey?'

Eadmund and Magnus are almost doubled up at the thought of Willelm quaking in his boots at Bearrucing. When Godwin shows they try to tell him my tale.

'Will the pair of you let me in on the joke? Or you can let Ivar tell me in his own words', Godwin rebukes them and scowls at his younger brothers. He looks to me next and asks, 'Are *your* brothers as foolish as these two? Sometimes I lose hope of even thinking of seeing them as earls – as they will one day be when I am king'.

'Svein is as gloomy and ponderous as was his grandfather, King Harald. As for Jarl Osbeorn, he is too fond of raking in the tithes from passing trade. No, Godwin, your brothers have much more of the Seaxan in them'. I laugh before finishing, 'Yet I would sooner have them about me than Leofric's sullen brood'.

'What, Eadwin and Morkere?' Godwin's eyes open wide in mock wonder, 'Against those two Stigand could be likened to a court fool!'

Magnus has to hold his stomach, as painful as he must be from laughing. Eadmund eyes his younger brother, chuckling to me,

'This one has a very ticklish funny bone!' He laughs throatily and takes a cup of ale from Gerda as she passes him on her way across the room with another cup of ale to a hooded, seated guest.

'-I th-th-thank you', I hear him, a frightened man, his speech reedy and faltering.

'Is *that* the snivelling turd who betrayed us to the Northmen?' Oslac thunders. Ealdsige jumps with fright, dropping his ale cup as Oslac strides across the room. His powerful smith's hands grip the old man's shoulders, pinning him down on the chair.

Ealdsige can hardly even croak for fear, let alone beg for forgiveness. Godwin prises Oslac's strong grip from the ceorl and gently pushes him away from Ealdsige.

'Why should I not let him rip you apart, old man?' Scratching his beard Godwin asks Ealdsige. 'I might think him within his rights to demand a reckoning for your self-seeking ways!'

'I did it for my *wife!*' Ealdsige moans wretchedly.

'So I gathered, this morning', I scoff at Ealdsige. 'Godthryth was not as happy with the Northmen's silver as you seemed to think she might be. Where is she now, by the way?'

'She is with her sister at Ansgar's hall', Ealdsige whines, and cringes when Oslac makes a fist at him.

'Where is the bag of silver that de Warenne tossed onto that table of yours?' I ask.

'I have it with me', Ealdsige whimpers.

'Give it to me', Godwin orders the old man.

'It is on my saddle', Ealdsige tries to stand, but is held down by

Magnus pressing down one-handed on his scrawny shoulders.

'Theodolf can get it', Eadmund hints and looks over to where the lad is talking to Gerda, 'if he has nothing better to do'.

Theodolf looks taken aback at me, unaware of what Eadmund has just asked him to do.

'Lord Eadmund has asked if you would kindly get the bag of silver from Ealdsige's saddle', I tell my friend, smiling, 'that is, if you have nothing *better* to do.

I smile at Gerda. She blushes and scurries away to the kitchen. Theodolf strides to the door and walks out into the thickening snowfall to the stable. Not long afterward he shows again in the doorway, laughing hysterically.

'What is there to laugh about?' I ask before anyone else does, 'Tell *us* what is so funny, *if* there is anything to laugh about'.

Theodolf holds up the bag, allowing one last coin to fall to the floor and laughs again,

'These Northmen are sly bastards. They gave Ealdsige an old bag with holes in it, and as he rode here, they nearly all fell out through the widening hole'.

He begins to laugh again before finishing,

'Some happy fellow will be following the trail of silver coins from the river Leag when this snow finally melts!'

There is a quiet in the room that we would only witness if someone near and dear had died suddenly. Then the laughing starts. Only when we are all too weak to laugh any more do we fall silent again.

20

Ealdsige begins to weep in low, drawn-out sobs.

'I think you had better have this last piece of silver, old man, as a keepsake to remind you of the day you became suddenly more wealthy than you could ever think in your wildest dreams... *and how you were robbed by your own witlessness!*' Godwin stoops and picks up the last coin from the floor and tosses it into Ealdsige's lap.

'By that I mean the loss, by your greed, of your *wife* not your coins!'

The old man looks at the coin in the open palm of Godwin's hand, holds his head in both hands, and rocks backward and forward, shaking. When he looks up at me his face is streaked with tears,

'I am sorry for my misdeeds, my Lord!' Ealdsige moans hoarsely.

'If it were only that easy to forgive', I answer. 'By your deeds, I think my friends and I would have been pegged out by the river for the gulls to peck out our eyes'.

'It does not bear thinking about', Saeward shudders and hisses hotly into my right ear.

'Do you think you have been punished enough?' asks Godwin, not looking at me.

'I have, my Lord Godwin, *aye I have!*' Ealdsige turns, whining like a beggar from me to my younger kinsman.

For one who had in mind to hand me over to a sworn foe for his own ends – *whatever* he says about it being for his wife - he feels only sorrow at his own loss, not for the deed itself. Neither Godwin nor I will be taken in by such a shabby act. His brothers keep their own counsel, but I would say they will lose no sleep over Ealdsige, whatever happens to him.

Godwin looks sideways at me, stern-eyed, and asks,

'Would you say it is for his wife to say whether he should be punished further?' He knows Ealdsige is watching us both like a hawk through his fingers, hoping for pity and finding none.

'What do you say, we send for her?' I offer.

'One of my huscarls will take some of the fyrdmen and call on Ansgar to ask for her. He will say her husband begs forgiveness for his sins and wishes to have her here when a priest hears him out. That way Ansgar is bound to send her. Her sister should come, too, to help Godthryth on how best to deal with Ealdsige', Godwin turns to Eadmund and asks for Aethelgar to be brought in.

Ealdsige suddenly bolts for the door. No-one stops him, but Magnus asks Oslac to see whether the old man takes his horse,

'You stay here, Ivar', Magnus tells me when I head for the door with my friend. He smiles at me, 'The old fellow has not gone to the stable. He will not get far, nor will he come back. I will send men out in the morning to look for him'.

I know what is in store for Ealdsige. We all know, and none will raise a finger to help him. He will be found dead in the morning by the River Leag, or floating in it. If he tries to cross, even if he *were* able to reach the western bank, he would be unable to find anyone close enough to take him in before the cold takes him.

A burly, thickly-bearded dark-haired fellow comes to stand at Godwin's side. He has buckled on his sword belt and awaits his lord's orders. My young kinsman looks up and smiles wanly before telling him,

'Aethelgar, I thank you for your swift readiness, but you can rest easy. The errand I had for you is no longer needed. You can rejoin your friends in marking the end of the Yulefeast'. Godwin turns away his huscarl and stares hard at me. Whatever Ealdsige has done, he still thinks I am blameworthy. 'We can all mark the end of the Yulefeast. I would say we have need of cheer now that this sad affair is ended. Someone can take the price of the horse to his woman at Eanefelde, and give her the weight of that last coin in silver pennies. They can tell her that it is Ealdsige's last will, that he wished her to have that at least. I do not think she will refuse it', Godwin tells us all before we sit to eat.

Eadmund shakes the bench as he climbs over the bench behind me, thumps down onto it with one heavy hand on my right shoulder and leans over toward me, asking,

'Perhaps you can *tell* us all now what you saw of Willelm's crowning at Thorney?' He grins at me as we put our hands together over the table, waiting for Godwin to begin, 'What is more, you can tell us who you saw taking their oath of loyalty to this new king. There will be a reckoning to pay when Godwin mounts the throne'.

Godwin clears his throat to let Eadmund know he means to begin. Everyone is silent whilst Harold's eldest hurries through his prayer. The hubbub begins anew before I tell them everything and answer my kinsmen's searching questions about the new order.

'...We need to keep an eye on him', Magnus sits back in his chair when I have finished recalling Ansgar's words to Cyneweard.

'Moreover, we need to watch them *all*', Godwin adds as he toys thoughtfully with his drinking cup and stares across the table at me. 'From what Ivar tells us, half the nobles in the kingdom have sworn an oath to him. How many will keep it, I wonder?'

Magnus chews on his lower lip and shakes his head, thinking of something to say but saying nothing.

'How long before Ansgar comes crawling to us, asking to see what he could gain from being your man?' Eadmund asks and grins at his older brother. He takes a draught of ale and finishes off the last of his meat before going on. 'If what Ivar says is right about him, any hope he may foster to keep his standing may be dashed'.

Godwin sums up my own thoughts on Willelm,

'As I read this king, his rewards will go to his own underlings for helping him win. The ones that helped him to the throne will be at the forefront to be given land, I think. If they have not done so already, someone may yet tell Willelm that Ansgar fought alongside father. The same underlings may also tell their lord that father's stallari also fought in Lunden, if he does not know already. How will it look if their duke does not send him packing and set one of his men up at the Shire Reeve of Middil Seaxe?'

'I think Willelm already knows about that', I tell them between mouthfuls of boar meat.

'No doubt Ansgar wonders for how long he can hold his post', Godwin says to anyone who is listening. 'As for being a stallari, I daresay Willelm has enough men willing to do his bidding on that score. What with his half-brothers, untold numbers of higher and lower vassals... He will not be short on offers'.

'You are right brother - now what of Waltheof, Eadwin and Morkere?' Eadmund belches, finishes his ale and holds out his cup for Ingigerd to fill before adding, 'I understand Eadgar was bought cheaply, Ivar. How was he rewarded for allowing the Witan to bypass him again?'

He looks closely at me as I answer, sipping from his cup and from time to time following Ingigerd around the room with his eyes..

'My understanding is Eadgar had no say in any of it. As for the earls, I do not know what has been offered for their oaths'. I hold out my own cup for filling before I go on to add a warning,

'I was hoping Ansgar would have told me before we took our farewells. On the morning of Willelm's crowning I would say he was not as forthcoming as he might have been. He kept his thoughts to himself on being Willelm's man'.

Eadmund looks levelly at me and asks of our youngest earl,

'What of Waltheof? Would *he* join us against Willelm, even though he has sworn the oath, or is he Eadgar's man?'

'Waltheof has little following in the south. His kin are in Beornica, at Baebbanburh. Morkere would not wish to help him, lest his own standing be threatened in Northanhymbra. The ealdorman Uhtred of

Bamburgh who ruled in the north before Siward was his mother's kin. Eadwin and Morkere are two of a kind. Two peas in a Miercan pod, you might say!'

'Now Ivar, about Stigand, what do you think of him, does he see himself where he is now in the years to come?' Without looking at me Magnus plays with his spoon. He half-knows the churchman's fate even before he asked.

'Why do you ask of Stigand?' Eadmund turns to his brother. 'His days are numbered anyway!'

'Stigand *was* one of your father's followers. When your father was killed his only real following came from Eadgar until he sold out to Willelm. The king will bring his own man', I underline Eadmund's thinking, 'from Northmandige. I think he will bring his household priest, Lanfranc. The Holy Father will not fret when Stigand is ousted from Cantuareburh. How long Stigand holds onto the archbishopric depends on how long it takes the Northmen to see his usefulness as fulfilled, when they think they can do without him'.

'Who have we left...Ealdred, now - what of him?' Godwin casts in the dark. In following his own claim to the throne on the strength of his father's shortened kingship, he wishes to know the feeling in the Church. Although Ealdred was shocked that Harold had pushed for the throne even as Eadweard was settling into his tomb, he still crowned him.

'As for Ealdred ... well your guess is as good as mine. He has deemed Willelm fit to rule as king over us all and must bear the weight of his own deeds if the Bastard does not act in the way his oath demands. He will not be long on this world, I think'. My thoughts go back to the way Willelm shook as he swore the oath before Ealdred, 'As it was, he had to take the oath in his own tongue, because he has not yet mastered Aenglish'.

'We who pay our dues will be ruled by a man who does not know how we pay them unless an Aenglish abbot tells him in his own tongue? That has to be the grounds for misrule, surely? Does he trust his men *that* much?' Magnus almost chokes with laughter, spraying ale across the table and earning dark looks from all around. Godwin glowers, but Magnus is not yet finished. 'How does he *know* if we pay him what we owe, unless he bleeds us dry with his own sword point?'

'Do that again brother and see how I gather my dues!' Godwin threatens Magnus, and asks me,

'Is there anything else you heard that might be useful to me?'

I sit back and look up at the curling smoke leaving the room through the hole in the roof. I lean forward again to lift my cup before shaking my head, and then recall Hereward's words.

'I met a thegn from Borna who answers to the name of Hereward. He told me that any following for you would be lacking in the Danelaw or anywhere further north. Although Morkere has become Willelm's man, his word is still law. Before Harald Sigurdsson was beaten your father gave the southern part of Northanhymbra over to Maerleswein's rule. He was showing how he could cut Morkere to size for not calling him in to help fight the Norsemen and Tostig. Morkere may have to put up with Maerleswein for a little longer. How long before Morkere has a rebellion on his hands he does not know, once they hear he has given his oath. he could be on his own'.

'He told you *that?*' Godwin angrily furrows his brow. 'He told me that I would be welcomed in the east!'

'I think what was meant was that you would be welcomed as far as East Aengla. From the fenlands northward, Lindcylne shire is still Morkere's earldom. Maerleswein holds the northern and eastern Danelaw -', Eadmund tries to put his brother right.

'All right, rub in the salt!' Godwin growls like a bear, glancing sideways at Eadmund as he does so.

'Would there be any following in the *south* that I can rely on, in Centland and Suth Seaxe or Suthrige?' he asks me.

'Without question, Godwin, *they* will. Everyone in your father's and grandfather's earldoms would always stand behind you. They recall your grandfather's unwillingness to punish the townsfolk of Dofnan for their rebuke of Eadweard's brother-in-law Count Eustace', I tell him to the best of my knowledge. Then to take Godwin's thoughts from his woes and to keep the spirit of the Yule feast I tell them about the eerie happening at the inn,

'...An odd thing that has to do with Eustace came to pass when we were on our way back from the West Mynster'.

'Aha! You are going to tell a tale of fetches to chill our bones in this midwinter, perhaps?' Magnus sits forward, mouth open as he did in childhood when Gytha told her grandchildren the grim heathen tales of the northlands.

They all sit up now, ears pricked, rapt as I tell them all about the inn near Ceolsey, and how the cock-sure Eustace entered the inn with another noble. They listen with bated breath as I talk of how he threw his weight about, demanding room and drink. When they hear of her stare that crazed him and made him leave without any of his demands being met, Godwin crosses himself and Eadmund laughs. I let them settle again, clear my throat and finish the telling,

'... Well, we stayed at the inn overnight. In the morning when we awoke we found the inn silent, bone-chillingly cold with no fire, no ostler to care for our horses, no householder or food to break our fast with. That was when I met Hereward. He told us of the inn having been empty for some time, that the old man who looked after our horses had died years before. We only saw in the morning that the inn was festooned with cobwebs, crawling with woodlice', I end the telling of my tale to the gathering.

Not a man or woman stirs – Ingigerd, Gerda and Winflaed have also come to listen at Burhwold's bidding - until knocking on the door breaks the spell.

Godwin roars, irked by the noise,

'See who it is at the door at this time of night! Put some more wood on the fire to keep the demons at bay!'

There is still something of the child in all of us, no matter what age we reach before our wyrd calls to claim us. Godwin's childhood has stayed with him in a way none of us would have dreamed. He believes deeply in the power of evil spirits, and this is the time of year when our greatest fears play on our thoughts. The long darkness of midwinter fills many a man's soul with foreboding. This is the time of old heathen ways. The evenings of the Yulefeast are for telling tales about hwicce craft.

Although tales of spay wives, fetches, shape-shifters and dead men walking fills many a man's deepest thoughts with dread, we still listen. Ingigerd and Gerda use the break in my telling to shake themselves from their fears and return to the kitchen.

'One of the men from Wealtham has come with word from Dean Wulfwin', Healfdan has answered the door and now stands in the doorway to the main room, awaiting an answer.

Godwin waves the young man to him.

'Bring him here, Healfdan. Bring him here, although I fail to see why he is here so late! There are wolves around again, I hear. We would not want one of Wulfwin's men to fall prey to our four-legged friends, would we?' Godwin's play on words brings laughter to break all feelings of dread after listening to my tale.

'Have they lost men to the wolves here?' I ask. Our horses are out in the stables. Knowing how wily wolves can be, they could very easily use the darkness to take our mounts one by one. Someone need only be lazy in putting his horse away, and not bar the stable doors. I have grown fond of Braenda, and would not want to lose her to the grey-coated sons of the woods.

'There have been losses aye', Godwin answers, 'due only to the foolishness of some in this household. Some do not listen to warnings and ride alone through woodland at this time of the year'.

When a man can warm himself by the fire in the mid-winter darkness why would he forfeit his own safety, and that of his horse? Of course he is right, but there are times when a man's duties lead him to risking life and limb.

'My Lord Godwin-', the rider begins, only to be stopped by Godwin, who holds up his hand and demands a reason for his foolishness.

'Did Dean Wulfwin tell you that you had to come out *now?*' Godwin demands of the poor fellow.

'He *did,* my Lord. This is *most* pressing!' the rider answers breathlessly. 'I am to await your answer before I return'.

'Can *anyone* here read?' Godwin blurts out, holding Wulfwin's vellum aloft. He does not hold with men who can read. Only Brothers can read, he says, because they are odd anyway. When I told him once I could read he sat shaking his head. His father told him to learn how to read and write, but he would run from the hall, yelling with fury.

That was *many* years ago, when he had first begun to learn how to hold sword or axe without killing himself and those around him. We found him later battling with Harold's huscarls, sweat pouring from him. '*Why* must I learn to read and write' he tearfully asked his father, 'there are more *useful* things for a man to learn?'

'You may one day find reading *and* writing useful', Eadmund echoes his father's words, earning himself a dark scowl. He holds out his hand, smiling, and offers, 'But you can give it to me. I will read it for you'.

Eadmund wrests the letter from Godwin's grasp, unrolls it and reads it through swiftly, wordlessly. He nods before passing it across the table to Magnus, who looks at the second-most name on the parchment and hands it to me without giving it another look.

'You may as well read it, as it is about you', Eadmund nods and sits back, arms folded, watching me closely as I scan through the other names listed before reading properly:

'*My good friend Godwin Haroldson*', it begins, adding words of friendly greeting before leading to the real meaning of the letter. '*I have knowledge of someone using my teaching Brothers' habits to gain entry to the chantry at the West Mynster for his own ends. Word comes to me from Abbot Eadwin, who tells me that our king is most upset about the matter and wishes to see such person or persons at Bearrucing Abbey who undertook this grave deed*'.

'Dean Wulfwin says he knows who they are speaking of, but will not press for an answer. However, he cannot deny the king the knowledge if he is put to the test', the rider adds Wulfwin's own words.

Godwin looks darkly at me and shakes his head slowly. He rises and strides around the bench, telling me as he comes,

'That errand you set yourself has been costly. A number of towns-folk were killed by the Northmen after freeing you. If this king of ours – however short his reign - presses his claim to your neck, others will suffer if we do not offer you up'.

'We cannot take Ivar to task for lives that were given in setting him free', Eadmund chides Godwin for his fecklessness. 'That would be wasteful. The Northmen would have carried out the killings one way or another if another of ours was taken in chains through the streets and freed at their cost'.

Each man seated around the table nods. Magnus thumps the table with his fists and roars at his eldest brother,

'Godwin, I am ashamed of you, for thinking of handing over our kinsman! *Ivar is one of us!* Blood ties should count strongly with us in our struggle to rid ourselves of this Northman king. I say again, *shame on you, Godwin!*'

'I was not thinking of handing him over. Nor will he be turned out into the winter snows. We would have to leave with him anyway if Willelm was given word that we were here! No, we sit out the winter further away until after the thaw, when the Northmen are more likely to come looking for you'. Godwin chews on his beard.

He chews his lower lip for a long time, plainly thinking, then tells us,

'We shall have to leave for the west a little earlier than I foresaw, that is all! What is your name, rider?'

'I am Aethelric, my Lord', the rider answers stiffly.

'Well, Aethelric, you can let Dean Wulfwin know I have taken his warning. We shall be on our guard from now on. Stay here overnight. Tell Dean Wulfwin that I told you so', Godwin bends a thumb toward Wealtham behind him. 'In the morning, when Oslac and Cyneweard have eaten, they can ride with you back to Wealtham'.

Godwin allows Aethelric leave to go and eat. With him goes Oslac to show him where to find food and drink, as our evening meal is over now.

'Can Dean Wulfwin keep his own counsel whilst being berated, do you think?' Godwin asks me when everyone has left the table for their beds and we are alone.

'Do you mean will he yield if the Northmen press him for my whereabouts?'

I search his eyes and add my own thoughts.

'He will hold true toward you, and give no-one away easily'.

Standing at the end of the table Godwin follows rings with his fingers and stares dully back at me as I tell him.

'True, he must take care of his canons and the Brothers who teach, but Willelm will not threaten him. Wulfwin is far too wise to be wrong-footed', I assure Godwin. 'We have time to think. Tomorrow is another day. Sleep on your thoughts and we will talk again'.

Godwin rubs his eyes, yawns and looks down at the floor. He comes to stand behind me and rests a strong sword hand on my right shoulder.

'Aye, Ivar. Tomorrow *is* another day. Hopefully we will find time for hunting, to put meat on the table for the New Year Feast'.

Sighing and stretching again, he strides toward the door. Turning to look at me before he leaves the room he asks simply,

'Do not drink us dry in drowning your cares, Ivar. Leave some ale for us to drink with our morning meal. Good night, kinsman!'

AGAIN, THERE IS A NEW BEGINNING